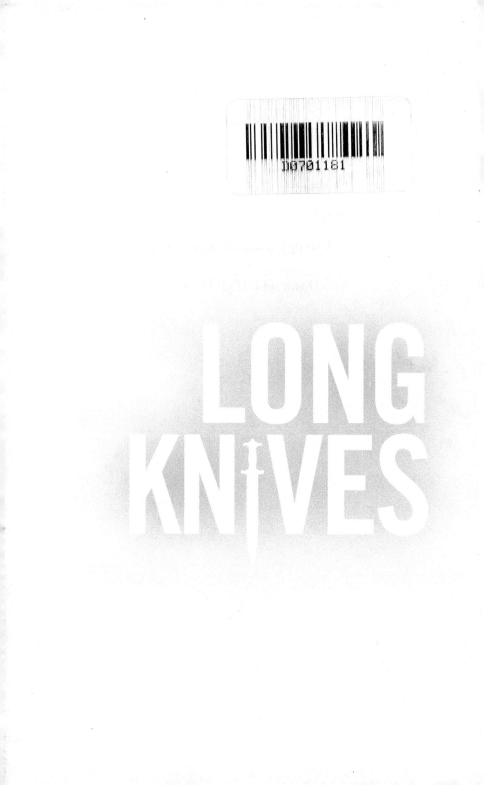

LONG KNIVES

Also by Charles Rosenberg

Death on a High Floor

CHARLES ROSENBERG

LONG KNIVES

A LEGAL THRILLER

WITHDRAWN

 THOMAS & MERCER

Published by Thomas & Mercer, Seattle

www.apub.com

Amazon, the Amazon logo, and Thomas & Mercer are trademarks of Amazon.com, Inc., or its affiliates.

ISBN-13: 9781477817520
ISBN-10: 1477817522

Cover design by Paul Barrett

Library of Congress Control Number: 2013915797

Printed in the United States of America

For Sally Anne
and for Joe

Jenna James

I had never been happier. That was, of course, because I couldn't see twenty-four hours into the future.

But let's start with the past. Five years earlier, I had decided, let's face it, on a whim, that I was done with Big Law. And so, aided by a bit of luck and the dwindling memory of my fifteen minutes of fame from saving Robert Tarza's butt from San Quentin, I left my law firm, Marbury Marfan, and transformed myself—poof!—into a tenure-track law professor at UCLA. I still worked hard, but I no longer spent my nights preparing for trial or my days battling the jerks, most of them of the male persuasion, who seemed to appear like clockwork on the other side of my cases.

It was only twelve miles from M&M's perch on the eighty-fifth floor of a downtown high-rise to the rolling hills of UCLA, but in terms of lifestyle it might as well have been a thousand. I found time to eat in good restaurants, I slept well at night and I stopped biting my fingernails. I enjoyed my colleagues and, although he wasn't perfect, I even had a guy in my life. I no longer made the kind of money I made at M&M, but I still lived quite well by anybody's standards.

Another way to put it is that after lunging at every carrot dangled in front of me from the age of five—the need to ace grade school, stride down the aisle as the valedictorian of my high school, nail acceptance to an Ivy League college and then go on to Harvard Law School and make the law review—I finally had a life instead of a résumé.

Okay, that's not quite true. There was still one last carrot dangling out there. I was up for tenure. It was November, and the decision would come no later than April. But with four well-received law review articles published in less than four years—two on civil procedure and two on admiralty law—I was pretty confident I had that final carrot nailed, too, if you can nail a carrot.

Teaching and writing about civil procedure, with eight long trials under my belt, was a natural for me. Teaching admiralty law had come as a surprise; I'd never even been on a sailboat prior to arriving at UCLA. But fate twists your life in funny ways. The week before classes started for my first year of teaching, Charles Karno, who looked the picture of health and had been teaching the admiralty course for more than twenty years, dropped dead of a heart attack while running a half marathon. The dean had prevailed on me to teach it. "You can learn it along with the students," he said.

I did and found I loved it, and particularly liked teaching the law of salvage—who has what rights to ships, and everything in them, when they sink to the bottom of the sea. In order to live the law and understand it better, I had even spent the past summer at sea as a lowly deckhand on a treasure salvor ship. And now, instead of my formerly pasty-skinned self, I was bronzed and, well, if not ripped, at least the most toned and buff I'd ever been in my life. In fact, I had been admiring myself in front of the mirror when my cell phone beeped to let me know that a text had arrived. I picked up the phone from the bed, where I had tossed it along with my clothes. The text was from the dean: "meet me Oroco's 8:30 A.M. tomorrow"

It was an odd time and an odd place, but I texted back: "ok what topic?"

No text came back in reply.

So tomorrow was going to be an odd day—a mystery meeting with the dean at 8:30 and, just before that, a meeting with Primo Giordano, a student in my Law of Sunken Treasure seminar. Several days earlier, Primo had put himself on my office hours sign-up sheet for 7:30 A.M.—the first time a student had ever signed up for that only-slightly-past-sunrise slot, which I made available as a kind of joke because no law student ever got up that early.

When I saw him later in class and asked him what he wanted to see me about at such an early hour, he paused and said, "I have something interesting to talk to you about," and hurried away. Given that he was a student, Lord knew what that might turn out to be.

I didn't think it was going to be a problem to meet Primo at 7:30—the meeting probably wouldn't take very long—and then, right after that, drive down to meet the dean at Oroco's in Westwood at 8:30. It was at most a ten-minute drive.

As it turned out, I should have texted the dean that I was too busy to meet with him, told Primo that I had a firm policy against discussing anything the least bit interesting with students, canceled my classes for the week and taken a nice long drive up the coast.

CHAPTER 1

Week 1—Monday

My office is on the third floor of a red-brick addition to the law school that some people still call the New Building. Built in 2001, it's in the southeast corner of the law school and can be reached by a separate entrance. That way, you don't have to walk through the old building and risk running into students. I arrived at the law school at about 7:15 A.M. At that hour I didn't expect to find anyone else around in any part of the building. Neither law professors nor law students are known to be early risers.

I climbed the steps to the third floor, wanting to arrive at my office several minutes before Primo. When I reached the top, I opened the heavy fire door and turned right into the hallway that leads to my office. My keys were in my purse, and as I walked I burrowed in it, searching for them. When I finally looked up, keys in hand, I stopped dead in my tracks. The door to my office was already open. Not only that, the light was on, and when I entered, Primo Giordano was already seated in one of my two gray suede guest chairs—chairs I had purchased with my own money to replace the butt-ugly ones the university had provided. He had with him a long red mailing tube, sealed on both ends with white plastic caps, which he had rested across the chrome arms of the chair.

He turned as I came in. "Hi, Professor. The door was open and the light was on, so I calculated that you were only away briefly. I hope it is not a bother to you that I entered. There is no place to seat oneself in the corridor."

"No worries, Primo," I said as I hung my black wool blazer on the back of the door, moved to my desk and took a seat in my red Aeron desk chair, another piece of office furniture I'd purchased with my own funds. In truth, though, the open-door situation was worrying. I always lock my door when I leave, and I was sure I hadn't failed to lock it the day before.

I must have been silent for a moment, while those thoughts went through my head, because I suddenly heard Primo saying, "Are you okay, Professor?"

"Oh yes, fine. Sorry, got up super-early this morning and need a cup of coffee to really start functioning. Would you like a cup, too?"

He smiled broadly. "I am Italian. What Italian would not want a cup of coffee?"

"Great." I turned toward the credenza, where my Braun coffeepot sat. I had ground the beans the day before, filled the reservoir with water and set the timer so the coffee would be ready at 7:30 the next morning.

"Hmm," I said. "It's not quite finished dripping. Let's give it another couple of minutes."

"Professor, do you always prepare the coffee the night before?"

"Almost always. I'm usually too sleepy to do it when I first get in." I smiled at him, and he smiled back. He was nice to look at. He had a terrific smile, not to mention that he was tall, dark and chunky handsome. Plus older than the average law student. Twenty-eight or -nine, maybe even thirty. Which was great, because I'd begun to tire of early-twentysomethings. Maybe I was getting old.

"Thank you for agreeing to see me so early, Professor."

"You're welcome, although this isn't all that early for me. I've been trying to get in by at least 8:00 A.M. every day this semester because I'm pushing to finish a law review article."

"You go to bed early, then?"

"No. I stay up late *and* get up early. I don't need a lot of sleep."

"You are, how do you say it, an owl of the night?"

I laughed. "We would say night owl."

"Ah, you will forgive me. My English is good, I think, but the metaphors sometimes escape from me."

I restrained myself from correcting him again and waited for him to tell me why he was there.

"Professor, is the law review article you are working on the one you spoke about in class? About sunken treasure?"

"Well, it's not only about sunken treasure. It's called *The Law of Sunken Treasure Salvaged*, but that's just an attempt at a cute title. It's about how the law of marine salvage should be applied to many things that are abandoned in the ocean. Sunken treasure's just one example. Most of the other examples are boring."

"But sunken treasure is why I am here, Professor. I have a map that shows the exact location of a sunken treasure."

"Is that what's in the tube, Primo?"

"Yes." He raised the tube off the arms of his chair and held it out to me. "I want to show it to you and receive your advices on how to claim the treasure."

"It would be 'advice,' Primo. Singular rather than plural."

"It is many advices that I need from you. Why is it therefore singular?"

"Who knows? Do you mind my correcting your English?"

"No, no, Professor. That aides me. Please fix my English when I make mistakes." He smiled his very nice smile again, showing a row of pure white, perfect teeth. He continued to hold the tube out toward me but then put it back across the chair arms when it became apparent that I wasn't immediately going to take it from him.

We sat and looked at each other for a few seconds without saying anything. What ran through my head was the dumb thought that in the multipage policy manual provided to professors by the law school, there was probably not a single word about what you should do when a student offered to show you a map to sunken treasure. But whether it was in the manual or not, it certainly made no sense for me to step over the line that separates *us* from *them* and give legal advice about a business venture to a student who was taking a class with me.

"Primo, even if it's real, I'm not sure I want to see it or get involved in it."

"But you are an expert, no?"

My mentor at my old law firm, Robert Tarza, had taught me that the quickest way to wiggle out of representing a client you don't want is to deny expertise.

"Well," I said, "I know something about the legal theory maybe, but I know nothing about how it gets applied in the courts on a practical basis. I've never practiced admiralty law. It's something I've become interested in—on a theoretical level—only since coming to UCLA."

"But I need your advices—I mean, your advice—and I trust you. If I go to a law firm, I will not know if to trust them. They could steal the treasure. I am sure you will not."

"Maybe I can recommend someone else you can trust. Before I do that, can I ask you a few questions?"

"I am disappointed. But, yes, ask me your questions."

"Where did you get the map?"

"I inherited it from my grandfather. It was received by me when he died three years ago."

"No one else claims the map?"

"My brother and I together own it. He also inherited it."

"Is the treasure part of a sunken ship?"

"Yes. A Spanish galleon, the *Nuestra Señora de Ayuda*. It sank in 1641."

I don't know if you can roll your eyes internally, but I think I did it just then. The wreck of the *Ayuda* is quite well known. The ship was a so-called Manila galleon, one of the Spanish treasure ships that plied the seas between Acapulco and Manila, carrying silver and gold outbound from Mexico to Manila and Asian trade goods on the way back. It sank just west of Santa Catalina Island, about thirty miles from where we were sitting.

"You realize, Primo," I said, "that the resting place of the *Ayuda* is hardly a secret. It's everyone's favorite Southern California Spanish shipwreck."

"Yes, but no one has found it."

What he said was true. But that was most likely because the ocean had long ago pounded whatever was left of the *Ayuda* into oblivion. Not only that, the ship had managed to sink in what was now a federal marine sanctuary, so good luck on getting a permit to dive for it. In Primo's defense, the treasure-hunting bug can bite deep when it first sinks its pincers into someone's neck, and Primo had clearly been badly bitten. There was little to be gained, though, in telling him that he was an idiot.

CHAPTER 2

The better strategy was to let him tell me his story, cluck sympathetically and then politely usher him out.

"Primo, where do you believe the *Ayuda* sank?"

He turned his head and looked around the office, first left, then right, then at the ceiling.

"What are you looking for?"

"Hidden microphones."

I laughed. "Well, if they were hidden, you couldn't see them, could you? But there aren't any recording devices of any kind here. In any case, what's the big secret? Everyone knows where that ship sank—just west of Catalina."

"No, it is much, much farther west."

"That can't be."

"Why not?"

"The Spanish records say it went down off Catalina after foundering on a reef. It's listed as being there on every treasure-hunting website."

"What we have discovered is that those records are not right. The ship is out farther."

"How much farther?"

"More than two hundred miles."

"How did you figure that out?"

"My grandfather, he found the navigator's survivor account in the old Spanish archive."

"In Seville?"

"Yes."

"Primo, dozens of serious treasure hunters have pored over those archives for hundreds of years. No one has ever reported finding such a thing about the *Ayuda*."

"I will show to you the survivor account he found. But I must ask you to sign first an agreement of confidentiality."

"I'll think about that, but I'm likely to say no. It would be very awkward for me, as a law professor, to enter into a binding contract with a current student, and that's exactly what a confidentiality agreement is—a contract."

"I understand," he said.

I had begun to worry that I was being recruited into some sort of scam. What Primo was saying made no sense. A navigator in 1641 couldn't possibly have calculated the exact location of his ship when it sank. Back then they couldn't even measure longitude accurately from a ship on the open ocean. I had just finished explaining to the students in my seminar how terrible navigation was in the seventeenth century. It was one of the reasons there were so many shipwrecks.

Primo, who had been in class the day we discussed that topic, must have sensed my disbelief. "My grandfather," he said, "took the story of the survivor and calculated approximately where is the ship. You must believe this."

I didn't think I needed to believe it. "When did your grandfather figure that out?"

"I am not sure. Perhaps it was in the early 1980s."

"How deep is the ocean where you think the ship is?"

"Many thousands of feet."

"Primo, I'm now totally disbelieving. Until the late 1980s only the US military had the technology to locate wrecks in thousands of feet of water."

"We started a company," he responded. "With family and investors. Two years ago we paid to have a sonar array towed over many miles of ocean bottom."

"Where?"

"Where we thought the wreck could be. After many, many weeks of searching we found the wreckage *precisamente*—precisely."

"How precisely?"

"It is spread over many meters of ocean floor. But we know where is that area."

"Well, that makes more sense as a matter of theory, although you would have needed millions of dollars and a good bit of luck to pull that off."

"We did. We spent many millions to find it. And we need now money to go down and seize the treasure from the bottom."

"What cargo do you expect to find when you get down there?"

"Gold and silver coins."

The whole conversation had begun to feel more and more unreal. A galleon that wrecked off Catalina would have been on its return voyage from Manila. Inbound from Manila to Mexico, the ship would have carried only trade goods to sell in Acapulco. Instead of challenging him in detail, I said, "There wouldn't have been gold and silver coins on that voyage. Or at least not very many."

"You are right," he said, "but Chinese porcelains are there, and they live well in the water of the ocean, even for centuries.

Plus many gold and silver jewelries made in China. Also of great value."

It would soon be time to get Primo out of my office and leave him to his fantasy. And I had no intention of helping him find another lawyer to assist him. Before he left, though, I did want to find a way to finagle a look at the supposed survivor account—if it really existed. That did intrigue me. But if I had to sign an agreement to see it, I'd just pass.

A small tone sounded, indicating the coffee was now ready. I grabbed two mugs from the bookshelf behind me. "Do you take sugar?"

"Again, I am Italian. So of course."

I removed the carafe from the warmer, poured the coffee into his mug and set it on my desk. Then I opened the bottom drawer, where I keep sugar for those who take their coffee adulterated, and took out a spoon and the sugar bowl.

"Two spoonsful or one?"

"Two, please."

I dished in the sugar and set the mug in front of him. "I'd give it a minute or two, Primo. It's probably still too hot to drink."

As I was about to pour my own cup, my cell phone rang. Or actually, it played "Yankee Doodle," which is what I had set it to that week. I glanced at the number and saw that it was from the 650 area code—Palo Alto. That meant it was probably someone from the *Stanford Law Review*, calling about my article. It was a call I didn't want to miss. I set the carafe back in its warmer and picked up the phone.

"Jenna James here . . . Yes, I can talk now. But can you hold on a moment?"

Primo was starting to get up. I put the phone against my thigh to mask my voice. "Primo, just stay here, please. This will be quick, and I can take the call in the empty office across the hall. Enjoy the coffee. Please pour yourself some more if you finish that one." I got up, came out from behind my desk, walked across the hall into the empty office that was directly across from mine and shut the door behind me. I'd try to get a look at the survivor account when I got back.

CHAPTER 3

The call took longer than I expected. The *Stanford Law Review* editor—for reasons lost to history, scholarly law journals are for the most part edited by law students—was insistent that my article needed additional footnotes to support several points I had made. We argued back and forth for a while until I caved. Then he went on to tell me about his recent ski trip to Mammoth—he was a great skier, in his opinion—and seek my advice on which summer law-firm clerkship he should accept. During the whole thing, I was feeling guilty that Primo was sitting in my office, waiting. At least he had great coffee to drink.

I finally got the guy off the line, dropped the cell into my pocket and dashed back across the hall. I was by now utterly desperate for my own first cup of coffee of the day, which the gods seemed to be conspiring to deny me.

To my surprise, my door was now closed, even though I knew I'd left it open. When I tried to reopen it, it was locked, which was even stranger, because it's a door that doesn't lock automatically when you close it unless you push in the little button on the side. Which I had for sure not done. What's worse, my keys were still in my purse, which was inside my office. I knocked, but there was no answer. Then I knocked louder. "Primo, are you in there?" There was no response.

Crap. He had no doubt gotten tired of waiting and left, not that I could blame him. Probably closed and locked the door as a courtesy.

I plucked the cell from my pocket and called campus security. They said someone would be there shortly to open it with a master key. Sure enough, only a few minutes went by before a skinny guy wearing a UCLA security uniform came walking down the hall.

"Good morning, Professor," he said. "I'm George Skillings from security. You lock yourself out?"

"Yeah. Kind of embarrassing, but I did, and my keys are in my purse, which is in my office."

"Happens all the time," he said as he unhooked a heavy ring of keys from his belt, chose one and inserted it in the lock. He turned the key, depressed the latch and pushed open the door. "There you go."

As the door swung open, the first thing I saw was Primo, slumped in his chair. His head lolled to the right, while his entire body also listed sharply in the same direction, held upright only by the chrome arm of the chair. His right arm drooped over the side, his hand almost touching the ground. He looked as if he might topple over at any moment.

"Jesus," George said, as we simultaneously moved in front of Primo.

From the front he looked even worse. There was drool coming from one side of his mouth, and he was breathing rapidly, with a horrible rasping sound escaping with each breath. His eyes were open but glassy.

I was frozen to the spot. George reached out and tried to straighten him up in the chair, then took two fingers and put them to Primo's neck. He held them there a few seconds while looking at his watch. "His heart rate's almost 180 per minute. Tachycardia." He punched a single number—clearly a speed dial—into his cell phone. I heard a click as someone picked it up on the other end. "It's George Skillings from security. I'm over at the law school. There's a guy in distress in Professor James's office. Possible drug overdose, heart attack or stroke. We need the UCLA ambulance here ASAP. We're in the southeast corner of the building." Then he gave them the room number, put the cell back in his pocket and turned to me. "Help me get him on the floor. It will help his breathing."

I nodded my assent. George moved up to the chair and put his hands under Primo's armpits. "Professor, why don't you get his legs, and we'll see if we can move him without dropping him? On my count of three, okay?"

"Okay," I said, as I moved over and grabbed Primo's feet.

"Okay, one, two, three!"

I lifted his feet while George lifted Primo's heavier upper body, and we managed to lower him to the floor without dropping him or hitting his head.

George tilted Primo's head to the side and reached into his mouth to try to clear some of the drool. "Don't want him to inhale his vomit if he throws up," he said. "I don't think there's anything else I can do for him until the EMTs get here with the ambulance, which should only take a couple of minutes. They're based on campus at the UCLA police station."

"What do you think is wrong with him?" I asked.

"No idea. Could be a reaction to drugs. Could be a heart attack or a stroke. Who is he?"

"Primo Giordano. A student in my seminar. He was meeting with me. But I got a phone call and took it across the hall so he wouldn't have to clear out. I told him to have some coffee and I'd be right back."

"How long were you gone?"

"I'm not sure exactly. Maybe six or seven minutes, maybe a little longer."

"Did you close the door when you left?"

"No."

"Weird."

Further conversation was interrupted by the arrival of a man and woman in crisp blue uniforms with patches on their shoulders that said UCLA Emergency Medical Services. They were pushing a red gurney loaded with a green backpack and other equipment I didn't recognize. From the look of them, they were students.

The guy, whose badge said his name was Carter Sullivan, looked at Primo and asked of the room in general, "What's going on?"

I repeated the story I had just told George Skillings. As Carter listened, he inflated a bag under Primo's legs and simultaneously cradled his head. Meanwhile the woman EMT, whose badge said her name was Susan Suarez, took a piece of equipment off the gurney, which I recognized as a blood pressure cuff tethered to a machine with a video screen. She wrapped the cuff around Primo's arm. As the cuff first inflated then deflated, she looked at the screen and called out, "Pulse is 190, pressure is 80 over 40. Really shocky."

Carter looked up at me. "What's his name, Professor?"

"Primo Giordano."

"Thanks." He put his mouth close to Primo's face. "Do you know your name?"

"Primo," he answered, but in a whispered voice, almost inaudible. Then Carter asked him, "Do you know where you are?"

"Law school." Again, it was hard to hear him.

"What happened, man?"

There was no response.

"What day is it?"

Again, Primo made no response.

While Carter spoke to Primo, Susan produced from somewhere a large, black radio phone with a stubby antenna and pushed a button. "Dispatch, this is Number 59. We're at the UCLA Law School. We have a white male law student in his twenties with shocky vitals. Essentially unconscious. No known cause. How long will it take the fire department paramedics to get here?" She paused and listened. "That's too long. We'll take him to Ronald Reagan UCLA Medical Center as a Code 3."

"What's a Code 3?" I asked

"Means we're going to use the siren."

"You're not going to wait for the paramedics?"

"No, they'll take about ten minutes to get here. With the siren we can get him to the ER at Reagan in two or three."

Carter was still down on the floor with Primo and had put an oxygen mask over his face. At that point I realized that the door to my office was still open and a small crowd of people had gathered in the hallway, watching. I saw four students I knew, plus my faculty colleagues Aldous Hartleb and Henrietta Gomez, and a third person I didn't recognize. I reached out and pushed the door shut. I don't think anyone else inside my office noticed that I had done it. They were all focused on Primo.

"Let's get him on the gurney," Carter said, looking up at Susan. "Sir," he said, addressing George Skillings, "can you assist?"

"Yes, I can."

Carter collapsed the gurney down to floor level, and the three of them hefted Primo onto it, blood pressure cuff still attached and oxygen mask still on. As soon as Primo was settled, Susan buckled him in with three leather straps, brought the gurney back up to chest height, reopened the door and began to pull the gurney backward out of the room. I followed them into the hallway. As I left the office, I glanced back and noticed for the first time that the red mailing tube Primo had been carrying didn't appear to be there. Or maybe it was just out of my sight line.

The group outside the door parted as we moved through, the faces of the crowd a mix of shock, concern and plain curiosity. I noticed that Henrietta was still there, but Aldous had gone.

CHAPTER 4

Carter and Susan were moving fast with the gurney. I trailed behind them, first down the hallway to the elevator bank, then into the elevator, which someone from security was holding open for us—where had he come from? Then they pushed their way out of the front door of the building, where, in the street, a white ambulance stood with its motor running, UCLA AMBULANCE emblazoned in blue letters across its double back doors. Another uniformed woman in blue, sporting a UCLA police badge, stood at the rear of the vehicle. As we arrived, she opened the doors, and the two EMTs slid the gurney into the ambulance and clamped it in place. Despite the oxygen mask over Primo's mouth, I could still hear his ragged breathing.

Carter looked over at me. "Why don't you ride along with us? We can continue debriefing you to see if you know anything else that might be helpful."

"Okay, I will."

"Hop in," Susan said, pointing to a bench on the right side, which was covered with a long flat beige plastic pillow, the kind you sometimes see on a chaise longue. I climbed aboard and sat down. Carter and Susan clambered in after me and seated themselves, one on either side of me. I heard rather than saw the rear doors slam. Seconds later we accelerated away as the siren began to wail. I had always wondered if the siren outside an ambulance sounded loud to people inside. It does.

As we got under way, Susan turned to me and asked, "When he showed up in your office, did you notice anything at all that seemed unusual? Please think hard, this guy isn't in good shape."

"No, nothing. It was just an ordinary conversation."

"Did he say anything about drugs or hard partying?"

"Nothing."

"Did he mention any health problems?"

"No."

"Why did he come to see you? Maybe there's a clue there."

What ran through my mind at that point was that if Primo was so nervous about the treasure map that he was looking for hidden microphones in my office, I shouldn't tell this unknown EMT about it. And besides, how could that have had anything to do with his collapse? But maybe I should tell them about it. After all, if it somehow came out that the map was important and I hid the information, wasn't it going to make me look bad? And what if it was missing? I suddenly realized that Susan was staring at me, waiting for my answer.

"Oh, I'm sorry," I said. "I'm a little shaken up by all of this. I don't really know why he came to see me. He put his name down on the sign-up sheet that's on my office door last week, and he'd only been in my office about five minutes when, like I said before, I got a phone call and went across the hall to take it. Up 'til then we were just exchanging pleasantries."

"For five minutes?"

"He's Italian," I said and smiled. "So yes, about five minutes of pleasantries, and during that time I was finishing up making coffee. I offered him a cup just before I left to take the phone call."

"Was there anything unusual about the coffee?"

"Not that I know of. I bought it at Coffee Chaos, where I usually buy my beans, and ground it the day before, right before I left to go home."

"Did he put anything in the coffee?"

"Sugar. A couple of teaspoons. Well, actually, I put it in, at his request."

"Sure. So nothing out of the ordinary there?"

"No."

"Did he drink it?"

"I assume so. I think his cup was sitting on my desk when I was let back into my office. I didn't look in it, but I assume he drank it. I can check when I get back."

"Did you have any yourself?"

"No. I was about to pour myself some when the call came. In fact, right now I'm dying for a cup of coffee. I haven't had even one this morning, and I'm kind of an addict. By now I would usually have had at least three."

"There's plenty of it around the hospital," she said.

Just then the ambulance, which had been twisting and turning its way through the campus to the hospital, came to a quick stop and began to back up. A few seconds later it stopped again and the back doors flew open.

"Professor," Carter said, "we're at the ER receiving bay now. I'm sure the docs here will want to talk to you, but right now we need to off-load the patient and tell them what we know. Nice to meet you." He stuck out his hand, we shook and he was gone.

I waited for them to roll out the gurney, where it was immediately surrounded by three or four doctors and nurses dressed in scrubs of various colors. Then I stepped down from the ambulance and watched as they pushed the gurney into an exam room and pulled the curtain closed.

I stood there, stunned. Not thirty minutes earlier, I had been sitting in my office—totally comfortable in my own world—talking to a student. Then, in what seemed the blink of an eye, I had been transported to an entirely different world, dumped off there and left to fend for myself while the denizens of that world went about their mysterious tasks—including whatever they were doing to Primo behind the curtain.

I had been standing there alone for perhaps a minute or two, lost in those thoughts and perplexed about what to do next, when suddenly a voice from behind me said, "And who might you be?"

I turned around and saw a short, slim man, perhaps in his midforties, with thinning black hair and a goatee that was beginning to be shot through with strands of gray. He was wearing a white coat and had a stethoscope tossed casually over his shoulder. His name, which was stitched in red just above the breast pocket on his white jacket, said *William Nightingale, MD*.

"I'm Professor James," I said. I don't usually use my professorial title in introducing myself, but I could sense that I was in a professional world where rank might somehow count.

"Professor of what?" he asked.

"Law."

"Ah," he said. "The enemy."

"Doctor, I'm an expert on the law of marine salvage, which is a subtopic of admiralty. I don't think that has much to do with medical malpractice claims, which is what I assume you're referring to."

He laughed. "You're right. And I suppose that means that on some level we're in the same business, since we salvage people who come here." He paused. "When we can."

"I suppose." I was still piqued at the hostility so often shown to lawyers as a matter of rote response.

"So," he said, "I understand you came in with the student who's unconscious?"

"Yes."

"Tell me what happened, please."

"I already told the EMTs."

"Yes, and I'm sure they're being debriefed by the people who are working on him in that cubicle over there." He pointed to the white curtain behind which Primo had disappeared. "But I'm the attending physician in the emergency department, and I'd like to hear it directly from you."

I sighed. "Okay." And I told him the whole story all over again, still sans treasure map.

"Interesting," was all he said.

Would he, I thought to myself, find it more interesting if I also told him about the map? More useful to Primo's recovery? I was on the edge of telling him when I remembered how important Primo thought maintaining confidentiality about the map was. And it couldn't possibly have any relationship to his illness. I decided again to skip it.

"Dr. Nightingale, is there someplace around here where I can get a cup of coffee? I'm something of an addict, and for one reason or another, I haven't yet had my morning fix."

"Sure. I'll take you out to the visitor waiting room and show you the machine there. It even takes credit cards."

"That stuff is usually horrible. You can't just sport me a cup from some stray coffeepot around here?"

He tilted his head. "I think I can do that. But I do need to get you out of here and to the waiting room. Let me walk you there."

I followed him past various cubicles, most empty and open, a few behind closed doors. When we reached the waiting room,

I grabbed a chair and sat down, and the good doctor departed with a cheery wave and an "I'll be right back with your coffee, Professor." And sure enough, he returned a few minutes later with a blue mug that said UCLA EMERGENCY DEPARTMENT on the side, filled to the brim with life-sustaining black fluid. He handed it to me and held out several small packages of creamer and sugar.

"Oh, I drink it black. But thanks for the coffee."

"You're welcome, Professor."

"What should I do now?"

"You're not family, are you?"

"No."

"Well, after you finish the coffee I think you should just go back to your office. Since you're not family, the medical privacy rules prevent me from telling you anything."

"Can you at least tell me if he's still alive?"

He pursed his lips and shrugged. "Sure. He's very much alive." He paused again. "I think he's going to be fine. We'll probably just keep him here for a few hours for observation and then release him."

"Thanks. What shall I do with the coffee mug when I'm done?"

"Why don't you just take it with you? That will give me an excuse to ask you out to dinner in order to retrieve it."

His remark irritated me, even though I was accustomed to being hit on—if less frequently since I'd left my twenties behind.

"I already have a boyfriend."

"Is he also a fiancé?"

"No."

"Then there's hope," he said, and turned and walked away, waving at me over his shoulder.

I sat for a few minutes after Dr. Nightingale left and savored the coffee. His parting remark had been charming, although not nearly charming enough to overcome my initial annoyance, especially given the setting, with my student still lying on a gurney behind a curtain. I put the empty cup carefully on the floor beneath my chair. Maybe he could ask my chair out to dinner if he felt like it.

CHAPTER 5

I looked at my watch. It was exactly 8:15 A.M. Amazingly, the whole episode with Primo, from office meeting to hospital, had taken only forty-five minutes. There was still time to get to Oroco's, which was only four or five blocks south of the hospital, in time for my meeting with the dean. I considered canceling but decided to go ahead with it. Among other things, the dean would probably want to hear directly from me what had happened with Primo, and I'd be able to tell him.

I left the ER waiting room and walked south toward Oroco's at a brisk pace. I suppose I should have worried more about Primo, but I just assumed it was some kind of drug issue. And since he was apparently going to be okay, I pushed the matter out of my mind. Instead, I tried, without success, to puzzle out what urgent matter had caused Dean Matthew Blender to summon me to meet him on such short notice at such an unlikely place. Oroco's wasn't a law-school crowd hangout—I had been there only once in my four years at UCLA—nor was it the kind of upscale establishment our dean frequented. It was, at best, funky.

At 8:30 A.M. sharp, I walked through the front door of Oroco's and spotted the dean, who was seated in the rear at a red Formica-topped table for two, studying his menu. I walked to the back and sat down across from him. He put down his menu, looked at me and said, "I heard about your student."

"You did? I was just about to tell you about him and give you the details."

"The security guy called the associate dean for student affairs—which is something you should have done, by the way—and told her about it. She called me about fifteen minutes ago."

"I'm sorry," I said, annoyed but trying hard to respond in a neutral tone. "I was rather preoccupied with going to the hospital in the ambulance with him."

"Well, no harm, no foul, Jenna. The important thing is, how's he doing?"

"A doctor there told me he was probably going to be fine, that he'll likely be released from the ER in a few hours."

"Good. I suppose it's just a blip then, and we don't need to worry further about it. Nor do I need to know the details right now, unless they somehow implicate the school. Do they?"

"No."

"Good. The associate dean will deal with it, then. Let's order."

"Okay."

During the entire conversation, as I sat there facing him, I had the same thought I had had the first time I met him: that he looked like a ferret. I know you're not supposed to judge people by their looks, and I try not to, but every time I encountered him that's what came immediately to mind.

For a couple of minutes we sat silently, studying our menus. Finally, Dean Blender put down his menu again, but instead of saying "Nothing on here looks quite right for a ferret," he said, "You know, Jenna, I'm quite surprised."

I hadn't a single, solitary clue what he was talking about. I elected to say so, although during that microsecond in which words move from brain to mouth, I decided to omit the so clearly called for profanity. "Dean Blender," I said, "I'm sorry, but I don't have any idea what you're surprised about."

"Jenna, you don't need to call me Dean Blender. As I've mentioned before, Matthew will be just fine."

"I apologize. I was taught as a child to be more formal when dealing with authority. But before we get into a serious discussion about anything, can we order coffee and breakfast? Especially coffee? I've had only one small cup this morning, and I need more than that to function well."

"Of course, of course," he said. "And I do apologize for asking you to meet me so far from campus at such an early hour. But it's close to another meeting I have scheduled at nine thirty. Plus, with my busy schedule and all my fund-raising, I rarely get to meet one-on-one with my faculty anymore, and this seemed like a grand opportunity to catch up."   I think my lips twitched slightly at his reference to *his faculty*, as if my colleagues and I were his personal possessions. But before I could say anything that would have further cemented my reputation as one of his faculty who always spoke her mind, a cute waitress, no doubt a UCLA undergrad, appeared at the side of our table, order pad in hand. She bore a name tag announcing her name as Tiffany.

"What would you guys like?" Tiffany asked, looking at me.

"A giant cup of coffee and a green onion scramble, please," I said. "And no salt on it, please."

"We don't have giant cups of coffee. Just one size, kinda small, actually."

"Then please bring me two."

"Okay. Toast or bagel?"

"Just the eggs, thanks. No side dishes."

The waitress turned to the dean. "And you, sir?"

"Coffee. One cup only." He gave her a wink. "And a toasted bagel with cream cheese. And please, the bagel cut in half, cream cheese spread on the first half only—in a thin, nongoopy layer—the second half left dry."

"Well, sir," she said, "we're short a waitress this morning, and they're short in the kitchen, too. So if it's okay with you, I'll bring you the cream cheese, and that way you can put it on just the way you like it. Will that work for ya?"

"Sure, sure," he said.

She turned and departed, leaving the two of us to resume our conversation.

"So," I said, "I think you were about to tell me what has so surprised you."

"Right, right. Well, candidly, I'm surprised that you've done so well here." He waved vaguely in a northerly direction, as if to acknowledge that *here* referred to the UCLA Law School, which was less than a mile north of where we were sitting in Westwood Village, the commercial area just south of the campus.

"Why's that surprising?"

"You're probably unaware of this, but there was quite a debate in the faculty as to whether to make you an offer of a tenure-track teaching position."

"I'm quite aware."

"You are?"

"Dean, secrets at the law school have a half-life of about three days. I hadn't even taught my first class before I heard that I was a controversial hire because I had spent too many years practicing law before I arrived—God forbid—plus I didn't have, in addition to my JD, a PhD in economics or political science or history or whatever's trendy these days."

He had put his right hand in front of his mouth and partly over his nose, a habit of his I'd noticed in faculty meetings that he often engaged in right before telling a lie. When he did that, his long, thin, turned-up nose tended to stick out from between his splayed fingers, which is no doubt why the ferret analogy came so easily to mind.

"No, Jenna," he said. "That wasn't it at all. Not at all. The discussion was whether, after a splashy career as a high-profile trial lawyer, you could really buckle down and do scholarly work. Whether you'd find it boring to do that instead of strutting around a courtroom."

"Well, the career, as you call it, was only eight years long. And I didn't 'strut around courtrooms.' That's a typical academic misperception of what real lawyers do in courtrooms, particularly from certain faculty who've never been in one, haven't really practiced law and treasure their PhDs."

"My apologies," he said. "I didn't and don't mean to disparage trial work or the value it can bring to scholarship." He took his hand away from his face. "But anyway, I asked you here so I could tell you that, to my surprise, you have overcome everyone's—or at least almost everyone's—doubts. Your scholarship has been outstanding. I've read every one of the four law review articles you've published so far and they're great."

Just then Tiffany returned, managing to balance three cups of coffee in two hands. She set one in front of the dean and two in front of me. "There you go," she said. "Be back with the food as soon as it's up."

The arrival of the coffee gave me the opportunity to decide not to cross-examine him and ask exactly who had *not* had their doubts erased. In fact, I suspected that the dean was himself one of the doubters. I had been hired during his first semester as dean, when he hadn't yet amassed enough power to block my appointment, and he'd never been particularly friendly or supportive. So I assumed his current praise was bs.

Instead, I said, "I'm pleased to hear that the general opinion—and yours!—is that I've done good work. Although I'm kind of surprised you asked me to breakfast at 8:30 A.M. just to tell me that."

"I thought you'd appreciate my telling you personally."

"Sure. But it hasn't escaped me, Dean, that you usually breakfast with *your* faculty at the Faculty Center. What do you really want to tell me, and why are we having what is in effect a secret meeting?"

"I simply wanted to have the opportunity to tell you, one-on-one, that assuming your big law review article on marine salvage gets the rave reviews everyone is expecting for it, you've pretty much got a lock on getting tenure. I mean, it's ultimately up to your Ad Hoc Tenure Committee, and then the Internal Appointments Committee and the faculty as a whole, of course, but I've got my ear to the ground, as they say, and what I hear sounds good."

"Dean Blender, not to be egotistical about it, but I think I already know that. So I'm still not sure why we're here."

Just then his cell rang, and he glanced at the screen. "I need to take this." He listened for a moment, then said, "Okay, keep me posted." He looked over at me. "That was the associate dean. She just learned that they've decided to admit Giordano to the hospital and keep him overnight. They're still not worried. It's just so they can run some tests. He'll probably be discharged tomorrow morning."

"Good," I said. "He's a nice guy; I hope he'll be okay."

A few seconds after that, Tiffany came back with the food and set it down in front of us, which interrupted any further discussion of Primo. The dean picked up his knife and began to spread cream cheese on half of his toasted bagel. He went on spreading while I let my scrambled eggs sit in front of me untouched. Finally, I said, "Dean, right before you got that call, I was saying I still wasn't sure why we're here."

"Well," he said, "let me put it this way, Jenna. There are two people up for tenure next year, and I think you're the only one likely to get it. Telling you that is a terrible breach of confidentiality, of course, so it's not something I wanted to talk about anywhere near the campus. But under the circumstances . . ."

I immediately understood what he was saying—that Aldous Hartleb, my next-door office neighbor, close friend and lover, would probably not be getting tenure.

"Have you told him?" I asked.

"No, of course I haven't. That would be presumptuous of me, because I could be wrong and, as I said, it's confidential. I'm not even supposed to be a part of it at this point. And the process isn't done yet. But I thought it would be a kindness to let you know my sense of things due to the, uh, situation."

"Would you like me to be blunt?"

"Are you ever anything but?"

I stared at him without responding.

While he stared back, no doubt wondering if I was going to explode, I took the time to think carefully about the tenor of my response. Since the moment I learned to talk, I had for the most part lacked a filter in front of my mouth. Overall, that approach had served me well. In recent months, though, I had been consciously trying to moderate my tone. Not because I enjoyed doing so but because it had seemed a better way to get ahead in an arena where civility, even if often faked, was so prized.

I went for unfiltered.

"Bluntly, I think that you're too chickenshit to tell him yourself and you want me to do it for you."

"That's not what I intended at all."

"Well, intended or not, I'm not doing it. Plus I'm no longer interested in dining with you." I screeched back my chair and got up.

"Where are you going?"

"To my office. I have work to do on my law review article."

As I reached the door of the restaurant, I glanced back at him. He had pulled my scrambled eggs over in front of him and was busy putting ketchup on them.

CHAPTER 6

M y car, of course, was still in the UCLA parking lot, up by the law school. I could have grabbed a bus to get back, but I needed time to think. So I walked back, or maybe stomped back is a better way to put it, making my way through the campus on foot.

As I passed the Ronald Reagan UCLA Medical Center, it occurred to me that I could go back to the ER, try to find Dr. Nightingale again and check on Primo. But due to the privacy rules, he probably wouldn't tell me anything beyond what the dean had learned, so I skipped it. In any case I wasn't particularly anxious to see Dr. Nightingale again.

When I got to Bruin Plaza, which is about a five-minute walk north of the hospital, I saw that the large metal sculpture of UCLA's mascot—the Bruin, a baby bear—had been boarded up inside a large, white wooden box. That meant the big game between USC and UCLA was imminent. Maintenance had boxed up the bear to prevent USC vandals from throwing red paint on it, as they had done a couple of years before. Over at USC, their maintenance team had no doubt done something similar to protect Tommy Trojan, their half-naked warrior statue, from *our* student vandals. One year UCLA students had cut off Tommy's sword and welded it to his behind.

Despite what I had just told the dean, I could tell Aldous if I wanted to. Or I could keep quiet about it. I mulled over my choices as I turned right out of the plaza and climbed up Bruin Walk, which runs up the steep hill beside the seriously hideous, modernist Ackerman Union.

If I told Aldous, it for sure wasn't going to help our relationship. Aldous was a proud guy, and although he'd probably appear to brush off the whole thing, I didn't think he'd be happy about his lover getting tenure when he didn't. And not all that pleased to have her deliver the bad news to him, although he'd hide that, too. On the other hand, if I didn't tell him, he'd find out sooner or later. And once he found out I'd kept it from him—the dean would no doubt figure out a way to let him know that I had—the deceit wasn't going to bring us any closer.

On some level my difficulty in deciding which way to jump—to tell him or not tell him—reflected the state of that relationship. We had met at the new faculty orientation more than four years earlier, but nothing had happened, at least not right away. Then we ended up by happenstance as next-door office neighbors and spent a ton of time talking. It took more than a year, but, facilitated by a three-martini evening, we finally ended up in bed.

The sex was hot, and the sex had stayed hot. We were a good match in other ways, too—both of us smart, curious about the world and willing to take risks and break rules. But somehow a deep emotional connection had never quite arrived. Maybe it was me, maybe it was him. Well, actually, I tended to think it was more him.

Part of the problem was that Aldous wasn't an emotional kind of guy. I'd never seen him break a sweat over anything, let alone cry about something or admit to even passing anxiety. He tended to confront problems, either solve them or fail to solve them and move on. He was pretty much the same with people. I sometimes had the sense that if I were run over by a truck, he'd just transfer his body to the next hot young professor down the hall. Maybe he'd stop first to put a flower on my grave. But only one.

I was, by contrast, an emotional kind of woman, or at least I liked to think of myself that way, even if maybe it wasn't obvious at all to other people. Which had to do with my steely-girl-with-steel-toed-boots reputation (in fact, Steel Boots had been my nickname in college). But inside, even if hardly anyone could see it, I was an emotional cupcake.

So while Aldous and I had a lot of fun together—including a two-week trip to France the previous summer after I finished my treasure salvor cruise—in the last few months I'd had the growing sense that we weren't going to last much longer. Staying in it just for the sex was tempting but didn't seem the right way to go.

I needed to talk to Aldous about all of that soon—not that we hadn't talked about it already three or four times. I hoped in the end we would be able to transition to some kind of friendship. But hiding from him what the dean had just told me wasn't going to help accomplish that.

Lost in those thoughts, I reached the top of the hill, turned right and started to walk through the grassy quad at the core of the campus, bookended by the red-brick, neo-Romanesque performance hall on one side and the undergraduate library on the other, both among the first buildings constructed at UCLA when the campus opened in the late 1920s. As was often the case, there was a crew filming a movie or TV show, or maybe a commercial, in the performance hall's colonnaded, arabesque walkway, which often serves filmmakers as a stand-in for somewhere in the Middle Ages or the Middle East.

They had stopped pedestrian traffic for a few minutes while they completed a shot; everything stops in LA for the movies. While I was standing there, I continued turning the Aldous problem over in my mind and discovered at least a temporary way out. I would indeed tell Aldous what the dean had said. But I'd also tell him that he should fight for his tenure. We'd figure out who his enemies were—there had to be two or three senior people who were causing the problem—and figure out how to crush them. It might even be fun, and maybe it could help salvage our relationship, or at least help transition it to a better place.

After a few minutes, they reopened the walkway, and I crossed the quad, walked the last two blocks to the law school and climbed the stairs to my office once again.

CHAPTER 7

On my way to my office, I noticed there was light coming out from under Aldous's door. I knocked gently and heard him say, "Come in," which I did.

Aldous's office is typical of academic offices. It's lined with wooden bookshelves, has a big oak desk with a black leather desk chair behind it, two cloth-covered guest chairs with blonde wood arms and the required notebook computer and printer. Aldous was facing away from me, his hands behind his head and his feet up on the windowsill, looking out of the window at Murphy Hall, across the street. Murphy Hall is UCLA's administrative office building—the place where the suits who run the university hang out.

I stood there for a few seconds, waiting for him to turn around, and when he didn't, said, "Earth to Aldous."

He dropped his hands, turned to face me and, on seeing who it was, got up and came out from behind his desk. "My God, Jenna, I just heard what happened this morning. Are you okay? Is the student okay?"

"Actually, Aldous, I'm a bit shaky." I realized I was tearing up, which was pretty rare for me.

He closed the distance between us and hugged me, although enveloped me in his arms might be a better way to put it. Aldous, at age forty-one, is a six foot four, chisel-chinned former college linebacker. I'm not quite five foot six and on the thin side, even thinner than I used to be since I became more diligent about stripping carbs from my diet. I leaned into the hug, and we stood there for a moment, rocking back and forth, until he let me go. He pulled back slightly, looked at my face and used his finger to wipe away my tears. Then he went back to his desk, took a tissue from a Kleenex box that was sitting there and handed it to me.

I wasn't quite sure how to react to either the hug or the Kleenex—Aldous wasn't normally a hugging kind of guy, and I'd never seen him go to the aid of anyone who was upset. It made me wonder if I'd been wrong about him. Maybe there *was* an untapped emotional well there after all. Or maybe the problem was that for whatever reason I'd been unable to tap it, despite a lot of trying.

"Well," he said, "it's understandable that you're a bit shaky. Who wouldn't be? But are you basically all right?"

"Yes."

"Good. How's the student? And who is it?"

"His name's Primo Giordano. He's in my Law of Sunken Treasure seminar. I guess he's okay. They're keeping him in the hospital overnight for some tests."

"I don't think I've ever run into him."

"He's a third year. Originally from Italy. I don't think he's cut a big swath as a student, so I'm not surprised you don't know him."

"Well, it's good he's going to be okay. With your tenure decision coming up, you really don't need the stress of dealing with a student death."

"Death? It never occurred to me that he might die, Aldous." I was taken aback. People as young as Primo didn't die unless they were hit by a car or drowned or something like that.

"I guess it's just my negative outlook on things, Jenna. Back when I did numbers, the guy who had the cube next to me died unexpectedly one day after drinking a soda. Now, whenever anything even slightly bad happens to someone, I automatically think they're going to die."

I knew that by "back when I did numbers," Aldous was making reference to the fact that, before attending law school, he had worked at a Wall Street investment bank, where he had been a quant—a guy who crunched reams of quantitative data to predict the price of obscure financial instruments. It had made him rich, and every once in a while I wondered if his wealth was the real source of my attraction to him. I couldn't make up my mind about that. It was true that I sometimes missed my big salary at Marbury Marfan, but I didn't think I truly needed the kinds of things Aldous's money could buy—first-class travel, five-star hotels, the ability to buy anything you wanted just because you wanted it and all of that. On the other hand, it was a nice way to live, and if Aldous ever decided to start spending his money that way—despite the fact that he didn't currently seem so inclined—I could work really hard to get used to it.

I decided to change the topic. "So," I said, "when I came in, you were staring out of the window. Daydreaming?"

"No. I was looking out at Murphy Hall, wondering if I'd be happier as an administrator than as a law professor."

"Why?"

"Because my academic performance is in question."

"By whom?"

"Just a couple of people. But they're important people."

"Name names."

"There's not a lot of point in that right now. Let's just say that the law review articles I've written over the last few years about unearthing securities law violations through metadata analysis haven't exactly gotten a rousing reception, either around here or from the academic elite at other law schools."

"I thought they were good. What was wrong with them?"

"Too quantitative. Too many numbers, not enough analytical text. 'Still a quant, not really a law professor.' Or something like that."

"I thought quantitative analysis was the rage these days. And in any case, I found them accessible."

"Thanks, Jenna. I appreciate your saying that. But two of our colleagues—who are most likely members of my Ad Hoc Tenure Committee—apparently found them otherwise. Or so the drums are telling me."

"The drums?"

"Sorry, an obscure reference to the way certain African tribes used to communicate. Call it the gossip, if you like."

"That doesn't mean it's really over. The decision hasn't actually been made yet."

"I think in this case, Jenna, the decision's all but made. The bottom line is that you're going to get tenure this year, but I'm not."

"And that's it? You're just going to accept it?"

"I think that's the easier, more pleasant path. I can easily get a job at a lesser law school, or even go back to Wall Street."

"Out of Los Angeles?"

"Probably."

"Shit, Aldous, I say you ought to stay here and fight. I'll lead the charge, and God knows I'm good at that."

"Getting yourself involved in a fight on my behalf makes no sense for you. It could even impact your own tenure."

"I'll get tenure no matter what."

"Maybe, but you don't want to polish your rep of being difficult to deal with. So stay out of it. Once you get tenure here, if you work hard for a couple of years after that, you'll have the cred to go on to Harvard or Yale or someplace like that. Or maybe Columbia, since I'll likely be in New York. Or do you already have feelers from other schools?"

"I do."

"So you might go to another city yourself."

"No. If I get tenure, I plan to stay right here."

"We don't," Aldous said, "have to be together in the same city to still be 'us.'" He gestured at a photo on the bookshelf that I hadn't noticed earlier. The photo showed the two of us in foul-weather gear, standing on his sailboat, heeled hard over in the wind, laughing into the camera. "One of the good things, Jenna, about being a law professor, is that you'll have lots of spare time to do things with me, even if we're in different cities for a short while."

As I listened to him talk, I realized that Aldous, despite our several conversations about it, didn't really think that our relationship was in trouble. I tried to send a message. And a not very subtle one.

"My God, Aldous, you have that picture on your bookshelf, right where everyone can see it. Even students."

"Jenna, what are you talking about? Everyone in this law school knows we're an item. Even . . . students."

"Well, please take it down. Given the uncertainty of our relationship these days, it makes me uncomfortable." It was a petty thing to say, but before I could take it back, Aldous had walked over to the bookshelf and turned the photo facedown.

"There," he said, smiling. "Photo evidence of relationship temporarily suppressed. Anyway, are we still going to dinner and the play tonight? We can go out afterward, have a few martinis and talk about how we can manage living in different cities."

I plunked myself down, heavily, in one of the guest chairs. "I say we skip the play, go out to dinner and talk instead about why you're being such a pussy about this tenure thing."

"I want to go to the play—it's about that pussy Hamlet. Afterward we can go to dinner and you can call me whatever disparaging names you like."

"Fine, we'll go to the play. But *pussy* isn't really disparaging."

He just looked at me.

"Well, okay," I said, "maybe it is."

"A typical Jennaism?"

"Yeah, I know, Aldous. Confrontational Jenna. I'm trying to do something about that, but without a lot of success."

"No worries," he said. "I find it charming."

"Thanks. I don't think a lot of people around here do. It worked better in a big law firm. Anyway, change of topic: I had breakfast with the dean this morning."

"Oh?"

"Yes, he took me to breakfast deep in Westwood to tell me pretty much what you've already figured out."

"Interesting. Did he suggest you tell *me*?"

"No, though I think he hoped I'd tell you and save him the trouble."

"The guy is a real piece of work."

"No doubt of that," I said.

"So were you," he asked, "going to tell me?"

"Of course I was going to tell you. Now you're told, and I need to go back to my office and get to work on the new footnotes Stanford wants. Assuming I can put what happened to Primo out of my mind, which may not be easy."

"You'll figure it out," he said.

"I guess so," I said. "See you later, Aldous." And with that I left.

As I walked toward my own office, I wondered to myself how a guy who had recently suggested, despite what I saw as our ongoing difficulties, that we should get married—and it would all somehow work itself out—could be thinking about moving out of town. Did he think I would ultimately just follow him? Professor Jenna Sheepdog?

CHAPTER 8

When I reached my office, the door was open and George Skillings was still standing where I'd left him when I followed the gurney out of the door almost two hours earlier.

"You're still here, George?"

"Actually, I just came back. For whatever reason, I'm suspicious of that coffee he drank."

"Why?"

"I don't know. Just a gut feeling. Anyway, I was thinking I ought to preserve it, just in case."

I thought to myself that I really ought to object to his having let himself back into my office without my consent. Then I thought better of it. Given the circumstances, this was a good situation in which to practice being nonconfrontational.

"Suit yourself, George."

"Do you have any plastic bags around, Professor?"

"Sure. I have a small box of them in my desk drawer." I walked around the desk, fished one out and handed it to him.

"Thanks. As a precaution, I'm going to bag his cup—there's a little splash of coffee left in it. Just in case there's something wrong with it. Did you make it from beans?"

"Yeah. I ground them yesterday before I left, and the pot went on automatically this morning, before I got here."

"Are the beans old? I've heard that weird toxic molds can grow on old coffee beans."

"Really? I've never heard that."

"I read it somewhere."

"George, do you really think it could have been the coffee? I've never heard of anyone getting sick from coffee. I read a lot of online coffee blogs, and no one's ever even mentioned it. Not even the people most obsessed with quality."

"Yeah, well, but are the beans old, Professor?"

I was beginning to think that George Skillings was some kind of nutcase, but I decided to answer his question anyway. "I don't think they're old. I just got them a couple of days ago from Coffee Chaos down in Manhattan Beach. This is the first coffee I've made from them. I brought the bag from home yesterday."

George extracted a vinyl glove from his back pocket, slipped it on his right hand and picked up Primo's cup. He dropped it into the plastic bag and sealed it shut.

"Maybe I should take some of the beans, too," he said.

"Help yourself. The bag is on the bookshelf over there."

"Got another plastic bag?"

"Sure." I got it out and handed it to him.

He walked over to the shelf, opened the beans, which were still in their Coffee Chaos bag, and poured some into the second plastic bag.

"What about sugar?" he asked.

I pointed him to the drawer where I kept it, handed him another plastic bag and watched while he took a sample of the sugar.

"Professor, did you drink any yourself?"

"No. I got that call just as I was about to pour myself a cup." I pointed to the empty coffee cup that was still on my desk, a supersized black one that says JENNA on it in big red letters. "So I hadn't filled mine yet."

"Well, if I were you, I'd toss whatever's left in the pot, and the beans, too. It's unlikely the coffee's the problem, but you never know, and you don't want to risk making anyone else sick."

"Okay, I will. By the way, did you see a big red mailing tube around here, with white caps on the ends?"

"No, why?"

"The student had one with him when he got here, but I don't see it anywhere."

"No, didn't see it."

"Do you recall seeing it when we opened the door?"

"No. But I wasn't really focused on looking around the office."

"Me neither."

"Well, I have to go fill out my report," he said. "To be candid, though, Professor, you look a bit stressed out, which is hardly surprising. Maybe you ought to take the rest of the day off, huh? You don't need to be a superhero about this."

"I'm okay. And I've got work I've got to get done. But thank you for your concern."

"Be sure to toss that coffee," he said as he left.

After he was gone, I took the carafe out of its holder beneath the drip spout and sniffed it. It did smell a bit strange. It even seemed to make me a bit nauseated, but then, it was probably more from the situation than from the coffee. Looking at the coffee made me realize I had an intense need for still more. I left the office, locked the door and went over to Lu Valle Commons, the casual coffee-and-food place that sits between the law school and the public policy school. I drank down two big cups. When I finished the second cup and set it down on the table, I noticed my hands were shaking slightly. Initially, I couldn't figure out why. Sure, it had been unnerving to have Primo collapse in my office and then be dragooned into going to the hospital with him in the ambulance. That was over, though, and he was going to be all right. In the end I just passed it off as what happens to your body when an intense adrenaline rush fades. Like what used to happen to me on the track team in high school right after I won a close race. I decided not to worry about it. Everything was going to be fine.

CHAPTER 9

I left Lu Valle Commons and walked back to the law school, unlocked my office and sat down at my desk. Then I tried to get back to work on my law review article, intending to make the small last-minute changes Stanford had requested. After maybe thirty minutes, I realized that instead of typing I was just staring at my hands on the keyboard. They were red all over, and rough. The thought that went through my head was that my hands had begun to look like they belonged to an old woman. Which was ridiculous, since I was only thirty-four. But still . . . Maybe I needed to get a manicure or something. Which was also ridiculous. I'd never had a manicure in my whole life. All I did to my nails was cut them. I didn't even use nail polish.

After a few more minutes of staring at my hands, I realized I was rapidly becoming a basket case, even as I simultaneously chided myself for my reaction. There was no good reason for it. It certainly wasn't my fault that Primo had collapsed in my office, and I had gone well beyond the call of duty in riding to the hospital with him. Really, George Skillings should have gone. That was his job. Maybe I was feeling the way I was because it was the first time I'd ever been the first person on the scene for something like that.

In the end, whatever the reason for my feelings, it was clear to me that I wasn't going to get anything at all done that day, and I might as well go home. I got up, stepped out into the hallway, closed the door behind me and locked it. And I made special note of the fact that I had indeed locked it. Tomorrow, if it turned out to be open again, there wasn't going to be any doubt in my mind about the locked state in which I had left it.

As I went by Aldous's office, I stopped and knocked, thinking it might be good to talk again, but there was no answer. Nor was there any light coming out from under his door. He was probably off teaching a class.

Just then, I heard a voice behind me say, "Professor?" I turned to see Julie Gattner, an attractive brunette who's a third-year student in my Sunken Treasure seminar. Julie had been one of the students hanging around in the hallway earlier in the morning, when I'd shut the door to block their view of the EMTs working on Primo. There were two other students with her, neither of whom I recognized.

"Professor," Julie said, "what happened to Primo? We saw him being wheeled out by the emergency people."

"I don't really know, Julie. One minute he was okay, then he wasn't. But I want to respect his privacy, so I think I'm just going to leave it at that, okay?"

"Oh, sure, I understand. Hope he's all right. He's a really nice guy."

"Agreed. And I don't mean to be unfriendly, but I need to get going."

"Oh, sure," she said again, turned away and headed down the hall in the direction from which I had come. As the group moved away, I heard one of the other students say to her, "Primo's into stuff, isn't he?" And then I heard another voice I didn't know respond, more faintly and harder to make out, "Yeah, maybe he just went too hard last night."

I stood for a moment and thought about that, then trotted down the stairs and out the door and headed over to my car, which was in Parking Lot 3. A pass for Lot 3—particularly a blue pass—was an important faculty perk. The lot's only about a six-or seven-minute walk from the law school, at least at the speed at which I usually walk, and is especially handy when it rains or the weather turns cold, keeping in mind that most Angelenos regard anything under fifty degrees as positively arctic. Had I been less lucky, I might have had to park in Lot 2, which was farther away, not to mention rather dark and forbidding inside.

My trusty Land Cruiser was there, waiting for me. It was ten years old by now, but I still loved it, and it still served as my home away from home, although the backseat, with its books, discarded plastic water bottles and at least two old pizza boxes, had become something of a disgrace. I really needed to clean it out. Maybe today would be a good day to do it.

I got in, put the key in the ignition and started the engine. I was about to put it into gear and back out of the parking space when my cell rang. I picked it up and glanced at the screen. It was the dean. I thought seriously about ignoring his call, but given all that had happened, I supposed I owed it to him to answer, so I did.

"Jenna, it's Matthew. Giordano died."

I was poleaxed. I tried to say something in response but found I couldn't speak.

"Jenna, are you there?"

It took me another second, but I finally found my voice. "Yes, I'm here. Did you say he died? That Primo died?"

"Yes. I got a call about ten minutes ago from the chief attending at the ER, a Dr. Nightingale."

"The same doctor who told me that he'd probably be fine."

"He told the associate dean the same thing. You were there when I got the call. I guess he got it wrong."

"What did Primo die from?"

"Dr. Nightingale wouldn't tell me anything. Medical privacy and all that crap. He just wanted to get information on next of kin."

"I have no idea who they are."

"I gave him what we have on file. Meanwhile, my phone's been ringing off the hook ever since they took him out of your office. A lot of people are saying he was a heavy partier. So maybe it was drugs."

"I guess. I hardly knew him. But whatever, I'm in shock."

"I can understand that. There's one more thing, though."

"What?"

"His brother, Quinto Giordano, just called me."

"Quinto? That's his brother's name?"

"Yes, why?"

"Well, Primo means 'first' in Italian. Quinto means 'fifth.' So does that mean there are three other brothers in between?"

"I have no idea. But he was calling about something in particular."

"What?"

"He wanted to know, and I quote, 'Where is the treasure map?' What is he talking about?"

"Oh, shit."

"What?"

"When Primo came to see me, he told me he had a map marking where a supposed Spanish galleon had sunk. Filled with valuable stuff, he claimed."

"Did he have it with him?"

"He said he did. He was carrying a red mailing tube, and he said the map was inside it. I never got to see it because right after he offered to show it to me, I went across the hall to take a call, and when I got back, he was already unconscious. I simply forgot about it."

"Where is it now?"

"I don't know. It disappeared at some point. I think it was already gone when the EMTs got to my office, but I only noticed it was gone when they were wheeling Primo out. In any case, it's not there now."

"How big was it?"

"Maybe three feet long."

"How could you fail to notice immediately that something that big was missing?"

"Hey, Dean Blender, when I got back from the phone call, I was focused on Primo, you know? He was unconscious and drooling. And then the EMT guys arrived and all of that. I wasn't exactly looking for the effing map."

"Okay, okay. Are you in your office now?"

"No. I'm in my car in Lot 3, about to go home."

"I think you should go back and look again for that map."

"All right, but it's not there."

"Try the trash cans. And let me know if you find it. This guy seems a little unhinged."

I turned off the car and jogged back to my office, thinking hard about the map. If it was really important—could it possibly be a real treasure map?—there had to be a logical explanation for what had happened to it. It was in my office for sure when I walked across the hall to take the phone call but apparently gone by the time I got back. Where could it have disappeared to in the few minutes I was away? I had no answer.

When I reached my office, my door was again wide open. This time there was a UCLA police officer standing inside, looking around. He turned as I walked in and said, "Could you identify yourself, please?"

"I'm Professor James. This is my office."

"Ah, I see. I'm Detective Drady of the UCLA Police Department." He handed me a card. "I'm doing an initial investigation of the death of a student." He looked at a set of notes he had in his hand. "Student's name was Primo Giordano. I understand this was the last place he was seen alive before they took him to the ER."

"Uh, I guess that's true. But how did you get in, Officer? I locked my office when I left."

"Campus security let me in. Said I could have a look around, even though you weren't here. Don't need a search warrant since it's university property. We don't usually exercise that right, but in the case of a death, it's different."

"Oh."

"Would now be a convenient time to interview you, Professor? It's best when things are fresh in someone's mind."

"Sure. You know, Officer, you look vaguely familiar."

"I was one of the LAPD officers who arrested Robert Tarza."

"I'm sorry, I don't remember that."

"Well, you do remember, don't you, that Tarza tried to flee to Chicago when he was the target in a murder investigation? For murdering the managing partner of his law firm?" The sarcasm was so thick I could have cut it. And although it was tempting to respond in kind, I decided to stick to the facts because I had no idea where, exactly, this upsetting conversation was going.

"He wasn't trying to flee, Detective. He was going to see a rare coin dealer to try to get to the bottom of things."

"Well, whatever. When he got back, we arrested him. I was one of the arresting officers. I testified briefly at the preliminary hearing. You cross-examined me."

Once he put it in context I did vaguely remember him. He had testified for something like two seconds. But I really didn't want to get into a further discussion of the case with him.

"I'm sorry," I said, "I still don't recall your testimony."

"Well, it's a long time ago now. Six years, maybe?"

"Something like that."

"Not long after that trial I left the LAPD and joined the UCLA force."

"Well, welcome to UCLA School of Law, Officer. Let's sit down, and you can ask me what you want to know, not that I know very much."

CHAPTER 10

The interview with Officer Drady took about ten minutes. We covered pretty much the same territory I had covered with everyone else. I went out of my way to mention that the coffee had smelled odd to me. Drady sniffed what was left in the pot, wrinkled his nose and suggested I toss it. I reminded him that if there was something wrong with it that had made Primo sick—like some weird fungus on the beans—it could be evidence. But he said Skillings had already collected samples and was going to hand them over to the police, so there was no need to keep it. Overall, he didn't seem particularly interested in that aspect of the story.

I also decided it was time to mention the supposed treasure map. He raised his eyebrows on that one but didn't press for more details about the map. When I told him it had gone missing, he helped me look around the office for it and confirmed it wasn't there.

As the interview was wrapping up, I thought to myself that the death had been awful, but the conversation about it with Drady had so far seemed rather anodyne. Then I berated myself for using that word, even in my head. It's one of those ten-dollar words law professors use to impress each other, and all it means is ordinary, inoffensive. It's certainly not a word I would ever use in front of a jury.

Which is exactly when the interview began to veer toward the offensive.

"So," Officer Drady said, as he slapped his notebook closed, "what's Robert Tarza doing these days?"

The truth was that Robert and I, despite his having been my mentor and close friend for close to a decade, were no longer on the best of terms. I hadn't spoken to him in several years. But I certainly wasn't going to share that with this asshole detective.

"Well," I said, "I haven't talked to him lately, so I don't really know exactly. Litigating in his downtown law firm, I suppose."

"He's lucky not to be up in Marin County instead, if you ask me."

"Which is what, Officer, a veiled reference to San Quentin, which, if I recall correctly, is in Marin?"

"Didn't intend it as veiled, really. I still think he had something to do with the murder of the managing partner all those years ago."

"You don't think all the others who were convicted had anything to do with it?"

"Yeah, I do. But I don't think it was the whole story."

"What do you think the whole story was?"

"I'm not sure, but to be candid, I think you had something to do with it, too, Professor."

I stared at him for a moment in disbelief.

"I didn't, Detective. And if you don't have anything else to ask me about today's situation, I have a lot of work to do."

"I'd only say this, Professor. The last time around they found the body of the managing partner in the firm's reception area with a knife in his back, and he turned out to be your boyfriend.

This time around there's a body and it's your student. What's a good detective to think?" He stood up and stuck out his hand. "Good to meet you."

"I wish I could say the same," I said, conspicuously declining either to stand up or to shake his outstretched hand.

He smirked, turned and waltzed out the door.

I sat there after he left with a rising feeling of unease. Was I about to be accused of killing Primo? That was too ridiculous even to contemplate, and I shoved it out of my mind. Or maybe I didn't shove it entirely out of my mind. When I looked down at my hands, they were shaking again, and they were redder than ever.

CHAPTER 11

After Drady left I looked around my office once again, hoping to catch sight of either the mailing tube or its supposed contents. I got down on my knees and peered under my desk. I opened all of my desk drawers, thinking perhaps someone had taken the map out of the tube and folded it up. I looked carefully on my bookshelves, even pulling out some of the books to make sure nothing had slipped behind them. It wasn't in any of those places.

Next I walked back into the empty office across the hall, where I had taken the phone call. The room was still utterly empty. I went down the hall and searched in the small kitchen, where there was a tall trash can. There wasn't much in the can, but I rooted through it anyway. I found nothing that even remotely resembled a map. I looked in the drawers and cabinets. I searched the trash can in the women's room and even in the men's room. Nothing.

I returned to my office and considered what to do with the coffee that was left in the coffeepot. I was about to take it to the bathroom and dump it when I had second thoughts.

Skillings had taken a sample, which Drady had said he was going to give to the police. If there turned out to be something wrong with the coffee, there were going to be consequences. My litigator instincts told me I needed to have my own sample. I decided it would be easiest to take the entire coffeepot home with me.

My next problem was what to do with the remaining beans in the cute little Coffee Chaos bag. If they were tainted in some way, it wouldn't be a great idea to leave them there lest someone else use them. But who could possibly use them without my knowledge? On the other hand, at least three people had entered my office without my knowledge in the last twenty-four hours—Primo, Skillings and Drady. There was no point in risking it. I grabbed the bag and shoved it into my purse.

I walked to Lot 3 for the second time, carrying the coffeepot, managing to get there without having the coffee slosh over the edge of the lid. I put the pot on the floor in front of the passenger seat, got back in the car and headed for home.

On the way, not far from campus, I spied a new nail salon. It had a big sign out front: ONLY NAILS. GRAND OPENING. Amazingly, there was a parking place right in front. I braked hard, slid my car into the space and went in. After some initial confusion, I was able to persuade them that I didn't want my nails done—that I just needed some treatment that might soothe my raw, red hands. The woman in charge, whose name was Thu Nguyen, and who I think was also the owner, suggested hot wax. I agreed. The treatment—wrapping my hands in plastic bags into which hot wax was poured—felt great. For the first time that day, I was able, at least momentarily, to forget about Primo and the missing map and just relax.

When they were done with the treatment, I thanked Thu, paid in cash and left a large tip. Then I got back in my car and headed home. On the way, though, I couldn't help but replay the day's events in my mind—over and over and over again. They still made no sense to me.

CHAPTER 12

Home is a condo—the penthouse—in one of the high-rises along the Wilshire Boulevard corridor, just east of Westwood Village. It looks north into the hills and has three bedrooms and a marble hot tub. I bought it when I was in my last year at Marbury Marfan and still making a mid-six-figure salary, and used my end-of-year bonus and a small inheritance for the down payment. Now, on my low-six-figure law professor salary, I had begun to find the mortgage payments and the condo association fees a bit of a stretch. I really ought to have sold it, but it reminded me of my prior, more glittery life, so I kept it.

The financial drain was one of the things that had prompted me to say yes when my cousin Tommy had called from Hawaii the previous spring, reported that he'd been accepted into the graduate molecular chemistry program at UCLA and asked if I'd let him rent my spare bedroom for the fall semester. He said he'd only need it while he got the lay of the land in Los Angeles and found a place of his own. He'd offered to pay me a thousand dollars a month.

Tommy is the only child of my Uncle Freddie, who is one of my favorite people on the planet. I'd first met Tommy the year after I graduated from high school. I'd spent that gap year before college living with Uncle Freddie in Hilo, Hawaii. At age sixteen, my parents had thought I was still too young to go directly to college and could instead have a more limited adventure with some adult supervision. At the time, Tommy was only nine. He was already tall for his age and had a mop of bright red hair. His hated nickname was Carrot. We got along in the awkward way that a sixteen-year-old out for adventure gets along with a nine-year-old who spends most of his time playing video games and collecting Bufo toads.

As I opened the door, Tommy was slouched on the leather couch in the living room with his red tennis-shoed feet propped up on the coffee table, reading a professional journal of some sort that displayed colorful hydrocarbon rings on the cover. Tommy had grown into something of an odd duck. He was now very tall and gangly, almost loose-limbed. His hair, still bright red, was now cut into a mohawk.

"Hi, Tommy," I said.

"Hi, Jenna. Why are you carrying a coffeepot full of coffee around?"

"It's a long story," I said as I put it on the kitchen counter. "The coffee may be bad, so don't drink it."

He gave me an odd look. "Okay, I won't. Hey, your father called you. About an hour ago."

"He did?"

"Yep. He said, 'Hello, this is Senator James.'"

"Did he say whether something was wrong?"

"No. He sounded pretty casual. Just said to call back when you got a chance. Didn't seem very interested in chatting with me. I'm not even sure he realized he was talking to his nephew."

"Oh. Did you identify yourself?"

"No. Guess I should have. Hey, I was pretty young when he was a politician. I've forgotten, what kind of a senator was he again?"

"The United States kind. From Ohio. Still fond of using the title, I'm afraid."

"Not a bad title, as hierarchy goes."

"No, not bad, I guess."

"Hey, someone also came by to see you."

"Who?"

"That real-estate agent who keeps bugging you to sell your condo to his client. Knocked on the door."

"What did you tell him?"

"Exactly what you told me to tell him the last time. That the condo's not for sale, and it's particularly not for sale to an anonymous buyer. I said you wanted to know who the buyer was."

"Did he tell you?"

"No. He just gave me his card again and said you should reconsider because they're offering a great price. The card's on the kitchen counter."

"I'll put it with the stack of his other cards."

"Hey, Jenna, can I ask you something personal?"

"Sure."

"Why are your hands so red?"

I didn't see that there was any point in telling him that it had arisen right after someone died—I didn't feel like sharing all of that with him yet—so I told him half the story.

"I stopped off and had a hot wax treatment. Felt great but seems to have left my hands kind of red."

"That's weird. An old girlfriend of mine used to have those treatments, and they never left her hands red."

I shrugged. "Maybe the wax was too hot."

"Can I suggest a different possibility, Jenna?"

"Sure."

"It could be stress. There's something called Raynaud's disease that can make your fingers red. It's often triggered by stress. Hold up your hands a second."

I held them up in front of me, and Tommy and I both stared at them.

"You're right," I said. "It's mostly my fingers that are red."

"Yes," he said. "And the tips are white, which is also characteristic of Raynaud's. Anything stressful going on with you right now?"

I felt, suddenly, as if Tommy had become my doctor. But it felt good to have someone care about me, especially after my go-round with Drady. I decided to tell Tommy what had happened.

"Something *very* stressful. One of my students just died—he collapsed in my office, and I had to go with him in the ambulance to the hospital. At first they thought he'd be okay, but a couple of hours later he died."

"Well, Jenna, I don't know much about Raynaud's, but that's the kind of thing that could do it."

"How do you know about it at all?"

"I went to med school in Hawaii for a year and then dropped out. But you ought to see a real doctor about it, because some forms of Raynaud's are benign, but some indicate a serious underlying condition."

"All right, I will. But right now I'm going to go call my father."

I tossed my purse on the big black leather recliner next to the couch and headed toward my bedroom so I could have some privacy. As I put my hand on the bedroom doorknob, Tommy said, "Hey, Jenna, what did your student die from?"

I turned to face him. "No one seems to know. Or at least not yet. Why?"

"Well, are you a suspect?"

I froze. And, despite the absurdity of the question, I felt my stomach clench. "Why in hell would I be a suspect, Tommy? I hardly even knew the guy."

He grinned. "Isn't the person who finds the body always a suspect?"

"I didn't find the body. He wasn't even dead when I found him." I realized, as those last words came out of my mouth, that I sounded defensive, which was ridiculous. I had no need to be defensive.

"I'm just pulling your chain, Jenna."

"Well, I don't find it funny. At all. Now, if you'll excuse me, I need to call my father."

I turned, walked into the bedroom and, resisting the temptation to slam the door, closed it quietly behind me. Then I collapsed against it. First George Skillings had collected the coffee from my office based on a "gut feeling"—before he even knew that Primo had died. Then Drady had all but accused me of murder. And now Tommy was "joking" about it. Were these people serious? I could feel myself beginning to hyperventilate.

CHAPTER 13

I walked over to my bed, sat down on the floor next to it, closed my eyes, folded my legs into a yoga position and took long, slow, deep breaths. I had learned the technique in a meditation class I attended while in law school in an attempt to beat back exam anxiety. Eventually, the slow breathing started to work, and my near-panic retreated. After a few minutes more, I felt more or less like myself again.

I got up, sat down on the bed and picked up the phone from the nightstand—I still have a landline, another extravagance—and punched in my father's number on the speed dial. As the phone rang on the other end, I wondered what his call could be about. Normally, my father only called me twice a year—on my birthday and, if it wasn't one of the years when I dragged myself back to Cleveland for the holidays, on Christmas.

The phone was picked up on the fourth ring.

"Hi, Dad, it's Jenna."

"Jenna Joy! What a pleasure."

I controlled myself from telling him, for the millionth time, not to use my hated middle name. But ever since my grandmother, his mother, whose name it had been, died last year at the age of a hundred, it had become harder to complain about it.

"It's nice to hear your voice, Dad. But you almost never call. What's up?"

"I'm coming to visit."

"When?"

"On Thursday."

"Why?"

"There's a conference at USC Law School honoring old Judge Jenkins. You remember, the judge I clerked for on the 9th Circuit, when I got out of law school."

"I don't recall him personally, Dad, because I wasn't born yet, but it sounds like fun. I hope I'll get to see you while you're here."

"I'm hoping to stay with you."

"You're certainly welcome to, but, you know, I'm a long way from USC, and the traffic in the morning is bad, and . . ."

"Oh, no worries there, Jenna Joy. I'll have a car and driver. And it will give us an opportunity to spend some quality time together."

I thought to myself that despite our checkered history, I really ought to make an effort to be more welcoming. Dad had just turned eighty, and since my mother's death two years earlier, he had clearly been lonely.

"Dad, I'm having trouble hearing you. I'm going to put you on my speakerphone. Sometimes, for reasons I don't understand, it works better than the handset."

"Okay, sure."

The truth was that I needed to put him on speaker because my hand had begun to shake so violently that I was having trouble holding the phone.

"Okay, Dad, can you hear me?"

"Yep."

"Hey, Dad, I'll look forward to seeing you. What day are you coming?"

"This Thursday. My plane gets in late in the afternoon. Don't worry about picking me up. I'll just take a cab. Can you leave a key with the doorman?"

"Sure. And Tommy may be here, too."

"The guy who answered the phone when I called?"

"Yes."

"Something romantic?"

"No, Tommy's your nephew, Dad. Uncle Freddie's son."

"Oh. Didn't realize he was living with you. Fred was always a bit worried whether he'd amount to anything. What's he doing now?"

"Grad student in molecular chemistry at UCLA."

"Guess he's straightened out, then. But I'm sorry you're not living with someone romantically. It would be good for you to get married, Jenna Joy."

I had never mentioned Aldous to him and didn't think this was the time.

"Dad, I'm going to get married when I want to get married."

"All right." And then he hung up. Which wasn't unlike most of the exits he'd made from my life over the years. Here one moment, gone to a chicken-dinner fund-raiser the next.

CHAPTER 14

After I hung up, I grabbed my iPad, which was sitting on the nightstand next to my bed, and looked up Dad's conference on the USC website. I kept missing the keys because of the way my hand was shaking, but eventually I found it. It was called *Harold Jenkins: A Judge before His Time* and was slated to start Friday afternoon with a cocktail reception and end Sunday at noon. So unless Dad was making other plans—unlikely—I was going to be forced to join him for dinner on both Thursday and Sunday, plus be expected to spend Friday morning and much of the day Sunday with him. Worst of all, he'd probably ask to attend one of my classes, and I'd be hard-pressed to say no. Unfortunately, the only class I'd be teaching during his time in LA would be my Sunken Treasure seminar on Friday morning—a class in which one of the students had just died under mysterious circumstances.

I stopped myself midthought. Why was I thinking of Primo's death as having happened under mysterious circumstances? Hadn't I overheard the students saying he was a heavy partier? It was probably drugs.

All of that was going through my mind as I sat on my bed staring at the telephone in its cradle. I finally got up and walked to the third bedroom, which I had converted into a study. It was the smallest of the three, and while the room I had rented to Tommy would have made for a more comfortable study, the third bedroom had the best view of the hills. I could even see the law school from its windows.

I had furnished the room rather starkly—Lucite desk in red, pushed right up against the windows, black mesh Aeron desk chair and a set of floor-to-ceiling blonde oak bookshelves fastened to the wall just to the left of the windows. The carpeting was the same industrial gray I had chosen for the rest of the condo, but I'd splashed a bright rug on top of it, something I'd picked up in Guatemala on the previous summer's treasure cruise. Against the back wall I had installed a pull-out sofa, also red. Not that it had gotten much use as a bed. It was rare that I had overnight guests. The only art in the room was a woodblock print of a monk in his red robes. It looked classic until you noticed that he was holding a brimming martini glass with a sliver of lemon hooked over the top edge.

I sat down and turned on my notebook computer, which was sitting on the desk. It was an exact match of the one in my office. I had finally tired of carting a computer back and forth and had elected instead to have two, one left at the law school and one in my condo. All my files were stored in the cloud, backed up automatically every few minutes. All I had to do if I needed a file was pull it down from the Net, without regard to where I had been when I created it. Aldous had warned me that this created a greater risk of data theft, but I had ignored him.

My first problem was what to do about my Law of Sunken Treasure seminar, which met for just over an hour and a half on Tuesdays and Fridays at 9:00 A.M. Tomorrow was a Tuesday. As I thought about it, there was something unseemly about meeting the day after Primo had died and just going forward as if nothing had happened. I would at least have to make some mention of it, and I really had no idea what to say. Or maybe the school was going to cancel classes for the day. No student had died during my almost four years at the law school, so I didn't know what the drill would be. I needed to ask.

I picked up my cell—my hand seemed to have stopped trembling—and punched in the dean's number.

He answered on the first ring. "Jenna, I've been sitting here waiting for your call for well over an hour. Did you find the map?"

"Oh my God, I'm sorry. I totally forgot to call you. I've been kind of distracted."

"Understood. Was the map there?"

"No, it wasn't. I searched everywhere but couldn't find it."

"Well, where is it?"

"I have no idea."

"We have a big problem then."

"Dean Blender, there's something you need to understand. All I ever saw was a red mailing tube. I have no idea whether there was a map or anything else in it."

"This Quinto guy insists that's what was in it. He says he helped his brother roll the map up in the morning and put it in the tube so Primo could show it to you."

"I sound like a broken record, but, again, I have no way of knowing whether that's true or not. I never got a look at the map, if it was even in there."

"All right, I'll take you at your word."

"That sounds ominous. Why would you *not* take me at my word?"

"I didn't mean it that way. It was just a manner of speaking. Anyway, please let me know if you learn anything new. I have to go now. I have a lot to do to try to put a lid on this mess before it spins out of control. It's one thing for a student to die, it's another thing for his family to claim a professor stole something from him."

"They think I stole it?"

"That's the clear implication."

"That's absurd."

"I know. Welcome to my job as dean. And as I said, I've got to go."

"Wait."

"What now?"

"Are you going to cancel classes tomorrow?"

"No, why would we?"

"A student died."

"Once in a while we lose a student, Jenna. It's tragic, but life goes on. We've never canceled classes before for that. We'll have a memorial service of some sort at an appropriate time. Assuming that's okay with the family, of course."

"I see. Maybe I'll just cancel my own class in the morning. The one Primo was in."

"That's up to you, but I think most faculty would just man up and teach it."

"I can't man up."

"Why not?"

"I'm not a man."

There was a small silence, as he, I hoped, absorbed what a chauvinist pig he was. Finally, he said, "I've got work to do. Let me know if you learn anything more."

"I will, but I don't know how you expect me to learn anything more."

There was no response. I looked at the cell phone screen, which said "disconnected." He, too, had hung up on me. I was tired of people doing that. In fact, I was tired of talking to people I didn't want to talk to. I powered off my cell phone.

Then I remembered the coffee, which was still sitting on the counter. I went back to the kitchen, poured some of it into a glass jar, put a lid on the jar and placed it in the refrigerator. That left almost half a pot of coffee still in the pot. I sniffed it and it smelled bad, so I hesitated to pour it down the drain, lest I smell up the sink.

There's a small balcony off the living room that I rarely use in the winter. It has a broad-leafed plant on it that I sometimes neglect to water. I figured I could just dump the coffee in the plant and it would kill two birds with one stone. I'd get rid of the coffee and give the plant some needed water. It seemed unlikely to me that the plant would be bothered by the smell or whatever fungus had sickened Primo. If that's what had really happened, which I doubted.

CHAPTER 15

I had agreed to meet Aldous at 7:45 P.M. at the Geffen Playhouse in Westwood for a performance of *Hamlet*. The curtain was at 8:00. It wasn't the Geffen's usual fare, which tended a bit more toward the modern. Nor was it mine; I very unsophisticatedly prefer movies. But I had been looking forward to it as a fun night out with Aldous.

After my strange phone call with the dean, in which he all but accused me of stealing Primo's supposed map, I had considered canceling. Yet it didn't seem likely that staying home would improve my mood—or my hands, which were still red and in which I could still detect an ever-so-slight tremor if I held them out in front of me. And perhaps Aldous would have some good advice. So I threw on a little black dress I had bought at Nordstrom, looped a string of pearls around my neck and slipped on my patent-leather heels. Then I retrieved my car from the valet and drove to the Geffen.

Parking is often an issue in Westwood, but since I had a UCLA parking pass, I just pulled into a nearby UCLA lot. Teaching at UCLA doesn't have a lot of privileges, but it has some.

When I walked into the stone-walled courtyard of the Geffen, Aldous was standing there waiting, looking handsome. The evening was cool but not cold—in the low 60s, not unheard of for mid-November in Los Angeles—and he was dressed in a nubby brown cardigan worn over an ecru shirt, sharply creased brown khakis and brown tasseled loafers. He looked like an ad out of a Brooks Brothers catalog, which fit, since he'd once told me he bought almost all of his clothes there.

He sprinted over to me. "Honey, I've been trying to call you all day, but you didn't pick up or return my messages. And you haven't been in your office. I've been by three times to look for you. Are you okay?"

I admit that I was a bit stunned to hear him say that. I couldn't recall the last time he had tried to track me down. For any reason.

"I'm sorry," I said. "I turned off my cell and forgot to turn it back on. And no, I'm not okay. I don't know if you heard, but my student died. I'm a mess."

"Of course I heard. It's all over the school. I've been worried sick about you."

"You could have dropped by my condo when you couldn't reach me."

As soon as I said it, I realized it had been the wrong thing to say. He was trying hard to care about me and I was being a jerk.

"Jenna, you've told me several times never to do that. Under any circumstances."

Which was true. I didn't like being dropped in on. Maybe some of the lack of intimacy was on my side. I'd never agreed to move in with anybody, despite several heartfelt invitations, and I didn't even like staying overnight with a guy.

In the end I didn't respond to what Aldous had said about dropping in on me but asked, instead, "What are they saying around the school about Primo?"

"Nothing specific. Just a lot of shock and supposed grief, although I haven't run into anyone who really knew him well."

"Nobody's saying what killed him?"

"No. Do you know?"

"No. I have no idea. I went with him to the hospital in the ambulance, but they wouldn't say much because I wasn't a relative. And anyway, at that point they seemed to think he'd be fine."

"Who told you that?"

"Some doctor who also tried to pick me up."

"Did he succeed?"

"Not yet."

"Not yet?"

"I'm teasing you, Aldous."

"You don't usually tease."

"I know, I know. I need to lighten up, don't you think?"

Before he could answer, the chime sounded and we went in.

Aldous had reserved seats in the middle of the third row of the orchestra. One of the things I've always liked about him is that he drives an old VW Bug and only flaunts his wealth in small ways. Which got me thinking, as we sat there waiting for the curtain to go up, that if I wanted to, I could become Mrs. Aldous Hartleb, retire and grow prize gladiolus or something. Sure, I'd have to overlook the lack of emotion in our relationship, but maybe all that stuff was overrated. And marrying Aldous would make my father happy. Maybe it would make me happy, too.

The play was, thank God, a classically staged *Hamlet*, not a jazzed-up, modern version with Hamlet wearing a pin-striped suit and living amid Danish modern furniture. As the actor began the soliloquy and spoke the famous lines, "To be or not to be," it hit me that Primo had been alive when the sun rose in the morning and was now dead. He was, and now he was not. And it struck me that Primo wasn't the only one who had gone through an arc. When I got up that morning, I had been a happy camper on my way to tenure. Now, not much more than twelve hours later, I had become an almost unhinged camper whose hands shook. In fact, when the curtain went up I had shoved my hands under my thighs to hide them from view, just in case that started again.

During the intermission we ran into a couple of other faculty members from the law school. We all drank champagne and made small talk. No one mentioned Primo, but his ghost was clearly present and walking around. I looked at the hand holding my champagne glass and was relieved to see that there was no tremor at all.

After the play ended, Aldous and I were standing on the sidewalk in front of the theater, talking about where to go to dinner.

"I'm thinking the Napa Valley Grille," he said.

"I'm thinking someplace less fancy," I responded. "Maybe a late-night burger place. Preferably someplace far from Westwood, where we won't run into anyone from the law school. I'm finding seeing people from there and not talking about Primo unnerving, even though I very much don't want to talk about him."

"Well, what about . . ."

He never got to finish his thought because just then a slight, dark-haired young guy wearing a black leather jacket burst out of the alley next to us, sprinted up to me and began shouting in my face, "Where's the map? Where is the damn map!?"

Aldous put his large hand on the kid's thin shoulder and pushed him gently backward. "Whoa, my friend. I don't know who you are, but please get out of the lady's face."

The guy backed off a couple of feet and said, "I'll tell you who I am. I'm Quinto Giordano, the brother of the man Professor James poisoned. The police can deal with that part. Right now I just want the treasure map back. Tonight."

"Poisoned?" I asked. "What the hell are you talking about?"

"I dropped him off near your office this morning, with the map. I watched him go into the building. A few hours later he was dead, and the treasure map he took with him to your office is missing. Put it together yourself, bitch."

Aldous stepped forward and placed himself between me and Quinto. "You're out of line, sir. If you have information about your brother's death, take it up with the police or the DA. But stop harassing—and slandering—Professor James. Got that?"

"Yeah, I got that. But you—" he stabbed his finger at me over Aldous's shoulder—"are gonna hear from me again. And if you know what's good for you, you'll get that map over to me. Your dean knows where to find me." He turned and strode off toward Ralphs, the big grocery store that sits next door to the theater.

"Are you all right, Jenna?" Aldous asked.

"No."

"Have you ever seen that guy before?"

"No."

"He said he was Primo's brother. Wasn't Primo Italian?"

"I thought so."

"This guy doesn't sound Italian."

"No, he doesn't. No accent. Perfect grammar."

"Are you sure you've never seen him before? He certainly seemed able to pick you out of a crowd."

"The first time I ever even heard of him was earlier today, when the dean told me that he was demanding a map the guy thinks I have but that I don't."

As I said it, I realized that I was holding back the gory details from Aldous, almost like they were dammed up behind an emotional wall. If I couldn't tell him, who could I tell? The wall broke.

"There's more, Aldous. The dean practically accused me of stealing the map."

"What? Why?"

"I don't know. Because it was in my office and now it's gone? It's ridiculous, but I *know* he thinks I took it. And then Drady practically accused me of murdering Primo."

"Who's Drady?"

"A cop who was involved in Robert Tarza's prosecution, way back when. Now he's on the UCLA force and is investigating Primo's death."

By that time Aldous had gathered me into his arms and was just holding me tight. "Jenna, you need to get a grip. We need to sit down, and you need to tell me everything. Maybe I can help."

"That would be great. I need someone I can count on." I was crying gently into his shoulder, and people in the crowd were staring at us. To my surprise, I didn't care.

"Jenna, do you still want to go to dinner?"

"No."

"What do you want to do?"

"Can I come home with you?"

"Of course."

CHAPTER 16

Week 1—Tuesday

I awoke, turned my head and looked at the clock on the nightstand. It was 6:30 A.M. and the sun was up, if barely. I turned my head to the other side but saw no Aldous in the bed. Then I heard him moving about in the kitchen and detected the smell of frying bacon.

I stretched my arms out in front of me. I was wearing red plaid flannel pajama tops with sleeves at least three sizes too long. The cuffs had been folded over multiple times but still managed to cover my hands halfway down my fingers. I lifted up the covers and confirmed that I was also swimming in matching, way-too-big bottoms. I didn't much remember putting them on.

Aldous appeared in the bedroom doorway, wearing a white T-shirt and jeans. "And how does milady feel this morning?"

"I'm okay. But was that stuff after the theater last night real? Or did I dream it?"

"It was real enough. And I think you need to do something about it."

"I can't imagine what. I don't have the map—if there even *is* a map. And I have no interest in ever seeing Primo's brother again—if he really is his brother."

"I'd like to try to look into both of those things. I have some resources I can tap."

"What does that mean?"

"It means I'm rich enough to hire a private investigator."

"I don't think I'm quite ready to do that yet. Or have you do it for me."

"You know, Jenna, maybe it's time you let someone try to take care of you a little instead of always playing the rough, tough trial lawyer."

What Aldous was saying, of course, wasn't that he'd take care of me by tucking me in every night and making me breakfast every morning but by spending money on me. So I ignored the take-care-of-you part and focused on the rest of it.

"I'm not playing at that, Aldous. I am a rough, tough trial lawyer. It's bred in the bone."

"I suppose. But why don't you give up being that way for just one day and let me arrange for you to meet with a PI? No commitment and, like I said, I'll pay for it."

"Please don't do that right now. Maybe later, okay? My focus at the moment is that I have a class to teach at nine, and all I have here is the black dress and pearls I arrived in. And these pajamas." I waved my arm with its flopping sleeve.

He smiled. "Maybe your students would like that."

"Maybe they would, but I wouldn't. After we eat the bacon you've got cooking—and maybe some eggs and coffee, too?—can you run me back to my car so I can drive home from there and change?"

"Where's your car?"

"In the UCLA lot near the theater."

"No problem."

"Can I use your toothbrush?"

"Yep, that, too. Brush your teeth, get dressed and I'll finish making breakfast."

After I brushed my teeth, I shed the pajamas, shimmied my little black dress over my head and glanced around to see if there had been any changes since the last time I'd been there. There hadn't. Aldous's bedroom still featured only a platform bed, two nightstands and a single set of blonde dresser drawers with nothing on the top. All of the lights were in the ceiling. Aldous believes in pristine.

The house itself is set into a hillside way up in Bel Air. It's what people in LA call a midcentury modern—canted wood-beamed ceilings, neutral-toned wall-to-wall carpeting, sliding doors leading to multiple redwood decks and what seems like acres of glass all around. The bedroom itself has an uncurtained view to the southeast, overlooking the city.

Aldous had asked me several times to move in with him, but, as was my habit, I had politely declined each time. Of course, my refusal, given how long we'd been going out, was certainly a sign that I had an intimacy problem myself. I was too smart not to recognize that. I had also declined to leave any clothes at Aldous's, although it would certainly have been convenient that day.

I ate a quick breakfast of bacon and scrambled eggs, plus two cups of strong coffee. Then Aldous and I walked out to the driveway, where his car was parked. I climbed into the passenger seat, and Aldous got in on the driver's side. I waited for him to turn on the ignition and back out of the driveway, but he just sat there, saying nothing. Finally, I said, "Are you going to drive me to Westwood or are we waiting for something?"

"I want to talk for a moment, Jenna."

"About how messed up I was last night?"

"Not just that."

"What, then?"

"Do you realize how long it's been since you stayed overnight here?"

I realized I didn't know the exact answer, except that it had been a very long time. "I don't really know."

"It's been over three months. And before that night three months ago, it had been over two months."

"Well, I have my own place, Aldous. And this is kind of far away from the law school."

"You know that's not true, Jenna. And yes, you have your own place, but we used to spend nights here, together. Not often, but at least once a week. And then something happened."

"I know."

"What happened?"

CHAPTER 17

I sighed. I didn't really want to have the conversation that was about to take place, which seemed to repeat itself like a fugue every few months. But I was stuck.

"I'm not sure what happened, Aldous. Since we got back from France, we've grown farther apart somehow. But maybe this isn't the right time or place to talk about it. I mean, we've tried talking about it at least three or four times, and we just end up going round and round, arguing about which one of us is the most detached person on the planet. So what's the point?"

"I'm guessing there will never be a better time or place to try again to talk about it."

"Why?"

"Well, you're feeling really open and vulnerable because of what happened yesterday with Primo. I've never seen you before like you were last night. I'm concerned about you, super worried, really. So maybe we're both more open to feelings right now, and to talking about them instead of arguing about them."

"Do you have a cigarette?"

He laughed. "You don't smoke, Jenna."

"I used to, as a teenager."

"You think that would really help?"

"Kind of."

I thought I had found the perfect out. Aldous loathed cigarette smoke and I doubted he had any around. He probably didn't even know where to buy them.

"All right," he said. "Just hang on a minute."

He got out of the car, went into the house and came back a few minutes later with a pack of Marlboros. He climbed back into the car and handed me the cigarettes, along with a pack of matches. "One of my nieces visited a couple of weeks ago and left these."

"Thanks."

I took the Marlboros from him, tapped out a cigarette, put it in my mouth and lit it. I took a deep drag and started coughing violently. Aldous opened the car door, plucked the cigarette from my hand and dropped it on the concrete driveway. Then he climbed out of the car, stood up, crushed out the cigarette with his foot, got back in and said, "Honey, I think your smoking days are long over. You've lost the skill set. So just tell me what you were going to say without the benefit of a cigarette."

There was, I thought to myself, no real reason to hold back. "I was going to say, Aldous, that we've grown ever more distant from each other and, to be direct, the problem is that I'm finding you ever more emotionally unavailable—despite your display of caring about me yesterday and today, which I don't doubt was genuine. And appreciated."

He sat for a moment without saying anything. Finally, he said, "Jenna, like you said, we've been down this road before, but do you think of yourself as someone who's emotionally available?"

"Sometimes I do and sometimes I don't. I can be cold, I know that. And wrapped up in intellectual things while feelings pass me by. But I laugh a lot. I can cry if I need to. I get angry once in a while. You never do any of those things. And I like to hug people I love. But you hardly ever hug me. You hugged me twice yesterday, and I think the last time before that was sometime last year."

"I laugh a lot, Jenna."

"That's true. I'm being unfair."

"And I could go to hug classes if you want."

I actually burst out laughing. "Now *that* is funny, Aldous."

He started the car and put it in gear. "I suppose it's not very emotionally connected to drive while we talk, but otherwise you're going to be late for your class." We drove for a couple of blocks in silence. Then Aldous said, "Jenna, would it surprise you to learn that I think of *you* as ever more emotionally unavailable?"

"Yeah, it would."

"Well, I see you as a person who's always on message, always focused on what you want, always determined to get exactly what you want and not inclined to let emotions get in the way. And you seem more like that every day."

"That's the steely girl on the outside, Aldous, the one who appears to ignore the stresses of everyday life. The one who used to appear in court and now makes appearances in classrooms. And maybe the march to tenure has made me more that way lately. But on the inside I'm not like that."

"You wouldn't know it from the way you present yourself."

I thought about that for a moment. "You know, if we're truthful about it, the problem isn't really that either one of us is totally emotionally unavailable. For some reason, we're just not available to one another. Or at least not most of the time.

I mean, you're friendly and kind and funny, and so am I. Well, at least I'm friendly and kind. But that's not the same thing as being mutually open."

"I think we are. Do you remember when we lay together on the bed in the bedroom of that small château in France and read Keats out loud to each another?"

"I do."

"That's what I think of as an emotional connection."

I didn't respond to that because I didn't see it the same way. Reading poetry together was warm and fuzzy, but it wasn't what I thought of as a true emotional connection. But he was trying. He was. And so was I.

We drove the rest of the way to the UCLA parking lot in silence. When we arrived I opened the door and started to get out of the car. Before I could say "thank you," Aldous said, "Jenna, I know we've got a long way to go to work this out, but are you willing to try? I don't want to lose you."

There was a part of me that wanted to say it was hopeless. But maybe it wasn't. Maybe it was worth going another round.

"Yes," I said. "I'm willing to try. But the idea of your living somewhere else is going to make it doubly hard."

"I know," he said. "And I suppose this isn't the best time to tell you, but I've had an offer to interview for a job at a brand-new law school that will require every student to get both a law degree and a graduate business degree. It's just the kind of place I've always wanted to teach, so I've got to go for it. I'm leaving for the interview the day after tomorrow. I'll probably be gone for at least three or four days, because there might also be a deanship involved."

"Where is it?"

"In Buffalo."

CHAPTER 18

I was back at my condo by seven thirty. Tommy still seemed to be asleep, or at least the door to his bedroom was closed.

I poured myself a third cup of coffee—safely ground the afternoon before from a bag of Starbucks dark-roast beans I'd had around for at least a week—showered and got dressed for class in my standard law professor outfit: black wool jacket, creased jeans, a cream-colored blouse and practical heels, black. If it had been a cold day, I would have added a dark red V-necked sweater, but it didn't seem cold enough to bother.

Then I pinned up my hair. After I left M&M, I had let my hair grow back, and it was almost down to my waist. But the uptight part of me didn't think long hair appropriate for a law professor, so I always put it up. Doing that also made it harder to see the roots, which revealed that although my hair looks jet black, it's actually dyed, because I'm naturally a blonde. I can't explain why I've never wanted to be a blonde; I just don't.

As I passed through the living room on my way to the study, I glanced out of the sliding glass doors onto the balcony and noticed that the plant into which I had poured the coffee the day before looked distinctly wilted. I slid open the balcony door and looked more closely. The plant was indeed looking sickly, its leaves droopy. Worse, the bottom leaves, onto which some of the coffee had splashed when I poured it into the plant, had what looked like small burn holes in them, with charring around the edges of the holes.

I stood there for a moment, staring at the plant. There was no way to continue denying that there was something deadly about the coffee, and it was probably not a weird coffee bean fungus. I didn't know a lot about fungi, but it seemed unlikely there was one that could burn holes in plant leaves overnight. The coffee must have been poisoned, and since the coffee had been brewed in my office, the poison must have been aimed at me, put there by whoever left the door open. It wasn't just my hands shaking now. My whole body shook. I went to sit down on the couch for a moment and waited for it to pass.

The shaking finally stopped. I needed to get a grip to figure this out. I needed to be the steely girl that Aldous saw.

The first question was, Why would anyone want to kill me? I couldn't come up with a remotely plausible answer. I would need, as my father liked to say, to "think on it." I also needed to talk to the police about it.

The threat I felt was another excuse to cancel my class if I wanted to take it. I decided to teach it anyway. If someone wanted to kill me, canceling the class wasn't going to help. They'd just do it after class. I needed a broader strategy than just hiding.

I called down to the valet for my car, then went into the study and printed out my class notes for the day. I put them in the thin cloth briefcase I usually carry and took the elevator down to the lobby. My car was waiting out front, and the valet was holding the door open for me.

"Good morning, Hector," I said as I started to get in.

"Good morning, Professor. Have a great day."

"You, too."

Hector had not yet closed the car door when a man wearing blue running gear jogged off the sidewalk into the driveway, stopped right next to me and reached into the broad pocket that ran across the front of his sweatshirt. I knew in a heartbeat that he was going for a gun. I looked around in a panic, trying to see if there was a way to clamber out the other door.

"Are you Jenna James?" he asked.

As soon as he asked the question, I knew that what was about to happen had nothing to do with guns. Assassins didn't check your name before shooting. Process servers did.

"Yes, I'm Jenna James," I said, as I took a large gulp of air and my heartbeat started to return to normal.

The man handed me an 8½ x 11 manila envelope. "You've been served."

"Whatever."

"Will you sign a receipt?"

"No."

"Doesn't matter," he said, "have a wonderful day," and jogged off.

"I'm sorry, Professor," Hector said. "I didn't see him coming."

"It's okay, Hector. Just some legal papers. Don't worry about it."

"All right. Well, have a nice day anyway." He closed my door.

The engine was already running, but I sat there for a moment, tore open the envelope and scanned the document inside. It was a lawsuit. The plaintiffs were Quinto Giordano and something called Altamira Società Recupero, SPA, both represented by a sole-practitioner lawyer I'd never heard of whose office was on mid-Wilshire. There were two defendants, me and the Regents of the University of California. It had been filed in the Los Angeles Superior Court in Santa Monica.

"Shit." I said it out loud.

The lawsuit wasn't very long. Its essence seemed to be that I had stolen a valuable map that belonged to Quinto. It sought an injunction to make me and UCLA return it and asked for a million dollars in compensatory damages, plus another million in punitive damages.

I saw Hector looking at me through the passenger window, worried. I rolled the window down as he said, "Are you really okay? You don't look so good."

"Thanks for being concerned, but really, I'm just fine. I'm running late, though, so I need to go." I slipped the lawsuit back into its envelope, tossed it onto the passenger seat and drove off. I tried really hard not to screech my way down the driveway. I mostly succeeded.

By 8:45 I had parked in Lot 3 and was climbing the stairs to my office, carrying the envelope in one hand and my briefcase in the other. When I got to Aldous's door, I knocked, but there was no answer. I took a pen out of my pocket and wrote a note on the face of the envelope: "Aldous—I've been sued. Please read and let's talk later. J." Then I crossed out the J and replaced it with "Love, Jenna." I slid the envelope under the door and headed to the room where my Sunken Treasure seminar was scheduled to begin at 9:00.

CHAPTER 19

I arrived a few minutes early for the class, took my place at the podium and watched as the remaining ten students, seven men and three women, filtered in and took their seats. The classroom was small and banked, with only four rows of seats rising upward in curved ranks toward the windows in the back. To keep the seminar enrollment low, I had employed two old tricks that are well known to all law professors. First, I made the full admiralty law course, which I taught only in the spring semester, a prerequisite for the seminar. Second, I arranged for the class to be scheduled to meet on Tuesdays and Fridays at 9:00 A.M. Most law students don't like to get up that early, and they treasure three-day weekends with no classes.

Lodged in the podium in front of me were controls for a veritable cornucopia of digital equipment, including a DVD player, a VHS tape deck and an opaque projector on which I could lay a book or document, as well as a PC linked to the Internet. With a touch on a control screen protruding from the console, I could project sound and images from any of the devices onto a large screen behind me.

Usually when my students arrived for the seminar they found an image already being projected on the screen, often a picture or sketch of a famous ship that now lay broken on the bottom of the sea. But today the screen was dark, and I was sure the students sensed the reason. I had decided to start the class by talking about Primo.

The class settled down and grew quiet as I stood there. I took a deep breath and began.

"Ladies and gentlemen, I'm sure you all know by now the sad news that one of your classmates, and a member of this seminar, Primo Giordano, passed away yesterday at the Ronald Reagan UCLA Medical Center. We don't know yet what happened, although I assume that in time we'll learn what it was, because an autopsy is going to be performed. The dean has shared with me that there will, at the appropriate time, be a memorial service here at the law school, according to the wishes of Primo's family."

I looked out at the students and saw ten sets of eyes staring at me amid the kind of silence in which you could hear a pin drop. "I'd suggest that we bow our heads for a moment of silence in Primo's memory, and then, if any of you would like to say anything, it would certainly be appropriate."

I bowed my head and stared down at the assorted electronics on the podium, where a tiny red light was blinking. I used its blink to count to sixty, then looked up and out at the class.

"Would any of you like to say something?"

Julie, the brunette who had asked about Primo the day before, and who was sitting in the front row, raised her hand and said, without waiting for me to acknowledge her, "He was a great guy. I'm going to miss him." I thought I detected a small tear in the corner of her eye. The two other women in the seminar, who sat in the front row on either side of Julie, nodded their heads in apparent agreement but said nothing.

Then Crawford Phillips, one of the guys in the back row—four of the seven men had chosen to sit together there—spoke up, saying, "He *was* a great guy. And a great pickup basketball player. We'll all miss him, both here and on the court. I'm really sad."

After that there was an awkward silence as no one volunteered anything further. Which didn't surprise me; Primo had said very little in the seminar, just as he had said very little in the admiralty law class the spring before. I had had the impression then that he didn't have any close friends in that class, although that hadn't struck me as unusual at the time. With more than three hundred students in each class year, and almost a thousand in the school overall, there are often students in my classes who have never before had a class with most of the others.

I let a moment pass and then said, "Well, it's a sad thing and we're going to miss him. But I don't know what else to say at this point. I should also mention that if you feel the need for counseling, contact the office of the associate dean for Student Affairs, and they'll arrange for you to see someone."

I waited a few seconds to see if anyone else wanted to speak, then reached down and touched a button on the console. The screen behind me lit up with a black-and-white picture of a mammoth Great Lakes iron ore freighter. "Today I want to discuss the wreck of the *Edmund Fitzgerald*—the ship, not the Gordon Lightfoot song." There was a short burst of laughter, which is what I had hoped for. Teaching is, after all, a performance art, and I wanted my opening to take us away from Primo.

I looked toward the back row. "Crawford, that ship, which sank in Lake Superior during a huge storm in 1975, is in only

580 feet of water. Its exact location is well known, and it's easily within reach of modern salvage robots. If we thought there was something valuable in the purser's safe, could we go and get it?"

"No, we couldn't," Crawford said. "It's in Canadian waters and the Canadian Underwater Cultural Heritage Act precludes it from being salvaged."

Julie raised her hand. "Not exactly," she said. "We could request a permit from the Canadian government to salvage it."

"Good luck with that!" one of the other students said. The comment triggered another burst of laughter, and we were off and running in a class that explored, as I had intended, the increasing conflict between treasure hunters and the marine archaeologists who want to keep the world's hundreds of thousands of shipwrecks as their personal scientific playgrounds. Or at least that's how I think of it.

When the class ended over an hour later without further mention of Primo, I breathed a sigh of relief and went off to see if Aldous had returned to his office.

CHAPTER 20

The light was on under Aldous's door. As I raised my hand to knock, a voice behind me said, "So I heard some poor student died in your office."

I knew who it was without looking. I would have recognized the deep, raspy voice of Professor Greta Broontz anywhere. Greta is one of the other civil procedure professors, and she hates me.

I considered opening Aldous's door without knocking and going inside without even acknowledging her, but it seemed the wrong thing to do. I sighed and turned around. And there she was: about my height but butt ugly, with stringy red hair cut in a pageboy, one brown eye and one blue, a squashed nose and deep acne scars. The students called her the Pineapple.

"Greta, he didn't die in my office. He died at the UCLA Medical Center. Of as yet unknown causes."

"Well, I heard he was poisoned by your coffee."

"And where did you hear that absurd story?"

"A little bird told me."

"What was the bird's name?"

"I'm sorry, I was told in confidence, and unlike some people, I do keep my confidences."

I knew she was referring to her suspicion that I was the one who, during my first year at the law school, had leaked to the UCLA student newspaper, the *Daily Bruin*, that she was moonlighting more or less full-time with a downtown law firm, pulling in at least two times her law-school salary. She had apparently assumed I was the paper's source because I had just arrived from a downtown law firm, albeit a different one.

"Greta, I didn't poison anyone."

"I didn't say you did, dear. I said he was poisoned *by* your coffee. Passive voice. Guilty conscience?" She grinned, exposing brilliant white teeth, which I had always assumed were dentures.

"Greta, please excuse me. I have an appointment with Aldous." I turned around, performed a perfunctory knock, opened the door and walked in without waiting. I closed the door behind me and collapsed against it.

Aldous was sitting in his desk chair, looking at me. "Wow. I didn't even get a chance to say 'come in.'"

"Sorry. The Pineapple just appeared out of nowhere and accused me of poisoning Primo."

"What?"

"Actually, she said he was poisoned by my coffee and then suggested she wasn't accusing *me* of personally poisoning him. Somehow it was just my coffee."

"That's not good."

"No, it's not."

"It's particularly not good that it's Greta."

"Why?"

"She's a member of your confidential Ad Hoc Tenure Committee."

I wasn't surprised. She was a faculty member who taught civil procedure, as I did. And she was very senior. So it made sense. I had been hoping against hope that if there was going to be a professor who taught civil procedure on the committee, it would be someone else. Now my hopes had been dashed. "That woman is the curse of my life, Aldous. She has the office next door to me, lives in my condo building and now you're telling me she's on my tenure committee."

"Do you get along better as neighbors than you do here?"

"No. She has the apartment beneath mine and is always playing her classical music at full volume in the middle of the night."

"Do you complain to her about it?"

"No. I just pound on the floor with a big wooden pole until she turns it down. I guess I've avoided mentioning that to you."

"For fear it would make me not want to stay overnight at your place?"

"You never have."

"I know. It was a joke, Jenna."

"Oh, I'm sorry. I guess my joke receptors are off today."

"Well, Greta does sound like a curse on you. Maybe you need to consult someone in Haiti about her."

"Not a bad idea. But wait a minute: How did you learn she's on my committee? That's supposed to be confidential."

"You don't really want to know."

"No, I do want to know."

"I developed some special computer skills back when I was a quant on Wall Street."

"You hacked into the UCLA computer?"

"Not exactly, and why don't we just leave it be? I shouldn't have told you."

"Well, however you found out, it's bad news because she hates my guts. But she's clever enough to cover it up and find some supposedly legitimate problem with my scholarship. And if she's a no, all I need is one more no, or one yes with reservations, and I'm sunk."

"Yeah, but there's also good news. The other two faculty on your committee are much more favorably disposed toward you."

"Glad to hear it."

"Do you want to know who they are?"

I hesitated for a few seconds, then, finally, said, "No."

He laughed. "Or at least you don't want to know right now."

"I need to sit down," I said. I moved away from the door and sank into one of the two guest chairs.

Aldous came out from behind the desk and plopped himself into the other chair. "I think I'll join you out here. It's weird talking to you from behind my desk. Not emotionally connected enough." He smiled.

"Very funny, Aldous. Ha ha. Somehow I'm not focused right now on who's sitting where, and I don't want to rehash our conversation of this morning."

"You're not having a good week," he said.

"Not hardly. Did you read the lawsuit?"

"Yeah, I did. You'll need a lawyer, obviously."

"I know. I was thinking about that as I was driving in."

"Got anyone in mind?"

"Yeah. Oscar Quesana."

"Who's he?"

"He was my co-counsel when I defended Robert against the murder charge. I learned a huge amount from Oscar. We had a rocky start, but we became good friends in the end. He's an unusual guy—a vegan who lives in a house that looks like it was decorated by the Vermont Country Store and doesn't believe in cell phones or fax machines, let alone e-mail—but a great lawyer."

"Ah, yes, you've mentioned Oscar before. But isn't he a criminal defense lawyer?"

"Yeah, he wasn't even in our law firm. We didn't do criminal defense. But I think he used to do civil cases, too, and he's aggressive. He'll figure out a way to get rid of this in short order."

"Okay," he said. "Sounds good. If he can't do it, I'm sure you know lots of others who can. In the meantime, though, I've got a class to teach. Do you want to stay here until you're sure Greta has gone away?"

"It doesn't matter one way or the other."

Aldous got up from the chair and reached for the doorknob, then paused. "You know, Jenna, you really can't blame Greta for being hostile to you."

"What? Why?"

"Because she thinks you leaked that she had that job downtown."

"I didn't *do* that."

"I know. But everyone around here thinks you did."

"That really pisses me off."

"I'm just telling you what I hear."

I had been having an internal struggle about whether to tell Aldous about the dying plant, and the conclusion I'd reached about who had been the target of the killer. On one level he didn't seem like the best person to tell because our relationship was so fraught. But on another he did care about me. I decided to tell him, even if we had only minutes left before he had to leave.

"Aldous, before you go, there's one more thing we need to talk about. And it's something I haven't wanted to bring up because it seems nuts."

"What?"

"I believe there *was* poison in that coffee; not just in Primo's cup but in the pot—I'll explain later why I think so. So I think someone was trying to poison *me*, not Primo."

"Seriously?"

"Yes, and I'm scared. Terrified, really. So afraid that when the process server served me with the lawsuit this morning, I thought he was an assassin. Not only that, I'm thinking of moving to a hotel until they catch the person who did it, and I've pledged to myself not to eat a single bite of anything that I didn't make myself."

Aldous sat back down in the chair. "I can be late for my class. Tell me the details of why you think Primo was poisoned and why you think the poison was in the coffeepot."

I told him. When I was done, he looked at me and said, "This is a lot more serious—for you—than I thought it was. When you came in here, I thought you were just being paranoid."

"And now?" I asked.

"Crazy as it seems, someone may actually have tried to kill you. Although I think we need to find out for sure what was in that coffeepot. Going to the police right away is a good idea. But I have another idea."

"Which is?"

"Why don't you stay at my house while I'm gone?"

"It's lonely up there. You don't even have any close neighbors."

"I can hire a security guard for you if you want."

I thought about it for a moment. It was one of those on-the-one-hand, on-the-other-hand conversations I was always having with myself. Oddly, one of the on the other hands was that despite sometimes being attracted to Aldous because of his wealth, I didn't want to be dependent on him and his money.

Which somehow, in my warped internal monologue, seemed to balance out my life being in danger.

"I don't think that's necessary, Aldous, but I appreciate the offer."

"Will you at least think about it?"

"I will, but I don't think I'll change my mind."

"Okay, I do really have to go now." He got up from the chair, opened the door and looked back at me. "There's one more thing, Jenna."

"What's that, Aldous?"

"Emotionally unavailable as I am, I love you."

He exited through the door and shut it gently behind him.

CHAPTER 21

As soon as I got back to my own office, I picked up the phone and called Oscar. It had been almost five years, but I hadn't forgotten his number. After a few rings, a mechanical voice answered and said that the phone had been disconnected and there was no new number. I tried information. Nada.

I sat and thought about it. Oscar was a major Luddite. He didn't own a cell phone and he didn't have a fax machine. He didn't use e-mail. There was one place, though, where he had to be listed. I went to my computer and looked him up on the California State Bar website. All active lawyers are required to provide contact information to the State Bar. That didn't work either. The only phone number listed was the one I had just called. A Google search, when I tried it, was equally unavailing. There were precious few references to Oscar, and those that were there were all at least two years old.

Had he died? I checked the obituaries in the *LA Times*. Nothing.

Strange as it seemed, and close as I had been to Oscar at one time, I didn't know a single person who also knew him.

Except for one—Robert Tarza. Robert liked to keep in touch with people, and he might well know where to find Oscar. But Robert wasn't someone I was super anxious to call. He hadn't been happy about my leaving M&M and had tried hard to talk me out of it. After that, despite the fact that he had been my mentor for more than seven years—we had done six long civil trials together, and he was the closest thing to a father figure I'd ever had in the law—our relationship had cooled once I left. I was going to have to suck it up and call him.

I chose calling because Robert was terrible at checking his e-mail, and I assumed, stuffy as he was, that he didn't text.

I dialed M&M's main number. It was picked up on the first ring.

"Marbury Marfan," the voice on the other end said.

I recognized the voice of Christine, the firm's longtime receptionist. "Hi, Christine, it's Jenna James."

"Oh, hi, Jenna, it's so nice to hear your voice. How are you?"

"I'm great. How about you?"

"Very good. Who do you want to talk to?"

"Robert, of course."

"Oh, I thought you guys were close, but I guess not so much anymore. Robert went senior—retired—five or six months ago. Didn't you go to his retirement party?"

"No, didn't make it." I decided to leave it at that and not mention that this was the first I'd heard of it, that I hadn't even been invited.

"Oh. Well, he still has an office here, but he almost never comes in, and I think he sold his house. So I don't really know where he is. But Gwen is still here, working for someone else, and she probably knows. I'll put you through to her."

"Thanks."

After a few rings, Gwen picked up. "Mr. Carlson's office."

"Hey, Gwen, it's me, Jenna."

"Oh, hi, Jenna. What can I do for you?" Gwen wasn't the chatty type.

"I'm looking for Robert. Do you know where I can reach him?"

"Yes. He's living in Paris."

"Really?"

"Uh-huh. With an old flame. Apparently."

Now that was an amazing piece of information. In all the years I'd known him, Robert hadn't had a single girlfriend. I wanted to know more.

"Someone we know?"

"Not I. I thought I knew everything there was to know about Mr. Tarza, but I now know there were some things he chose not to share with me."

I smiled to myself at the sharp note of disapproval in her voice. Gwen had worked for Robert for more than twenty years. They had seemed to all of us almost like a married couple. But apparently he'd been cheating on her, if failing to disclose a girl-friend to your secretary was cheating.

"What's her name?"

"Tess."

"Interesting. I suppose we're all entitled to a few secrets."

"Maybe."

"So do you have a number for him?"

"Yes. Tell me your e-mail address, and I'll send you the con-tact information there."

I gave her my personal address. It wasn't a good idea to use my UCLA e-mail, which the university could read if it wanted to.

"I'll tell him you said hello, Gwen."

"Don't bother."

I suppressed a laugh. "Uh, all right. You have a good day."

"You, too."

After I clicked off the call, I sat there and thought about it. Robert, in Paris with an old girlfriend. What was that all about? A ping on my cell announced that an e-mail had arrived, and when I looked it was from Gwen with the contact information. His address was in care of someone named Tess Devrais in Paris in the 5th arrondissement, which put it somewhere on the Left Bank. I knew from my recent visit that it was quite a chic area.

I did a rapid time zone calculation. Paris was nine hours later than Los Angeles, which meant it was not quite 7:30 in the evening there. I didn't know what outrageous amount my cell-phone carrier was going to charge me for a call to France, and I didn't feel like using Skype, so I figured what the hell and punched in the number.

CHAPTER 22

Robert Tarza

When Jenna's call came through, I was sitting on the couch in Tess's apartment, sipping a vodka martini and looking out the window at Notre Dame, just across the river. Tess was in the kitchen, whipping up a soufflé of some sort. It was early by her standards, but she had adapted—more or less—to my American desire not to wait until ten o'clock to have dinner.

Tess is the French equivalent of a Silicon Valley multimillionaire, except her many millions are in euros. She used to run a large tech company that she founded. Now she just dabbles in the things that retired multimillionaires dabble in. A charity here, an investment fund there, helping out some young entrepreneurs over there. Whatever keeps her busy. I had first met her in a bar in Paris, almost fifteen years earlier, before she was really rich, during my first and only sabbatical. The bar of the George V, to be exact, one very raw night in March.

I can command a room if I want to. Tess, whether she wishes it or not, demands the room. When I walked into the place that night, she was sitting at the bar, doing just that. Every person in the bar was looking at her, openly or furtively.

It's hard to say exactly why Tess has this effect on people. If you look carefully at her, no one part of her is truly world class. She has a pretty face, but not one that would put her on the cover of *Vogue*. She has high, firm breasts, but not of a size that attract a lot of men these days. And while she has great legs, they aren't so stellar that they would need to be insured, à la Betty Grable.

Nor is it the way she dresses. Understated and tasteful, but with clothes just as likely to have been bought at Bon Marché as at Dior. It could be her hair, but there are a lot of women with tousled mops of jet-black hair.

Perhaps it's her eyes, a deep green that can be as warm and inviting as a forested glade on a summer day or as cold and distant as the edge of a freshly calved iceberg. That night, though, the bar was sufficiently dark that I doubt anyone could have seen the color of her eyes unless they were sitting right next to her, which no one was.

I was riveted by her, too, but chose to sit in a booth in the far reaches of the place, as far from her as I could get. I had always done okay with women, but it was clear to me, just from glancing at her, that she was out of my league.

For whatever reason, she came over, drink in hand, sat down opposite me in the booth and said, "Hello, *monsieur l'Américain*." I had apparently been given away by my shoes.

Much later Tess told me that she had simply liked the way I walked when I came in, which is when she also noticed my shoes. Who knows if that's really true? She just wanted me, and Tess has been used to getting what she wants since she first learned to walk. Probably even before that.

Later that night, to my utter disbelief, I ended up at her elegant apartment overlooking Notre Dame and the Seine and stayed for two months. When it was time for me to return to M&M, Tess argued with great fervor—in English, a language she speaks passably well, although far from perfectly—that I should quit the firm, stay in Paris and live out my life with her. I pointed out at the time that I was forty-nine and she was thirty-two, and that, therefore, she would likely still have a lot of life to live after I had become a drooler, but she was not amused.

In the end I couldn't bring myself to do it. I just couldn't picture myself as an expatriate, even with Tess at my side. At first, upon my return to Los Angeles, we had exchanged a few desultory notes on paper. Then that had dwindled down. Not even an e-mail had followed.

When I retired I decided to treat myself to a summer in France. I started by checking into the George V in Paris for a few days—one of my favorite hotels anywhere—while I looked for a monthly rental. The first night I was there, I went down to the bar, which seemed unchanged from the last time I'd been there, fifteen years earlier. When I walked in, Tess was, to my shock, sitting at the bar. I started to turn and walk back out, but before I could get out the door, I heard her say, "*Alors*, how long have you been in Paris, *monsieur l'Américain*? And why have you not called me?"

Six months later I was once again living with her in the very same apartment—no one in Paris gives up a good apartment until they die—and not planning to go back to the US anytime soon. Nothing much had changed between us, really, and she, at least, still looked great at forty-seven. Indeed, but for a small crinkle of fine lines in the corners of her eyes, she had changed hardly at all. I, on the other hand, was, at sixty-four, badly in need of joining a gym and getting my hair cut.

The phone had stopped ringing, and my reverie of the past was interrupted by Tess standing in front of me, holding out the portable phone. "It is some American girl for you."

I took the phone. "Hello?"

"Robert, it's Jenna."

Jenna was the last person in the world I expected to hear from.

"Hi, Jenna. How did you find me?"

"Gwen."

"Of course. She's still my keeper, I guess."

"I don't think she approves of who you're living with."

"Probably not. My sin was never telling her about Tess. Someone I met on my sabbatical. Oh, but you wouldn't know about that. You weren't at the firm yet. Come to think of it, you were probably still in grade school."

"How long ago was your sabbatical?"

"Fifteen years ago."

"I was in my junior year of college."

"Oh. Well, now that we've got the chronology out of the way, what's the reason for your call?" I knew that sounded a bit abrupt, even cold, so I added, "Are you coming to Paris? Is that why you're calling?"

"No, I'm up for tenure this year, so it's nose to the grindstone, no travel. I was actually calling to see if you know how I can reach Oscar. His phone is disconnected and I can't find him."

"That's easy. He was here just a month ago with his new wife."

"He got married again?"

"Yes. Wife number six. Nice lady."

"I hesitate to ask: How old is she?"

"Thirty, I think."

"Younger than me."

"How old are you now?"

"Thirty-four. How old is Oscar?"

"I'm not really sure. A couple of years older than me, I think. You can look him up on the Cal Bar website and figure it out."

"I suppose. But how do I reach him? The number he lists there is disconnected."

"I'll give you his cell number."

"He has a cell?"

"Believe it or not, he has an iPhone. The new Mrs. Quesana is trying to modernize him."

"Will wonders never cease?"

"I'll text the contact info to you, including his—believe it or not—e-mail address."

"Great."

As our conversation continued, I found, to my amazement, that despite our virtual estrangement since Jenna had left Marbury Marfan—and had, in my view, left me in the lurch at a critical moment—my old, warm feelings for her were somehow bubbling up.

"Jenna," I said, "back in the old days you would have told me from the get-go why you needed to reach Oscar. I hope you're not in any kind of trouble."

"Some serious trouble, actually. A student died after falling ill in my office, and the police are investigating his death. I need Oscar to talk directly to the police about it. And I've been sued in a crazy civil suit. The brother of the student who died claims I stole a treasure map from him. I need Oscar's help with that, too."

"A treasure map? That's odd."

"It's a long story."

"Well, long or short, why are you calling Oscar about it and not me? He hasn't done civil stuff in years." And then I said, actually shocking myself at the words that came out of my mouth, "I'm willing to help a bit with that if there's some way I can do it from here."

"Well," Jenna responded, "it didn't occur to me to ask you because we've been out of touch for a long time and, let's face it, as close as we used to be, we'd drifted apart . . ."

"I guess that's right."

The conversation had reached that awkward stage at which one of us either had to change the topic or break it off. Breaking it off seemed the best thing to do.

"Well, Jenna, I'm glad you called. If you do find yourself in Paris, I hope you'll let us know you're here. And I meant it when I said I'm willing to help with the civil suit."

The change in my tone from the beginning of the conversation, which had come unbidden, truly astonished me. Perhaps it was nostalgia for a life that was now gone. One in which I worked full-time at a time-consuming job and Jenna was, in effect, my adjutant.

"Okay," Jenna said, "if I do come to Paris, I'll be sure to call. As for the civil suit, I think that's best handled by someone who's here in LA. Now I need to go. Be well."

"You, too."

Tess appeared, carrying a plate of soft white cheese and crackers. She eased herself onto the couch beside me while simultaneously putting the plate on the coffee table in front of us. "Robert, who is this American girl, this Jenna, where her call puts first a frown and then, later, a smile on your face?"

"You were eavesdropping, eh?"

"What is this word, eavesdropping?"

"In French, *espionné*. Spying."

"Yes, I spied on you and your old girlfriend on the phone."

"She was not a girlfriend. I will explain."

"I will wait to hear."

That wasn't much of a reprieve. Tess isn't a person who likes to wait. I was going to need to explain my relationship with Jenna well before the clock struck midnight.

CHAPTER 23

After dinner, Tess and I took a walk along the Seine, which was something we did often. It was a cool evening, with a slight drizzle. I was wearing a light wool topcoat, the kind that sheds the rain if the drizzle isn't too heavy, and a dark fedora for which I had paid much too much. No one paid me the least bit of attention. Tess was wearing black midcalf boots, dark wool pants, a blue navyesque pea jacket with gold buttons and a red knit cap. As usual, she turned almost every head.

After we had walked awhile, we stopped briefly to admire Notre Dame in its flood-lit glory, then headed for our favorite café, a place we often stopped at the end of our walks. Since it was raining, the tables had been put up, and we went inside. Tess moved toward a small table for two in the back corner, which was relatively isolated from the other tables. I knew that, with privacy, she was about to reopen her inquiry into Jenna.

"*Alors*," she said, once we were seated, "who is this Jenna . . . exactly?"

"Exactly, she was an associate in my law firm."

"She was only associated with it? She did not work there?"

"No, sorry. An associate is an employee of a law firm. I was a partner—I still am, technically. The other lawyers who work there—who don't own a part of the firm—are employees and are called associates. I don't know why they're called that, but they are."

"This is confusing still."

"Think of it this way, I was Jenna's boss."

"Ah, there are many types of bosses in this world."

Before I could ask her what she meant, a waiter appeared and took our order. Tess ordered an espresso. I ordered a brandy. I thought I might need it. After the waiter departed, I tried to follow up on her comment about bosses.

"What did you mean when you said there are many types of bosses in this world?"

"When I had twenty years of age, before I commenced my own company, I worked for a small company and had a boss. *Patron* is the word we use. The *patron*, he squeezed my ass every day."

"I never squeezed Jenna's ass." Which was absolutely true. I could have joked that it was tempting, but I decided that saying that, even in jest, would complicate our conversation.

"Did you squeeze anything, Robert?"

"No. Look, Jenna and I were never romantically involved. Not even a little. We worked together a lot. I was her mentor."

"We have this word in French, too. It is like a teacher, no?"

"Exactly."

"But a teacher, he also squeezed my ass."

Just then the waiter arrived with the espresso and the brandy. He must have overheard Tess's remark about the teacher, because he gave us both an odd look as he set down the cup and the glass. And the bill. French waiters in cafés always leave the bill at the start.

"It sounds," I said, "like your ass was constantly at risk."

Tess picked up her cup, sipped it and just smiled at me over the rim of the cup. "Yes. But when I was *le patron*, it was not."

"I have no doubt of that. But Tess, why do you care so much what my relationship was with Jenna? Even if we had had a romantic relationship—which we did not—it would be over. I was married, too, once upon a time. You've never been jealous of my former wife."

"I am not jealous of this Jenna girl. It is just that when you spoke on the phone, at the end your face lit itself up. Like you spoke to a lover you had lost."

"I didn't think my face lit up."

"It did."

"Well, if it did, the look said only that I was once fond of Jenna and hadn't talked to her in a long time."

"Ah, and why not?"

"She left the firm to become a law professor, and I was super pissed off at her for leaving."

"You did not think she was permitted to leave? Like she was a slave?"

"No, of course not. It was just that the two of us had been planning to open a new practice in our firm—a high-end, white-collar criminal defense practice. We had worked hard on the plans for months. We had persuaded the firm to support the idea and presented the plans at a firm meeting. We had even persuaded Oscar to join us."

"And then?"

"She waltzed in one day and told me she had an opportunity to teach at UCLA, and she felt she couldn't pass it up, that it was something that wouldn't come her way again. Of course, it was an opportunity she had, quite clearly, aggressively pursued. In secret. It didn't just fly in the window and land on her desk."

"What did you say to her then, Robert?"

"Not much. I was so angry I didn't speak to her for the rest of the time she was at the firm. And I've continued to be angry. I didn't even invite her to my retirement party last spring."

Tess picked up her coffee cup, took a sip and leveled her gaze at me across the top. "Do you imagine this was the good way to behave?"

"No. It was childish of me."

We sat for a couple of minutes drinking our coffee and not saying anything. Finally, Tess said, "In this time before you were angry with Jenna, you were not ever with her in a romance, and you do not wish to be, is this correct?"

"Correct."

"So she will not interfere with us? Like your firm interfered with us fifteen years ago, when you went back to it? Your firm was like a wife."

"She will not interfere."

"Good. Because I have jealousy sometimes, you know."

"I do know. You look annoyed when I even look at other women."

"You look at other women? I am shocked!" And then she burst out laughing, so loud that the others in the café turned and looked at us.

"Seriously, Tess, there's no reason to be jealous of Jenna. Jenna and I did six long civil trials together. That means we were together almost constantly. And it means I taught her many things, but she also taught me a lot of things. She is, among other things, a tougher negotiator than I am." I paused and thought how best to sum it up. "Tess, Jenna was like a daughter to me, really."

"More than the daughter you have? The one you do not talk about? Or to?"

"Yes, much more than that one."

"But she is now a second daughter you do not talk to—or, until tonight, about. This is a problem for you, that you throw daughters out of your mind."

I smiled. "We would say 'put daughters out of mind.'"

"Whichever you would say, do you not think it is time to be less like a child?"

"Yes. You are right. And now she's in some kind of trouble and I should help her. Much like she helped me when she represented me in the criminal trial."

"I thought it was Oscar who helped you."

"He was the lead, but Jenna figured it out. She's the one who truly saved me."

"I understand now," Tess said. "And if you wish to help her, I will wish to help her, too."

"That's kind of you, Tess. I don't know what you can do to help, though. But I appreciate that you said it. And to repeat, she is no threat to you and me."

Tess held up her cup. "To you and me and for you and me to help your friend Jenna. And, as we say in French, from the Bible, '*Maintenant que je suis un homme, j'ai fait disparaître ce qui faisait de moi un enfant.*'"

"Meaning 'the time has come to set aside childish things'?"

"*Oui.*"

I picked up my brandy glass and touched it to her cup. "To all of that."

CHAPTER 24

Jenna James

Week 1—Late TuesdayAfternoon

Now that Robert had given me Oscar's phone number, there seemed no reason to put off calling him. But Oscar is a what-exactly-do-you-want sort of guy, so I tried to think through what I really did want from him, other than the comfort of a competent voice in my ear. I composed in my head what I wanted to say and punched in his cell number. The phone rang for a long while, and I had begun to assume my call would go to voice mail when he answered.

"Oscar Quesana."

"Hi, Oscar. It's Jenna."

"A pleasant surprise indeed. But I thought I was well hidden. How did you track me down?"

"Robert gave me your number."

"That's the damn problem when you're forced to let a telephone live in your pocket. Anybody can give out your number, and then someone else can call you up anytime they want."

"Am I just anyone?"

"No, no, of course not. You're a person I like. But I haven't talked to you in what, three years? So you aren't likely calling to invite me to a garden party. What might you want?"

"I'm in trouble."

"Oh, I'm sorry. I wouldn't want you to be in trouble. I apologize for my abrupt manner. It's just me getting used to being so reachable. What kind of trouble are you in?"

"Well..."

The tiny pause I had injected in the conversation by saying *well* gave me time to take a blank piece of paper that had been sitting on my desk and fold it in half. "Two kinds of trouble, Oscar. First, I've been accused of stealing a map of sunken treasure from a third-year law student named Primo Giordano, and I've been sued for the return of that map. Which, by the way, I've never seen and I don't have."

"You need a civil litigator to defend you, which I'm not. In any case, you should be able to get your insurance company to hire one for you, at least to cover the defense costs." As he spoke, I folded the paper in half again. I'm fortunate in being able to talk and fold at the same time. I've been practicing since childhood.

"You're right, Oscar, except the insurance company won't take care of my second problem."

"Which is?"

I folded the paper in half a third time. "There seems to be a bizarre rumor going around that I killed Primo by poisoning him. He died yesterday."

"Well, you know my usual first blunt question in a criminal case. Did you do it?"

"No."

"Did you poison him?"

"No."

"Kill him in some other way?"

"No."

"Harm him in any way at all?"

"No."

"Do you know if someone else did kill him?"

"No."

"Do you know someone who wanted to kill or harm him?"

"Don't know that either."

"Do you know what he died from?"

I folded the paper in half a fourth time. How did I want to answer that question? *Had* the coffee killed him?

"No to that, too."

"You paused slightly before answering that one. Is there something more?"

"No, I was just distracted by something here."

"Okay. Are the police investigating you?"

"I'm not sure. A UCLA cop was in my office looking around, and someone from campus security bagged up the coffee cup the student had been drinking from."

"With your coffee in it?"

"Yes. Freshly made."

"At some point I'll need to hear the whole story, but it's clear you're already being investigated as a suspect, if not a target. Anything else you know of going on in that investigation?"

"Yes. The UCLA cop who was in my office is Detective Drady. Used to be on the LAPD and was one of the cops who arrested

Robert on the plane. He testified briefly in the preliminary hearing."

"Can't say as I recall him."

I was staring at the much-folded paper as we spoke. Folding it in half a fifth time is always hard, particularly if you want the folds to be nice and crisp.

"Tall and fat with a red face."

"Oh, yeah, I do remember him now. But he's a cop, so the media never called him fat. They used some more friendly euphemism like 'beefy.'"

"Probably."

"Jenna, why does anyone suspect your coffee?"

"I don't really know if they do yet, other than that it smelled bad, Primo drank it and he died a few hours later."

"What else?"

"I dumped the leftover coffee on a plant yesterday, and by today the plant was well on its way to being dead."

"Do the police know that?"

"Not yet. But sooner or later they're going to analyze the coffee sample they have and figure out that it's poisonous."

"And since it was in your office, they'll conclude you're the one who put the poison in it?"

"Yes, but please consider, Oscar, that whoever poisoned the coffee may well have been trying to poison *me*."

"That seems unlikely. What was their motive?"

"I don't know. I mean, what was the motive to kill Primo?"

"We don't know enough about Primo to even speculate about that, but there no doubt is one."

"Maybe."

"Jenna, you know a lot about your own life and you just said you can't come up with a motive that would make you the target.

So what we need to focus on is moving the police away from the idea that you could be Primo's killer."

Oscar's response was exactly the problem, of course. Everyone was going to suspect that I tried to kill Primo by poisoning his coffee in order to get the effing map. Whereas my gut told me that because the poison was in the pot, someone had tried to poison *me*.

While I was listening to Oscar and thinking those thoughts, I had managed to fold the paper over for the fifth time. I smoothed it down really hard with my thumbs. It was crisp enough, although not perfect.

"The good news," Oscar was saying, "is that it's a pretty circumstantial case against you. Not to mention that it makes no sense. If someone as smart as you wanted to poison this guy Primo, you wouldn't do it and then leave the poison sitting around in your office."

"Yes. The whole thing is bullshit."

"As you well know, even bullshit cases can take on a life of their own. And I hate to say it, but both the LAPD and the DA's office likely still remember you left them with egg on their faces after Robert's case. They might trump something up just to get even."

"That's what I'm afraid of. Detective Drady even brought up Robert's case in a not-so-friendly way, and he mentioned that I've now been associated with two dead bodies."

"That's ominous. But Jenna, let's go back to the civil case for a minute. If the student is dead, who's suing you for return of the map?"

"The student's alleged brother and some mysterious company in Italy."

"So this is already very complicated."

I looked at the folded paper and decided not to attempt folding it a sixth time. It was certainly doable, but it always looked gross unless you used a really, really thin piece of paper to start with, which I hadn't.

"Yeah, Oscar, it is."

"You want me to represent you in the criminal investigation?"

"Yes, if there really is one."

"There is one already."

"Okay."

"It will be awkward to charge you a fee."

I smiled. "Then don't."

"Tell you what: for the initial investigation and consult, I'll do it gratis, except for expenses. In exchange, you can take me and Pandy to dinner."

"Pandy's your new wife?"

"Yes, ma'am. You'll like her."

"Well, congrats on that, and I'm sure I will. Is that her real name?"

"No, it's Pandora, but, as you can understand, she's kind of sensitive about it."

"Uh-huh. I get it. So when can we get together?"

"That's going to be awkward to do in person right away, because I'm living in New York. Pandora has a really nice place here."

"When will you be back in LA?"

"Don't know."

"All right, let's play that one by ear, then."

"Okay."

"One more thing, though, Oscar."

"What's that?"

"Will you represent me on the civil end, too? The two things are obviously connected."

"I don't do civil stuff anymore. No longer know how."

"But it's a perfect fit. Since there's really no discovery to speak of in criminal matters, we can use the discovery in the civil case to find out what's going on on the criminal side."

"Yeah, that can work sometimes, but I'm not your guy for that."

"Who would you recommend?"

"You must know a zillion civil lawyers, Jenna, and, like I said, the insurance company will probably appoint someone to represent you."

"I want my own lawyer, too."

"Ask Robert to do it. He needs to get out from under that Tess woman for a while."

"I'm reluctant to do that."

"Are you and Robert on the outs?"

"Kind of. He was pissed when I left the firm. Didn't even invite me to his retirement party."

"I wondered why you weren't there."

"Now you know."

"I asked after you, Jenna, when I was in Paris visiting Robert, and he explained that he was angry at you, not just because you left the firm but because you sneaked around about it and ended up cratering the new department he was trying to set up—one that I was going to join and you were going to run, remember?"

"I remember."

"Why did you do that? Sneak around about it?"

"Because I was afraid if I told Robert about wanting to go teach, he'd talk me out of it, using brilliant, persuasive arguments. Probably presented on flip charts."

"Oh, okay. Knowing you and knowing him, that makes some sense. Well, in any case he's perfect for advising you about the civil suit. Since he's retired he might do it for free. I suggest you two make up."

"Maybe that's already happened. When I talked to him to get your number, he said he was willing to help if he could do it from there. And although he didn't ask me to, I'm going to fax him a copy of the complaint."

"Good. I think he's just the right person for it, but he'll have to come back. I sensed he'd like to be in the States for a while anyway. Now, let me give you some additional guidance on the criminal end of it. First, don't talk to the police."

"Oscar, I can't decline to talk to them. The guy was a student in this law school. And he died. I can't refuse to participate in the investigation and hope to keep my job."

"All right. I take your point. But say as little as possible."

"Okay."

"Good. In the meantime, buy yourself a computer that UCLA hasn't paid for, stop sending e-mail about this stuff via the university's servers or Wi-Fi, even if it's through your own private e-mail account and use a cell phone that you paid for and with monthly charges that aren't paid for or reimbursed by anyone else."

"Is the new stuff to have some restricted use?"

"Yes. Use only that new cell phone to call me or your other lawyers. Don't give anyone else the number and don't call anyone else on it. Use the new computer to write up any notes related to this matter and put 'prepared in anticipation of litigation/attorney client privilege' at the top of every page. Don't type anything else on it. Use the new computer to set up a new e-mail address, and use that e-mail only to communicate with your lawyers. Put the same heading on every e-mail."

"Wow. You're really up on your technology these days."

"Pandy made me go to an introduction to the Internet class, and I could immediately see that all of this stuff is a prosecutor's dream."

I laughed out loud. "I see."

"I don't see what's so funny about it. But once you get clean equipment, write up the details of all of this and send it to me. Did Robert give you my e-mail address?"

"Yes."

"Okay, good-bye."

"'Bye."

After we clicked off, I tossed the folded paper into my purse so as not to leave it behind in my office. Aldous had come in one day and noticed fifteen or twenty folded papers in the wastebasket. He'd been teasing me ever since about being OCD. There was no point in leaving him further evidence to support his diagnosis.

CHAPTER 25

After the call with Oscar, I spent a few minutes in my office trying to work on the added footnotes Stanford had requested for my law review article. It was no use; I was just staring out of the window. I needed to get out of there or I was going to start folding paper again.

I locked up my office, walked to my car and headed for Best Buy. The nearest one was about fifteen minutes away. When I got there, I bought a notebook computer and a cell phone. I registered the cell to Verizon because my old one was with AT&T. I also bought a new coffeepot for my office.

As I exited the store, lugging my haul, I almost bumped into Julie Gattner, the student from my Sunken Treasure seminar. As usual, she was well dressed, in this case wearing black wool slacks and a standing-collar red blouse, covered by a jet-black knit wool sweater. And topped off with a jaunty red beret.

"Oh, hi, Professor."

"Hi, Julie."

"I'm glad I ran into you, Professor. Do you have a few minutes? There's something I want to talk to you about."

"Something about your research paper for the seminar?"

"No. Just some information I have that might be of use to you."

"Oh. Shall we find a place where we can grab a cup of coffee? We can't just stand here in the entryway to Best Buy."

"I'm kind of in a rush. What if we just sat down over there?" Julie pointed to a nearby green bench that was bolted to the sidewalk.

"Sure."

We walked over to the bench and sat down, and I unloaded my bundles beside me.

"Well," Julie said, "this gets a bit personal, but here goes. I want you to know that I dated Primo for several months and I know some things."

I was immediately wary. Relationships between professors and students, once they went outside the normal realm and got into students' personal lives, even if volunteered, were problematic. There were so many rules about confidentiality and privacy and a host of other things, and it sounded as if Julie might be about to cross some line.

"Julie, I'd like to hear what you have to say, but I want to make sure you aren't about to violate anyone's confidences or invade anyone's privacy."

She paused for a moment, clearly thinking about it. "I don't think so. And also, once someone's dead, they don't have any privacy rights anymore, isn't that right?"

"Well, that's not my field, but I think that's generally correct, as long as you're not violating some statute or reg."

"Well, I never had any confidentiality obligations to Primo to start with, did I? I mean, I'm not a government or a university he attended or a company he worked for."

"I guess that's right. Although if you contractually obligated yourself not to disclose something . . ."

"Yeah, I see. But, whatever, I'm going to risk it. Stop me if you think I'm getting into areas I shouldn't."

"Okay." I have to admit that I very much wanted to hear what she was about to say, while I was, at the same time, distressed at the legal dance we'd just performed. In essence, I'd given Julie legal advice without learning all of the facts and ignoring whatever conflicts I might have.

"Like I said, Professor, Primo was my boyfriend. We dated for about three months, and we broke up about six weeks ago."

"Maybe this is too personal, Julie, but what do you mean by 'dated'? That covers a wide range of, uh, activities."

"Until we broke up, we were living together. In an apartment in Santa Monica. The inexpensive part of Santa Monica, south of Colorado and inland from the ocean."

"And?"

"The lease was in his name, so I had to find another place. When I heard yesterday that he had died, I went back to the apartment because I still had a few things there and I wanted to get them. I still had a key. I waited until I was sure no one else was there. When I was looking around for my stuff, I opened a drawer and came upon his diary under some shirts, and—I guess I'm still angry—I took it."

"How do you know it was his?"

"It's his handwriting, and it mentions some things only he and I could know about."

"So you read it."

"Yes." She turned bright red. "I shouldn't have, but it was, you know, almost irresistible." She paused. "Okay, it *was* irresistible, obviously."

"What does it have to do with me?"

"It says he was planning to show you a copy of a map so he could get you involved in a project involving sunken treasure. I think he wanted to ask for your help with the legal aspects of recovering the treasure."

"Uh-huh" was all I said. It seemed best not to volunteer anything, at least until I got a better sense of where this all was going.

"I thought you'd maybe be interested in seeing it."

"For the Sunken Treasure seminar? Is that why you thought I'd be interested in the diary?"

"No, something else. The diary says that his brother—his name is Quinto—didn't want him to approach you about the project. He was threatening to kill him if he did. Or, you know, at least that's what it says."

"Does it say why?"

"No."

"Is there anything else in the diary that, uh, pertains to Primo's death?"

"No."

"Don't you think you should turn it over to the police?"

"Part of me does, but part of me says you should see it first."

"Why?"

We were sitting side by side on the bench, our heads turned toward one another. Julie leaned closer and spoke in a whisper. "Professor, people are saying you killed him. And the diary exonerates you. If I give it to the police, and it disappears, it won't do you any good."

So the rumor had spread. Now I had to decide whether to acknowledge it or act surprised and offended. I chose a middle ground. "Julie, I heard from another person that that rumor was going around. I guess I shouldn't be surprised that it's spread even more widely. It would be really helpful to me to know where it's coming from. If I might ask, who told you that?"

"You know, I'd really rather not say exactly who told me. At least one professor and one student. Plus, you know, there was a reporter from the *Daily Bruin* snooping around the law school, asking questions."

"Are they saying how I killed him?"

"Uh, poisoned coffee."

"Do you believe that, Julie?"

"No, I don't."

"You know, if you think the rumor is false, don't you think the right thing to do would be to tell me who's spreading it?"

"I just don't want to get involved, Professor. Beyond telling you about it, which I've done."

I didn't say anything in response. After a moment Julie said, "Uh, Professor, I really have to go. Do you want the diary or not?"

"Yes, I guess I do. But why don't you just make me a copy?"

"I don't want to copy it. I just want to get rid of it, frankly."

"All right, then. Just leave it in my box at the law school. In a plain envelope."

"If I do that, someone might take it."

"That's true. Why don't you just slip it under my office door?"

"That sounds risky, too."

I sighed. "So what do you suggest?"

"Do you know where the botanical garden is at UCLA?"

"Sure."

"How about this? I'll walk up the steep main path there at 9:15 A.M. That's right after it opens. You walk down the path at the same time, and I'll hand the diary to you as I go by."

"Isn't that a little too much like a spy novel?"

"Yes, maybe. But I'm nervous about the whole thing."

"Okay. Well, I'll see you there. And thanks, Julie, for letting me know about this."

"No worries, Professor. And, uh, again, I know you didn't do it."

"Thanks."

She got up and walked away. I watched her saunter slowly over to her car, which was in the parking lot, and get in. After she drove away, I realized there were all kind of things I should have asked but hadn't. Well, there was always tomorrow. After I got a look at what was, in essence, a stolen diary.

CHAPTER 26

Week 1—Wednesday

I tossed and turned all night. At 5:00 A.M. I finally gave up trying to sleep, got up, reheated a leftover cup of coffee in the microwave and drank it down. Then I got dressed and walked into Westwood. It was only five or six blocks, and the walk in the chilly morning air helped drive away my sleepless night. It was still dark when I got to the Coffee Bean & Tea Leaf. The only other people there were various Ronald Reagan UCLA Medical Center workers—the med center was only two blocks away—in their various-colored uniforms, tossing down final cups of coffee before their shifts started.

I bought a super large double latte, along with two blueberry muffins, and plunked myself down at one of the little round tables. Which was when Dr. Nightingale walked in. Unfortunately, he saw me before I could scoop up my coffee and muffins and depart. He came directly over to my table. "Mind if I join you, Professor?"

"Suit yourself," I said.

"That's not very friendly," he said as he tossed his iPad down on the table, marking his spot.

"Well, why should it be? My student was in your ER, dying, and you were trying to pick me up."

"That's not what happened. Let me get a cup of coffee and then I'll set you straight."

I watched him standing in line and ordering, not exactly looking forward to being set straight but not seeing any easy escape. After a few minutes, he came back over, pulled out a chair, set his coffee cup next to his iPad and sat down.

"So now you're going to set me straight, Doctor?"

"I'm sorry, that wasn't a great way to put it. Can we just start over?"

"Sure, why not?"

"Look, when I came back to the ER waiting room with your coffee, I had no idea your student was at risk of dying. We had rehydrated him and he had regained full consciousness. He was chatting happily away with us, and his vital signs—heart rate, blood pressure, oxygen level—had all returned to normal. Not long after that, his vital signs began to head back downhill. We stabilized him and decided to admit him to the hospital. An hour or so after that, he crashed."

"Crashed?"

"His heart stopped. And we couldn't restart it. Ten of us tried everything we could think of for almost an hour."

"What caused it?"

"We have no idea. All of our tests and X-rays were negative. We assumed when he recovered so quickly with hydration that he'd had too much to drink the night before, although there was no alcohol on his breath. Or we thought it was maybe a mild overdose of prescription meds."

"The lab tests didn't show anything at all?"

"I shouldn't be talking about that at all, really."

"How about just a little?"

"All right. Let me speak hypothetically. When you're brought in like that, unconscious, very shocky, with no obvious trauma, the blood tests and imaging we run on the spot only tell us in more detail what kind of shape you're in. But unless it's a heart problem or some lung-related condition like an embolism, they probably won't tell us right away exactly what's causing your symptoms. There are some exceptions, but they weren't applicable to him. And the tox screen we do for drugs and some other chemicals doesn't come back instantly."

"Can you give me an example?"

I realized this was like taking someone's deposition. He clearly realized it, too, because he took a long sip of his coffee before answering, which is what witnesses in depositions often do when they want a little extra time to think.

"For example, maybe your potassium is really low. But if we've ruled out the likely causes—especially if you're young and otherwise healthy seeming—the tests won't usually tell us, or at least won't tell us quickly, *why* your potassium is low. Instead, we might just try to bring it back up rapidly. Maybe we push potassium into you."

"Push?"

"Inject."

"I see."

"Can I steal a little piece of your muffin?" he asked.

I picked up the one muffin I hadn't yet attacked and handed him the whole thing.

"Wow. Thanks. Is that a peace offering?"

"Not necessarily."

I took a bite out of my remaining muffin and chewed for a moment before continuing. It sometimes helps to slow down the pace when you're questioning someone. If they feel at ease, they may open up more.

"What did your preliminary tests show you?"

"Nothing of importance about the underlying cause of death. None of the tests we ran predicted he was about to die, and none of them told us anything about why he did. It was as much a surprise to us as to you."

"What will it take to find out?"

"The autopsy will tell a tale, and the tox reports the coroner will run from blood samples and tissue will likely tell a fuller tale. An educated guess would be that he ingested something unusual that did him in."

"There's no quick way to find out?"

"No, and in addition to the autopsy, there will be a police investigation, and there will likely be a coroner's investigation, too. If you know, where did he collapse?"

"In my office."

"I probably knew that at one point, but I'd forgotten it. I'm surprised the coroner hasn't already sent an investigator to check out your office."

"For all I know, maybe they have. My office seems no longer to need my presence for people to wander in and out."

"Well," he said, "I need to get going." He paused. "Given that we agreed to start all over again, will you take my phone call?"

"Sure. What will you be calling about?"

"Dinner." He got up, turned and walked out the door, whistling. I couldn't quite make out the tune. The truth is, I had been tempted to accept his dinner invitation on the spot, which surprised me. Hadn't I been put off by his propositioning me while Primo was still in the ER? Hadn't I just, in effect, agreed to try harder with Aldous? Hadn't Aldous just told me he loved me?

He had. But, then again, it was also true that I had failed to respond in kind when Aldous said it.

I sat at the Coffee Bean for another hour and a half, reading a *Wall Street Journal* someone had left behind, then an *LA Times* I ducked out to buy from a newspaper rack across the street. I managed to limit my coffee intake to just one additional cup.

At about 9:00 A.M., I walked onto the campus and up toward the top gate of the botanical garden. The garden, set on several acres on a steep hillside in the southeast corner of the campus, contains hundreds of tropical and subtropical trees and shrubs. On sunny days it's shady. On rainy days you can shelter there without getting wet.

I loitered about half a block from the entrance, waiting until I saw them open the gate. At 9:15 sharp I headed onto the steep dirt path that winds down toward the bottom gate. Sure enough, Julie was walking up the path. She was wearing a beige trench coat, which seemed a bit over the top to me, but maybe it was just something she wore all the time on cool days. As she approached me, she swiveled her head back and forth, clearly looking to see if there was anyone around. There wasn't, and as she passed she handed me a brown manila envelope and walked on. The whole thing was absurd, but then, the last two days had been absurd all around.

I walked the five blocks back to my condo and took the elevator up. When the doors opened on my floor, Greta Broontz was standing there. After I got out, she entered the elevator without acknowledging me and studied the ceiling until the doors closed. It seemed odd, since her condo was a floor below mine. There were three other units on my floor, so perhaps she was visiting someone. I turned away from the elevators and walked down the hall to my own condo. I unlocked my door, went into my study, shut the door behind me, sat down at my desk and ripped open the brown envelope.

CHAPTER 27

The envelope, now open, sat before me on my desk. Suddenly, a little voice in my head said, *This could be evidence. Do you really want to have your fingerprints all over it?* Even though there was no one there to see it, I shook my head in the negative. I got up, went into the kitchen, knelt down in front of the sink and pulled out a box of disposable vinyl gloves I keep there to use when I'm cleaning. I pulled out a pair and skinned one onto each hand. Then I got up and headed back to my study.

"Cleaning on a weekday morning, Jenna?"

It was Tommy. He was sitting in his usual spot, tennis shoes up on the table, chemistry book of some kind in his hands. That day, the shoes were an iridescent green.

"Yes," I said. "I'm getting rid of the dust bunnies in my study. They're starting to drive me crazy."

"Huh. Haven't noticed any in my room. Maybe it's because your study faces the street. All those cars."

"Yeah, maybe. Were you here when I came in?"

"Uh-huh. You blew right by me without saying a thing. Both coming and going. I don't think you even saw me."

"Hey, I'm sorry. I'm a bit distracted. Cleaning probably will help clear my mind."

"Jenna, if it won't take you away too long from cleaning, can I ask you a legal question for a second?"

"Sure."

"Do you know much about wills?"

"Hardly anything. Why?"

"My dad is bugging me to make a will. He says now that I'm an adult, it's important."

"Could be. Do you want me to give you the name of a lawyer who can help you out?"

"That would be good. But let me ask you, if I don't bother and I die without one, who would inherit the little that I have?"

"It varies by state, but probably, unless you get married or have children in the meantime, your dad. And if he isn't around when you die, my dad, and if he isn't around either, your first cousins, I think."

"Which would include you?"

"I guess."

"Do you have a will yourself?"

"No."

"How come?"

I smiled. "The cobbler's children never have any shoes."

"Okay. Well, thanks. When you get a chance, please give me the name of a lawyer you'd recommend."

"Will do."

I walked back into my study and shut the door. Tommy, if he noticed, would likely find it odd that I had closed the door in order to tackle dust bunnies, but he would just have to find it odd.

Now properly gloved, I sat down at my desk and extracted the contents of the envelope, which consisted of a thin, spiral-bound notebook with a green cover. The pages inside were narrow ruled. Being OCD, I couldn't help but count them. There were only ninety-nine, despite the fact that the cover of the notebook stated that it contained one hundred sheets. I also counted the pages with writing on them. There were fifty-one.

There was no writing on the cover, and the first page was blank. The second page was covered, margin to margin, top to bottom, with handwriting in blue ink. The writing was cramped but followed the narrow-ruled lines with precision.

I began to read. I had half-expected it would be written in Italian, but instead it was all in English. In fact, the first entry said he was going to try to write in English to try to improve his language skills. The diary seemed to me very likely to have been written by Primo because it contained the same awkwardness of phrasing he displayed when he spoke. Despite the fact that Primo was dead, I felt like a voyeur. The journal was very personal.

Most of it was about how unhappy he was—unhappy with law school because his grades were poor; unfairly so, he thought. Unhappy with Julie because she wasn't treating him right, and unhappy with his brother Quinto because they couldn't agree on how to go about some secret project, although the diary didn't say what the secret project was. Maybe it was recovery of the treasure? Primo was also homesick for Italy, and in particular for his small village there.

Assuming the dates on the pages were accurate, he had started the diary about three months before he died, sometimes writing every day, sometimes skipping several days in a row. For the most part, on each day he wrote he filled only a single page. There was a temptation to skim through it all and look for the entry Julie had mentioned about Quinto threatening to kill him. But as a lawyer, I had learned that chronology is a powerful ordering tool, and that if you were going to review a set of documents for the first time, it was best to read them first in chron order. So I steeled myself and began to read.

In one of the entries, dated about six weeks earlier, he had written that he was "tired of Julie's spirit," which I assumed was some Italian idiom misrendered in English, and that he was going to throw her out. I guess that confirmed that they were living together, as Julie had asserted. The complaints he lodged against her were failing to keep their apartment clean, doing better than he was in law school, lording it over him and secretly dating someone else. The latter accusation, of course, seemed to me like the most important one. I had never heard of anyone evicting a girlfriend for failing to clean. At the very end of the page, he called her a *troia stupida*. I would need to look that one up.

It had taken me quite a while to read the first thirty pages, which were in some ways like a poorly written soap opera. Before starting on the last pages, I got up and went to the kitchen for a cup of coffee, passing Tommy, who seemed not to have moved. There was still coffee in the pot from the morning, but it was cold, so I poured a cup and put it in the microwave for fifty-seven seconds, which I had determined to be the best time for reheating coffee in that particular oven. The better to pretend I was still cleaning up dust bunnies, I took a roll of paper towels and a can of Endust out from under the sink and headed back to my faux task.

As I walked past Tommy, he looked up from his book. "I'm surprised there are any bunnies left."

"Only a few. This stuff will deliver the coup de bunny, so to speak."

He tipped his head slightly and looked at me. "I didn't know you were witty, Jenna."

"Oh, witty as witty can be, Tommy," I said over my shoulder as I headed back to the study. Once there I sat back down, swigged down a big swallow of coffee and turned to the remaining pages. After reading for another ten minutes or so, I reached the last written-on page, which was dated the day before Primo died. On that day—there was no entry dated two days before he died—Primo wrote only about a fight he was having with Quinto about the best way to carry out their secret project. But, again, there was no mention of exactly what it was. Then I came to the last paragraph, which said:

I have said to Quinto that he has the wrong in this and that I will ask Professor Jenna James to help us and will show her the map to get her to be part of our project so she is aware we are serious. She has much legal expertise about sunken treasure.

Upon reading that, I actually said, "Aha!" out loud. The secret project did involve the sunken treasure: presumably, how to recover it.

The diary paragraph continued:

Quinto does not want her because she is the girlfriend of Professor Aldous Hartleb, and he argues that this professor is not to us a friend. We have shouted about this. Today he said if I show her the map to involve her in our project, he will kill me. I do not think he means it, but if he does, I am not afraid. I will do this in a way that is mine. I am first and Quinto is fifth and he must know his place.

Aldous was involved? As my grandmother would have said, you could have knocked me over with a feather.

CHAPTER 28

I sat at my desk for a few minutes, staring out at the hills to the north. It was by now late morning, and although the day was still gray, it was no longer drizzling. I swiveled my chair toward my computer so I could look up the meaning of *troia stupida*. I put the phrase into Google Translate, and it came up in English as *stupid bitch*. *Troia*, by itself, translated as *slut*. Either way, hardly a term of endearment.

I considered my options.

The diary, assuming it was genuine, was potent evidence that I didn't kill Primo. It suggested that if he wasn't killed by something he ate, drank, injected or inhaled, or by some preexisting medical condition—if his death was, as a coroner might put it, "at the hands of another"—then the most likely hands belonged to Quinto. Or maybe even Julie. So the most intelligent option was to turn it over to the police just as quickly as I could get over to the campus.

Another option was to keep the knowledge of its existence to myself and wait. *Wait for what, Jenna Joy?* an inner voice asked. (Okay, I admit it, when I talk to myself, I sometimes use my hated middle name in my internal monologue. It's probably me as the sneaky ten-year-old I once was.) I answered myself out loud: "Hold on to it until it will do me the most good." That was a reference to the time I hid my parents' video camera under a pillow on a high bookshelf and used the tape to nail my mother for snooping around my room—*after* she vehemently denied it.

Finally, the inner voice of Jenna—the mature one—spoke up: *You're out of your depth, kid. Sure, you did a good job defending Robert, but you never did set up the criminal defense department at M&M like you promised to do, so you're in no way a real criminal defense lawyer. But you do have one now. Call him.*

Oscar answered on the second ring, and I explained the situation to him.

"You know," he said, "you're proving as stupid as your former law partner."

"Robert's not stupid."

"No, but he was situationally stupid when there was a threat to his own hide."

"Well, what the hell did you want me to do? Tell her I didn't want it?"

"You could have tried to persuade her to give it directly to an investigator. Or you could have had somebody nearby who could testify that she gave it to you and could then have taken it from you and secured it."

"As long as I give it to the police right now, I still don't see . . ."

"Jenna, you're now unfortunately part of the chain of custody. The police, trusting as they are, and especially as fond of you as they are, will say you had an opportunity to cook the evidence in some way."

"How could I possibly do that?"

"How about by ripping out a page?"

"If I'd ripped a page out, Oscar, the binding coil would be filled with those tiny little shards that get left behind. But you can see that there aren't any."

"Maybe Julie ripped out the page herself and removed the shards before she gave the diary to you, Jenna."

"Setting me up?"

"Right. You mentioned that there's a diary entry three days before he died and one the day before he died, but not two days before he died. The police will suspect you tore out that missing day and removed the shards yourself."

"He didn't write in the notebook every day."

"Maybe not, but if the notebook had a hundred pages to start with, there's a page missing, right? So no matter how often Primo wrote in it, *someone* tore out a page."

"Okay, so I screwed up. How can we fix it?"

"Frankly, I'm not sure yet. But in any case, we do have to get it to the police so you're not also accused of obstructing justice by hiding evidence. But that doesn't mean it has to be this minute."

"Meaning what?"

"Meaning if we give it to the police, they'll never agree to share it with us later for forensic analysis, or at least not without a lot of trouble and expense."

"So?"

"I used to use a private forensics guy down in Venice. He can do a bunch of tech stuff, including sampling the ink. I'm gonna call him. Can you get down there this afternoon?"

"Sure. I don't have any classes today."

"Do you have a copy of Primo's handwriting?"

"No, students type or e-mail almost everything."

"We're going to need to find something to prove authenticity."

"Come to think of it, there's his signature on the sign-up sheet for appointments. It's on the wall beside my office."

"Are you at the law school now?"

"No. I'm at home."

"Do you have a copy machine there?"

"Yes."

"Okay. First, put your gloves back on and make a copy of every page of the diary, front and back, including the cover, the back and the blank pages. Then put it back in its envelope and put the envelope in a plastic bag. After you copy the diary, go up to the law school and grab the assignment sheet and put it in a separate envelope. Then take both envelopes down to my guy in Venice. I'll e-mail you his name and address."

"Shouldn't your guy be the one to copy the diary?"

"He'll make a copy of it, too, but I want a copy for us while he works on the forensics. It might take him a day or two."

"Will he turn it over to the police when he's done?"

"No, I will. I'm coming back to LA to deal with this. Tonight, if I can get a flight."

"Last minute. That will be expensive."

"Not a problem."

"Why not?"

"You're paying for it."

CHAPTER 29

I put a pair of gloves back on, extracted the diary from its envelope and started to copy it, page by page, on my slow ink-jet printer. On page four the black ink cartridge ran dry. I opened the desk drawer and shuffled around the junk, looking for a spare. Nada. Buying a couple of new ones had been on my list for a while, but it was, unfortunately, still on the list. It didn't seem to me a big risk to copy it at the law school.

I was also going to look for Aldous. He had some explaining to do, that was for sure. He had kept from me his involvement with Primo's project, and it was hard to imagine what excuse he could have. How could we have slept in the same bed without his mentioning it?

I looked at my watch to check the time. So few of my generation even wear watches anymore, but I still wear the one my grandparents gave me for my high-school graduation. They had been under the sweet misapprehension that watches were still valued as gifts. Wearing it reminded me of them, which was a nice memory because they had been my emotional port in a stormy childhood, what with my mother's mental instability and my father's drinking problems, both of which had been routinely hidden from public view by my father's senate staff until it all came unglued the year I turned twelve.

Since it was no longer raining, I decided to bike up to the campus instead of driving. I needed the exercise.

My bike lives in my study. It's a red Cervélo R5 racer, which I bought when I was still at M&M, at a time when its cost wasn't much of an object. On some level it was a stupid purchase, because I no longer race it, and its value makes it a prime target for thieves. In fact, the chain I use to lock it up when I have to park it outside seems at times like it weighs almost as much as the bike. On the other hand, I look great on it, especially in black Lycra.

I went into my bedroom—Tommy had disappeared from the living room—put on my riding gear and a helmet, lifted the bike from its rack in the study and headed down the freight elevator. The route from my condo up to the law school was easy and involved mostly backstreets. Instead of pedaling down six lanes of traffic on Wilshire Boulevard, which is always scary as hell, I just crossed Wilshire at a nearby traffic light, took mostly backstreets up to the edge of the campus, then pedaled uphill to the law school, which is more or less at the top of the set of hills that encompass UCLA. It was enough of an uphill that, despite all the gears, I worked up a minor sweat.

I carried my bike up the steps to the third floor of the law school. As I headed toward my office, I saw that Aldous's door was open. He was standing at one of the bookshelves, reading a book that was open in his hands. I stood in the doorway, holding my bike in one hand, and said, "Hey, handsome, how you doing?"

He turned his head to look at me. "Oh, good, it's you. I feared it was some student making an awkward joke."

"Awkward because you're not handsome?"

"No, awkward because it's not cool to be hit on by a student, even in jest."

"Had that experience of students hitting on you, have you?"

"Not recently."

"I see."

We both laughed, and then, as I walked in and leaned the bike against the wall, I said, "You know that lawsuit I gave you to review? The one where Quinto Giordano is suing me?"

"Uh-huh. Don't you remember? I read it this morning and told you to hire a lawyer."

"Right. Well, here's my question: Do you know either of the plaintiffs?"

He sighed. "Only the Italian company, not Quinto."

"Don't you think you should have told me that?"

"Here's the way it went down, Jenna. Last summer I spent a few weeks consulting for my old company on some pitches they'd received for investment. One of them was a pitch for investing in the recovery of deep-sea treasure. They were looking for twenty million, I think, to recover sunken treasure that had supposedly already been located on the ocean floor. The company pitching it was one of the plaintiffs in your suit—Altamira Società Recupero."

"How the hell could you not have mentioned that to me? Especially after you saw the lawsuit, in which that company is a plaintiff?"

He sighed again. "The company I worked for signed a super-tight confidentiality agreement that binds me, too. It precludes even mentioning the project or the names of those involved in it to anyone. It was very awkward to keep it from you, but I thought I needed to honor it."

"Can you at least tell me what you recommended?"

He paused for a moment and pursed his lips. "I guess now that you know about my role in it I ought to tell you a tiny bit—although I really shouldn't even now—but please don't tell anyone I told you."

"I won't."

"I recommended that they pass on it. Too risky, and it didn't look like the people running the company had the right experience. I wrote up a memo and suggested that if the company could first raise a couple of million in additional money, use it to get better side-scan sonar of the actual ship on the bottom—the pictures they had could have been of almost anything—and bring some folks with more experience on board, it might be worth a relook later."

"Did you ever talk with Quinto or Primo about it?"

"No, there was some other Italian guy—a good deal older—pitching it. I don't recall his name off the top of my head. I'd have to see if I can find it."

"I looked that Italian company up on various databases and couldn't find out anything about them."

"They're a private investment company, and they try to stay beneath the radar."

"Why didn't you ask me about the deal? That's my area of expertise, you know."

"Jenna, please forgive me, but you're an expert on the law of deep-sea salvage, not how to do it and make money from it. From an investment point of view, it was a nonstarter. If I'd thought it had any chance of success as an investment, then of course I would have tried to get permission to consult you. Jeez."

I was mollified, at least somewhat. And his story, if true, explained why Primo and Quinto knew who he was, but he didn't know who they were. Or so it seemed. And then I remembered what Ronald Reagan had once said about the ballistic missile treaty: *Trust, but verify.*

"Aldous, do you still have a copy of your memo? I'd like to see it."

"My client company probably considers it to be confidential, but since they didn't invest, I don't see any harm in showing you my report, redacted a bit maybe—but not the company's proposal—as long as you don't copy it and keep it confidential. I'll dig it up and you can sit here and read it."

"If we get married, as you've suggested, will I be required to read important stuff only in your presence?"

I knew that was a harsh and sarcastic thing to say. But I was really trying to answer the question in my head: if I had been in Aldous's shoes, would I have withheld the information just because of a "tight" confidentiality agreement? How can you say you love someone and do that?

I was about to express that exact thought when Aldous said, "Dear God, Jenna. You're impossible. Let's change the subject. Have you gotten a lawyer yet to defend you in the lawsuit?"

I decided to skip the confrontation, at least for the moment, and said, "I talked to Robert Tarza, my old law partner, and I think he'll pitch in from Paris, which is where he's living. It's not like I need to do anything on that front in the next day or two, and I can probably get someone here to work with him. And I've hired Oscar Quesana to be the interface with the police on Primo's death."

"Okay, good."

"You know, Aldous, another option on the civil suit would be for you to represent me."

"Well, first, Jenna, because of my research, I would have a conflict doing anything involving the Italian company. But even if that weren't a problem, I teach securities law and, when the associate dean makes me, first-year contracts. I wouldn't have a clue what to do."

"We could ask for a conflict waiver—you were just a consultant. And you would know what you were doing if I were standing behind you, telling you what to do."

"I'd rather have you standing in front of me."

"What the hell is that supposed to mean?"

"It was a clumsy attempt to compliment you about how great you look in Lycra."

"Oh, really?"

"Yeah, you do. Anyway, hire Robert Tarza."

"I'll think about it some more. Right now, I need to get going."

I didn't really need to get going, but I wanted to get away from Aldous and consider whether his story made any sense. I had been planning to show him the diary but decided that could wait. I did want to know where he'd be, though.

"When are you going to Buffalo, Aldous?"

"Tomorrow."

"Well, call me when you're there."

"I will. And the offer to stay at my place is still open. I'm going to give you my spare house key." He reached into his desk drawer, extracted a brass key from the very back of the drawer and tossed it to me.

I snagged it out of the air and put it in my purse. "I don't think I'll use it, but thanks."

"The entry code is the six digits of my birthday plus the number nine and the star key punched twice. I'll tell the security service you might be coming."

As I headed for the door, he said, "You know, I hear Buffalo's actually a great place."

I chose not to respond.

CHAPTER 30

I went back to my office, checked my e-mail—nothing of any consequence—then went to the copy room and copied the notebook. I figured if anyone saw me, I'd just say I was copying some notes I'd made when I was out on the treasure-hunting ship over the previous summer. If they asked about the vinyl gloves I was wearing—I had brought an extra pair with me—I'd say I was having some kind of hand treatment. Or something like that.

As it was, no one came in while I was copying. When I got back to my office, I lifted the sign-up sheet off the wall—it still had Primo's signature on it—and put it in a plastic bag, as Oscar had instructed. I would have to replace the sheet, but since I didn't have office hours on Wednesdays, I could do that later.

I had to get the original down to Oscar's guy in Venice. I decided that, instead of biking back to my apartment and then driving to Venice to see Oscar's guy, I'd just bike there. I checked Google Maps. It said that by bike it was nine miles and would take me about an hour. The ride would clear my head, and after I dropped off the packages, I would have dinner by myself at some small café by the shore and then take myself and my bike back to Westwood on a bus. The Santa Monica buses all have bike racks on the front.

I realized that my plan involved staying away from my apartment for as long as I could, and it was because I was still afraid. Maybe it was worth staying at Aldous's after all. But I didn't want to stay there until he was out of town.

I put the three plastic bags—one with the original of the diary, one with the copy and one with the sign-up sheet—in a saddle-bag on the side of the bike and carried the bike down the steps. I placed it in the street outside the law school, mounted and began to pedal away. Just as I was picking up speed, I noticed a man in a dark coat and a broad-brimmed hat that obscured his face walking along beside me. He had two dogs with him. Suddenly, the man gave the large dog a sharp kick on the side, and it ran into the street, directly in front of me. I swerved to avoid it and somehow managed, in the process, to hit the curb straight on. The bike stopped dead and I went flying over the handlebars. My shoulder hit the still-wet grass and skidded along until my head bonked the sidewalk with a distinctive sound. The world whorled and went dark.

I woke up just as they were unloading me from the ambulance at the UCLA ER. I tried, feebly, to get up but found I was tethered to the gurney with leather straps. I heard the EMT say, "Take it easy, Professor, you had a bit of a spill, and it looks like you hit your head, although, fortunately, not very hard. All your vital signs are stable, and your color has come back. But the docs here are going to take a look at you just to be sure you're okay."

"All right," I said. "Where's my bike?"

"When we came to pick you up, someone from the law school was standing there—a tall guy who said he was also a law professor—and he said he'd keep it safe until you got back. He gave me his card to give you. It says his name is Aldous Hartleb. I'll bring the card in to you after they get you settled in an exam room. Initially, he wanted to get into the ambulance with you, but we didn't feel comfortable with that."

"No need for the card," I said. "I know him well."

Shortly thereafter, they wheeled me into an exam room, where most of my clothes were removed. I was immediately surrounded by several doctors and nurses, who hooked me up to some sort of beeping machine, pushed and pulled at me, moved my arms and legs around and clucked and chatted among themselves in incomprehensible gibberish. Then someone else came and wheeled me to another room on another floor, where they did a CAT scan of my head and upper body, then took me back to the exam room and got me into a blue hospital gown.

After a while I was alone in the little room. Just me and the machine to which I was tethered. I thought about trying to get up, but the rails on the narrow bed were up, and I couldn't immediately figure out how to lower them. I fell asleep. When I woke up and cracked my eyes open, there was a doctor in the room looking at me. I realized with horror that it was Dr. Nightingale.

"Well," he said, "the bad news is that you're pretty banged up, particularly your shoulder and your face, and you're going to be black-and-blue in various places for a while. The good news is that you don't appear to have any bleeding under your skull or any other sign of a severe concussion, and you don't have any broken bones or, so far as we can tell, torn ligaments. So you're lucky."

"When can I get out of here?"

"We'll discharge you just as soon as you can arrange for someone to pick you up. Is there someone you can call?"

"Probably. Can I borrow your phone to make the call?"

"Sure." He handed it to me.

I reached Aldous on his cell, and he told me he had rushed down to the hospital and was out in the waiting area because they wouldn't let him in to see me.

I handed the phone back to Dr. Nightingale. He wasn't bad looking, really. And he was, for the moment, my only conduit to what had killed Primo. Perhaps I needed to follow my thoughts of the morning to their natural conclusion and accept his dinner invitation.

"Dr. Nightingale, I'm grateful to you for taking care of me tonight, and I realize that I've been kind of rude to you in the last couple of days. If it's still open, I'd like to accept your dinner invitation."

He smiled. "Good, but I don't think it's ethical for me to finalize a dinner with you until you're no longer a patient here. So call me if you still want to do it when you wake up tomorrow morning, okay?"

"Okay, I will."

"I'll go and sign your discharge papers. Be sure to arrange a follow-up with your personal physician tomorrow. If you begin to experience a bad headache or other symptoms, please return here immediately. And it's probably best to avoid driving for the next day or two."

"Okay."

"Do you have any Tylenol at home?"

"Yes."

"Well, you're probably not very sore right now, but you'll likely be really sore tomorrow, and maybe even more so the next day. Tylenol should do the trick, but if you need something stronger, call the hospital pharmacy. I'll leave a script there for you."

Shortly thereafter, I was discharged. I shed my blue, open-backed hospital gown, put my slightly abraded Lycra back on—the only clothing I had—and went out to the waiting area to find Aldous. The Lycra did look a little incongruous in that setting. Aldous was sitting in a chair, reading something on his iPad. He got up, picked something up off the floor, walked over and handed it to me. "I put your bike in my office before I came down here, but I brought this. I thought you might want it." It was the saddlebag from my bike.

"Oh, thank God. I was worried that had been lost."

"What's in it?"

"Well, can you drive me to Venice?"

"Sure."

"I'll tell you what's in it on the way there."

He looked at me. "You know, I'd like to give you a hug, but it looks like that might hurt."

"Yeah, probably best to avoid it for now."

We left the ER and went out to get into Aldous's red VW Bug, which he had left with the valet. I decided I needed to start trusting people more, and that Aldous was a good place to start. On a certain level, it was crazy, because he'd withheld the information about the Italian company from me. But on another level, after thinking about it, I concluded I would probably have done the same thing if faced with a tight confidentiality agreement.

Making him my lawyer for the day—so what I said to him would be privileged—I told him about the diary and pretty much everything else I had discovered. He made no comment, just kind of grunted.

Then I asked him the question that had been bugging me, but that had seemed so paranoid I'd hesitated to ask it.

"Aldous, did you see my accident?"

"Yes. I was looking out the window when it happened."

"Did some guy intentionally push that dog into the road in front of me? A guy in a big black coat with his hat pulled down over his face?"

He laughed. "I saw the accident, and you misinterpreted what you saw. That guy walking along was old Professor Sikorsko. He's a retired chemistry prof. He was out walking his little dog when the bigger dog—a stray, I guess—started bothering the little one. Sikorsko smacked the big dog on the side to make him go away, and it ran out into the road in front of you. He felt terrible about it."

"But not terrible enough to come to the hospital and see how I was."

"He's like ninety years old."

"Oh, okay. I just had to ask."

"I understand."

When we got to Venice, I went up to a large brown door at the designated address, lifted the brass knocker and let it fall against the metal kick plate. A small man with a handlebar mustache and a shaved head opened the door and looked at me.

"I'm Jenna James. I have some things for you. Oscar Quesana told me you'd be expecting me. He also told me to ask your name so I wouldn't give these things to the wrong person."

"Oh, yeah," he said. "Right. I'm John Smith."

That was the right name.

"Just a minute," he said, and closed the door. A couple of minutes later the door opened again and, still standing in the doorway, he gave me a clipboard with a sheet of white lined paper on it. He also handed me a pen. "Please list the name and description of what you're leaving, one item to a line. Then date and initial each entry."

I put the clipboard against the doorjamb, so I'd have something to steady it while I wrote, and filled the items in as requested. Then I handed it back to him.

"Thanks," he said and closed the door in my face.

Aldous had parked around the corner. I walked there and got back in the car.

"How'd it go?"

"Let's just say the guy wasn't exactly charming."

"Well, I don't know exactly what forensic examiners do, but I've never imagined them as the life of the party."

"Let's go to dinner, Aldous. I'm starving. And maybe you can tell me what I need to know about staying at your house." I had decided that while I wasn't committed to staying there, it was good to have the option, just in case.

CHAPTER 31

Robert Tarza

Week 1—Wednesday
Paris, 10:00 P.M.

In my gathering old age I had taken to going to bed early, at least during the week. Tess usually stayed up reading or watching TV or old movies. She had a particular affinity for Monty Python movies, although I was never sure whether she really, truly got all of the jokes.

I had put down my copy of *Le Monde*, which I admit I could only read with a French-English dictionary close at hand, and was already drifting off when the phone rang. Tess would get it, I knew, and, in any case, hardly anyone ever called me at her place. My friends always called my cell.

I put the pillow over my head. After a few rings it stopped, and I fell back asleep. Then I heard Tess calling me from the other room. "Robert, wake up. It is your friend Oscar."

I struggled awake again. "Tell him I'm asleep and I'll call him back tomorrow." There was a pause, and then Tess again, louder this time. "He says it is important, and he knows you do not sleep because he heard you say you were in sleep."

"All right, all right." I struggled back to full wakefulness and picked up the bedside phone. "What do you want? It's late here."

"I apologize. I'm calling to ask your assistance in something urgent."

"What?"

"Jenna has been sued."

"I know. She told me, and late last night she faxed me the complaint."

"Did she also tell you about the student who died?"

"Yes."

"Well, this is all becoming a mess, and the two things are intertwined. I've been dealing with the cops, but I need you to come back and deal with the civil suit."

"Did Jenna suggest that I come?"

"More or less."

"I told her I was surprised she hadn't asked me about it to start with, and I guess I said I was willing to help if I could do it from here. But I wasn't thinking of coming back. I could recommend several good people at my firm. In fact, Jenna probably knows them all."

"Robert, Jenna has worked hard to get tenure, and I think this is going to derail it. You know her better than anyone, and I think you'll be in the best position to counsel her on how to handle this. Otherwise, I think the whole thing is going to blow up in her face. And candidly, my friend, you owe it to her."

"Well, when you were here we talked about the whole situation, and I'm feeling much better about Jenna and hoping to resuscitate some sort of relationship with her. But I don't think that translates into making a transatlantic trip.

"You should do it because you owe her. Without her, you'd be working in the library at San Quentin right now."

"I think you could have done an equally fine job."

"I don't think so."

"I'll think about it and call you in the morning. Now I want to go back to sleep."

"Okay. I'll send you an e-mail with more details."

"Okay."

"And Robert?"

"Yes?"

"Do the right thing."

"Good night, Oscar."

CHAPTER 32

Jenna James

Week 1—Thursday Morning

After our dinner in Venice on Wednesday evening, Aldous had dropped me off at my apartment. He had first offered to take me back to his place, but I had declined. My fear had begun to abate. After all, I could've been killed in the bike accident, so perhaps I needed to stop worrying about an assassin.

As for the bike, there was no way it could fit into his VW, so we chose to leave it in his office at the law school. He told me he'd get it back to me later.

By the time I got through my front door, my bruises were really beginning to hurt. I had two things to do before I tried to go to sleep.

First, I booted up my computer and searched for Professor Sikorsko. To my astonishment, he not only had a Facebook page but had left it totally open, so I could see everything about him—his newsfeed, his friends, his photos and his "likes." The page said he had been retired for twenty-five years. His profile picture showed him holding a small dog named Corky. None of his friends seemed to have any connection to the law school, sunken treasure or anything else remotely connected with Primo's death. His photo albums mostly showed pictures of his adult grandchildren, who lived in Pennsylvania. There were no pictures of big dogs. I also checked out his posts for the last year. There was nothing of interest. His only "like" was Häagen-Dazs ice cream.

Second, I left a note on Tommy's pillow, asking him, if he could find the time, to do me a favor and go to Home Depot and buy the best dead bolt he could find. I said cost was no object. To just get the *best*.

Then I took two Tylenol and tried to sleep.

Sleep had been slow in coming and fitful, and I was still tossing and turning when the alarm beeped at 6:00 A.M. the next morning. I reached out to turn it off. A sharp pain shot through my arm, but I managed to shut off the alarm anyway and fell instantly back asleep, into my only deep sleep of the night. I woke again with a start at 9:00, when my cell phone rang. I usually leave it on the nightstand beside my bed. When I grabbed for it, I managed to knock it off and then had to reach down and scrabble for it on the floor with my fingers, which reminded me again, as my muscles protested the entire thing, of the accident the previous afternoon.

I finally got the cell to my ear. "Hello?"

"Jenna, its Bill Nightingale."

I was still pulling myself out of sleep, the way you do when you're suddenly awakened by a phone call, trying to make sense of who's calling. It took a second or two to clear the fog from my brain, and I finally managed to blurt out, "So you have a first name." I didn't think he would notice my slightly delayed response.

"Yes, of course I do. Did I wake you? You sound kind of sleepy."

"No, no, not at all."

"Okay. Well, I'm not calling about dinner. You need to call *me* on that, as we discussed last night. But first, how are you feeling?"

I stretched a bit more and felt my muscles protest again. "I'm okay, I guess. A bit sore."

"That's to be expected. Do you have a headache?"

"No. Do you always call your patients the next day to check up on them?"

"No, I usually ask one of the nurses to do it."

"So is this just to encourage me to call you about dinner?"

"No, actually not. I got a phone call this morning from someone at the coroner's office that I think you should know about."

"Okay."

"They've completed Primo's autopsy and are moving into analysis of tissues and fluids for toxins of various kinds. They usually send that out."

"Uh-huh."

"But they have some newfangled device that gives them a preliminary read on certain toxins."

I sat up and swung my legs over the edge of the bed. My legs didn't seem to hurt. "Should I be taking notes on this?"

"No, I don't think so."

"Okay. Go ahead."

"Anyway, he asked me if we had any sodium azide in the Emergency Department and, if so, if it might have somehow gotten on our patient."

"What's sodium azide?"

"It's a common laboratory reagent, used a lot in bio and medical labs."

"Why did he want to know, and what did you say?"

"Apparently, using this new whizbang instrument, they detected some in a small coffee stain on his shirt."

"What's sodium azide?" Even as I asked the question, I had a bad feeling about what the answer was likely to be.

"It's similar in some ways to sodium cyanide."

"Well, do you use it in the ER, and could you have spilled it on him?"

"No, we don't, so no, we couldn't have. Which is what I told him."

"What happens if you ingest it?"

"I just looked that up. A fraction of a gram will kill you, and the initial symptoms sound similar to the ones Primo presented with when he was brought in."

"And therefore?"

"I just looked at Primo's chart on the computer. It says you told the EMTs that he drank some coffee in your office that you prepared."

"That's true."

"Well then, assuming you weren't trying to commit suicide and take a student with you, someone tried to poison you."

His statement jolted me. Up until that second, I had maintained the faint hope that the coffee hadn't actually killed the plant. That maybe bugs had come in the night and eaten holes in the leaves that looked like burn marks but really weren't. Or that maybe the coffee really did have some weird, naturally occurring fungus in it that was poisonous. Now the poison had a name, and it didn't grow on coffee beans.

"I hate to say it," I said, "but that confirms something I've kind of assumed, except until now I didn't know the name of the poison. Does the coroner's office also have Primo's UCLA chart?"

"Of course. Or if they don't, they will shortly. The coroner's office will also be analyzing his blood and other fluids and tissue to make sure they didn't somehow spill the sodium azide on his clothing themselves. It's only a preliminary result."

"Do you think," I asked, "that sodium azide could burn a hole in a plant leaf if some of it splashed on it?"

"I don't really know. But it's pretty strong stuff, so it might."

"That only confirms that someone is trying to kill me."

"I meant that only as a joke, Jenna."

"I don't think it's a joke at all. That poison wasn't just in Primo's coffee cup. It was also in the coffeepot in my office. Someone put it there, and I don't see how Primo could have been their target. It had to be me."

"Why would anyone want to kill you, Jenna?"

"I have no idea, but that won't make me any less dead if they try again and succeed."

There was a pause in the conversation. I don't know what he was thinking, but I was thinking I needed a friend with some scientific expertise.

"Dr. Nightingale, I think I want to take you up on the dinner invite."

"Bill will do fine for a name."

"Okay, Bill, I'd like to confirm what I said yesterday. I'd like to go out to dinner with you."

"Name a day."

"Well, my dad's coming into town today and will be here through Sunday afternoon. So how about Sunday evening?"

"Sounds good. I'll call you on Saturday sometime and we'll pick a time and place."

"Great. And thanks for the heads-up about the coroner's findings."

"No problem."

I pushed the button to end the call, got up from my bed and walked very slowly into the bathroom to wash my face and brush my teeth. When I looked in the mirror over the sink, I actually shrank back. The entire right side of my face, from right above my lip to right above my eyebrow, was black-and-blue. It didn't hurt that much until I made the mistake of touching it. "Ouch." I said it out loud and promptly decided not to wash my face. I did brush my teeth, although the back and forth motion of my arm in brushing was slightly painful.

I took two Tylenol.

I heard my phone ringing again. I padded back to the bedroom, where I had left it, and picked it up.

"Hi, it's Matthew Blender."

"Oh, hello, Dean."

"I heard you were in a bicycle accident yesterday, and I'm calling to check up on you and see if you're okay."

"Yeah, I think so. They took me to the ER and I had a CAT scan, but I don't seem to have anything really wrong with me except that one side of my face looks like I was beaten up."

"Do you have classes today and tomorrow?"

"Yep."

"No one would blame you for canceling them for the next couple of days."

"No, I think I'll just man up and teach them."

There was a slight pause on the other end.

"Jenna, I'm sorry I said that the other day. I've never lost a student, or at least not so directly, and I just wasn't being sensitive to what that must feel like. I apologize.

"Apology accepted."

"So where were you headed on your bike?"

That seemed to me an odd question. I mean, what did it matter? I couldn't fathom why he was asking, so I decided to tell a white lie. "I had ridden up to the law school earlier, for the exercise, and was just heading home."

"I should start doing that. Get away from my desk more."

"Well, if you do, watch out for darting dogs."

He chuckled. "I will. You take care, and if you need anything, please call me."

"Will do, boss."

I looked at the clock on the wall. It was already 9:15. I had a class to teach at 10:00. I needed to get a move on. As soon as the class was over, I needed to put a plan in place—one that would protect me and at the same time figure out who was trying to kill me.

CHAPTER 33

On Thursdays at 10:00 A.M. I taught civil procedure, a first-year course. That made it different from all the other courses I taught at UCLA. The students were still in their first semester of law school and thus, for a brief moment in time, slightly afraid of their law professors.

The fear stemmed from two facts. The first was that they had all arrived thinking they were smart because, on the basis of their college grades and LSAT scores, they had gotten into UCLA Law, a so-called "highly selective" school that accepts only a small percentage of applicants. The second was that it was only November, so first-year students had not yet received any grades. As a result, they had no way to know how they would stack up against all the other self-designated smart people who sat around them. The first stack-up would soon be measured by the only metric law schools really care about—end-of-semester grades.

As a law professor, I was one of the temporary gods with the power to sort the students at semester's end by giving them grades. That's a terrifying power, on both sides. Most of us tried, of course, in the modern academic way, to be approachable and helpful, but in the last analysis we were gods, at least for a little while.

So now I, one of the gods, was standing in front of the gathering class at 9:55 A.M., looking like someone had beaten me up. The question in my mind was, Would any one of the seventy students in the class mention it? Would anyone say, "Hey, God, what happened to you?" I was curious about it, if only because, during my first year of teaching, I had turned to eating to cover my anxiety—coffee alone hadn't done an adequate job—and had porked on fifteen pounds in the first semester, then lost it again over Christmas. No student ever mentioned it.

I waited a moment or two for a few stragglers to hurry in. Unlike a few of my colleagues, it wasn't my habit to close the classroom doors at 9:59:59 and start talking at 10:00 A.M. sharp. As I waited, I sipped coffee from my red M&M mug, which I continued to use as some sort of talismanic reminder to the students that once upon a time I was a real lawyer and please don't forget it.

At 10:03 I began. "Good morning, everyone." Would anyone, I wondered, say anything?

Jordan Brown, a student in the first row, answered that question within the first few seconds by blurting out, "Professor, what happened to you?"

"Bike accident," I said.

At that point, of course, I had a choice. I could elaborate, or I could just plunge ahead. I chose a semiplunge.

"Thank you, Jordan, for asking. I appreciate it. The good news is that I wasn't badly injured. The bad news is that you'll get to watch my face"—I pointed to it with my right index finger, being careful not to touch it—"turn from its current black-and-blue to a nice yellow over the next couple of weeks. But now, since you were the first to speak today, let me ask you the first question."

"Okay," he said, looking a bit rueful that opening his mouth had led to his being called on.

"What is a deposition, Jordan?"

"It's when, in a civil suit, you take someone's testimony under oath but before trial and outside of court."

It was odd how sometimes what went on in the classroom reflected my life outside of it. As soon as I got my legal team fully in place, I wanted to take Quinto's deposition. There were a zillion questions I wanted to ask him. He'd be under oath, and we might get some straight answers.

"Not a bad seat-of-the-pants definition, Jordan," I said. "But what does Rule 30 of the Federal Rules of Civil Procedure, which governs depositions, actually say?" I was forever trying to train the students to start with the actual rules and their actual language.

He quickly looked down at his notes. "I don't recall exactly, Professor. I'd have to read it from the book."

"Let's do that together." I flipped a switch on the podium and projected the text of Rule 30 onto the large screen behind me. It said:

Rule 30.

Without Leave. A party may, by oral questions, depose any person, including a party, without leave of court except as provided in Rule 30(a)(2). The deponent's attendance may be compelled by subpoena under Rule 45.

I picked up my laser pointer from the podium, turned slightly and aimed its small red dot on the words *Without Leave*. "What does that phrase mean, Jordan?"

"It means that you don't have to get the permission of the court—the court in which the suit is pending—to take a deposition."

"Right. Well, when *do* you have to get the court's permission?"

"There are a variety of circumstances set out in Rule 30(a)(2) when you do." As he spoke I moved my laser dot to focus on the reference to Rule 30(a)(2).

"Well, Jordan, we don't have Rule 30(a)(2) projected at the moment, but did you read it?"

"Yes, I did."

Just as he finished answering, the classroom door opened. It made a squeak, and I jumped. My first thought was, once again, that it was someone with a gun. It wasn't. It was Greta Broontz.

"Hello," she said, addressing the class but not me. "I'm Professor Broontz. I'm here to evaluate Professor James's teaching as part of the ongoing evaluation for her tenure application. Apologies for being late. I'll just take a seat up in the back row. Please ignore me."

I was infuriated. No one ever showed up unannounced, let alone late, to do a teaching evaluation. Greta had either intentionally failed to let me know in advance or, most likely, had just made up the whole assignment. Even worse, she hadn't even acknowledged that it was my classroom. She hadn't even looked at me.

I could have thrown her out, of course, and maybe I should have. But a little voice in my head said that I could make use of the outrage, and it would be better if I didn't flip out myself. Instead, I just said, "Well, welcome, Greta," intentionally skipping the professorial honorific.

CHAPTER 34

I waited a few seconds for Greta to take her seat in the back row and for the class to settle down from the interruption. I picked up where I had left off with Jordan Brown.

"What would happen, Jordan," I asked, "if you tried to take someone's deposition more than once? What does 30(a)(2) say about that?"

"You're not allowed to. So they probably wouldn't show up, or they'd ask the court for sanctions, because you can't take the same person more than once, at least not without the permission of the court. "

"Very good, Jordan. So, ladies and gentlemen, no matter how familiar you think you are with the procedure, always go back and read the applicable rules over again, so you don't"—I looked at Belinda Walker in the back row—"so you don't what, Belinda?"

"So you don't," she said with glee, "screw up."

This brought a burst of laughter from the class. All semester long I had harped on how embarrassing it is to "screw up" through a niggling procedural error because you failed to read the rules. I hoped, by doing that, that in the long professional lives that lay before my students, they would remember that and be better lawyers. It had become such a theme in my civil procedure classes that last year's class had given me, as an end-of-year gift, an embroidered sampler that said, "Don't Screw Up." It now had pride of place on the wall of my office.

"Thank you, Belinda."

I noticed that Greta had been scribbling furiously in a notebook all during the discussion about not screwing up. She was the sort of academic prig who didn't appreciate humor in the classroom, and I was sure she'd find some way to object to it in her report—if there really was going to be a report at all.

I scanned the class, moving my gaze from Belinda Walker to the class as a whole. "Now that we have a small piece of the procedural detail out of the way, I'd like to talk a bit about the strategic use of depositions."

Litigation strategy—the real world—was something I enjoyed talking about. Unlike admiralty law, which I'd had to learn nearly from scratch in order to teach it, civil litigation procedure was at the heart of what I'd used and abused for more than seven years at Marbury Marfan. Unlike a few professors who preferred to skip the practical, I thought I had something to bring to the class that the students weren't going to get just by reading the cold rules and the court cases that interpreted them.

For the next forty minutes, we had a rollicking discussion of deposition tactics, including how to get around witnesses who stubbornly refuse to answer questions, how to deal with the ubiquitous I-don't-know answer and whether it's best to let the deponent—the person whose deposition is being taken—know what you're going to ask him or her at trial, or whether it's best to avoid the direct question and save it as a surprise. Usually, it's best to ask, but there are circumstances when it isn't.

As the class was coming to an end, I heard the door to the classroom open again—I didn't flinch that time—and saw Oscar come in and take an empty seat in the front row.

"Well, class," I said, "we have the honor of a visit by an old friend and colleague, Oscar Quesana, who is one of this city's best criminal defense lawyers."

Oscar did a slight bow of his head, as if to acknowledge the praise.

"But," I added, "he doesn't know squat about *civil* procedure."

Oscar looked around the classroom, in which all heads had now turned to look at him. "Well, Professor," he said, "what have you been discussing?"

"Tactics in the taking of depositions."

"Have you discussed whether it's best, if you're a defendant, to take the deposition of the plaintiff early in a litigation or just before the case is about to go to trial?"

"No, we haven't, Oscar," I responded. "Do you think that's important?"

"Yep."

I knew, of course, that we would soon face the same question about taking Quinto's deposition. Do it now or do it later?

"Ladies and gentlemen," I said, "I think Mr. Quesana has brought up a very interesting question, which we'll discuss in the next class, after—" I paused—"I have had the opportunity to get the benefit of the wisdom he brings from the perspective of his, um, advanced age."

Over the general laughter, I said, "See you all tomorrow," and closed the rule book in front of me. As I did so, I saw that Greta had come down from the back row and was moving quickly toward the classroom door, ready to escape. I jumped down from the podium and caught up to her just as she was starting to leave.

"Greta, I really don't appreciate your coming to my classroom unannounced. Don't ever do it again."

"You must not have gotten the e-mail, dear, or maybe you don't check your e-mails."

"There was no e-mail, Greta. This is harassment, pure and simple. The dean is going to hear about it."

I realized I had no doubt antagonized the Pineapple even more. But since she was already a sure no vote on my tenure committee, there was no reason to care. Not only that, it felt good.

I noticed that a clutch of students had gathered nearby, all of them listening intently. On one level I didn't care. On another I needed to de-escalate the situation so that it didn't, judolike, end up bouncing back on me. I stepped to the side, so we were no longer face-to-face and said, "We'll talk later, Professor." I stretched out the word *professor*, separated the syllables and let my voice fall an octave, so that anyone listening would have sensed that I might just as well have said *dog shit*.

CHAPTER 35

After Greta had departed, a few students, as almost always happens at the end of a class, came forward with questions for me. As I answered them, Oscar stood politely a few feet back, waiting his turn. When they had gone, he walked up to me.

"Hi, stranger," I said and started to wrap my arms around him in a bear hug before drawing quickly away. "Ow! I keep forgetting that I'm injured."

He stepped back and looked me up and down. Had it been anyone other than Oscar, I might have been offended.

"Well," he said, "you don't look much different as Professor James than you did back when you hung out on the high floors downtown. Maybe a bit thinner and a bit more toned, from that brief feel of you. And, uh, a bit more black-and-blue."

I smiled. "Pandy won't mind your feeling?"

"Not in a hug and, anyway, she's not the jealous type. I mean, how could she be as wife number six?"

When I had first met Oscar, I assumed his many wives meant he was a womanizer. But I later learned that his first wife ran away with the mailman, the second was killed in a car crash, the third divorced him because he worked too hard, and four and five were women he married—without requiring anything in return—so they could get green cards.

"I can imagine," I said, "that might make her more jealous."

"I take your point."

"You flew in last night?" I asked.

"Uh-huh. I'm staying at my old place. Pandy has a tiny place in Malibu, but she stayed in New York, and my old place is a lot more convenient if I'm going to do some real work."

"I hope there won't be a lot of work to be done, at least of the kind of work you do, Oscar. I'm praying this is going to be entirely a civil matter and not a criminal one. But let's go talk about it in my office. We'll be a lot more comfortable there." I looked around. "Plus students from the next class in this room are beginning to filter in."

On the way to my office, we caught up on things. I told Oscar about my newfound interest in admiralty law and actually going out to hunt for sunken treasure. He told me about Pandy, who, he reported, was a professional psychic. I avoided asking what the difference was between an amateur psychic and a professional one. He also informed me that Pandy was only twenty years younger than he, so he expected it would work out a lot better than his last marriage, which had been to someone who was twenty-five years younger. I refrained from rolling my eyes.

I also told him what Bill Nightingale had said about the sodium azide found on the coffee stain on Primo's clothing. He said he'd never heard of it but would have his forensics guy check that out, too.

Once in my office, I apologized to Oscar for the lack of coffee. "I bought a new coffeepot, and some new beans, but I haven't had time to bring them over here and get it set up. We can grab some in the coffee room, though, if you want."

"Doesn't matter," he said. "I've given up coffee as it's not very good for me."

"Oscar, have you given up drinking Manhattans, too?"

"No, never. They're health supportive. Are you still drinking martinis?"

"Of course."

He put his hands behind his head, leaned back and said, "Jenna, these reminiscences are great. There are no times like old times. But in light of what you just told me about sodium azide, we should get down to the legal business at hand. Don't you think?"

"Yes, but first we should talk about the cost of that business. I don't think, on a law professor's salary, that I can afford to pay you what you charge. I know you said you'd do the first part for free, but I think it may go on for quite a while."

"You could be right, but we'll work it out. But here's the thing: before I boarded the plane yesterday, I called Robert in Paris. Woke him up, in fact. He called back this morning and said he'd represent you without charge. Call it what friends do for friends. He'll do the stuff on the civil suit you've been served with—although I haven't gone over all of the details with him yet—and I'll put in my two cents' worth and do the criminal, if there turns out to be any. Which I hope there won't be."

"I'm both stunned and grateful."

"In Robert's case, he's the one who should be grateful to you for what you did for him five years ago. In my case let's just say that way back then I started out being dismissive of you, but now know how wrong I was. So it's my way of saying 'sorry about that . . . Professor.'" He leaned forward in his chair and did a small bow.

I was close to tears. Oscar was in many ways the most talented lawyer I knew, and his bow was a great honor.

Oscar waited for me to compose myself, then said, "Let's talk depositions."

"Whose?"

"Quinto's."

"When?"

"Remember the question I posed in your class—whether it's best to take a depo of the opposing party earlier or later?"

"Sure. And the answer is that it should almost always be later, after a lot of other discovery and investigation is done, so you know what to ask about. Because you can only depose someone once and . . ."

"Right, right. But don't forget that for the first ten days after a lawsuit is served, the defendant has the sole right to notice a deposition. So I say we notice Quinto's deposition right away, before he notices yours, which will give us priority."

"But actually take his depo later."

"No, let's take it now and find out what this is really all about. Where the map came from, who the Italian company is, who is financing all of this and a whole bunch of other stuff."

"That's risky because we may get only one shot at him."

"We can always ask the court later for leave to take his depo again, and my bet is we'll get permission, given how weird this case is."

"Okay. But I thought you didn't take depos since that's the civil litigation world, and Robert's in Paris. He can do the paperwork from there but not the stuff that has to be done in person."

"I'm not going to take the depo. Robert is."

"Robert's coming back from Paris to help me?"

"Yes, he's coming. In fact, he's on his way."

"That's wonderful."

"I thought you'd be pleased, Jenna."

"I am. It's great to be cared about. But now I want to turn to the question of who's trying to kill me."

"Okay, but I'm not persuaded anyone *is* trying to kill you. Motive is key, and you haven't found anyone with a motive."

"Well, I've made a list of everyone who I think might even remotely have a motive." I reached into my pocket and pulled out the folded piece of paper on which I had written the names. I handed it to Oscar. He unfolded and read it.

"You have three names here."

"Right."

"I don't know who any of these people are. Let's go through them."

"Sure."

"Okay. Who is Aldous Hartleb?"

"My lover. He's also a faculty member here."

"And you're serious that he's a suspect?"

"Sort of."

"What would his motive be, Jenna?"

"His case for tenure looks weak. Mine looks strong."

"So you're saying if he bumps you off, he'll get your slot?"

"No, because tenure isn't awarded here on the basis of 'slots.' If you're good enough, you get tenure no matter how many people are eligible in a year."

"So he has no motive."

I got up from my chair, walked over to the bookshelf, pulled down a volume and handed it to him.

Oscar looked at the book and read the title aloud. "*Social Choice in Leadership* by Gunter John Schmitson." He opened the book and paged casually through it. "Okay, what's the point of this? I obviously don't have time to read it right now."

"That book is a study by an eminent psychologist. He says that in almost all human communities, if there's a contest for leadership between two individuals and one of the individuals falls out at the last minute due to some external calamity, the group will almost always choose the remaining candidate even if he's not qualified, and even though the other one would have won hands down."

Oscar got up and slotted the book back into the space on the shelf from which I'd taken it. "Let me get this straight, Jenna. You think that if Aldous got rid of you, he'd be more likely to get tenure from the group in power here as a kind of consolation prize?"

"Yes."

"And because of that he might want to kill you?"

"Yes."

"Is his career the be-all and end-all of his life?"

"Probably not."

"Do you have any other evidence that he's the person trying to kill you?"

"Well, come to think of it, there are two other things about Aldous that might point to him. He was in the hallway outside my office when the EMTs were working on Primo, but when we emerged with Primo on the gurney, he was gone. That seemed suspicious."

"And the other thing?"

"When a dog ran out in the road in front of my bike, supposedly accidentally, Aldous was nearby."

I had become, I realized, a study in contradiction. If I really suspected Aldous, why had I trusted him and told him everything? I couldn't explain it, except that when I made the list I had to stretch for suspects. Two hadn't seemed enough.

I looked over at Oscar, who had gone back to studying the list. "What do you think about Aldous as a suspect, Oscar?"

"I think you're losing it."

CHAPTER 36

Week 1—Friday

Two calls had come in quick succession on Thursday afternoon, and they had collectively rearranged my Friday schedule. The first was from my father, who said that he had arranged to stay with a friend who lived near USC instead of with me because the friend could be "helpful" to him. He didn't say helpful about what. He hoped I wasn't offended. I wasn't. He proposed that, instead of doing dinner on Thursday, we get together for lunch on Friday. I suggested we meet at 1:00 P.M. at the Faculty Club. He declined directions and said his driver would find it.

The second call was from the dean, who called right after my father and proposed we meet on Friday morning, once again at Oroco's in Westwood. We agreed on 7:30 A.M., which would give me enough time to get to my Sunken Treasure seminar at 9:00. He didn't name the topic, but I figured it had to be about Primo and the impact that was going to have on my tenure application.

* * *

When I got to Oroco's, the place was crowded. The dean had already arrived and was in the process of grabbing the last table for two. As I headed toward him, I saw Tiffany, the waitress from earlier in the week, and caught her eye. I held up two fingers, and she nodded.

"Good morning, Jenna," the dean said as I pulled out a chair and sat down. "Still pretty banged up, I see. Does it hurt a lot?"

"Not too much. Tylenol seems to keep it under control."

"That's good."

Tiffany appeared with my two cups of coffee and plunked them down in front of me. One of them spilled over slightly, but she seemed not to notice. "Need time, guys, or ready to order?"

"I'm ready," I said. "I just want an English muffin, no butter."

"Well," the dean said, "since you're going light and we don't have much time, I think I'll have the same thing, except lots of butter on mine. And a small glass of orange juice, please."

Tiffany looked at the dean. "You sure you don't want only half of it buttered, like last time?"

"No, both sides."

She made a note on her little pad and departed.

"So, Dean," I said, "what's today's secret topic?"

"Your tenure."

"I thought it was assured, per our last secret meeting."

"No, what I said was that it looked good, assuming your big article scheduled for Stanford got rave reviews. But I also said that it was ultimately up to your Ad Hoc Tenure Committee, the Internal Appointments Committee and the whole faculty."

"Right. I remember. So I assume we wouldn't be here unless there was about to be some hiccup. It can't be the law review article. I gave drafts to the Ad Hoc Tenure Committee a month ago, and I'm confident in it. What's the problem?"

I knew, of course, what the problem was going to be. But I thought my brewing outrage, when it finally exploded, would be more effective if I pretended ignorance for the moment.

"The problem is Primo Giordano's death."

"I didn't know that having a perfect record of student survival was a precondition to tenure," I said, hoping the dean, who was sometimes slow on the uptake, wouldn't miss the dripping sarcasm.

"It's not so much the fact that a student died, Jenna, as that the University of California is now being sued, along with you, for recovery of his missing map, which was last seen in your office."

"Assuming," I said, "that there ever was a map and that it really is missing. Because neither I nor anyone else has ever actually seen it."

"Well, assuming or not assuming, there's a lawsuit pending."

"So?"

"Jenna, can't you see the problem?"

"Candidly, I can't."

"If the university grants you tenure, and the lawsuit isn't quickly settled, it's the kind of thing that's going to be all over the papers, the Internet and local TV. *Student Death, Missing Treasure Map Linked to UCLA Prof* is just too good to pass up."

"All right, so I'll be the subject of news stories. I thought tenure was based on scholarly performance, teaching quality and community service."

"It is."

"Well, my scholarship is great, I won the student teaching award last year and in terms of community service, I've busted my butt on two different faculty committees."

"All true. But tenure always has some political element to it, even if it's unspoken. If we were to deny tenure to a person of color, for example, it wouldn't pass without comment."

"Which means what? That since I'm white, no one will give a shit if I'm denied tenure because of a baseless lawsuit connected in some bizarre way with a death that had nothing to do with me? Is that what you're saying?"

I had apparently raised my voice because several of the diners at nearby tables turned and looked at us.

"Calm down, Jenna. What I'm trying to do here is to have a preliminary conversation with you about an awkward situation. And what's awkward is that if you're granted tenure in the face of unresolved allegations of stealing from a student, that's going to cause a shit storm, to put it indelicately."

"You've got to be kidding."

"I'm not kidding. And of course it's a situation that may quickly resolve itself and not affect your tenure at all. I'm just giving you a heads-up, okay?"

"Like the heads-up you gave me that all was well, except that now all is not well?"

"I guess. But I also came with a suggestion."

"Which is what?"

Before he could offer his suggestion, Tiffany arrived with our English muffins and his orange juice and put them down on our table.

"You guys need anything else?"

"No," we both said in unison.

"Okay, then, you both have the greatest day."

As Tiffany moved off, I decided I needed to rein in my growing hostility—at least temporarily—to try to learn what I could about what was going on and then talk to Robert and Oscar and develop a strategy to deal with this development, too.

"I'm sorry, Dean. This is all kind of unnerving. I mean, I'm still hurting from the bike accident, and now you're suggesting my tenure might be in doubt. So I'm trying to take it all in, and I'm sorry if it's made me a bit excitable."

"That's understandable, Jenna. But my suggestion was only that you might consider deferring your tenure decision for a year. Lots of people do that, you know. You're only in your fifth year of teaching, and you have a three-year contract at this point. So you could defer the decision by one or even two years and still be fine."

"I see. Have you discussed that possibility with anyone else?"

"Yes, with two very senior members of the faculty."

"Did you bring it up or did they?"

"They did."

"Was one of them Greta Broontz?"

"I'd rather not say who it was."

"I'll take that as a yes."

"Take it any way you want. But speaking of Greta, I'm not telling you anything confidential in saying she's been quite vocal about not being a fan of your scholarship."

"Yes, she's told me that to my face. And since we're discussing Greta, I called you about her yesterday afternoon and you didn't return my call."

"Yes, and I know what that's about. Greta came to see me yesterday, distraught that she had apparently failed to tell you she was coming to your class to evaluate your teaching for your tenure review. She thought she had e-mailed you."

"So that really was her assignment?"

"Yes, of course. As you know, we do a teaching review for both the third-year review and the later tenure review."

"Well, that's weird, because the last time, for my third-year teaching review, the e-mail scheduling the review came from the associate dean."

"It was just a mix-up all around, and everyone feels awful about it."

"Do you really believe that?"

"I do."

"Well, I don't, because while Greta was carrying out the 'mistake,' she was incredibly rude to me. And there was nothing mistake-ish about it."

"Greta has been having some personal issues, Jenna, and you should cut her a bit of slack."

"Like what?"

"Some health issues, and I can't say any more than that."

"So Greta gets to come and disrupt my class—and, in effect, disrespect me in front of my class—because she has some supposed secret health problem?"

"Candidly, Jenna, Greta's mistake—and it *was* a mistake—is just a blip on the problem. The larger problem is that up 'til now your critics have been a very small minority, but this whole brouhaha about Giordano will create an opening for them to try to gain some traction. Which is another reason to defer while you get the controversy behind you."

"It's also a reason not to defer, since it gives them even more time to gain traction—whatever that means."

"You could look at it that way, but my years as dean tell me that once the lawsuit and the controversy surrounding it are gone, everything will calm down, you can get tenure—which would please me—and we can all get back to work."

"I see."

"Jenna, will you at least consider it?"

"I will."

"And get back to me in the next couple of days? The Ad Hoc Tenure Committee will be issuing its confidential report soon, so if you're going to defer, you need to do it promptly."

"Okay."

My calm *okay* had come via an enormous effort at self-control. Because I was, in fact, enormously angry; seething, really. What I actually wanted to do was reach across the table and twist his pointy nose, like something you might do to an enemy in middle school. I understood, intellectually, that on some level, he was just doing his job and was trying to be helpful, in his own distorted, ferrety way. So with a supreme effort of will, I had just buried those feelings—for the moment—and given him the wimpy response he was looking for.

"One more thing," he said. "Have you heard anything yet about the cause of Giordano's death?"

He had switched from my pending academic death to a real death; how appropriate. Well, how should I answer his actual question? I thought about it like this: all I'd heard was a confidential *secondhand* report that a *preliminary* analysis had identified a *potentially* toxic substance in a coffee stain on Primo's shirt.

"No, I haven't heard anything. Have you?"

"Haven't heard a thing. And I understand that we won't hear much until the coroner finishes his work."

"Let's," I said, "talk about something else."

He agreed, and we finished our English muffins in relative harmony. We talked about UCLA football and whether the Bruin statue was adequately protected this year against vandals.

On my drive back to the law school, I left a message for Oscar, asking him to set up a conference call or an in-person meeting between him, Robert and me. Things were clearly spinning out of control, and I was spinning out of control. I needed to do something about it. Something very aggressive.

CHAPTER 37

I arrived at my classroom to teach my Law of Sunken Treasure seminar a little earlier than usual, with about ten minutes to go before the start of the class. I stood at the podium, looked out at the still mostly empty seats and thought about the fact that I was still pissed off. I wondered if anyone could see that my jaw was clenched.

I loved teaching at UCLA, and I had been looking forward to getting tenure. Not because tenure meant that I would have a job for life but because it was an accomplishment that didn't measure success by how good I was at screwing over the people on the other side of a lawsuit. I could own tenure as a pure reward for my hard work, teaching and scholarship over the last four years. Now it was all bizarrely threatened through no fault of my own, and I was going to have to return, at least for a while, to the dog-eat-dog world of litigation. It made me both sad and angry at the same time.

"Professor? Could I talk with you for a moment?"

It was Julie, standing in front of the podium. I'd been so lost in thought I hadn't noticed her approach.

I looked up at the clock. "We don't have long before the class starts. Can we talk afterward?"

"Sure. I wanted to find out if you read the diary."

"I did, and I've got some questions about it. But let's talk afterward, okay?"

"Works for me."

As I watched her move back to her seat in the first row, one of the thoughts that went through my mind was that Julie wasn't on my list of people who might be out to kill me. But she was certainly on the list of people who might have been out to kill Primo. Maybe I should be making two lists. Maybe they were somehow related.

By 9:00 A.M. most of the rest of the students had taken their seats. I flipped a switch and projected on the screen, as usual, the image of a ship. This time it was the *Nuestra Señora de la Concepción.* Once everyone was settled in, their notebook computers popped open in front of them, I aimed the beam of my laser pointer at the ship and asked, "Anyone know what type of ship that is?"

The only hand up was Julie's. I gestured toward her in the symbol that means, in classrooms everywhere, "Go ahead and answer."

"It's huge," she said, "so I'm gonna guess it's one of the Manila galleons we read about early in the course."

"Please remind your classmates what they were."

"They took silver and gold from western Mexico out to the Philippines, where it was traded for porcelains, spices and other trade goods from China. Then the ships brought all that stuff back to Mexico on a return voyage so it could be shipped on to Spain."

"Right. And the ship *was* huge. In addition to its cargo, it could carry a thousand passengers and crew. What do you suppose happened to it, Julie?"

"Well, since it's up on the screen in this class, I'm guessing it sank somewhere because somehow or other . . . the crew screwed up." She smiled a broad smile, no doubt pleased to remind me that she'd taken my civil procedure course when she was a first year and was still in on the joke.

"Good guess, although it may not have been the crew's fault. In any case, it crashed on the rocks on the coast of Saipan in 1638. What do you think happened after that?"

"If it was close to shore, the cargo was probably salvaged."

"It was, or at least most of it was. The Spanish were such meticulous record keepers that we could actually visit the archive in Spain and find out precisely what was salvaged and what its value was, even though the salvage happened almost four hundred years ago."

I looked out toward the back row, where Crawford Phillips was in his usual seat, chin on his chest, clearly struggling to stay awake and losing the battle. "Crawford," I asked, "how many shipwrecks do you think there are on this planet?"

On hearing his name, his head jerked up. "I'm sorry, Professor. Could you repeat the question?"

"Late night, Crawford?"

"Uh, yeah. Studying 'til late."

There was a collective guffaw.

"Well, whatever you were doing last night, the question was, how many shipwrecks do you think there are on this planet?"

"Since the beginning of time?"

"Yes, since men first sailed the seas."

"I'm guessing hundreds of thousands."

"Actually, the current estimate is three million. But where are most of them, Crawford?"

"Close to shore."

"Why?"

"Because in ancient times most trade was coastal, so ships mostly hugged the shore. And shores and harbors are the most dangerous places for ships. That's where all the rocks and reefs are. A lot of fog, too."

"Good answer. Now let me turn to the really interesting thing. If we went to the Spanish archive in Seville right now, we could find detailed records of all the Manila galleons that ever went missing. We could discover their names and whether they were on their outbound or inbound voyages. We could find out what their cargoes were and their value at the time. We could learn their expected routes and the approximate dates they sank. There'd be a lot of them. During the two hundred fifty years that the Manila galleons plied the seas, more than fifty of them disappeared without a trace and are presumably on the bottom of the ocean."

I stopped looking at Crawford so he could go back to sleep and swept my gaze across the other students. "If the galleons didn't sink within sight of shore," I asked, "could we salvage them?"

The woman who sat to Julie's right, Consuelo Hernandez, answered. "Depends on how close they were when they sank. But if they sank really far offshore, we probably couldn't find them to salvage. There was no radio communication and usually no survivors, so they're just out there on the bottom somewhere in the thousands of miles between Mexico and the Philippines."

"How many mile are we talking about, Consuelo?"

"Something like eight thousand."

"Right. And so the main problem for treasure hunters goes something like this: if a ship sank near shore, it's probably already been salvaged. If it's not near shore, but is within two hundred miles of the shore, it's difficult. Sovereign countries claim that area within their exclusive economic zone. So as with the *Edmund Fitzgerald*, you'd need to get a permit and share the prize with some government."

"But the government," Crawford piped up without being called on, "did nothing to deserve any part of the prize. No matter which government we're talking about." Crawford had demonstrated during the course of the seminar that he was something of a free marketeer.

"Crawford, I don't know about that, but I see that the idea of governmental regulation has awakened you."

"I wasn't asleep."

"Uh-huh. Well, in any case you could make some arguments on behalf of a sovereign state's right to a share of the treasure. But, in any case, if you can find a ship that's salvageable with current technology, you're much better off finding one that's well beyond the two-hundred-mile limit, so national salvage laws won't apply unless . . . well, unless what, Crawford?"

"Unless it's a warship."

"Right. Assuming you can find it with precision. Because there may be billions of dollars in gold and silver out there somewhere in the ocean depths, but unless you can find it, until the oceans are drained it's just going to stay there, sovereign rights or no sovereign rights."

We went from there into a discussion of the *Nuestra Señora de las Mercedes* case in Florida, in which Odyssey Marine Exploration salvaged a half-billion dollars in gold from a ship that sank off the Strait of Gibraltar in 1804. But the Spanish government got it all in the end because it proved to a court's satisfaction that, even though the ship was carrying cargo, it was also a Spanish warship, and governments never abandon their claims to warships. Most of the students found it horribly unfair.

As soon as the class ended, Julie approached me once again. "You said you had some questions about the diary?"

"I do. But let's walk back toward my office so we can have a little privacy, plus we need to clear out of here before the next class comes in. Better yet, let's go sit in the little courtyard out back. I have something very specific I want to ask you."

CHAPTER 38

We walked down the hall, then out of the double glass doors to the patio and sat down across from one another at one of the square white metal tables that dot the big concrete tiles. It's a pretty space, called the Shapiro Courtyard after its donors, with red-brick buildings on two sides. The trees that shade it are neither young nor old, but date from the time the courtyard was added, back in the 1990s. The day had turned warm, and I would have loved to just sit there and soak up the sun. But Julie was looking expectantly at me, so even though she had approached me to discuss the diary, it was clear that I was going to have to kick off the conversation.

"Julie, some of the things I want to ask you are kind of personal, and you should feel free not to answer. Normally, I don't pry into the private lives of my students."

"I'm okay with it. I wouldn't have given you the diary if I weren't. What do you want to know?"

"When you were living with Primo, did Quinto live there, too?"

"Yes. He had the second, smaller bedroom. But he wasn't there all the time. Maybe only three nights a week, and never on weekends. I don't know where he went the other nights. I tried to ask him a few times, but he wouldn't answer. He always changed the subject."

"Primo's diary says Quinto threatened to kill him. Do you know anything about that?"

"No. I was surprised to read that, and I never heard him threaten Primo."

"Do you think Quinto was capable of it?"

She paused. "I'm not sure. Maybe. He had a violent temper sometimes, but it was mainly raging arguments with Primo about who was most important and who had the right to do things first or have the biggest piece of pie, or whatever. It had to do with their birth order. It always seemed stupid to me."

"Weren't those arguments in Italian?"

"Sure. But I spent a semester abroad in Florence during college, and my Italian's good enough that I was able to follow most of it."

"Did you tell them you could speak Italian?"

"Of course not. It was more fun pretending to be a dumb American who spoke only English."

"Kind of dishonest."

"Maybe, but kind of useful, too, huh?"

I was appalled—but maybe I should have been more appalled when I learned she stole the diary, and equally appalled when I took it from her. I decided to move on. "Okay, well, what do you know about the birth order thing?"

"I only know that some rural Italian families name their sons 'first,' 'second,' 'third' and so forth. Quinto was the fifth child, and he told me one night that all of the older kids picked on him when he was young. But he thought he was way smarter than the rest of them."

"So he was one of five?"

"Yes, and the youngest."

"Did you read the stuff in the diary about a map?"

"I did. And I heard Primo and Quinto talking about it a few times. But I never saw any map."

"Did they say where it came from?"

"From their grandfather. But they talked about how they had gotten it updated at some point a couple of years ago—in a way that really pinpoints where the ship went down."

"Do you know how they managed to do that?"

"No. That was one topic they never discussed in detail in front of me, and if I came into the room when they were clearly talking about it, they stopped talking."

"If I ask you a question, can you keep the fact that I asked it confidential?"

She hesitated. "I'll have to be able to tell Consuelo. You know, the girl who sits beside me in class."

"Why?"

"Well, Primo and I didn't end so well, you know. But at one time I thought I loved the guy, and I feel like I have an obligation to find out how he died."

"Don't you think you should leave that to the coroner?"

"I'm not talking about what physically killed him. I just have a gut sense that whatever happened, someone did it on purpose, and that it's wrapped up with this map thing."

"Why do you have to talk to Consuelo about it?"

"She's been my best friend since college, and I just need to have someone to confide in."

"Julie, do you have any experience in investigating crimes?"

"Not really. Well, actually, I won at murder mystery night at my sorority."

"What's that?"

"It's like a dinner theater where there's a supposed murder, and there are clues, and the guests try to guess who did it."

"And you guessed?"

"Yeah. I was the only one who got it."

Frankly, Julie's statement about her investigative credentials made me wonder how she'd gotten into our highly selective law school, but it didn't seem like the right time to diss her. Instead, I just said, "I see. Well, that's not much of a credential, and you need to be careful. If it really was a crime, investigating it could make you a target."

"That's true. Anyway, what did you want to ask me that I need to keep secret?" She leaned toward me, her eyes wide, waiting.

Looking at her eager face, which reminded of the way Nancy Drew was depicted on the covers of all those girl sleuth novels I'd read as a kid, I wondered whether I should be telling Julie, let alone Consuelo, anything. In the end it seemed worth the risk because I had two lawyers helping me but no detectives, and I had turned down Aldous's offer to hire one for me. Now that he was at least a remote suspect in my mind, I couldn't accept the offer, and I didn't think I could afford one on my own. Julie might be able to help.

"I'll tell you, Julie, but you'll have to promise to tell no one but Consuelo, and pledge her to secrecy. Do you promise?"

"I promise."

"All right, then. There's a preliminary report—very preliminary—that Primo could have been poisoned by a chemical called sodium azide."

"What's that?"

"It's a reagent, often used as a preservative in biology and medical labs. It's closely related to sodium cyanide."

"Wow."

"What?"

"Quinto is an undergrad here, majoring in biochemistry."

"That's interesting, to say the least."

"Yes. Maybe I'll try to find out if Quinto has access to sodium . . . what did you say its full name was again?"

"Sodium azide."

"Okay. I can remember that now."

"Good. See what you can find out, Julie, and let me know."

Having Julie research it seemed, in fact, like the perfect solution. I had wanted to research sodium azide myself but had hesitated because I didn't want to leave a computer trail.

"Hey, Professor, do you have any more questions for me?"

"I do, but I'm late for something, and it might take a while. Can I catch you later?"

"Sure."

What I wanted to question her about, of course, was whether she had ripped any pages out of the diary. But now that I'd engaged her as my detective, it didn't seem prudent to ask right at that moment. Ask her I would, though. But later, after I'd gotten what I needed from her.

CHAPTER 39

At one o'clock I stood waiting for my father on the sidewalk outside the UCLA Faculty Center, which is only about a block from the law school. It's housed in a contemporary one-story A-frame clad in tan brick, wood and glass. Built in the 1950s, it's very Frank Lloyd Wrightian in style, and something of a relief from all the neo-Romanesque architecture nearby.

I hadn't seen my father since Christmas the year before, when I had made my way back to Cleveland for the holidays. My mother had been dead at that point for a little over a year, and I remember thinking that, at age eighty-three, my father looked hollowed out. Nothing to do and nowhere to go.

There had been a horrific snowstorm while I was there—it was the first time I'd ever heard the term Snowmageddon—and we had been housebound for four days of my seven-day visit. On some level that was good. We got to talk a lot. On others, particularly on the level that my brother, Henry, had come in from London, where he's some kind of investment banker, it was bad. My brother and I have never gotten along. Actually, Henry is my half brother, older by almost ten years. He's the son of my father's first wife. I'm a late-in-life second child by Dad's second wife.

We spent a good deal of time discussing politics, or rather my father and my brother spent a good deal of time discussing politics, while I mostly just listened. Henry is the political junkie in the family and was old enough to travel with my dad during two of his senate campaigns. I was too young to go at that point, and by the time I was old enough to do it—something I pined to do—the disaster had been visited upon us. That was the allegation that when my dad was on the Cleveland City Council he had taken bribes in exchange for voting to approve certain real-estate projects. The scandal and the subsequent federal trial gobbled up two years of our lives, and by the time the acquittal came in—the allegation was proved to be the utter fabrication of a bitter political enemy—he had been defeated and his political career was kaput.

My reminiscences of all that was interrupted by the arrival of a sleek black town car, which pulled up directly in front of the Faculty Center, just missing a couple of bicyclists as it swung to the curb. The driver got out, went around the car and opened the rear passenger door for my father. I really hadn't expected him to arrive in anything less impressive. Once you've been a US senator, you're a prince of the realm for life.

My father stepped out of the car and strode toward me. He seemed to have a renewed spring in his step, and his face was aglow. He was still senatorially handsome—six foot tall and square jawed, with steel-blue eyes and a large shock of Kennedyesque hair gone white, and clad in a deep blue pin-striped suit that fit him like the tailor-made garment it no doubt was.

"Oh my God," he said, "what happened to you?" He was looking at my face.

"Bike accident. But I'm okay. Just bruises."

"Can I hug you?"

"Better not. It still hurts."

He stood and looked at me as only a father can. "Well, other than that, you look great, honey."

"Is that," I asked, "similar to the old joke, 'other than that, Mrs. Lincoln, how did you enjoy the play?'"

"I guess it has some similarities."

"Well, *you* do look great, Dad. Shall we go in and get some lunch?"

"You bet."

The Faculty Club features a dining room sprinkled with small tables for four, each covered with a white tablecloth, with silverware already in place. But at lunch there's no actual table service. You walk to a room to the side, order from various food stations and then carry your lunch on a plastic tray back to a table in the main room.

Dad ordered a roast beef sandwich with everything on it. I asked for a mac and cheese. Not exactly what I needed to maintain my trim physique, but like Baby Bear's porridge, it seemed just right for the day it was turning out to be. By the time we had ordered, picked up our food and paid for it, Dad had become best friends with two of the short-order cooks and the cashier. He knew their names. They knew his. Not for nothing had one of the Ohio newspapers once called him the best retail politician in Ohio in over a century. I just stood there holding my tray and watching.

Finally, we made it into the dining room, sat down to eat and caught up for a few minutes on the usual: Dad's aging friends and their various ailments, the neighbors who never turned off their lights at night and the health of our old dog, Taft, who had been a puppy when I was sixteen but was by now, at age eighteen, the Methuselah of border collies. When we had finished the catch-up talk, my father took another bite out of his sandwich, put it down on his plate, crooked his head to the side and gave me an appraising look.

"Jenna Joy, is something wrong?"

"No, Dad. Why?"

"Well, you're usually bright and cheery, but today you kind of look like you just lost your best friend."

There's always a question about how much to tell your parents, especially when the parent you're talking to is eighty-three. I decided to skip the tenure thing and the Primo thing and talk about Aldous.

"Dad, you've always been perceptive about people. What's going on is that I have a very serious boyfriend. A guy named Aldous Hartleb, who's also a professor here. I hadn't told you about him because I wasn't sure until recently that it was serious."

"Why's that a reason to have a hangdog look? I don't understand."

"Because, for a variety of reasons, he's probably going to leave UCLA and move to—wait for it—Buffalo. He's on his way there for interviews."

"Nothing wrong with Buffalo. I mean, it gets lake-effect snow, sure. But sizewise, it's not that much smaller than Cleveland, and if you wanted to run for Congress, you could probably make a go of it. You've got great credentials for it, and there's even an admiralty practice of sorts there that you can engage in while you build your political base."

"Dad, I don't want to run for Congress. In Buffalo or anywhere else. I want to stay here in LA, where I've lived for more than ten years, where all my friends are and where I have a great law-school teaching job." I realized that I was starting to tear up.

Of course my tears weren't due to the prospect of Aldous leaving. They were due to my world rapidly falling apart.

"Oh, I'm sorry, honey. I'm making light of something that's clearly really important to you." He took a white handkerchief out of his breast pocket, leaned across the table and dabbed at my tears. I looked around to see if anyone had noticed. It didn't appear that anyone had, thank God.

"I'll be okay, Dad. And who knows, maybe I really will move to Buffalo with him."

As I said that, I realized that my emotions about Aldous seemed like a yo-yo going up and down on a string. Earlier in the day, the yo-yo had been spinning at the bottom. Aldous was emotionally unavailable, and maybe trying to kill me. Now, at midday, the yo-yo had climbed its string back up to the top. I felt better about Aldous for no reason I could put my finger on, and the idea that he was trying to kill me seemed so ridiculous that I was sitting there telling my father I might actually follow the guy to Buffalo.

"Well," my father said, "to cheer you up, let me tell you my piece of good news."

"What?"

"I'm going to run for Congress again. For the House of Representatives."

"What's the punch line?"

"There is no punch line. I'm serious. The seat is opening up because the incumbent is going to run for the Senate. Our house is right in the middle of the district, so I don't have to move to run. And it's where I got my start in Congress, before I ran for the Senate."

"Dad, you can't be serious. You'll be eighty-four next month."

"I know. And so when I tell people I'll only stay for three terms, they're going to believe it. Term limits are still really,

really popular around there, but I've already got the experience without having to stay a long time. I think my campaign slogan will be 'Doesn't Need to Learn on the Job.'"

"I don't think you should do it."

"There'd be a role for you, too. You told me you thought you were about to get tenure, so I figured after that you could take a six-month leave and help run the campaign. Your brother got a chance to participate in the old days, but you never did. So now it's your turn, huh?"

"No, Dad. Count me out."

"You know, when you scrunch up your face like that, so serious and determined, you look just like your mother."

"Like crazy Mary?"

"You shouldn't speak of her that way. She's dead and can't fight back. And she wasn't crazy."

I looked around the dining room again to make sure there wasn't anyone at nearby tables, because I didn't want what I was about to say to be overheard by anyone at UCLA. "Dad, you were gone in Washington three or four days out of every seven. And even when you were in town, you were out at some event, usually 'til late at night. So you didn't get to see crazy Mary melt down and talk to the houseplants."

"She didn't do that."

"Yes she did. She particularly liked talking to the schefflera. Although she worried that it was trying to get under the bedroom door at night."

"You're exaggerating."

"I'm not. It was a nightmare for most of my childhood. Do you recall that I graduated from high school when I was sixteen?"

"Of course."

"Well, I worked hard to get out early so I could get out of there and go off to college. Though you thought I was too young for college, so you sent me off to live for a year with Uncle Freddie, in Hilo. Which was fine. He was really into growing certain plants, but at least he didn't talk to them."

My father just sat there, kind of twitching his mouth around. "I'm really sorry, honey. I didn't realize how bad it was. If I'd known, I would have tried to fix it."

I knew I was expected to say it was all okay, but I wasn't in a forgiving mood. "You know what worries me the most, Dad? It's that I'm going to end up like her. I have her intensity, but I also have some quirks, and maybe they're going to get out of their cage."

"Like what?"

"Have you ever seen me fold paper?"

"I recall you used to do that as a kid."

"Well, I still do it."

"Oh."

"Do you know that I sometimes drink ten cups of coffee in a day?"

"No, I didn't."

"So enough. Let's go back to talking about Taft or something. This conversation is going off the rails."

"Okay, good idea, good idea."

We chatted on about nothing in particular, but as we got toward the end of the meal, he said, "By the way, I wasn't thrilled to hear you're living with Freddie's boy."

"You mean Tommy?"

"Yes."

"Why?"

"He's odd."

"There are a lot of odd people in the world, Dad."

"It has to do with when he came to visit us."

"I don't remember that."

"He was about fourteen. I think you were away at college."

"Did something go wrong during the visit?"

"Sometimes he stayed up all night."

"Well, that's hardly unusual for a teenager."

"Maybe not. But he also used to roam the house at night, looking into cupboards and drawers."

"That's probably still within the normal range of teen behavior, Dad, if perhaps a bit out there. And he doesn't do that now."

Or did he? I really didn't know, since I usually closed my door at night and put on white noise to help me sleep.

"Okay," my father said. "But if I were you I wouldn't let him cook for you."

His comment took me aback. Poisoning food—which was clearly what my father was talking about—seemed uncomfortably close to poisoning coffee. "Dad, are you suggesting he might poison my food?"

"No, no, just another way of saying he's odd."

I decided to drop it. I changed the topic again and, when we had finished our meal, walked him out to his car, which was waiting. As he got in, he said, "By the way, I'd like to meet this Aldous guy while I'm here."

"He's on his way to Buffalo, remember?"

"Oh, yeah, right. I forgot. Well, come to Cleveland for Christmas, and bring him along."

He gave me a kiss on my left cheek, the one that wasn't bruised, got into the car and was driven away.

CHAPTER 40

Robert Tarza

Tess and I arrived in Los Angeles on Thursday afternoon. Initially, I hadn't wanted to spend the money on a business-class ticket and had insisted on buying for myself a coach ticket, which was pricey enough, given that it was bought on the day of the flight. Tess had insisted on flying business class and also buying me an upgrade. I had put up token resistance and accepted.

On the way across the Atlantic, Tess pushed me to tell her the details of Jenna's situation. Even though I couldn't think of any real way for Tess to help out, I eventually gave up and told her. Then I tried to sleep the rest of the way, but without much success. At one point I opened my eyes and noticed that Tess was on her laptop looking at real estate in LA; the plane had Wi-Fi much of the way across. She was probably, I thought to myself, planning to buy an estate. Then I went back to sleep.

After we arrived at LAX and collected our baggage, a cab took us to the Hotel Bel-Air, where Tess had arranged for us to stay. The Bel-Air is a luxurious, Spanish-style hotel tucked into the hills above Sunset Boulevard, set amid twelve acres of gardens. The Bel-Air would find it hard to justify its existence in any other city. It features its own burbling brook, complete with ducks and swans, and the bar still requires men to wear jackets. The mission-style guest cottages are hidden away amid profusions of bougainvillea. Prices start at a thousand dollars per night and go up from there. With a staff that is the very essence of discretion, it's always been the best place in LA for a late-night tryst.

Upon arrival at the hotel, we surrendered our luggage to the valet, walked across the bridge and went into the lobby. I started to identify myself, but the man behind the reception desk focused immediately on Tess. "Ah, Madame Devrais," he said, rolling the *r* as if he were a native speaker. "We have been expecting you. You are preregistered. Did you have a pleasant trip from France?"

"*Oui*. Very pleasant, thank you."

"You and monsieur are in the Grace Kelly Suite. May I give you a small map to guide you? Or would you like someone to show you the way?"

"I know where it is," I said. I thought I detected an ever so slight elevation of his eyebrows at the news that I, so clearly below the salt, was familiar with the location of one of their priciest suites, but it may have been my imagination. We exited the lobby and followed the winding trail, through ferns and syc- amore, to the cottage. The door was open. The living room fea- tured a bone-white couch and two white chairs around a small round table. A fire crackled in the fireplace. The bedroom was to the right, behind a sliding wooden door.

"Nice place, Tess," I said. "And so very Hollywood. Planning on making movies while we're here?"

We both laughed. Tess threw her arms around me. Suddenly we were in a full embrace. As always, she was hard in all the right places, soft in all the other right places. She put her hands on my shoulders, pushed me back, studied my face for a few seconds—with what I call the Tess squint—and wrinkled her nose. "Welcome back to America, Monsieur Tarza."

"Thank you. It's good to be back."

"And now we must get to work to help your friend Jenna."

"We can do that tomorrow. It's 2:00 A.M. in France right now and I want to go to sleep."

Which is what I did, although I tossed and turned all through Thursday night, as I often do on the first night after long-distance travel. I woke up at 4:00 A.M. Friday morning—1:00 P.M. in the afternoon in France—tried to get back to sleep, had trouble with it, got up, ordered snacks from room service, read for a few hours and finally fell back to sleep on the couch in midafternoon. At one point Oscar called and woke me up. He wanted to talk details, but I told him I was too brain fogged to do it. He suggested instead that we meet at his office at 6:00 P.M. He said Jenna would also be there.

I struggled awake at 4:30, shaved and change my clothes. Tess was nowhere to be seen and hadn't left a note. I grabbed a cab and arrived at Oscar's office at 6:00, as we had agreed. Oscar was already there. Jenna wasn't. I was still feeling severely jet-lagged.

It was the first time I'd been to Oscar's office in almost six years. Back in the day, when Jenna, Oscar and I were strategizing my own defense against murder charges, I'd almost lived there. The office hadn't changed at all—still in an old apartment building in the Venice section of LA and still nothing more than a converted one-bedroom apartment with the living room serving as a cluttered work space. Its chief feature was a large,

CHARLES ROSENBERG

wooden conference table placed in the middle of what had once been the living room, with four swivel chairs, each pushed up to one of the sides of the table.

"Welcome back, Robert," Oscar said. "Grab a seat."

"Okay," I said and sat myself down in the chair that had its back to the window and faced the door. "When's Jenna coming?"

"In a few minutes. I gave her a slightly later start time for the meeting so you and I would have a chance to talk a little."

"So talk. Even with a night's sleep, I'm still pretty jet-lagged. It's three in the morning Paris time right now. It will be easier if you do the talking."

"Bottom line, I think our girl is in big trouble."

"Why big? I thought we were dealing with a frivolous civil case that's been brought against her for a theft of documents she didn't take—some kind of crazy mix-up—but that it's going to ruin her chances for tenure unless it's nipped in the bud in the next few days. You said it should be easy for me to take care of."

"Well, that's only part of it, as it turns out."

"What's the other part?"

"A law student died shortly after being carted unconscious out of her office."

"She already mentioned that to me and said the police were investigating it. But why should that make trouble for her?"

"There's a crazy rumor going around UCLA that she killed him. That she poisoned his coffee and served it up to him shortly before he died."

"What could her motive be for that? Were they lovers?"

"No, the supposed motive—wait for this—was to get her hands on a secret map he had showing the location of sunken treasure."

I put my fingers to the bridge of my nose, rubbed my eyes and shook my head slowly back and forth, in the manner of someone trying to wake up from a deep sleep. "Say what?"

"Yeah, it's passing odd, and I'd normally be inclined to dismiss it. But my sources on the UCLA police force tell me it's being taken seriously, and my sources in the coroner's office tell me that a preliminary tox report says the student died of a deadly chemical that's soluble in coffee, and that a coffee stain with that very chemical in it was found on his shirt."

"Oscar, when you persuaded me to come back here, you kinda lied to me."

"No, I just didn't give you all the details."

"How is the civil case for theft related to all this?"

"The clear implication is that she killed him in order to steal the map."

"I read the lawsuit. Jenna faxed it to me. It doesn't say that. It's just about recovering the map and seeks damages for stealing it. The poison coffee aspect is clearly a criminal matter, Oscar. I'm a civil litigator. I'd be happy to go into court and ask that the civil theft case be stayed while the criminal matter gets resolved. That's what people usually do in these mixed cases. The motion is almost always granted."

"True, but in this case we can use the parallel civil case to do the kind of discovery we could never do in a criminal case, where there really is no discovery. So it's in our best interest to keep the civil case alive and use it to our advantage, particularly in discovery."

"What kind of discovery?"

"To start, we can take the deposition of the lead plaintiff, this Quinto guy."

There was a knock on the door and Oscar got up to answer it. When he opened the door, Jenna was standing in the doorway.

"My God, Jenna," Oscar said, "what happened to your face?"

"Bike accident. Doesn't hurt much, though. Nothing to worry about."

"Maybe," he said, "I shouldn't give you a hug."

"No. I'm off hugs for a while. Maybe in a week?"

"Well, how about a fist bump, then?"

"You do fist bumps now, Oscar?"

"Something Pandy taught me."

Oscar held out his fist and they bumped, and then bumped again and laughed.

I had gotten up from my chair and was just standing there, several yards away, unacknowledged. I felt the same kind of awkwardness you feel when a friend you're with runs into someone he knows whom you don't, and your friend doesn't bother to introduce you. Maybe I deserved it. Suddenly I felt a wash of guilt that I had been so cold toward Jenna when she decided to leave Marbury Marfan. I owed her an apology for that.

Finally, Jenna walked over to me. "Hi, Robert. Thanks so much for coming."

"Of course I came. And I need to apologize to you for the way I treated you when you left."

"There's no apology needed. Or if there is, your coming back from Paris for this is more than apology enough. Let's just let bygones be bygones."

"All right, let's. Do I get a bump, too?"

"You bet."

We bumped, but only once.

Oscar had been standing to the side, watching all of this. "Hey, guys," he said, "back in the old days, when we used to meet here, we didn't whistle while we worked, but we did drink. Who's up for a martini?"

"Count me in," Jenna said.

"Oscar, between that and the jet lag, if I have a martini I'll be on the floor."

"I'll make you one anyway and you can just sip at it."

"Okay, I guess. But don't fill it all the way up, please."

Oscar went into the kitchen and came back with a large pitcher of clear liquid in one hand, three martini glasses gripped precariously in the other. "Martinis," he said, putting both pitcher and glasses down in the middle of the table.

"What about you?" I asked.

"I'm still drinking Manhattans." He went back into the kitchen and returned after a few minutes with a tall glass filled with an amber liquid.

"So," Oscar said, "I think we should take the deposition of this Quinto guy. Under the rules we have an exclusive right in the first ten days after the suit is served to notice depositions."

"Sure," Jenna said, "we do. But we have to give them ten days' notice, so it's not going to happen right away. And as I was just telling my civil procedure class, we only get one shot at the guy, even in a state court. We really ought to wait until we've done other discovery and investigation and know what we want to find out from Quinto. Otherwise we're going to waste our shot."

Oscar got up and began pacing around the room, his hands behind his back. "I don't agree. Let's notice his depo for Tuesday. If they show up, we can learn a lot even without all the prep. The worst that happens is that they don't show up. But I bet they will, because they're anxious to get the map back and they think you have it, Jenna. They'll expect you to come to the depo, too, and to get to discuss that with us informally. By the way, do you have it?"

"No, I don't have the effing map, and I don't effing know where it effing is."

"You used to use the f word full on, Jenna. What happened?"

"I'm losing my edge, I guess."

I finally spoke up. "Since I'm the one you guys think ought to take the depo, I should get to make the decision. I think we should go for it, crazy as it is. Although I'm betting they'll just send us an objection and not show up."

"What," Oscar asked, "are the stakes for that bet?"

"How about dinner at the world's highest restaurant, including the airfare to get there?"

"It's a bet," Oscar responded. "Where is it?"

"According to Tess, it's At.mosphere, which is on the one hundred twenty-second floor of the Burj Khalifa in Dubai. And by the way, they spell it with a period after the *t*."

"I'm not in on this bet," Jenna said. "It's above my pay grade, no pun intended."

"The loser of the bet," Oscar said, "gets to pay for you, too."

CHAPTER 41

I let Jenna and Oscar imbibe while I sat and sipped sparingly at my own martini, drinking enough to be polite but not enough, I hoped, to do any serious mental damage to my jet-lagged brain. For a while we just sat there, drinking and chatting about old times. Finally, I said, "Well, you guys want me to take a deposition of someone we know almost nothing about in a case about which I know almost nothing. Assuming this Quinto even shows up, of course. So I think we should spend time on preparation now."

"I think," Oscar said, "Jenna and I can get you up to speed pretty quickly. We do have at least some information." He reached into a folder that had been sitting on the table and handed me a thick set of pages that were stapled at the top. "This is a copy of Primo's supposed diary. The last entry is dated the day before he died and mentions the map. It also mentions Jenna and his brother Quinto, among other things of interest."

I took it from him and paged through it. "It's handwritten," I said. "How do we know it's actually Primo's handwriting?"

"Jenna gave me a copy of Primo's known handwriting. I gave that and a copy of the diary itself to a questioned-documents examiner. He reports that if the handwriting on the sample is truly Primo's handwriting, then so is the handwriting in the diary."

"Okay, Oscar," I said, "that's good enough for now, and I suppose Quinto, since he's Primo's brother, will be able to further validate the handwriting."

"Assuming," Jenna said, "that you choose to show the diary to him."

"Right. Assuming that. There might be a good argument not to right now. What else have you guys got for me?"

Oscar responded. "Not much, really. I'm having a PI run an investigation on both Primo and Quinto, but so far it hasn't turned up very much of interest except for the fact that Quinto, unlike Primo, was born in the United States—in Pittsburgh— and is a junior at UCLA. We don't know what he's majoring in."

"Primo's former girlfriend told me he's majoring in biochemistry," Jenna said.

"Does either one of them," I asked, "have a social media account of some kind?"

Jenna laughed. "Robert, do you even know the names of any social media sites?"

"Actually, Jenna, I do. I admit I didn't used to. I even have a Twitter account."

Oscar looked at me and raised his eyebrows. "You do? Hey, I do, too. What's your handle?"

"You go first."

"I don't remember. Pandy set it up, but I've never twittered anything."

"The proper way to say it," Jenna said, "is tweeted. You guys are too much. Let's go back to the depo prep, although this is a lame kind of prep. And by the way, I looked and, surprising as it seems, neither brother has either a Facebook or a Twitter account. If they used to have them, they've been taken down in a way that left no trace."

"So much for that," I said. "In terms of paperwork to use as a basis for questioning, then, we have only two things. The first is the lawsuit itself. We can ask Quinto questions about the allegations in it, but it's a suit that's scarce on details, so we won't be able to drill too deep with that. Second, we have the diary. Anything else?"

"No more paperwork," Jenna said, "but we can ask him what he knows about the map and where it came from—Quinto must know a lot about that. And maybe we can make use of the chronology of what actually happened after I arrived in my office. Like what Primo told Quinto his plans were for the meeting in my office. In fact, I've prepared a detailed chronology. Here it is."

She handed me several sheets of paper with a series of columns, headed *Date, Time, Event* and *Notes*. At the top, the paper said "Prepared in Preparation for Litigation. Privileged." That designation would make it harder for the other side to discover. Then she handed a second copy to Oscar. Oscar and I sat studying it. The chronology started several days before her meeting with Quinto and continued through the present. It was pretty thorough.

"This is helpful," Oscar said, "although Quinto isn't likely to be able to add much to this since he wasn't there. And let's not forget that what we really want to focus on is information that will tell us who killed Primo. Maybe learning what happened to the missing map will tell us that, but it's otherwise irrelevant."

"Well," I said, "you guys are talking about stuff that goes right over my head. I'm seeing the chronology for the first time,

Oscar, since you intentionally withheld most of it from me in your attempt to lure me here."

"It worked," Oscar said, exuding a Cheshire cat smile.

"Yes, it did. But now I need to know even more. Jenna, this chron is good. But I'd like to hear it from you in even more detail. Why don't you tell me what happened, with as much precision as you can recall, in exact chron order, starting with the first time you ever set eyes on Primo or even heard about him."

"Okay, good idea," she said.

Some fifteen minutes later, when Jenna had finished telling me her story—in much more detail than she had been able to write down—I said, "Well, that fills me in, and who knows, maybe Quinto will turn out to know some useful things, like exactly where Primo was before he came to see you."

"I think," Oscar added, "there are two basic questions to be answered, and the answers to those questions will tell the tale, although whether Quinto knows them I don't know."

"Which questions?" Jenna asked.

"The first is how the door of your office came to be open when Primo got there early in the morning."

"And the second?" I asked.

"The second question, assuming for the moment that Primo was poisoned by sodium azide, is how it got into his coffee. And I suppose two subquestions are how that chemical works— quickly, slowly?—and where it came from. Stolen from a UCLA laboratory? Bought on the Internet? Obtained in some other way?"

"Knowing you, Oscar," I said, "I assume you've already given some thought to those questions."

"I have, Robert, I have."

"And?"

"Well, at first glance it would seem that the question of where the poison came from would be most fertile to investigate. But I think not. The better key to this is, somehow, who unlocked the door, how and when."

"It's possible," Jenna said, "that I just left it open the night before, when I left."

"I think," Oscar responded, "that that's unlikely, Jenna. You are OCD in the extreme, so you're unlikely to have skipped something so routine. Plus you remember locking the office when you left. I'm going to assume that, between the time you left your office the evening before and when you got there the next morning and found Primo sitting in a chair in front of your desk, someone unlocked the door."

"Okay," I said. "Why will that unravel the mystery?"

"Because, assuming Primo didn't commit suicide, it's extremely likely that whoever unlocked the door also poisoned the coffee."

"Have you figured out who it was, Sherlock?" Jenna asked.

"No, of course not. But I've made a speculative list of how it might have happened." Oscar pulled a piece of paper from his shirt pocket, unfolded it, placed it on the table and smoothed it out in front of him. "To start, there are two main possibilities: someone opened it with a key or someone picked the lock."

"That sounds right," Jenna said.

"Okay," Oscar replied, "the candidates for having a key are law school personnel from maintenance, the cleaning crew, UCLA security and, I assume, the dean's office. Would the dean have a master key, Jenna?"

"I assume so, but I don't think I can just, at this point, go ask him."

"No, probably not. But beyond those people, who would be in a position to get a spare key made?"

She sat and thought for a moment before answering. "Well, I keep a spare office key in my apartment, in a drawer, and I suppose someone could copy that. But the only person who's in my apartment regularly is my cousin Tommy, who's a kind of temporary roommate. Other than that, someone would have to steal it from my purse and make a copy, but my purse is rarely out of my sight."

"Or," I said, "there's the other possibility: that someone copied the master key from maintenance, the cleaning crew, UCLA security or the dean's office."

"You know," Jenna said, "the most likely explanation is the second one on Oscar's list—that someone picked the lock."

Oscar looked thoughtful. "What makes you think that?"

"Because even I could pick that lock."

CHAPTER 42

Y ou can pick locks?" Oscar looked genuinely surprised.
"I can," Jenna said. "And it's not difficult to get a pick kit.
Would you like to see mine?"

I had forgotten that Jenna could pick locks, even though I
had personally witnessed her do it five years before.

Jenna reached into her purse, pulled out an elongated leather
kit about eight inches long and three inches wide and put it on
the table. We all stared at it. Oscar reached over, picked it up and
moved it to his side of the table. "Jenna, you shouldn't be carrying this around when the police suspect you of a crime. But tell
me, where did you learn to do that?"

"Oh, when I visited Uncle Freddie in Hawaii during my gap
year after high school. He's a PI, and he has all kinds of interesting skills. I think it amused him to teach me, and I got quite
good at it. He had a set of six practice locks, each one more difficult to pick than the one before it."

"How'd you do?" Oscar asked.

"I eventually nailed them all." She grinned.

"You know," I said, "I think I'm going to focus my efforts on figuring out who might have copied a key. Call it a gut sense, but I say key."

"Why?" Jenna asked.

"Because not very many people know how to pick locks, and if you're standing there in a UCLA hallway using a lock pick on someone's door, you're at big risk of being caught. No one much notices someone opening a door with a key."

"Well, I say pick," Jenna said.

"Well, you say potato, I say potatto, but I'm the one taking the depo. I'll cover both possibilities, of course. Somehow. And I guess I'll call Gwen to see if I can talk her into filing a notice of appearance in the lawsuit for me and serving a notice of deposition on Quinto's lawyer. For what day do you think? Tuesday?"

"Maybe Wednesday," Oscar said. "That's at least a tad more reasonable notice."

"Let's roll with it," Jenna said. "But Robert, don't you have to get the firm's new business committee to approve your taking on a new client?"

"Probably. But I'm just going to ignore that for now, and if Gwen will do what needs to be done, I'll deal with it later."

"Sounds good," Oscar said.

"I have one more question," I said.

"What's that?" Jenna asked.

"You must have some theories about who poisoned Primo. Who are your main suspects?"

Oscar let out an actual guffaw. "She does! And all of them are crazy, if you ask me."

"Well, who are they?" I asked.

Oscar looked over at Jenna. "Madame, you have the floor."

"The first one is my boyfriend, Aldous Hartleb. He's a faculty member and has the office next door to mine. It's complicated, but I was thinking he's after my tenure slot, even though there are no real slots."

I smiled at her. "I know you well, Jenna, from all our years of working together, including your verbal ticks. You just said, 'I *was* thinking.' Does that mean you've now changed your mind?"

"Sort of," she responded. "I realize now that my feelings about that are overheated, so although I haven't crossed him off the list, I've demoted him to last place. As I said, my main reason for including him was the thought that he was after my tenure slot. But the more I think about it, the more I see that he doesn't really care that much about getting tenure here. He seems really excited about going elsewhere."

"Who's in first place now?" Oscar asked.

"My colleague, Professor Greta Broontz. She has the office next to mine on the other side, so if I did leave the door open, she had an easy opportunity to plant the poison."

"What's her motive?" I asked.

"She hates me. For various reasons."

I raised my eyebrows. "Is that it?"

"Yes, but if you knew her, you'd think it was enough."

"Who's the third person on the list?" I asked.

"Before we get to that," Oscar said, "would anyone like another drink?"

"I would," Jenna said

"I would not," I said. "I've hardly touched this one."

"Okay," Oscar said, "two refills."

He scooped his and Jenna's glasses off the table, got up and went into the kitchen. While he was out of the room, Jenna reached over, retrieved the pick kit from his side of the table and dropped it back into her purse. She looked at me and placed her index finger gently over her closed lips.

I considered ratting her out to Oscar but then thought better of it. Jenna was an adult, and if she wanted to walk around with a pick kit in her purse, that was really her business. Besides, I was doing the civil side of the case.

Oscar came back into the room a few minutes later, set a refilled glass in front of Jenna and his own at his place at the table and said, "Jenna, I see you took the pick kit back. I can't make you give it to me, but at the very least you should leave it at home."

"I'll think about it, Oscar."

I was tired of the argument about the pick kit and wanted to get back to the core issue. "Who," I asked, "is the third person on your list, Jenna?"

"The third person is my cousin, Tommy, who's also my roommate."

"Why him?"

"Tommy knows where my office is—he's been there quite a few times and could have taken the key from my apartment because he lives there. He also majors in molecular chemistry. So he would have easy access to sodium azide. Plus the other day he rather casually asked me if I had a will, all in the guise of wanting to have his own will done."

"Would he," I asked, "inherit your assets if you died?"

"Well," she said, "only if both my father and his father died first, and then he'd have to split it with my half brother and maybe also with the three other cousins I have. But I'm not sure."

"Do you have a lot of assets, Jenna?" Oscar asked.

"No."

I thought about it for a moment. Perhaps it wasn't totally far-fetched. But there was a timing question that was critical.

"Jenna, did Tommy ask you if you had a will before or after Primo died?"

"After."

"So that means," I said, "that if he tried to kill you, he didn't bother to do his homework before the attempt. I mean, who would even bother to try without first learning if you had a will? Because if you did, it might provide that you were leaving your money to Friends of Dogs or something."

Oscar had been quietly sipping his Manhattan. Finally, he spoke. "Jenna, you've had experience with two murders, this one and back when your boyfriend was killed. I've represented defendants in several dozen homicides. There's always a theme, and the theme is that someone wants something—they want your car or they want your money or they want their husband or wife back. Sometimes they want their stolen dignity back. Or they want revenge. But usually, particularly if they get away with it, they get what they wanted."

"So?" Jenna said.

"So each of your suspects here may want something, but I don't see how killing you is going to get it for them. Tommy won't get your money if you die. Aldous isn't likely to get tenure just because you're dead, and Greta Broontz gets nothing at all."

"That's not correct," Jenna said. "She gets me gone. And in her warped universe, that would be enough, I suspect."

"No," Oscar said, "it wouldn't. People who kill out of hatred alone want two things. They want the victim to suffer in terrified agony before dying, and they want the poor soul to know who did it. Neither fits this murder."

CHAPTER 43

Week 1—Saturday Morning

I could have gone downtown to Marbury Marfan to prepare for Quinto's deposition. I still had a small office there, the lifetime perk of being a retired partner at the firm. But with the Internet and my notebook computer, it was easy enough to prep at the Bel-Air, and a hell of a lot more pleasant. Plus Tess was force feeding me cheese and crackers and fine wines as I worked.

I had a bunch of paper strewn on the coffee table and on the floor all around me, including the diary, which I had disassembled into its individual pages. It was like being surrounded by a paper beach, except with red Post-it notes scattered all over the sand.

Tess was standing in the doorway between the living room and the bedroom, surveying the scene. "You are quite the mess, monsieur."

"Preparing for a deposition can be messy. And this one is particularly messy."

"What is this deposition?"

"You put the person whose deposition is being taken—we call him the deponent—under oath and ask him questions, which he must answer."

"It is like a trial?"

"No, because although the person takes an oath to tell the truth, there's no judge. Just the lawyer asking the questions, the deponent and his lawyer are there. What the deponent says can sometimes be used later at the trial, if there is one. But sometimes not."

"It is in the courtroom, then, this deposition?"

"No. You're in an ordinary conference room, usually at a law firm."

"It is recorded?"

"Sometimes even by a TV camera. But always with a court reporter, who takes down, word for word, the questions the lawyers ask and the answers the deponent gives. Then the court reporter puts the testimony into a typed booklet, which we call a transcript, and the deponent signs it."

"Do you like this deposition thing? Or do you like a trial?"

I thought about it for a moment and shrugged. "They each have their charms. And their risks."

"Like women."

"One way to look at it."

"What is the main charm of a deposition?"

"If the witness is a party to the lawsuit, you can ask the witness anything you want and not worry about the answer. In a trial you need to be very careful what you ask because you'll be stuck with the answer."

"I do not understand."

I sat and thought for a moment, trying to figure out how to explain something that's actually complicated, plus has a hundred exceptions, in a way that Tess would understand.

"Let me explain it this way, Tess. Suppose you were in a French court suing a husband for divorce. And suppose to get a divorce you had to prove that the husband cheated on you."

"He would not be in court. He would be dead."

"Just suppose. It's a hypothetical."

"It is a hypothetical I do not like, but okay."

"If your husband is on the witness stand in a trial, and you want to prove that he cheated on you, you could ask him, 'Did you cheat on Tess?' He can say yes or he can say no, but he can't elaborate on his answer."

"What other question could you ask?"

"You could ask him an open-ended question—one that doesn't have to be answered only yes or no. For example, you could ask him, 'Why did you cheat on Tess?'"

"He would have no good reason."

I ignored her and went on. "If you asked him that open-ended question at trial, he could talk on and on about how bad you were in bed, what an awful cook you were and how old-fashioned and out of style your clothes were."

Tess picked up a pillow from the couch and threw it at me. I ducked, and it missed.

"You are a sheet, Robert."

"It's pronounced *shit*."

"Do not correct my English."

"Well, do you want to know what's different between a deposition and a trial or not? Because I'm not done."

"Yes."

"In a deposition you *want* to ask open-ended questions and get the deponent to tell you everything he's thinking or knows. That way you can know in advance what the other side will try to have him say at trial, and you can also learn things to ask other witnesses."

"I see. But this is byzantine. It would be better just to have people tell their stories in what way they wish. Without all these rules of the Anglo-Saxons."

"I'm sure the French have many similar rules, some even more byzantine."

"That is impossible. Our system is perfect."

I smiled. "Well, even in your perfect system, this depo would be a challenge."

"Why?"

"Because normally when I take a deposition of an opposing party in a lawsuit, I already know almost as much as the person I'm deposing, and all I want to do is confirm what I know. And, if I can, I want to trick the witness into putting his foot in it."

"Foot in what?"

"Never mind, it's a metaphor. But essentially, the problem here is that I know virtually nothing. I'm going to have to wing it, and I'm not a wing-it person."

"*Wing it?*"

"Tess, I need to buy you a book of English idioms."

CHAPTER 44

Jenna James

Week 1—Saturday

Saturday began for me as a day of nothing much happening. I slept late, got up, peered at myself in the mirror—the bruises were beginning to fade to yellow—got dressed and poured myself a bowl of high-protein cereal that I thought of as assorted sticks and stones. And I made myself a large cup of coffee. Then I sat down to read the *LA Times* over breakfast. Tommy had brought the paper in and left it on the kitchen table. Tommy himself was nowhere to be seen.

I was feeling at peace. For reasons I couldn't quite explain, I felt less afraid, and I had stopped trying to refine my list of who was after me and why. Maybe it was because, as Oscar had pointed out, my current list didn't make much sense. I paged through the *Times* to see if there was any mention of Primo's death. There wasn't. Nor had there been any mention of it in the paper on any of the previous days since his death. Nor, strangely, had there been any mention of it in the *Daily Bruin* or in the usual online places. Except for the lawsuit filed against me, the whole thing had disappeared without a trace. Maybe the suit could be resolved quickly, and it would all go away and I could go back to my life.

Around 10:00 A.M., Robert, who was preparing for Quinto's deposition—it was his MO to start days in advance—called to get more details about what had happened. Among other things, he wanted to know whose fingerprints had been found on the diary. I told him I didn't know, to ask Oscar, because his forensics guy still had the original diary.

It was a beautiful day, sunny and crisp. I decided it would be relaxing to go for a bike ride down by the beach. But first I had to make sure my bike hadn't been damaged in the accident. I had retrieved it from Aldous's office earlier in the week and brought it back to my condo, but without really inspecting it. Now when I examined it, except for a few scratches here and there, it appeared to be in fine shape.

I got into my Lycra outfit, put two bottles of water into the bike's saddlebag, picked up the bike and headed for the front door. Just as I got there, there was a knock on the door and, almost simultaneously, a loud voice said, "Police, we have a search warrant, please open the door."

I looked out through the spy hole and saw a man in a blue uniform with a badge. The thought flashed briefly through my mind that the whole thing could be a setup. "Officer, can you hold your identification up for me to see?" Almost immediately, an LAPD badge was visible through the spy hole. I opened the door.

Six cops, all in uniform, were standing in the hallway, one in front and five behind. "I'm Officer Krentz," the door-knocker cop said, "Los Angeles Police Department. We're executing a search warrant. Please stand aside so we can come in."

I wasn't really surprised. I hadn't thought specifically about the possibility of the police searching my condo. But once they concluded there was poison in the coffee from my office, it made utter sense for them to do it.

I did as requested, and the six of them strode into my living room. Officer Krentz looked at me and asked, "Are you Jenna James?"

"Yes."

"I'm required to give you a copy of the search warrant." He handed me a sheaf of papers. "We'd appreciate it if you could wait here in the living room while we execute the search."

"What are you searching for?"

"It's all right there in the search warrant, and we'll be giving you a receipt for what we take."

I leaned my bike against the wall, walked over to the couch on which Tommy habitually planted himself, sat down and began to read the warrant. I didn't teach constitutional law, but I did recall that the Fourth Amendment required search warrants to particularly describe the place to be searched and the person or things to be seized. This warrant seemed to fit the bill and then some.

Under place to be searched, it listed my "living room, kitchen, bedrooms and study, and the closets and drawers therein." Under things to be seized, it listed "all coffees, coffee beans, coffee grounds and paraphernalia for holding or making coffee, including coffeepots, grinders, filters and bins," as well as "all boxes and containers that could hold coffee beans or ground coffee." It also listed "all briefcases, saddlebags or other containers large enough to hold coffee, coffee grounds, coffee beans or paraphernalia for holding or making coffee." It also listed "all coats and jackets with pockets" capable of "holding same." I wondered why they had missed pants with pockets, or my shoes. People always hide things in shoes.

Most ominously, the warrant listed "sodium azide" and "any dry, powdered or liquid substance that might resemble it." I wondered how they would be able to tell what resembled it. I had looked up sodium azide in a chemistry handbook I found in Tommy's bedroom—the only research I'd done—and learned that, at least in solid form, it was a white powder. Were they going to take all of my sugar and salt?

I looked up from the paperwork, intending to protest the gross invasion of my privacy and the obvious overreach of the warrant. Officer Krentz, though, was no longer in the room. He had moved to the kitchen, and I could see that he was busy opening cupboards and drawers and handing things to another cop, who was sitting at the kitchen table. That kitchen-table cop was wearing blue vinyl gloves, with a pile of ziplock plastic bags piled in front of him. Each time Krentz, who was also gloved, handed him an item—he was at that instant handing off my small red coffee grinder—the cop at the table bagged it and made an entry on a log that was sitting on the table in front of him. A one-pound bag of sugar was sitting on the table, awaiting bagging.

I strode over to the kitchen and addressed Krentz. "Are you planning to take every single thing in my apartment?"

Krentz stopped pulling things out of a cupboard and turned to answer. "No, just the things listed. And don't worry, like I said, we'll be giving you a receipt."

"Well, when will I get them back?"

He sighed deeply, as if this was a particularly dumb question he got asked on a regular basis. "That's up to the court that issued the warrant." He resumed burrowing in the cupboard.

"Officer, can I walk around and watch what you're taking?"

"Yes, but we'd *much* prefer that you just sit down and stay out of our way."

His tone seemed threatening, so I went back to the living room. Then I called Oscar, who answered on the first ring.

"Oscar, the LAPD is executing a search warrant on me."

"Where?"

"My condo."

"Not surprising, really."

"You seem unperturbed."

"Well, that's kind of SOP. They'll give you a receipt for what they take."

"Which looks like it's going to be almost everything I own."

"I'm sorry, but that's kind of the way it goes. Are they taking your computer?"

"It's not on the list."

"Hmm. That's surprising. Must mean they're looking mainly for some sort of physical evidence, or that they're going to access your computer data via your cloud account."

"When will I get all this stuff back?"

"It's up to the court that issued the warrant."

"You're not much more helpful than the cops. So what should I do?"

"Well, don't leave. It's good to stick around and observe what they're doing. But don't get in their way either. You don't want to be accused of interfering with an investigation."

"This really pisses me off."

"If you told me you liked it, you'd be the first client I ever had who enjoyed having a search warrant executed on them."

"This is all the doing of Officer Drady."

"Could be. But, hey, I've got to go, Jenna. After they leave go down to FedEx or some other place with a fax and fax me copies of the warrant and the receipt."

"Okay."

"And don't be upset if they leave your apartment in a mess."

In the end that's exactly what they did. Dishes taken out but not seized had been piled on the kitchen counters, and clothes removed from drawers and closets but not taken had been dumped on the floor and left there. They did, upon departure and as promised, provide me with a four-page receipt of "items seized," which listed a large number of coats and jackets and four of my identical black wool blazers. One of the items listed was the jacket I had bought at Nordstrom a couple of weeks before and had intended to wear out to dinner with Dr. Nightingale on Sunday: "One Rebecca Minkoff woman's jacket, red, silk." That was annoying. More upsetting, however, was the last thing listed—"one glass jar with lid containing dark liquid." That was, of course, the sample I had saved from my office coffeepot the day Primo died. I had forgotten it was still in the refrigerator.

CHAPTER 45

I looked through my closet to see if anything else seemed appropriate for my date with Dr. N. Nothing looked quite right. Shopping isn't exactly my favorite thing, but it looked as if I needed to go out and buy something new to wear. Not to mention that I would have to buy, once again, a new coffeepot.

The question was, should I clean up the apartment first or do it later? I decided on later and called down to the valet to ask them to bring up my car. The answer, which was usually, "We'll have it for you in five," was, instead, "Uh, I'm sorry, Professor, but the police took your car."

"What?"

"Yes, a few hours ago they served the valet service with a search warrant. They drove a tow truck down into the garage and took your car away. They left a receipt, though."

"Why didn't you call me?"

"They told us we weren't permitted to. Something about people sometimes getting upset and violent if they learned their cars were being taken."

Officer Krentz had left his card stapled to the search receipt. It listed his cell phone number, and I called it.

"Krentz here."

"Officer Krentz, this is Jenna James. Don't you think you might have told me you were going to tow my car?"

"I could have, I guess, but I thought you'd just get even more upset."

"I didn't think I was upset."

"Yeah, you hid it fairly well, but I could tell. Your hands were clenched into fists every time you talked to me."

"Well, I guess that's neither here nor there now. When do I get it back?"

"That's up to the court that issued the warrant."

"F you," I said and broke the connection.

So that meant I had to shop for a rental car first. I called the valet service back and asked them to call me a cab. When the cab came, I asked the driver to take me to the rental car agency in Beverly Hills that specialized in high-end cars. I looked at various choices, rejected the less ostentatious ones and selected a red Ferrari. I'm not sure why I did it, exactly. Maybe it was because renting something out of my league and—let's face it, show-offy—seemed a good, if temporary, antidote to having had all of my possessions pawed through by the cops.

The rental guy seemed as surprised at my choice as I was. "Are you sure?" he asked. "It's pretty pricey and your insurance is unlikely to cover it. We'll have to add an insurance supplement."

"I'm sure, and that's fine."

After he ran a credit check on me, checked my insurance and had me fill out the paperwork, the rental guy tossed me the keys and said, "Live it up."

First I drove the couple of blocks to Neiman Marcus, which is one of the few upscale stores in Beverly Hills with valet parking. I went into the store and explained to a salesclerk, a woman of a certain age, that I had an important date and needed something that would show off my figure without being too blatant about it.

"All right," she said, "do you want black or do you prefer color?"

"For sure not black. How about white? Or maybe off-white? Something casual but sophisticated."

"I think I have just the piece for you."

She disappeared around the corner for a few minutes and came back with a white dress still on its hanger. "This is," she said, holding it up, "designed by Roland Mouret. His dresses are architectural and have a good bit of stretch. It's really elegant."

"Wow. It's also really tight."

"You'll look great in it. Try it on." She pointed to the fitting rooms.

I took it from her, went into a fitting room, dumped my jeans and T-shirt on the floor, slipped on the dress and zipped it up. It hugged my body in all the right places. I hadn't put on a dress that tight since law school. The top of the dress, at least, was modest. It rose all the way to my neck and featured little cap sleeves.

I walked back out and stood, rather awkwardly, in front of the saleswoman. "What do you think?"

"I think it looks fabulous. You don't even notice . . ."

"The bruises on my face?"

"Right."

"I'm thirty-four. I don't know if thirty-four-year-olds normally wear dresses like this."

"In this zip code they do."

"Why not? I need to live it up. Now I need some shoes to go with it."

"I have some nude sandals I think will be perfect."

"Might be a bit cold."

"This is Los Angeles, dear. No one ever admits that it's cold."

CHAPTER 46

The balance of Saturday was uneventful. Nobody served me with a lawsuit. Nobody searched my condo or towed my car. No further meetings were called by Oscar or Robert. I didn't hear from my father. The dean didn't call to press me about deferring my tenure decision. Nobody else died. And the no doubt temporary lull in my fear factor had continued. I did, however, get out my list of suspects to look at. Except for Aldous, they still seemed like good ones to me.

I also spent some time asking myself why, on top of the extravagant car rental, I'd just bought a dress that cost almost two thousand dollars. With the condo mortgage and fees already stressing me financially, it made no sense. Yet somehow it felt like taking control of a life that had suddenly and inexplicably spun out of control. I knew a lot of people would say that spending all that money on a dress represented just the opposite: lack of control. Somehow my theory made more sense to me.

Dr. N—that's how I'd come to think of him in my own mind—called midday to confirm our date on Sunday. I asked him if he'd mind going out Saturday night instead because on Sunday I wanted to get some work done finalizing my law review article. I also wanted to show off my new dress before I lost my nerve. To my surprise, he agreed to change the date and offered to pick me up at 7:00 P.M. I told him I'd pick him up instead, and he could just tell me when I got to his place where we were heading for dinner, since he'd obviously need to make a new reservation. He said he would e-mail me his address. Maybe that was just a sneaky way for him to acquire my e-mail address, although maybe not, since he could just as easily have found it through the UCLA Law School website.

I felt a little guilty about stepping out on Aldous. Who was in Buffalo. Of his own free will. There was no way I was moving to Buffalo.

As the time neared for me to leave to pick up Dr. N, I put on my new dress and the sandals and examined myself in the full-length mirror in my bedroom. The dress looked spectacular, emphasizing every curve and plane of my body, although I didn't know how I was going to feel appearing in public in something so "architectural," as the saleswoman at Neiman had put it. Of course, my Lycra bike outfit was also formfitting, but somehow its arguable function—reduced wind resistance—made it seem less disclosive, to coin a word. The dress had no excuse.

I looked through my jewelry box, took out a thin gold chain and looped it around my neck. The chain had an intricate set of interlocking links. If you looked closely, you could see that every other link was a tiny lion, and next to each lion was a link depicting a gazelle on its side. If you got really close, you could see that the lion link was feasting on the gazelle link. Robert had given it to me after his trial, with a note that said, "To the hunter go the spoils." I wasn't sure what that meant exactly, because I didn't feel as if I'd hunted anything other than a dumb prosecution or that there were any spoils other than two minutes of fame. But I did love the necklace, and I did love the look on the faces of those who got close enough to decipher the design.

A final decision I had to make was whether to wear a coat. The weather was unseasonably warm—a Santa Ana wind was blowing in off the desert—and I wasn't planning to do anything other than get in the car and move from the car to the restaurant, where there would inevitably be valet parking. I decided to leave the coat at home.

At 6:30 I called down to have the Ferrari brought up. When I got there, it was waiting in the driveway, with several men gathered around it. As I strolled out of the door, I heard one of the men say to Hector, the valet, "Whose car is this?" I walked up to the car and said, "It's mine." All of the heads snapped around to look at me. I ignored them, got in the car, put it in gear and drove off. In the rearview mirror I could see all of them gaping at me. Or maybe it was the car.

Dr. N lived in Hancock Park, a leafy neighborhood halfway between UCLA and downtown filled with large, stately houses, all with manicured lawns running down to flawless sidewalks on which children ride their overpriced bikes, watched over by the best nannies in town. In truth, it has always reminded me of the tonier parts of Cleveland. I'm sure the residents of Hancock Park would be horrified at the comparison.

The area was developed in the 1920s by people connected with big oil, then fell into disfavor in the 1970s as people fled the smog by moving west toward the ocean. In the last few decades, as the smog was abated and in-city living once again became popular, the area again became the lair of prosperous lawyers, doctors and corporate chiefs.

Dr. N's house was a two-story fake Tudor. Looking at it from the front, my guess was that it was about five thousand square feet, most likely with a pool and pool house out back. I pulled up in front and honked. There was no way I was stepping out of the car. After a moment the door opened and Dr. N emerged, wearing khakis, an open shirt and a blue blazer. At least in sartorial style, he looked a lot like Aldous.

"Wow," he said as he got into the car. "Is this what law profs drive these days?"

"This law prof does," I said.

"You're from a rich family or what?"

"Actually, Doctor, it's a rental."

"You're going to continue to call me *Doctor*? I thought I told you my name is Bill."

Calling him Bill was another step toward intimacy. But then again, I *was* going out on a dinner date with him, however much I might have excused it in my own mind as research on who poisoned Primo.

"Well then, Bill, where are we going?"

"We're going to Craft in Century City."

"I've never been there, but I've heard it's elegant, has great food and is pricey."

"All of those things but worth it. You know where it is?"

I put the car in gear. "Yes, I know where it is. Jeez. On Constellation, right off Avenue of the Stars."

"You know, Jenna, Avenue of the Stars is a very famous street."

"Because it has a dumb name?"

"No. It's because the pedestrian bridge that crosses the street is where they filmed one of the major scenes in *Planet of the Apes*."

"Wait. How old are you, Bill?"

"Forty-three."

"You couldn't have seen that movie when it was originally released."

"Right, it came out in 1968, before I was born."

"So you're some kind of sci-fi movie geek?"

"Kind of. What about you?"

"I don't do science fiction."

"What do you do?"

I realized that was a rather open-ended question, but I wasn't sure whether it was intended that way, or just a clunky way of asking what kind of movies I liked. I decided to interpret it the second way.

"I just like good movies. No particular genre, really, but I shy away from westerns, political movies and fart-joke movies. And science fiction."

"You equate the last two things?"

"I never thought about it that way, but yeah, they're about on the same level for me."

We spent the rest of the drive to the restaurant doing what people in LA who don't know each other well often do—talking about movies. It's the local equivalent of sports.

CHAPTER 47

Craft is in an elegant, modernist building that features walls of glass. When I pulled up to the valet stand, I was pleased to see that my car got admiring attention. My old Land Cruiser doesn't get much respect from the valetosphere. As I got out of the car, I saw one of the valets glancing at the windshield sticker that reveals that the car is a rental. Perhaps it was my imagination, but I thought he wrinkled his nose when he detected it.

Craft itself is a visually stunning place. Built with rich woods that set off the acres of glass, including thin wood beams that arch overhead, it manages to be both modern and warm at the same time. We were seated promptly at a good table, not too far from the door. When I looked around, I saw that the place was nearly full.

"You know, Bill, I've heard this place is one of those restaurants where it's really hard to get a reservation on short notice. And it's Saturday night. How did you do it?"

"It's my universally recognized charm."

"Sure. What's the real answer?"

"One of the senior people here believes I saved his life when he was brought into the ER a couple of years ago."

"Did you?"

"Well, I suppose it depends on how you look at it. I guess he might have died if he hadn't gone to an ER promptly, but pretty much any competent doc in any ER could have saved him."

"But you haven't told him that."

"No, I have, actually. But he insists I saved his life. It's a better story than my version, and he enjoys telling it. He's a writer on the side, and he says his version of the story is more literary." He smiled, and I noticed that he had teeth that were perfectly white.

"Do you get many perks like that as a doctor?"

"Not as an ER doc. Maybe if I were a high-end heart surgeon or something. What about as a law prof?"

"I've only been law proffing for a little over four years, so none of my former students are old enough yet to have landed important positions."

The waiter appeared with the menus and asked if we would like something to drink. I ordered a Jack Daniel's, neat. Dr. N ordered a scotch on the rocks. The drinks arrived quickly. I put my menu aside and looked across the table at him.

"I'm curious, Bill. Why are we here, exactly? Is this a date, or follow-up with a patient, or what?"

He pursed his lips, took a sip of his scotch and said, "I think, in truth, it's some combination of thinking, when I first saw you, that you're pretty, and assuming that if you're a law professor, you're smart—I like smart women—and noticing that you're not exactly young, so you've been around the block and . . ."

"Around the block? You mean I'm old? Do you think some-one old could wear this dress?"

"No, no, I'm not using *around the block* to mean old. I just mean that you've lived a bit. Last year I dated a twenty-five-year-old, and she didn't really seem to know much about the world yet. And, uh, you look great in that dress. More than great. Stunning, really." He took a larger swig of his scotch.

"So this is a date."

"I'd call it a getting to know you, which is maybe somehow less than a date."

"I see."

"But let me ask you, Jenna, why did you agree to come?"

"Curiosity. I don't know many doctors, so I thought maybe hanging out might introduce me to a new world. I like new worlds. It's one of the things I used to like when I was a litigator in a big law firm. I got to explore new worlds with every new case."

"What about Mr. Boyfriend? Is that an exclusive kind of thing?"

"It has been, but without formalizing it. Right now he's in Buffalo, looking for a new job, and that's a place I'm not going."

"What does he do for a living?"

"He's a law professor at UCLA, but he suspects he won't get tenure, so he's looking elsewhere."

"Are you likely to go with him to elsewhere, as long as it's not Buffalo?"

"No." I paused. "Well, maybe if it were Chicago or New York, but probably not those either."

"I suppose I should feel good about that, but I'm such a nice guy that I don't. I mean, it would give me a better shot, but I know how hard it is to build relationships that last."

I didn't want to start down that path, so I said, "Let's order. I can't afford to make this a late night."

"Been burning the midnight oil?"

"More burning the midnight stress. Ever since my student died. I shouldn't be saying this, but some people seem to think I did it."

"Did you?"

"No. Like I told you on the phone, someone is clearly after me. And part of my stress is caused by constantly looking over my shoulder. There are lots of ways to kill people other than by putting poison in their coffee."

"True."

"I've become almost paranoid. Every little noise makes me jump. Every stranger on the street who gives me a glance makes me nervous. I've even started locking my office door from the inside when I'm in there by myself. For whatever reason, though, I've been more relaxed about it today. I'm sure that will change, though. The basic circumstances aren't any different than they were yesterday."

Just then the waiter arrived to take our orders. I chose squid ink tagliatelle with Manila clams. That made twice in the last two days that Manila had entered my life, once as galleons and once as food. I also ordered an asparagus side dish. Dr. N ordered Alaskan halibut with olive relish and a mushroom side dish called Hen of the Woods.

After the waiter had departed, I looked at him and said, "I wonder why those mushrooms are called Hen of the Woods."

"It's because they grow in big bunches at the foot of deciduous trees, and some people think they look like a hen fluffing up her feathers. You've never seen them?"

"No. But it's a nice name."

"Its scientific name is kind of nice, too. *Grifola frondosa.*"

"Where do they grow?"

"Mostly in the northeastern US."

"Big range," I said.

"Yeah, it is. Did you grow up anywhere in that area?"

"In Cleveland."

"There are probably lots of those hens in various woods around there, although it could be a little too far west."

"My family didn't do much walking in the woods."

"Why not?"

We were about to go down the personal path again, and I decided to divert it. "It's a long story. Let's just say my parents were too busy."

"That's sad. If we're ever in the East together, we can take a woodland hike and I can show you some."

The thought that went through my mind at that moment was that it would probably be very pleasant to go for a walk in the woods with Dr. N. It sounded as if he could appreciate the simple pleasures. Aldous's pleasures seemed to require boy toys like sailboats and expensive things like five-star hotels and twenty-year-old wine. On the other hand, Dr. N and I were sitting at Craft, which wasn't exactly a down-market burger chain, and I had arrived in a Ferrari wearing a two-thousand-dollar dress.

"Hey, Jenna," Dr. N asked, "are you still with me?"

"Oh, I'm sorry, I was just thinking about how nice it would be to stroll in the woods—any woods—and get away from the stresses of my life."

"Well, the walk-in-the-woods offer is open any time. Any place, any woods."

"Okay."

After that we chatted on easily for a while, avoiding the personal. Then dinner came. The food was exquisite, and we mostly talked about the food and exchanged bites of the various dishes. We skipped dessert but ordered coffee, and when it came Dr. N said, "You know, I wasn't sure whether I should bring this up, given how stressed out you've been, but I did some research on sodium azide. I think what I found out will be helpful to you."

"Helpful how?"

"Helpful by showing that it's unlikely someone brewed the poison in your coffeepot. More likely it was put in your student's cup before the coffee was poured into it."

"Tell me."

"Well, first sodium azide, at least in powder form, is unstable. Too much vibration and it can explode."

"Why would that be helpful to me?"

"Would you want to put something unstable in a coffee grinder with the beans and subject it to grinding, whirling blades in a small space?"

"I see your point. What else did you learn?"

"It's unstable around certain metals. They can turn it into a toxic gas. So, again, you wouldn't want to put it into a metal coffee grinder with metal blades."

I sipped my coffee. "Anything else?"

"Too much heat can make it explode."

"How much is too much?"

"Over two hundred seventy-five degrees."

"Coffee doesn't get that hot."

"No, it doesn't. But no one in his right mind would brew sodium azide in a drip coffeepot. I looked it up, and the water in the holding tank of a good coffeemaker can get up over two hundred degrees."

"So what's your expert scientific opinion, Dr. Nightingale?"

"To a reasonable degree of medical certainty"—he was, with a wry smile, using the magic words expert medical witnesses are required to say to make their testimony admissible—"if it was added anywhere, it was added to his cup in liquid form either before the coffee was poured in or right after. Less heat, no vibration, no metal."

I cocked my head. "Hmm. That makes sense, I suppose. But let me ask you this: could it have been put in the coffeepot directly after it was brewed?"

"I suppose so. That wouldn't expose it to vibration or heat that was quite as high."

"Do you remember," I asked, "my telling you about the plant leaves getting burn holes in them?"

"I had forgotten that."

"Well, the coffee that burned the leaves came from the pot, so that tells me it was added both to the pot and to Primo's cup, maybe at the same time."

He looked thoughtful. "Could be."

"Does it come in a liquid form?" I asked.

"Yes. You can buy a five percent solution without a permit, and that's plenty potent enough to kill someone, especially if they turn out to be unusually sensitive to it."

"Well, Bill, that's all quite helpful. I'll turn the info over to my lawyers. I have two of them now, if you can believe that. I appreciate your looking into the whole thing. Thank you."

"You're welcome."

"Now I think it's time for me to take you home. This has been a lovely dinner and, well, I'd like to do it again, if you would."

"I would."

We ordered the check and then struggled over it. He insisted on paying; I suggested we split it. In the end he paid it, and I left the tip. How romantic.

CHAPTER 48

As we were waiting for my car to be brought around, another car pulled up, and Robert and a woman I'd never seen before emerged from it. He saw me immediately and walked over. The woman hung back a bit.

"Hi, Jenna. What a nice surprise."

"Indeed. Let me introduce you to my date. Robert, this is Bill Nightingale. Bill, this is my mentor of many years at my old law firm, Robert Tarza."

The two of them exchanged the usual pleasantries and shook hands. Then the woman, who had been hanging back, came forward, and Robert introduced her, too. "Jenna and Bill, this is Tess, who is visiting from France."

As soon as Robert said "Tess," I realized who she must be, because when I had called Robert in France, she had answered the phone and said her name. We shook hands all around. Then Tess said to me, "That is a very pretty necklace you wear."

"Thank you."

"The design, it is just like my bracelet." She held up her wrist so that I could see the dangling chain of gold lions biting into prone antelopes. I was speechless, in part at the surprise of the matching designs and in part because I had no idea how to traverse the emotional terrain I had just stumbled into. I assumed that Robert had given her the bracelet, and that it must be pretty obvious he had given me the necklace. I couldn't read Tess's face at all, and I didn't know if she was making light of the whole thing or was going to read something into the necklace that wasn't there.

Robert tried to solve the problem himself. "You know," he said, "I inherited both the necklace and the bracelet from my grandmother, who got them on a safari she took to Kenya long ago. I gave one to each of you because, like her, you're both very special to me."

"That's a very special story," I said, intentionally mimicking his words and wondering to myself if it was true. "I never knew that."

"I did not know it," Tess said, giving Robert a look that seemed to mirror my own doubts as to the story's veracity. At the same time, though, Tess looked more amused than upset.

"They're certainly unusual pieces," Dr. N said, no doubt trying to steer the conversation away from who had given what to whom and when.

"Well," Robert said, "we're running late for our reservation, so we should get going, but I think the two of you—" he gestured at Tess and me—"would like each other, and we should all have lunch soon. You, too, Bill. But like I said, we've got to hustle. So 'bye for now." And with that he put his hand on the small of Tess's back and led her toward the entrance. Tess glanced back at me over her shoulder as they went. I wished, at that moment, that I'd worn a different dress.

In the meantime my car had arrived and the valet was holding the driver's door open for me. "Nice necklace," he said, and
winked as I got in.

"Thanks," I said, checked to see that Dr. N was in and had
fastened his seat belt, then headed off down the street.

"What was that all about?" Dr. N asked.

"Tess is Robert's new squeeze. She's French, and he was living
with her in Paris before he came back to help me with my legal
situation."

"Were you romantically involved at some point?"

"No, never."

"I couldn't tell if she was unhappy or just amused at Robert's
rather awkward attempt to make the whole thing go away."

"I thought she looked amused. But I don't know her at all,
so I can't say for sure. Anyway, let's talk about something else.
Maybe she's as uncomfortable with the whole thing as I am."

"How about music," he said. "What do you like?"

"I'm stuck in a past that's not really my own. I like bands like
Fleetwood Mac and the Eagles. And I like No Doubt, which is at
least more from my own time. What about you?"

"Similar, but I'm at least a little closer in vintage to bands like
those."

We talked about music the rest of the way. We did turn out
to have remarkably similar tastes. Unlike me and Aldous, who
tended to prefer Wagner. Eventually we pulled up in front of
his house. I put the car in park but left the engine running. We
had arrived at what I used to call, when I was a teenager, the
Moment, although usually I was the one in the passenger seat.

"Well," I said, "I guess this is it."

"Uh-huh, I guess so. Do you think a kiss would be appropriate?"

I thought about it for a second. Inviting him to kiss me would be the final admission that things with Aldous were over. I wasn't quite ready for that, though, despite the fact that Aldous was still at least marginally on my suspects list. Talk about cognitive dissonance.

But I couldn't really say any of that out loud, so I just said, "Do you know, Bill, that in my head I still call you Dr. N?"

He laughed. "No, I had no idea."

"Given that, I think probably a kiss on the cheek would be best."

He leaned over and gave me a quick peck, then opened the door to get out. As he exited, he said, "I'm going to make it my goal to move my name inside your head to Bill."

I thought he had a good chance of accomplishing that, and getting the kiss, too.

I watched him walk up the pathway and waited until he put his key in the lock and opened the door. Then I drove away and thought to myself that he had learned at least something about me over dinner, but that I hadn't asked a thing about him, other than an inquiry about what music he liked. Which was rude of me. Maybe it could be excused by my current situation. Or maybe not.

CHAPTER 49

Robert Tarza

Week 2—Tuesday

You need a place to take a deposition, and the location is usually up to the lawyer who notices the depo. I considered noticing Quinto's depo for Oscar's unusual office in Venice but rejected it on the grounds that it would send the wrong message. In the end I opted to schedule it at my old law firm, Marbury Marfan, whose imposing offices occupy the top ten floors of a downtown skyscraper, including the penthouse floor on eighty-five. I hoped the setting would say to both Quinto and his lawyer, "Don't mess with Jenna."

As a retired partner in the firm—someone who, in the firm's lingo, has gone senior—I'm still entitled to avail myself of the firm's conference rooms and other facilities, so long as no one more important needs them. While trying to book a conference room for the depo, I learned that when you're senior every other person in the firm is more important.

My first choice was the elegant main conference room on eighty-four—da Vinci, as it's called—with floor-to-ceiling windows and a sweeping view of the hills to the north and the Pacific Ocean to the west. It had been reserved for the time I wanted it, however, by a second-year associate who would be hosting a meeting of his Los Angeles County Bar Association committee on gender bias in the profession. In the end I had to settle for a small conference room on the seventy-eighth floor that was named Cochise. It had no windows and was being remodeled. Its normal complement of contemporary furniture had been removed and temporarily replaced with stuff inspired by early disco. The small, oblong conference table sprouted like a mushroom from a fluted, white plastic base, and it wobbled. Its top was made of some material that screamed, "I am made from something fake." The room had only six chairs, which would make for a very snug fit around the table—two chairs on each side and one on each end. Upon seeing the room, I shuddered, but there was nothing else, and the alternative was either to change the date or move the depo to Oscar's place.

Gwen had been helping me tour what was available after I'd been turned down on Monday for da Vinci and Alligator. When I finally settled on Cochise, she made a note on her ever-present pad and said, "How the mighty hath fallen."

"What's with you, Gwen?" I asked. "Once upon a time we were a close-knit team. And this isn't about me. It's about helping Jenna."

"Well, Mr. Tarza, that was then and this is now. And Jenna doesn't work here anymore."

"But she's now a client of the firm, and this deposition is key to getting rid of the ridiculous case that's been filed against her."

"Thank you for reminding me about our obligations to clients, Mr. Tarza."

"This is about Tess, isn't it?"

"No. I've never met her and I'm sure she's a fine woman. This is about keeping secrets from your team back then."

"Keeping secret, when I got back from my sabbatical fifteen years ago, that I had had an affair while I was in France?"

"Yes, when you got back from that sabbatical—while you were gone I had to work for Mr. Klug, by the way—I specifically asked you how your sabbatical had gone and you said 'It was fine. Nothing much happened. I mainly sat in the Tuileries and painted bad landscapes.' So that was a lie, wasn't it?"

"I suppose it was. But it was a lie designed to protect my own sensitive feelings."

"You had feelings?"

I decided to ignore that. "Gwen, if I say I'm sorry I didn't tell you way back then, can we enter into a peace treaty?"

"If you say it and mean it."

"I'm truly sorry I didn't tell you, and I mean it with all my heart."

"All right, then."

After that the frost melted and Gwen became helpful to me in getting ready for Quinto's depo. Which was a blessing, because I hadn't taken a deposition in maybe ten years. I was about to find out if it was like riding a bicycle.

CHAPTER 50

Week 2—Wednesday

We had set the depo for 2:00 P.M. That way if we didn't finish by 4:30, which I didn't think we would, it wouldn't be much of a problem to reach agreement with Quinto's lawyer to resume the depo on another day. Or if no agreement could be reached, to persuade a court to order it to resume. On that later day, I would hope to be better prepared, with more material with which to question Quinto.

At the appointed hour, Jenna, Oscar and I were seated at the table in Cochise, waiting. Jenna was to my immediate left, Oscar farther to my left at the end of the table. The court reporter, who had arrived at about 1:45 with her steno machine, was at the other end. The two seats across from me had been left open for Quinto and his lawyer.

We didn't know, of course, if they were actually coming. They hadn't called to confirm that they were coming, but there was no requirement that they do so. If, on the other hand, they wanted to block the deposition as improperly noticed, they had needed, technically, to send me a written objection. They hadn't done that either. But under the circumstances of so outrageously little notice at the very start of a lawsuit, no court was likely to sanction them if they just plain failed to show up.

"By the way," Jenna said, "UCLA was named as a defendant in the lawsuit, too. Did we notify them of the depo?"

"I did that," Oscar said. "And I called their general counsel's office. They said that UCLA hasn't yet been served with the lawsuit, so they weren't going to attend. They'll just read the transcript of the depo. I said I'd send them one."

"Did you ask them if they're at least going to provide me with a defense to this stupid suit? I'm an employee, so they should."

"I asked them that, too, Jenna. They said they were studying the matter and would get back to us on it."

We all sat there for a while longer.

By 2:15 I had pretty much concluded that Quinto and his lawyer weren't coming.

"Oscar," I said, "when do you want to take us to Dubai for our dinner at the top of the Burj Khalifa?"

"They're coming," he said. "The way this town works, you're not really late for a depo until at least an hour has gone by. Especially if it's downtown. It's a bitch to get here."

Jenna began to rock in her chair, and I put my hand on the back to steady it.

"At least they don't squeak," she said.

I was about to respond when the conference-room phone rang. I picked it up and heard the receptionist announce that they had arrived. "Okay," I said. "Please have Gwen bring them down."

"Well, I think," Oscar said, "that, to mix a metaphor, the bet is now on the other foot, Robert, and you should take us to Dubai in early April. I hear the weather is pretty nice there that time of year. Still a bit rainy, but not yet hot."

"Uh-huh," I said. "We'll see if Quinto himself is actually here and not just a couple of lawyers."

A few minutes later, the conference-room door opened, and Gwen escorted Quinto and one lawyer into the room. I'd never set eyes on Quinto before, but he looked pretty much as Jenna had described him to me: young, slight and dark-haired, with a craggy face and deep-set brown eyes. He was wearing a not-very-well-made brown suit, a white shirt and a bright green tie, of a hue that you usually see only on St. Patrick's Day. His lawyer, by contrast, whose improbable name was Thaddeus Stevens, was tall, thin and blond and was dressed like he might be headed to the beach after the depo—casual, open-collared shirt, bone-white khaki slacks and brown leather sandals, all rather expensive-looking. He was also wearing an iridescent wrap bracelet on his right wrist, made with tiny green stones.

There were handshakes and introductions all around—even Quinto and Jenna shook hands—and the ritual offer of coffee, tea or soft drinks, which were set up on a credenza against the wall behind me. I also introduced Quinto and his lawyer to the court reporter, Hilda Vacarro by name. Treating court reporters like human beings instead of blocks of wood is not only polite but useful. Court reporters have to take down accurately what's said in a deposition, but if they like you, they can clean up all your ums, uhs and other grunts and pauses. If they don't like you, they can make you sound like the village idiot.

"Mr. Giordano," I said, "are you sure you wouldn't like some coffee before we begin?"

He looked at me, then pointed at Jenna. "Not while she's anywhere near the stuff."

There was dead silence in the room.

Jenna's response was to take a rather noisy swig from her own already filled coffee cup—a very large one that said JENNA on it in big letters—that she'd had ever since I first met her. "Whatever," she said.

Stevens, on the other hand, got up from the table, walked to the credenza, poured himself a cup—black—without any apparent concern and sat back down, clearly ready to begin.

I had looked Stevens up before the depo and discovered that he'd gone to a law school I'd never heard of in another state. But I had long ago learned to take seriously every lawyer who'd managed to pass the California bar—the hardest in the country—without regard to their credentials or their dress code. Caring about those things was a rookie mistake I'd made in my first year of practice, when I'd been drubbed by a lawyer from a no-name school who appeared to own only one suit and tie, and a particularly ugly tie at that.

It was almost three o'clock, and I did have at least two hours' worth of questions I wanted to get done. I didn't want them to announce at four o'clock that they had to leave to beat the worst of the traffic. It was time to get started.

CHAPTER 51

I turned to the court reporter. "Ms. Vacarro, would you swear in Mr. Giordano, please?"

She turned to Quinto. "Mr. Giordano, please raise your right hand."

He complied, and she asked, "Do you solemnly state that the testimony you will give in this deposition proceeding will be the truth, the whole truth and nothing but the truth?"

"I do," he said.

Before I truly began the deposition, there was something I needed to do. I had thought about doing it off the record but decided to make it a formal part of the deposition. "Mr. Giordano," I said, looking across the table at him, "before I begin today, I understand that you lost your brother early last week, and I want to extend my condolences."

"Thank you."

"I lost a sibling myself many years ago, and I know how difficult it can be."

"I appreciate your understanding."

"It wouldn't surprise me if things are probably still quite emotional for you, so if anything I ask you is upsetting such that you need to take a break, please let me know and we'll be sure to do that."

"Thank you. I don't think that will happen, but I'll let you know if it does."

I did, of course, actually feel for him. But my reason for offering condolences and the opportunity to take a break is that I didn't want him to have the excuse at trial to change his testimony by saying, "Oh, I was so emotional that I just couldn't give a straight answer, and that guy Tarza wouldn't let up on me."

With that out of the way, it was time to begin in earnest.

"Mr. Giordano," I said, "have you ever had your deposition taken before?"

"No."

"Okay, well, first, the court reporter, Ms. Vacarro, who is to your left, will be taking down my questions and your answers and will later give them to you in printed form to review."

"Okay."

"Although your counsel has no doubt gone over with you the procedures we'll be following today, I'd like to review them with you quickly myself, so that we're all on the same page about what we're doing here."

"Okay."

I then went over with him the list of what lawyers call the admonitions, admonishing him, among other things, to be sure to give his answers audibly, rather than just shaking his head yes or no, to be sure to listen carefully to each question and let me know if he didn't understand it—I'd be happy to rephrase—and reminding him that although his lawyer might make an objection, he needed to go ahead and answer the question unless his lawyer instructed him not to, that any objections would be ruled upon if and when the case went to trial. He rather docilely answered "Okay" to all of the admonitions. But then, most people do.

"And do you understand, Mr. Giordano, that when you give an answer today, it is under the same obligation to tell the truth as if you were in a courtroom with a judge present?"

"Yes."

Then I hit him with something I only rarely do, but this seemed like the right occasion. "And do you understand, Mr. Giordano, that the penalty for perjury—for not telling the truth today—is, pursuant to Sections 118 and 118.1 of the California Penal Code, up to four years in prison?"

Many lawyers in Stevens's position would have objected to that as harassment and complained that I was suggesting that Quinto was a liar. Stevens did something different.

"Isn't there a fine, too?" he asked.

I was flummoxed. I had never had an opposing lawyer do that before, and not only that, I didn't know if there was a fine. I wasn't sure what to say. A point for him.

"I don't know," I said. And then, trying to recover, "Mr. Giordano, do you understand the penalty for perjury?"

"Yes," he responded. "I understand the prison thing, and I guess the two of you will let me know if there's also a fine." The little schmuck actually grinned, and I wondered if he and Stevens had arranged it all in advance.

I now faced a choice. I could start with softball questions about things like age and education, or I could go right to the heart of what I really wanted to know. I usually start with the softballs, because one of my goals in a deposition is to lull the deponent into a fuguelike state in which he'll forget that his lawyer and everyone else are in the room and just want to talk to me—to answer my questions. Softball questions at the start are one way to try to achieve that.

"Mr. Giordano, how old are you?"

"I'll be twenty tomorrow."

I decided not to wish him a happy birthday. Under all the circumstances, it seemed not the right thing to do.

"And where were you born?"

"Pittsburgh, Pennsylvania."

"So you are a citizen of the United States?"

"Yes."

"Are you also a citizen of any other country?"

"Yes. I have dual citizenship with Italy."

"Any other citizenships?"   "No."

"Where did you go to high school?"

"I graduated from Marconi High School in Pittsburgh."

"Currently, do you have any degrees other than your high school diploma?"

"No. I'm a sophomore at UCLA, so I hope to have a BS in biochemistry in a couple of years."

"Mr. Giordano, I have premarked as Exhibit A to this deposition the Complaint—the lawsuit—in this matter, and I'm going to hand it to you. I've also brought courtesy copies for your counsel." I handed the marked exhibit to him and also gave copies to Stevens, and to Oscar and Jenna.

"Mr. Giordano, have you read the complaint in this matter?"

"Yes."

"To the best of your knowledge, is everything stated in the complaint true?"

"Yes, it is."

"All right, let me direct your attention to paragraph four, in which it is alleged, and I quote, 'Primo Giordano was my brother.' Do you see that?"

"Yes."

"How old was your brother Primo?"

"He was twenty-nine. Would have been thirty in March."

"Was he a full brother or a half brother?"

"A half brother. He and I have the same father but different mothers. His mother died and our father, who lives in Rome, remarried."

This was going well. He was volunteering things.

"Where was Primo born?"

"In Rome."

I thought to myself that it was interesting that Stevens had not objected to any of these questions, even though relevancy objections weren't appropriate in depositions, or otherwise tried to get in the way of the questioning.

"Do you have other siblings?"

"Objection, relevancy," Stevens said.

As is the case with most witnesses upon the first objection being made, Quinto didn't answer the question. He just kind of sat there confused, despite my earlier admonition to him that unless his lawyer instructed him not to answer a question, he should go ahead and answer it.

I didn't respond to the objection—you never should, unless the objection causes you to revise your question. For example, if probing the objection a bit more might help you improve your question and avoid any chance a judge will sustain the objection and block the answer from being admitted at trial.

"Please answer the question, Mr. Giordano."

"Well, I have three other siblings."

"Could you please name them and tell me their ages?"

"Objection, relevancy."

"Well," Quinto said, ignoring the objection, "there is my brother Secondo, who is twenty-seven, my sister Terza, who is twenty-five and my brother Quarto, who is twenty-three."

"So you're all named in birth order, First, Second, Third and so forth?"

"Yes. It's an old Italian tradition for sons. But my father was very modern and applied it to girls, too. So my sister is Terza—third. If she'd been a boy, she would have been Terzo."

"Thank you. Mr. Giordano, let me now direct your attention again to paragraph four, where it says, 'My brother Primo had possession of a map showing the exact location of sunken treasure.' Do you see that?"

"Yes, I do."

"Did Primo own the map?"

"Objection. Calls for a legal conclusion from someone who is not a lawyer. And you haven't established that he has any other qualification to answer the question."

"I'll rephrase," I said. "Mr. Giordano, do you have reason to believe that Primo owned the map?"

"I'll renew the objection," Stevens said, "but go ahead and answer, Quinto, if you're able to. Keep in mind that Mr. Tarza isn't asking you for a legal opinion, just what your understanding of the matter is . . . if you have one."

Quinto sat up straighter in his chair. "Primo never owned the map. I own it."

"So, to your understanding, Primo didn't have an ownership interest in the map prior to his death?"

"No."

"Do you have any reason to believe that any of your other siblings have any ownership interest in the map?"

"They don't."

"Do you have any reason to believe anyone else has an ownership interest in the map?"

"No."

"Do you have any reason to believe anyone other than you has an interest of any kind in the map, even if it's not as an owner?"

"No."

"Would it surprise you to learn that Primo told Professor James that the two of you were co-owners of the map?"

"No. He was always making that false claim."

"How did you come to own the map?"

"Objection. Calls for a legal conclusion."

"I inherited it from my grandfather."

"Your father's father?"

"No, my mother's father."

"What was his name?"

"Sven Johannsen."

"Do you know how your grandfather came into possession of the map?"

"He found it in the Spanish state archive in Seville."

Now we were getting somewhere.

"Doesn't that mean the Spanish government owns it?"

"Objection, calls for a legal conclusion."

"They might own the original, but our copy has had data added to it that show the exact location of the sunken treasure."

"Do you know when your grandfather found the original?"

"I think it was in the early 1980s, but I'm not sure."

It was worth a shot in the dark with a broad question that didn't have any foundation.

"Do you know how he knew where to look for it?"

"Objection," Stevens said, "no foundation. Assumes that his grandfather knew where to look for it."

"Yes," Quinto answered, "he did look, and my mother had told him where to look."

"If you know, how did your mother know where he should look?"

"She's a research librarian at the University of Pittsburgh, and her specialty is records in the Spanish state archive. She had a hunch, so she sent my grandfather to check it out."

"Did your grandfather speak Spanish?"

"Yes."

"Did he speak it well?"

"He said so."

"How about your mother?"

"Yes, and she speaks it well."

"Did your grandfather tell you what he found there?"

"Yes, he told me that he found records relating to the wreck of the Spanish galleon *Nuestra Señora de Ayuda*, which sank in 1641."

"Did he tell you if he studied those records?"

"He said he did."

"All right, then, let's move on to what he found there."

Jenna suddenly spoke up. "I hate to do this, but I really need a bathroom break. Too much coffee today, I'm afraid. Would that be okay?"

I looked over at Stevens, who nodded his assent.

"Okay," I said. "Let's take ten." I knew, of course, that Jenna was asking for a break because she had something to tell me.

CHAPTER 52

Jenna had the good sense to actually go off to the ladies' room as we took our break, so it looked like her request had been legitimate. Not that any experienced litigator would have believed it. When Jenna returned, Oscar and I were hanging out in the hallway—we'd left the conference room to Quinto and Stevens—and the three of us ducked into an empty office down the hall.

"Listen," Jenna said, "you can't just move on to what Quinto's grandfather supposedly found in the archive because what he's saying about his going to Seville and doing research there is absurd. Documents from the mid-seventeenth century in that archive are in old Castilian handwritten script. Modern Spanish speakers can usually understand the words and the syntax, but they often can't make out the handwriting. It's like trying to read the handwriting of the people who wrote our Constitution, only much, much worse. Here, let me show you."

She put her iPad down on the table, punched in some letters and numbers, then flipped it up where we could all see. The image of a crinkled document with a small chunk of paper missing on the left side appeared on the screen. "This," she said, "is a document from the archive in Seville relating to the very ship Quinto's talking about—the *Nuestra Señora de Ayuda.* Except it's from 1599, so I don't really know if it's the same ship or a different ship with the same name."

"Like you said," Oscar remarked, "it's really hard to read. I speak pretty good Spanish, and I can't make out a single word of it."

"Right," Jenna responded. "A document like that, even if you were there in person, would be hard to make out."

"What," I asked, "does the document relate to?"

"Oh, it relates to the departure of a galleon of that name from the Guadalquivir River—the river that runs through Seville— to somewhere in the Spanish colonies in New Spain. That was their name, at that point, for the New World. It could be the same *Nuestra Señora de Ayuda* as was supposedly lost in 1641, although that would make it an awfully old ship. But I don't know what the average service life of a Spanish galleon was."

"So what's your point for this depo?" Oscar asked.

"My point is that neither his grandfather nor his mother could have done this research alone. They would have needed an experienced archival researcher to help them."

"How do you know," I asked, "that such people even exist?"

"Because, Robert, I was there myself two summers ago. I got a grant to do some research in the archive in Seville about sunken ships that might have contained treasure and that haven't been salvaged. For some ships they even have records of the salvage. It was background research for my law review article."

"Well," Oscar said, "it's amazing there are such accurate records from so long ago."

"The Spaniards," Jenna said, "were the Germans of the sixteenth and seventeenth centuries. They wrote down everything."

We went back into the conference room. Everyone refilled their coffee cups and I restarted the deposition.

"Mr. Giordano," I resumed, "I'll just remind you that you're still under oath."

"I understand."

"Do you know if your grandfather had help in researching the records in Seville?"

"He told me he did."

"Did he tell you what kind of help?"

"Yes, he told me he hired an archival researcher named Pedro Cabano."

"Did you grandfather tell you what Mr. Cabano had done on his behalf?"

"Yes, he said he helped him look for the account of a survivor of the shipwreck of the *Nuestra Señora de Ayuda*."

"Did he help your grandfather with anything else?"

"I don't know."

"Did they find the survivor's account?"

"Yes."

"Did they find more than one survivor's account?"

"No."

"Do you have a copy of the one they did find?"

"Yes."

"Have you read it?"

"Yes."

"Do you have it with you?"

"No."

"Please summarize for me what it says."

Stevens spoke up. "Objection. Calls for confidential business information."

"Mr. Giordano," I said, "please go ahead and answer the question."

"I'm going to instruct him," Stevens said, "not to answer the question."

"You know, Mr. Stevens, that that's not a proper instruction. For one thing, 'confidential business information' isn't a recognized privilege. And even if it were, the proper procedure is to suspend this deposition and go into court to seek a protective order."

"Well," Stevens said, "we can go argue about that in court later if you like, but Mr. Giordano is not answering that question today."

I knew that I then had to ask Giordano a required follow-up question to make the dispute one a judge would consider ruling on.

"Mr. Giordano, are you going to follow your counsel's instruction and refuse to answer my question?"

"Yes, I am."

I made a note to come back to try later in the depo to find out more about the survivor's account without trespassing on information they considered confidential.

"All right, let me move on, then. Have you ever met Mr. Cabano yourself?"

"No."

"Do you have any contact information for Mr. Cabano?"

"No."

"Do you know of any way to reach him?"

"No."

"Do you know where he lives?"

"No."

"If I went to Spain, do you know how I might find him?"

"No."

I had the sense from Quinto's body language and the slight smirk on his face that he indeed knew something about how to get in touch with Cabano but wasn't about to volunteer it unless I asked him a question that, somehow, was exactly on the button.

Which meant going into thorough mode. At times taking a deposition is like scrubbing the bottom of a pot you can't see. For the pot, you have to use a pattern of swipes across the unseen bottom to try to get it all—back and forth one way and then the other, clockwise and counterclockwise, then diagonal and the other diagonal and so forth. In a depo you have to use a careful pattern of questions to scrub the bottom of the factual pot. Here I clearly hadn't yet hit quite the right pattern of questions.

"Does your mother know Mr. Cabano?"

"I don't know."

"Does your mother have his contact information?"

"I don't know."

"Do you know if your mother put your grandfather in touch with Mr. Cabano?"

"I don't know."

I turned and looked at Jenna, who had been tapping on her keyboard, no doubt trying to find some reference to Cabano on the Internet. She shook her head in the negative. I could, at that point, have given up the pursuit and assumed we'd find him by other means, but since I might not get the chance to ask Quinto again under oath, I decided to spend a little more time trying to unearth what he was hiding.

"Mr. Giordano, have you been in contact with Mr. Cabano by any means, including e-mail or phone?"

"Objection, compound." Stevens had decided to be difficult, but I decided not to argue about it.

"I'll rephrase. By e-mail?"

"No."

"By phone?"

"No."

"By postal mail?"

"No."

"By any other means?"

"No."

I was more or less out of ways to ask about where I could find Mr. Cabano when Oscar slipped a note in front of me. I read it and then asked, "Do you know anyone else who, to your understanding, has been in contact with Mr. Cabano?"

"Yes."

"And who would that be?"

Quinto smiled a very broad smile. "I believe that Professor Aldous Hartleb has been in touch with him."

Jenna, who had been slouching in her chair, leaned over to me and said, "Ask for a break."

"Mr. Stevens," I said, "I need to confer with my client for a few minutes before we proceed. So let's take another break."

Stevens looked at Jenna. "Small bladder?"

"You know, Mr. Stevens," Jenna said, "I should really report you to the State Bar for that sexist comment."

"Go ahead. I don't think there was the least thing sexist about it. Some *people* can't drink the amount of coffee you drink without needing frequent breaks. If you think that fact has to do with gender, that's your problem."

I didn't think we needed a spat in this depo, which had, so far, been fairly peaceable. "You know," I said, "I have a proposal. How about we ask the court reporter to simply delete from the transcript everything after my request for a break? Is that agreeable, Mr. Stevens?"

"So stipulated."

"Good. Madam Court Reporter, please leave the other repartee out of the transcript."

"I will," she said.

Whereupon Jenna, Oscar and I headed back to the empty office. This time we went there directly.

CHAPTER 53

After the three of us entered the empty office, I closed the door and said to Jenna, "So if I remember correctly, Aldous Hartleb is your boyfriend, right? The one on your suspect list."

"Right."

"Do you have any idea how he happened to be in touch with Cabano, the research guy?"

"I can make a good guess. Aldous told me that he did some work for an investment firm that was considering investing in a venture that was being put together to finance a search for the *Ayuda*. He did some of the due diligence on the deal. So I assume he talked to Cabano as part of that."

"Did Aldous's company," Oscar asked, "invest?"

"No, they passed on it."

"Well, then," Oscar said, "let's call Aldous up."

"Right now?" Jenna asked.

"Why not? I assume you have his cell number."

"He's in Buffalo."

"I bet his cell works even in a place like Buffalo. Let's do it." Oscar pointed to the speakerphone that sat on the desk, the surface otherwise bare.

Jenna picked up the handset and punched in a number on the keypad. Even though she was holding the handset to her ear and hadn't activated the speaker, I could hear the call ringing on the other end. Just as I thought it would go to voice mail, I heard a voice answer, although I couldn't make out what was said. Then Jenna spoke.

"Hi, Aldous, it's Jenna."

She listened for a moment, then said, "No, nothing's wrong. I'm calling about something specific. We're taking the depo of Quinto Giordano today, and something's come up that you might be able to help us with. I'm here with my lawyers, Oscar Quesana and Robert Tarza. Can I put you on speakerphone?"

Jenna put the handset back into its cradle and pushed the speakerphone button. "Can you hear us, Aldous?"

"Loud and clear."

"Good. Hey, I don't think you've met Oscar or Robert, so let me introduce them."

Which she did, and, in the usual awkward dance of introductions on the telephone, we all "met."

"Aldous," Jenna said, "when you were doing the due diligence on the *Ayuda* deal, did you talk to a researcher in Seville?"

"If I tell you the answer to that, can I be sure no one will let on that I'm the one who told you?"

Jenna looked around at me and Oscar.

"Aldous, this is Robert Tarza," I said. "I promise you your name won't be mentioned."

"Okay, then," Aldous said. "I sure did talk to someone. His name was Cabano. Hard guy to forget. Very slick."

"What did you talk with him about?"

"I was following up on a document that referred to a search in the Spanish archive made by Mr. X and Mr. Y, or maybe only one of them. It wasn't clear. I now assume those were code names used for Quinto and Primo. In any case, whichever one of them did the search had supposedly used Cabano to help look for a key document in the archive. Cabano himself actually found the document, or at least that's what I understood."

"Do you recall," Oscar asked, "what document it was?"

"Uh, yeah, I do. But the company I was working for signed a confidentiality agreement, and I'm bound by it. So I really can't tell you. But"—he chuckled—"if you were to take my deposition, I'd have to tell you, wouldn't I?"

"Right," Oscar said, "but if we noticed your deposition, I'm sure they'd go to court and try to get some sort of order to prevent you from answering that question. Anyway, Quinto has already told us it was a survivor account, and Primo told Jenna the same thing before he died. So that piece of confidential info is already out of the bag. Can you add anything to it?"

"I don't think I should."

I broke in. "Aldous, this is Robert again. I'm the one who's taking the depo today, and at this point what I most want to know is how we can get in touch with Cabano."

There was a long pause on the other end of the phone. Finally, Aldous said, "I suppose I can tell you that without violating the confidentiality agreement. But all I have is his cell number, or at least what it was last summer. I don't have an address or an e-mail."

"That would be a great start," I said.

"Okay, let me dig it out of my database." After a few seconds, Aldous came back on and gave us the number.

"Thanks, Aldous," I said. "Is there anything else you can share with us that might be helpful?"

"I'm afraid not. It was a pretty tight confidentiality agreement and, you know, I'd like not to be dragged into this thing."

"Understood," I said. "Thanks for your help."

"You're welcome. Sorry I can't be more forthcoming."

"Oh, I understand. By the way, what are you doing in Buffalo?"

"Looking for a job. Jenna can bring you up to date on that."

"Okay, well, have a good day."

"You, too. Hey, Jenna, can you pick up for a moment, honey?"

"Sure." Jenna picked up the handset, which caused the speakerphone to go off.

They talked for a few moments while Oscar and I chatted about other things.

Finally, I heard Jenna say, "Talk to you soon. 'Bye."

After she hung up, I looked over at her. "He's looking for a new job in Buffalo?"

"Yep."

Oscar had been drumming his fingers on the desktop. "Jenna, if I understand correctly, and please forgive me for being so direct, you sleep with Aldous, right?"

"Sometimes. Yes."

"Well, maybe you can get more out of him via a little pillow talk."

"I can try, but Aldous isn't a talker in those circumstances. He prefers . . ."

"Never mind," I interrupted. "I'm sure we can all imagine what he prefers." I was famous for being something of a prude, and living in France hadn't really changed me on that score. "Let's leave it, Jenna, that you'll give it a try if the situation presents itself. In the meantime, now we have Cabano's phone number, so we ought to be able to talk to him ourselves if we play it right."

CHAPTER 54

On my way back to the depo, I headed to the men's room. Stevens was standing at one of the two urinals. I went to the second one, which was right next to the first. For a while the two of us just stood there in silence, doing our respective thing. As I stared at the wall, I thought to myself that it wasn't unheard of for male lawyers to conduct serious business in that setting. I had no idea what the deal was in women's bathrooms. Did they talk stall to stall? In any case, apparently nothing was going to happen this time, and I wasn't about to initiate any conversation.

Then Stevens said, as he was zipping up, "Do you guys want to settle this thing?"

"Sure," I said. "But it's a little difficult to know how."

Stevens was by that time at the sink, and I could hear the water running. I was still facing the wall.

"Well, Mr. Tarza," he said, "the easiest way to settle it would be for your client to give the map back to Mr. Giordano. Once he gets it, he'll drop the suit and give your client a complete release. It will be totally over. Among other things, that means there won't be any wrongful death suit in your client's future.

And who knows, maybe the police will lose interest in the whole thing."

"Jenna didn't kill anyone, Mr. Stevens."

"I believe the police think differently."

I zipped up and moved to the sink. Stevens was already pulling paper towels out of the dispenser and starting to dry his hands.

"You know," I said, as I washed my own hands, "your solution would be a perfect solution but for one thing."

"What's that?"

"Jenna doesn't have the map."

"I think she does."

"I don't understand why you guys think that."

"Ask my client that question and he'll tell you."

"I'll do that, plus at least one more question that's been bothering me."

"Feel free," he said as he grabbed the door handle using the wadded-up paper towels, opened it, then tossed the towels in the wastebasket as he went through the door. Clearly a guy concerned about germs.

When we were all back in the conference room and settled in, I skipped the cordialities and started right in.

"Mr. Giordano, you're aware you're still under oath, right?"

"Yes."

"What leads you to think that my client, Professor James, has a map that you claim belongs to you?"

That was not, of course, a very good question. Among other flaws, it called for a narrative answer, which, although not technically objectionable, most lawyers will object to in order to send a message to their client: don't blather on. Make him ask you more narrowly focused questions.

Quinto looked over at Stevens, as if expecting some sort of objection. Instead, Stevens said, "Go ahead and tell him the whole story, Quinto."

Quinto folded his arms in front of him and said, "Here's the deal. The morning my brother died, I drove him to the law school in my car. Before we left to go there, I helped him roll up the map and put it into a red cardboard mailing tube. Then I watched him walk into the law school with it. He told me he was going to show it to Professor James. That was the last time I saw it."

Quinto stopped talking, folded his arms in front of him and just stared at me.

"Well, sir, why does that persuade you that my client has your map?"

"Because my brother had an appointment with Professor James at seven thirty. Like I said, I dropped him off right in front of the law school not long before that. I assume he went straight to her office. I understand he met with Professor James, became ill and was taken to the hospital. So during all of that, Professor James was the person with the best opportunity to take the map."

"Any other reason, Mr. Giordano?"

"Yes, come to think of it. When Primo didn't return to the car—that was before the hospital called me—I went to Professor James's office. When I got there, her door was locked, and there was no one there. The police told me that when they searched the office later, no map was found. So figure it out yourself."

"Are you aware that my client went with your brother in the ambulance?"

"Yes, I've been told that."

"Well, if she went right out the door with your brother, when do you think she had the opportunity to take the map?"

"She probably had a friend standing by, ready to take it."

Jenna pushed a note in front of me. It said, "Ask him if I knew Primo was bringing the map."

"Do you have any reason to believe," I asked, "that Professor James knew in advance that your brother was planning to show her a map?"

"He told me, right before I dropped him off, that he'd mentioned it to her, and that she was looking forward to seeing it."

Jenna pushed another note in front of me, but I knew what it was going to say and asked her question before even looking at it. "Do you recall his exact words?"

He hesitated slightly, and then said, "Something like 'I told her I was going to show her a treasure map.'"

When you take a lot of depositions, you learn to read pauses and hesitations, and I read Quinto's initial hesitation as saying "I'm not sure."

"Are you sure, Mr. Giordano?"

"Pretty sure."

I looked down at Jenna's note. It said, "He told me that he had something interesting to talk to me about."

"Is it possible, sir, that your brother told you that he mentioned to Professor James only that he had something interesting to talk to her about?"

"Objection," Stevens said. "Anything is possible, so the question is vague and ambiguous."

He was trying to get in the way of the answer. I rephrased. "Mr. Giordano, didn't your brother actually say to you that he had told Professor James he had something interesting to talk to her about?"

"I don't recall it exactly that way."

"What way do you recall it?"

Stevens interrupted again, trying to protect his witness. "He already told you how he recalled it."

"Mr. Giordano said he was 'pretty sure.' That gives me the right to probe his answer. Madam Court Reporter, please read the question back to him."

The truth is that I could just as easily have repeated the question. It wasn't complicated or long, but sometimes having the question read back by the court reporter gives it added gravitas and makes the witness more inclined to answer it.

Looking down at the screen on her stenotype, she read the question out loud:

"'Mr. Giordano, didn't your brother actually say to you that he had told Professor James he had something interesting to talk to her about?'"

"He might," Quinto answered, "have said that, although I think he said that he had told her he wanted to discuss a treasure map. I'm not sure."

I thought about pursuing that further, but it was good enough for now. At the very least, I had started to mess up their timeline about how Jenna had supposedly arranged for the map to disappear. One of the things you learn as a lawyer is to leave a good enough answer alone.

Stevens looked conspicuously at his watch. "It's getting kind of late. We'd like to get out of here before the traffic gets really bad."

I knew, of course, that what he really wanted was to get his witness out of there before I pursued the current line of questioning further. "I have only two quick areas to go into," I said, "on a different topic."

"Okay," Stevens said. "If it's really quick, go for it."

"Mr. Giordano," I asked, "do you have a copy of the map yourself?"

"Yes."

"With regard to the map you believe your brother took to Professor James's office, was it a copy or an original?"

"It was a copy."

"So if it's a copy that's missing and you have a copy yourself, why do you want the copy your brother allegedly took to Professor James's office back?"

"Because that copy has some information on it that my copy does not, and I don't know of any other copy with that information on it."

"What's the information that's on it?"

"That," Stevens said, "is business confidential and is objected to on that ground. I instruct the witness not to answer the question."

"To save you the trouble of asking," Quinto said, "I'm going to follow my counsel's instruction and decline to answer."

"Okay," I said. "Maybe we can work out a stipulation as to confidentiality. But to save us all a lot of work in the meantime, Mr. Stevens, how about if you permit the witness to answer the question now, and we'll all instruct the court reporter to mark the pages as confidential until such time as we can get the court to hear our motion, in case that's necessary?"

"What guarantee do we have that you won't disclose it in the meantime?" Stevens asked.

"Well, I'm an attorney, Mr. Quesana is an attorney and Ms. James, even though she's a professor, is still a member of the bar. So we'll give you our pledge as officers of the court not to disclose the information prior to entering into a stipulation or obtaining a court order."

"Are you all agreeable to that?" Stevens asked.

"Yes," Jenna said.

"Yes," Oscar said.

Stevens leaned over and whispered to Quinto. I saw Quinto nod his head in the affirmative.

"Okay, then," Stevens said. "Mr Giordano, go ahead and answer the question, if you recall it."

"I recall it," Quinto said. "And the answer is that the information on the copy is the exact longitude of the wreck, out there in the Pacific."

"Is that on your copy as well?" I asked.

"No. You see, I hate to say it, but Primo and I didn't quite trust each other. So when we hired a company to drag sonar arrays across the area where the ship likely went down, we asked the captain of the search ship, after he found the wreck, to put the exact latitude of the wreck only on my copy of the map, and the exact longitude on Primo's copy."

"So neither one of you had both pieces of information?"

"Correct. We planned, after we raised enough money to bring up the treasure from the ocean bottom, to combine our data so we would know where to go to do it."

I sat and thought about it for a few seconds. In many years of taking depositions, I had developed a nose for stories that smelled bad, and this one certainly had an aroma. But I couldn't figure out exactly where the smell was coming from, so I just plowed ahead with a few more questions.

"Mr. Giordano," I asked, "didn't your brother have other copies of his version of the map, the one with the longitude on it?"

"I assume he did, but I've been unable to find them."

"Do you have extra copies of your version?"

"Certainly."

"So if you have the exact latitude and longitude of where a wreck is, you don't really need a physical map, do you?"

He smiled. "Nope."

"Why did you and your brother bother to use a map at all?"

"It's so much better," he answered, "to give investors a map with an X on it to mark the spot. It's more romantic."

"Romantic?"

"Sure. Lots of people invest in this sort of venture out of a sense of romance. It's much more exciting to tell your friends at a cocktail party that you've invested in looking for sunken treasure than to tell them you invested in a totally quiet garbage disposal."

"But you couldn't put the actual X on any investor copy, right, because it would give away the location?"

"Right. We put an X on a map, all right—we used that old map my grandfather found in the archive—but we told the investors that the X we placed wasn't at all close to where the ship actually lies. The Pacific is large, and even if you put the X a hundred miles from where the ship really is, no one will ever find it. Or at least not with the amount of money anyone other than some government is willing to spend."

"If someone invested, did they get more precise location information later?"

"We told them, 'Hey, if you invest and we get enough other investors, we'll give you a map with the real X on it.'"

"Has anyone invested?"

"Not yet."

It was all very interesting—if true—but we were clearly running out of time, so I decided to close with something else.

"I have one final question today. Mr. Giordano, do you know how to pick a lock?"

Stevens, rather than objecting, just sat there, kind of stunned at the question, clearly trying to think up an appropriate objection. But before he could, Quinto answered, "No, I don't."

"All right, then. I'm going to ask the court reporter to e-mail me a rough-draft transcript of today's testimony. And I'd like to find a date to resume sometime next week. We're allowed a total of seven hours for a deposition, and we haven't come close to that today."

Stevens looked at his smartphone, clearly paging through his calendar. "No can do, I'm afraid. It'll have to be sometime after Thanksgiving."

I had expected that, of course. "That's fine, but let's actually pick a date before we leave." And we did. December 20. Which meant, having picked a date five days before Christmas, that it wouldn't actually happen until at least January.

After Stevens and Quinto cleared the room, I looked around and asked, of no one in particular, "So what's next?"

Oscar answered. "I think that you, Robert, should try to get in touch with this Cabano guy and see what you can learn. And Jenna, you and I need to get together and talk."

"Talk about what?" Jenna asked.

"Right before the depo started I got a call from the district attorney."

"*The* district attorney or an assistant district attorney?"

"The man himself."

"I'm embarrassed to say," Jenna said, "that I'm not even sure who that is now. I didn't vote in the last election, and I didn't pay much attention to who was running."

I spoke up. "The new district attorney is Charlie Benitez."

There was a dead silence in the room while Jenna took that in.

"You mean the assistant DA who prosecuted you, Robert?" Jenna asked. "The one I beat in the preliminary hearing?"

"The very same one," I said. Looking at her, I could tell she was taken aback by the news.

"He probably holds a grudge," she said.

"I don't know," Oscar said, "whether he holds a grudge or not. He seemed friendly enough in the call and just wanted some information. My suggestion, Jenna, is that you and I meet in your office tomorrow morning to go over what he wants."

"Okay," Jenna said. "I'm planning to make a really big push on finishing up my law review article tomorrow morning, so how about we start early, like 7:00 A.M.?"

"That's not really early in my book," Oscar said, "but if you insist on starting late, it's okay by me."

CHAPTER 55

Jenna James

Week 2—Thursday

Seven in the morning might not have been early in Oscar's book, but it was nevertheless still dark as I rode my bike from my condo to the law school. As I pedaled up the last hill, I thought about the fact that Oscar hadn't told me in advance exactly what the DA wanted. On the other hand, I hadn't pressed him to tell me. Maybe he thought not knowing would allow me a better night's sleep. Maybe I thought so myself. I had hardly slept a wink.

When I wheeled my bike into the hallway that led to my office, Oscar was already there, waiting.

"Hi, Jenna."

"Hi. I'm glad to see you found the door to my office locked."

"I even tried it. It's locked tight."

I got out my keys, unlocked it and we went in. I leaned my bike up against the wall and tossed my helmet onto one of the guest chairs.

"Grab the other chair, Oscar. Do you want some coffee? I bought a new pot, but I've stopped setting it to make coffee automatically before I get here, so it'll take a few minutes."

"Sure. Whenever you've got it ready."

I opened up my purse and took out a fresh bag of Peet's dark roast coffee, preground. I took out a measuring spoon and spooned the proper amount of coffee into the cone-shaped permanent filter. Oscar just sat and watched me do it.

"You're no longer using special beans?"

"Nope. I just buy coffee already ground at the grocery store and carry it back and forth with me in my purse. Someone tried to kill me, and I figure they might try again."

"Makes sense, I guess."

"Perfect sense."

Instead of taking the seat I had offered him, Oscar was standing, looking at the books in the floor-to-ceiling bookshelf that occupied one wall of my office. "You have a lot of books about ships," he said.

"Not just ships. Also books about admiralty law and sunken treasure. Since I got interested in all of that four years ago, I've turned into something of a collector. Feel free to browse while I go and get some water for the coffee. I'll be right back."

I walked down the hall to the kitchen and filled the carafe. When I got back, Oscar was thumbing through a large-format book with a colorful cover, which he had pulled from the bookshelf.

"I never realized," he said, "how many ships there are on the bottom of the sea."

"Well, you're looking at Pickford's *Atlas of Shipwrecks and Treasure*. It's pretty authoritative, and if you look in the back, it's got great maps, divided by world region, showing known or suspected shipwreck sites."

He flipped to the back of the book. "Is the *Ayuda* in here somewhere?"

"No."

"Does that mean it's not real?"

I shrugged. "Who knows? It probably means that at the very least Pickford didn't consider it certain enough to list in his atlas. You can find mention of the *Ayuda* on online treasure sites, though, of which there are a ton."

"What's your best guess about it?"

"Best guess? A Manila galleon by that name probably did sink on the west side of Catalina Island in 1641, but its cargo was likely salvaged not long after the ship sank. What was left of the ship has been pounded by the Pacific Ocean for, at this point, more than four hundred fifty years."

"A long time."

"Right, and it was made of wood. So it's either been dashed apart, rotted or buried so deep in the sand that no one is ever going to find whatever's left of it."

"I thought wood didn't rot under water."

"Some does, some doesn't. Depends on the type of wood, the amount of oxygen in the water, its acidity and a lot of other factors."

"So given all of that, why did Primo think he and his brother had found it?"

"All Primo would tell me is that they dug up some information in the Spanish archive—the survivor account that was mentioned in the depo yesterday—that suggested the ship sank much farther offshore than all the legends say it did."

"Do they know exactly where the ship is?"

"He claimed they'd actually located it with precision."

"Which Quinto said in the deposition, too. But you sound dubious."

"I am."

"Why?"

"Because in 1641 mariners could measure latitude pretty accurately while aboard a ship at sea, but not longitude. That wasn't figured out for another hundred years. So even if Quinto and Primo somehow managed to figure out the latitude at which the *Ayuda* sank—assuming it wasn't near Catalina—all that got them was the ability to draw a thin line on a map. One that stretched west from Catalina toward China, all the way to Manila."

"How far is that?"

"Something like seven thousand miles, maybe even eight."

"And yet they seem to think they, using a sonar search, found out where the ship really is."

"Yes, but taking off on the point Quinto made in the depo about how vast the ocean is, if you can only guess that a wreck is somewhere along a couple of hundred miles of latitude—and you don't even know the latitude with precision—you're not going to find it. Not unless you spend tens of millions of dollars or have the kind of luck you need to win a Powerball jackpot."

I decided to interrupt the conversation for something even more important than latitude and longitude. "Do you," I asked, "want some coffee, Oscar? Enough has dripped in that I can pour you a cup."

"I'd love some."

I poured him a cup, then poured one for myself. He sat down in the chair that didn't have my helmet on it. I went to sit behind my desk.

"Oscar, this is all very interesting, and I've come to love the lore of sunken ships, but let's cut to the chase. What did the DA want?"

"He wanted to tell me some things, and he wanted to ask me some things."

"What things?"

"He wanted to tell me that the autopsy shows that Primo died from respiratory failure secondary to being poisoned, and that the preliminary toxicology results say the poison was sodium azide."

"Which we already knew, more or less."

"Right."

"What else did he want to tell you?" I took a large gulp from my coffee. I assumed the news wouldn't be good.

"That the dregs of coffee from Primo's cup contained sodium azide in a high enough concentration that drinking a modest amount of it could kill you."

"Okay. We suspected that, too. What else?"

"He told me that the search of your apartment turned up a receipt for the purchase of a five percent aqueous solution of sodium azide, purchased at a local chemical company for cash. A printed-out receipt with your name on it was in a pocket of one of your blazers."

I leaped out of my chair. I couldn't believe it, but it was vividly obvious who was behind it. "Tommy!"

"What?"

"That little shit must have bought the stuff. He could easily have put the receipt in my blazer pocket. Or in one of them. I have four of those blazers, all identical. So I was right to put him on my suspect list. In fact, he's now number one."

"Well, for whatever reason, the DA still thinks it could have been you."

I banged my cup down on my desk so hard that some of the coffee slopped out. "This is absurd. What is my motive supposed to be for poisoning Primo?"

"The map, I guess."

"Oh, dear God. I don't have the map. I never saw the map. I don't know where the map is."

"It's somewhere, last seen in your office."

"Well, maybe so, but as we learned at the depo, there really isn't any 'map.' It's just an old piece of paper they found in the archive that they put some numbers on, along with a meaningless X."

"Well, the DA is willing to listen to an explanation. His request is that we permit the police to interview you about this whole situation."

"I already talked to the police. Detective Drady interviewed me the day Primo died."

"They want a more extensive interview now."

"I don't want to talk to them. They'll just take whatever I say and twist it to fit their ridiculous theory. I'm better off saying nothing."

"I think we might be able to blow this whole thing out of the water by agreeing to do it. You and I will go over everything carefully beforehand and get rid of the case. Point out all the absurdities to them."

"That's your advice?"

"It is."

"Let me sleep on it."

"All right. But sleep on this, too: If it was Tommy who bought the poison and you're going to blame it all on him, what was his motive for trying to kill you? Or Primo, for that matter? Or for trying to frame you? You still haven't come up with good answers to those questions."

CHAPTER 56

A fter Oscar left I tried to work on the additional footnotes Stanford had requested for my law review article. My conversation with the editor had been only ten days earlier, but it seemed like a year had gone by. I had trouble getting back into it. Not only that, I was going to have to go back to the library to finish up. Some of the materials I needed weren't available in my own collection or online.

I had told Oscar that I wanted to sleep on the decision about whether to submit to another police interview. As lunchtime approached it was becoming more and more clear to me that if I wanted to avoid another sleepless night, not to mention a workless day, I needed to make that decision sooner rather than later.

I decided to consult a pastrami sandwich. Although I usually avoided all that fat and all those carbs, pastrami sandwiches had always seemed able to speak clearly to me in times of trouble. I had even consulted one about whether to leave M&M for a teaching job. I walked to Northern Lights, a small eatery on the north side of the campus, and ordered a double pastrami with extra mayo, a large bag of chips and a supersized Coke.

The sandwich said Oscar was a great lawyer, and you should always follow your lawyer's advice.

I called Oscar while the pastrami rush was still with me. "Let's do it," I said.

"All right, when?"

"The sooner the better."

"The DA told me they they want to do it late today."

"No. Not today. And tomorrow I have my sunken treasure seminar at nine. So early tomorrow morning or in the afternoon will have to work. Where do they want to do this?"

"Since it's going to be Detective Drady doing the interview— you were right about that—I assume at the UCLA police station on campus."

"I'm not going there. If they want to interview me, they can come to my office. If not, they can stuff it."

"I'll try to put it in more acceptable language, as a request."

"Put it in whatever language you want. I'm not going to the police station like I'm some perp. It's me someone's trying to kill. I don't understand why they can't get that through their thick heads."

"I think the sodium azide receipt in your pocket didn't help."

"*You* don't think I did it, do you?"

"No."

"All right, then, let me know what time. My office or nowhere."

After I hung up, I really wanted to order a second sandwich, but I resisted and instead walked back to my office. Once there I scooped up my notebook computer and headed for the library. To get there I used a door on the third floor that leads from the faculty office hallway directly onto the third floor of the library.

The door is alarmed to prevent students from taking books and leaving without checking them out. Faculty are given keys that fit into a wall lock a foot or so to the left of the door. The trick is to open the door and then turn the key before the alarm goes off. It's hard to turn the key in time. A couple of times I haven't made it. I've always suspected the alarm was set up with such a short fuse because library staff would really rather have you walk through the main entrance. This time I made it through without setting off the alarm.

The admiralty law collection is housed in a funky area of the library called the Mezzanine. It's a sort of half floor sandwiched between the main floor and the second, dating from the founding of the law school back in the '50s, and it looks it. Instead of carpeting it has concrete floors, and instead of rich wood shelving it has rows of orangish metal shelving that run from floor to ceiling, densely packed with books. The aisles between the rows are narrow.

The Mezzanine is reached by an internal concrete stairway off the main reading room. Along the back wall are small study carrels with beige Formica desktops and beige wooden Boston chairs with curved arms and upright slats on the back. They always reminded me of the chair I had to sit in when I was called into the principal's office in high school, which was frequently.

I liked working in the carrels because no one bothered me there. I'd arrive, turn off my cell phone and just work. When I began my Stanford law review article, I commandeered one particular carrel and simply left the books I was using in it, topped with a big DO NOT RESHELVE sign in red. In the more than a year that I'd been working on the article, no one had touched my stuff. It was a cozy place, away from it all.

When I got to my carrel, it looked like it had been rearranged slightly. I hadn't been there in almost two weeks, so I brushed it

off as a false memory. I sat down and got to work. After working steadily for about an hour, I heard the alarm bell on the
third floor door go off. The bell was so loud that it sounded
throughout the library, even on the Mezzanine. Some poor faculty member had no doubt failed to turn the key quickly enough
and had been nailed by the door's alarm bell.

I worked for maybe another ten minutes, then reached for
Volume 6 of the *Benedict on Admiralty* treatise, which I had
kept in the exact same place in my carrel for almost a year—top
shelf, right-hand side. It wasn't there. Nor could I find it anywhere else in the carrel, which, admittedly, was something of
a mess, with forty or fifty books scattered about, some shelved,
some just stacked six or seven high on the desktop. Probably
someone else had needed Volume 6—it was about international
admiralty treaties—and had reshelved it in the stacks instead of
putting it back in my carrel. No biggie.

I got up and walked down the row of stacks that began right
next to my carrel. As I entered the row, I heard what sounded
like a woman's high heels coming up the concrete steps. I didn't
think anything of it. Quite a few of the women law students had
returned to wearing them, although only God knew why.

The thirty-three volume *Benedict on Admiralty* treatise was
always shelved in the middle of the row on the very top shelf,
high enough up that at five foot six, I could barely reach it. I
peered up at it. Volume 6 was missing. I would have to ask the
librarians to search for it. In the meantime I could make do with
one of the treaties in Volume 5. I didn't much feel like stretch-
ing up, so I glanced around to see if I could locate one of those
rolling library stools to stand on. That's when I heard a slight
groaning noise, like metal bending, and realized that the entire
book stack was toppling toward me. I instinctively raised my
arms to protect my head.

I'm not sure how many books hit me. All I know is that I was suddenly being pummeled by dozens of heavy volumes. The thunder of all of them coming down and hitting the floor—and me—more or less simultaneously was deafening. It was all over in a few seconds, and I found myself trapped in a kind of dark, dusty book cave. My arms were over my head, but I couldn't lower them because there were books jammed beneath my armpits. The metal shelving had bent forward—it had been kept from falling over entirely and killing me only because it hit the shelves on the other side—but it had so weighed down the books on top of me that I couldn't raise my arms. Every time I moved my torso even a little, the books above and around me shifted. Plus I was pinned back against the still-upright shelf behind me.

I screamed.

For what seemed like forever, but was probably only a minute or two, no one came. Then I heard a voice shouting "Is anyone in there?"

"It's Professor James. I'm in here." I realized I was yelling, but my voice came out muffled because dust was choking my mouth and throat.

"Are you hurt?"

I tried to yell louder. "I don't know. Please get me out of here."

"We're trying."

I heard still more voices, and then the books began to move and shift again as people pulled them from both ends of the aisle and, finally, from over my head. I could glimpse two or three people at each aisle end, trying to push the shelf back off of me.

"Keep calm," someone said. "We'll have you out in a moment. We called the EMTs."

I'm not sure how long I was buried. Someone later told me it took almost five minutes to dig me out. When I emerged, somewhat dirty and feeling a bit bruised, particularly on my arms, I had to duck to get out from under the still-leaning shelf. I stood up when I got out, only to be greeted by my EMT friends from the UCLA ambulance—Carter Sullivan and Susan Suarez. They were standing there with their blue cart.

"Oh, it's you," Carter said. "We couldn't see who was in there. How do you feel?"

"Upset. Someone's trying to kill me."

"We need to check you out. Could you lie down, Professor, so we can do that?"

"Sure."

Carter and Susan moved to my sides and eased me gently down onto their gurney, which they had lowered to floor level. Susan put the blue bag under my legs and inflated it, while Carter put on the automatic blood pressure cuff and inflated it.

"Professor, can you tell me your name?" he asked.

"Yes. Jenna James. Assistant professor of law."

"Do you know where you are?"

"The law library, on the Mezzanine."

"What happened here?"

"I was looking for a book and the whole stack fell on me."

"Do you know how that happened?"

"No."

Susan spoke up. "Her vitals are pretty good. Blood pressure's a little high, pulse is a little high, not surprisingly."

"Did any of the books," Carter asked, "hit your head?"

"No, I had my arms up, so they hit my arms."

He examined my arms. "They're going to be a bit bruised."

"What else is new?"

"Can you move your arms and legs without pain?"

I moved my legs up and down, then flexed my arms over my head. "No problems."

"Good. You probably haven't broken anything. But we'd like," he said, "to transport you to Reagan. You could have a concussion without knowing it, and given what happened to you last week, it would be prudent."

"You were the crew for that?"

"Yes."

"I was unconscious."

"Right."

"I appreciate what you say, Carter, but I'm not going anywhere. I'm going to wait right here until someone shows up and explains to me exactly what happened."

One of the librarians spoke up. "Someone from engineering is on the way, and someone from the UCLA police department. But we can't let you stay here, Professor. It's not safe. We're going to have to clear the Mezzanine and close it until we find out what happened."

"Like I said, I'm not going anywhere."

CHAPTER 57

Carter made one more attempt to get me to agree to go to the hospital. When I declined again, he handed me an Against Medical Advice form and asked me to sign it. I skimmed it. It said I released the Emergency Services Agency from all liability and mentioned that the possible consequences of refusing medical treatment could include head injury, broken bones and internal organ injury, and included consequences "up to and including death." I scribbled my signature on the form. Carter then asked one of the librarians to sign as witness to the fact that I'd signed it. After that the librarians all departed. Who could blame them?

Simultaneously, a UCLA police officer arrived. When they told me they'd called the police, I feared Detective Drady would show up, but instead it was a guy in uniform who identified himself as Officer Perez. Perez asked me what had occurred and I told him. He, too, looked at my bruised arms and clucked.

"You were lucky you weren't more badly injured."

"I know, Officer."

"This is the first library accident I've ever investigated."

"This was no accident."

"What makes you say that?"

"I heard someone coming up the steps right before the shelving started to fall. From the sound of it, it was a woman in high heels."

"Don't people come up here all the time?"

"Not very often, really."

"But they do, right?"

"Sure."

"So it may just have been a coincidence."

"I don't think so. Someone has been trying to kill me for almost two weeks."

He raised his eyebrows. "How's that?"

"Don't you know about Primo Giordano, the student who died after drinking coffee in my office?"

"I've been on vacation for the last two weeks, so I've heard about it, but I'm not working that case."

"Well, that happened because someone was trying to kill me."

"Tell me more."

Suddenly a light went on in my brain that said: *stop volunteering stuff to the police.*

"I would, Officer, but I think I should let my attorney do that. But, bottom line, this so-called accident was an attempt to kill me. Please write that down."

"Okay. I will. Do you have anything else to add about what just happened? If not, I need to interview some other people and take some photos."

"No, I don't really have anything else to add, except that I wish the police department would start worrying about who's after me."

Just then someone else showed up, a middle-aged Asian man with a totally shaved head. "Hi, I'm John Chen from engineering," he said, addressing Perez. "I just took a quick look around downstairs, right below this area, and it doesn't appear that there are any obvious structural problems with the building, so this is probably a local event. But I'm going to suggest that we clear the building while I check it out a little further." He looked at me. "Are you the professor who got hit with the books?"

"Yes."

"Were you hurt?"

"Just bruised arms, I think."

He looked around at all the books on the floor and at the tilted shelf. "You're lucky you weren't more badly hurt."

"So I've been told, multiple times."

"Hey, I'm just trying to be sympathetic."

"I know. I apologize."

"Can you tell me what happened?"

As he asked he was visually inspecting the shelving, including the ends of the metal vertical shelf supports that normally connect into the ceiling but were now floating free and twisted at the ends. He reached up and felt the tips.

I repeated the story, noticing Officer Perez taking more notes. Maybe he was trying to find inconsistencies in my story. Did he think I pulled the shelf over on myself?

"Do you have any idea, Professor," Chen asked, "what caused this? I know it's my job to determine that, but sometimes people who witness an event have their own useful ideas about causation."

Officer Perez spoke up. "She thinks someone was trying to kill her."

Chen stopped inspecting the shelving and looked directly at me. He was probably thinking, *Uh-oh, a nutty professor.*

Instead, he said, "She might be right. It looks to me as if someone has removed the bolts from the ceiling end of the metal uprights that support the shelves. Although I don't know if that would actually enable someone to shove over the whole stack."

"Well," Perez said, "maybe so, but how would they know when the professor was going to be here, and whether she'd be in this particular aisle?"

"Because," I said, "the carrel at which I work is right at the end of this aisle." I pointed to my carrel. "Everyone knows that carrel is mine and that I'm there a lot."

"Still seems unlikely," Perez said.

"Either way," Chen said, "I think we all ought to get out of here. I need to bring in an engineering crew to test the stability of the other shelves on this floor—there are dozens of them—and, in the meantime, have it closed off."

Chen looked at me. "You look a bit shaken up, not surprisingly. Do you need a ride somewhere?"

"I appreciate that, Mr. Chen, but I think I'm okay. I'm just going to go back to my office and try to resume my day."

"Okay," he said. "Here's my card. Please call me if you think of anything further."

Chen and I left, but I noticed that Perez stayed around and was busy cordoning off the area with yellow crime scene tape. It occurred to me that perhaps I should start carrying around my own roll of it.

When I got back to my office, I first tried the door, to be sure it was still locked. It was. I unlocked it, went in, locked the door behind me, sat down in my desk chair and sobbed. For quite a while. It was some combination of the physical pain and the fear. Someone was truly trying to kill me. Why on earth couldn't

I persuade anyone to take the threat seriously? Surely this event would change everyone's minds.

When I finished crying, I took some Kleenex from a box I keep in my desk drawer, dried my eyes and face and looked around my office. It was crazy, but I was still trying to see if the map was there, and I had somehow just missed seeing it. Even though I was beginning to doubt whether there really had been a map in that tube.

I called Robert but only reached his voice mail. Then I called Oscar, who picked up.

"Hi, Jenna. What's going on?"

I told him. In detail.

"Listen, the idea that someone pushed the shelves over on you is too baroque. It's much more likely an engineering screwup or something. You need to put it out of your head—I know that's hard—and move on."

"Hard? It's impossible. My arms are even more bruised than they were from the bike accident, and I'm flat-out terrified. I've been sitting in my office sobbing, and my hands have started to shake again." I held my hands out in front of me. "If you were here, you'd see that this time they're actually twitching."

"That happens to me, too, after a lot of stress."

"Oscar, for God's sake, we're not talking about ordinary stress here. Don't you finally believe someone is trying to kill me? I mean, what has to happen before you believe that? Do you have to stumble on my cooling body?"

I was practically yelling at him.

His tone softened. "Hey, I don't mean to be insensitive, kid, but I need to be honest with you. I don't think there's any real evidence anyone is trying to kill you. It just makes no sense."

"You don't think a set of heavy bookshelves being pushed onto me is proof?" I realized I was now actually yelling, and that I had gotten up from my desk and was pacing around my office. "No," Oscar said. "I don't think that's proof. I've been in that part of the library, and to make this work as a murder, you'd have to be an evil genius and a great engineer to boot, and you'd need perfect timing, too. I'm sorry, Jenna, but there are simply no facts to support your theory that the shelves were pushed."

"Maybe you're right," I said, although I was just saying that because clearly I wasn't going to persuade him. "But look, let's at least put off tomorrow's interview, okay?"

"Jenna, I don't want to ask to postpone the interview. It will make us look weak. Although we'll certainly mention the library incident and ask the police to look into it."

"The UCLA police are already doing that." Not, I thought to myself, that it would do the least bit of good.

"Great. Unfortunately, I'm busy with something else right now or I'd come over there. Among other things, I'm reviewing the report on the diary from my forensics guy. Plus I need to get ready for your interview with the cops tomorrow. Speaking of which, here's what I propose: let's meet early, say 7:00 A.M. tomorrow to prep for a Drady interview at 8:00. After that you can go teach your class at 9:00."

"I don't know if I'm even up to teaching that class."

"With a good night's sleep you'll be able to do the interview and the class. By the way, with your class scheduled for nine we'll have an excuse to cut the Drady interview short. You can always say you have more prep to do."

"All right, see you at seven."

"Good. And always remember what the Bard said."

"What's that?"

"'Screw your courage to the sticking-place.'"

After we ended the call, I thought about what he had said. He was right. My whole life was at UCLA. I wasn't going to let this insanity drive me out. Out loud, I said, "I need to stop feeling sorry for myself. I need to screw my courage to the sticking-place and move forward."

I had first heard that phrase when I was nine years old, playing on my neighborhood girls' Little League team and striking out in every at bat in every game. I told my father I wanted to quit. He told me to screw my courage to the sticking-place and figure out how to make myself into a better player. Of course, he had to tell me that over the phone because he was off at some political event in some other city at the time. Back then I didn't know what the phrase meant, and I certainly didn't know that Shakespeare penned it as a line for Macbeth's wife to utter as she tells him not to get cold feet about murdering Duncan.

As a child I instead pictured it as a large wad of chewing gum stuck to my bedpost. In any case, I stuck a wad of gum on my bedpost right after my dad hung up the phone that night and then started going to the batting cages until I emerged as the star slugger on my fifth-grade team. The gum is still there.

I didn't know what the law-school equivalent of the batting cages might be, but I was damned if I was going to let them drive me out. Whoever they were. Eff them. No, fuck them.

CHAPTER 58

When I got home at about 6:00 P.M., Tommy was in his usual spot on the couch, feet up, chemistry book in hand. For the first time ever, he was wearing black penny loafers. No pennies in them, though.

"Hi," he said. "I bought that dead bolt you asked me to pick up. It's on the kitchen table."

"Thanks. How much was it?"

"Twenty-six dollars plus tax. The bill's in the kitchen, too. You can pay me back whenever."

"Okay."

"Hey, that real-estate agent was by again. He wanted your cell number. Said he had an offer for you you'd be crazy to turn down."

"What did you say?"

"I told him I couldn't give him your cell number and that your answer is still no."

"Good. Was that the entire conversation?"

"No. I was curious, so I asked him what the offer was, but he said he could only talk to you about that."

"I don't care about the offer amount. Although I'm curious about who the mystery buyer is."

Tommy shrugged. "Do you want me to press him on that the next time?"

"You can if you want. But don't let him think that means I'm interested in selling, because I'm not."

"Got it."

"Tommy, I have a question to ask you. Several, actually."

"Shoot."

"Where were you the day they searched the apartment?"

"I went surfing."

"In November?"

"Wet suit."

"You grew up in Hawaii."

"Yeah, but I've lived here for quite a long time now, and the water's not warm very many months of the year. So I learned to use a wet suit. Want to see it?"

"No."

"Why do you ask, Jenna?"

"It just seemed odd. Usually you're here on weekends."

"Jenna, are you getting paranoid or something?"

"No. But I have a couple more questions. First I want some coffee. Do you want some?"

"No thanks."

Tommy went back to reading his book. I went into the kitchen and made myself some coffee, extracting the ground coffee from the Peet's bag in my purse. While I worked at it, I tried to think how to approach the subject I wanted to ask Tommy about. Without pissing him off, if that was possible. Maybe it wasn't possible.

I went back to the living room with my cup of coffee and sat down on the opposite end of the couch. I put my feet up on the table. Maybe that would make it seem more casual. "Tommy, my lawyer told me today that the police had found a receipt in one of my jackets for a chemical called sodium azide, bought for cash and made out to me."

"That's strange."

"Why?"

"Because that's a reagent used in labs, especially medical and biology labs. Why would you need it?"

"Exactly. So I'm wondering if maybe you bought it instead."

"Whoa. Are you accusing me of having stuff shipped here in your name?"

"I'm not accusing you of anything. I'm trying to figure out how this happened, since I certainly didn't buy it or ask anyone to buy it for me."

Tommy put down his book, got up from the couch and went to lean against the windowsill. He put his hands in front of him and cracked his knuckles. "What is this all about, Jenna? I'm really confused."

"What it's all about is that the coroner's report says the student who died, Primo Giordano, was poisoned by someone putting sodium azide in his coffee. The coffee I made."

"So someone's framing you."

"Maybe."

"And you think it's me."

"Like I said, I don't think anything." Then I thought to myself that I was about to make a baby lawyer's mistake and not actually ask the question, taking his incredulity as a denial. "Well, Tommy, let me just ask you directly. Did you buy that stuff?"

"No."

"Did you put that receipt in my pocket?"

"No."

"All right."

"Do you want me to move out, Jenna? I mean, this is crazy."

"No, no. But please understand, I need to get to the bottom of this. So I need to ask uncomfortable questions. Of all kinds of people."

"I'm your cousin. We've known each other since we were kids. I mean, why would I want to do a thing like that?"

"I don't know."

"I think I should go."

"No, don't do that. I'll just be more afraid if you're gone. And I'm sorry. I just had to ask." As I said that, I wasn't quite sure why I had now suddenly assumed he hadn't done it. Maybe it was because he sounded so offended. Maybe I just needed a friend, and he was offering to be one.

"Jenna," he was saying, "do you want some help figuring out who bought the chemical and where it came from?"

"Sure."

"Do you have a copy of that receipt?"

"Not yet."

"Okay, when you get it, let me see it."

"I will."

He unlimbered himself from the windowsill. "I'm going out for a while, Jenna. I might be late getting back. I'll try to be quiet when I come in."

"Where are you going?"

"Just out. I need to start thinking about another place to live."

"Don't do that."

"We'll see."

So much for having a friend.

Tommy picked up a hoodie that had been lying on one arm of the couch, headed for the door and opened it. Without turning around, he said, "Don't forget to lock your bedroom door."

I felt really awful. Like I had been unfair to someone against whom I had very little evidence at all, if I really thought about it.

But what if it *had* been Tommy who poisoned the coffee? He had just told me he was going to come back late. I'd be asleep. If he was the killer, he'd have a new and perfect opportunity to off me. Of course, he had had that opportunity every night.

I considered what to do. One option was to go to Aldous's house. I still had the keys. But that didn't seem like a good option. It was lonely up there, with no neighbors within two hundred feet. If it was Aldous who did it—unlikely as that now seemed to me—his house on a dark and lonely night would be the perfect place to have someone else do me in. Not only that, but as soon as I punched the code numbers into the security system, it would notify his cell phone, even in Buffalo, that I was in his house. He had explained to me once how that all worked.

In the end I chose to stay where I was. But before I went to sleep I barricaded my bedroom door with a heavy dresser and put a pot on top of it, right by the front edge, so that it would fall off if the dresser was moved even a little. I also removed the carving knife from the kitchen, and right before I climbed into bed, I put it under my pillow.

CHAPTER 59

Week 2—Friday

No one came to kill me during the night. I got up, made coffee, ate breakfast and drove to the law school.

When Oscar arrived in my office at 7:00 A.M., I had already made a full pot of coffee. He arrived bundled in a winter coat, wearing a black fedora and carrying a battered brown leather briefcase. He tossed his coat and hat on one of the guest chairs, sat down in the other and put the briefcase on the floor next to him.

"Are you cold?" I asked.

"Yeah. For some reason. I know it's not really very cold out, but I woke up freezing."

"It is kind of damp, though, Oscar. Do you want some coffee to warm you up?"

"No thanks."

"You know, every time someone turns down an offer of my coffee now, I think it's because they're worried I'm trying to poison them."

"That's not it at all. It's just that I'm trying to back away from caffeine. Pandy says . . ."

I finished for him. "That it's bad for you."

"Right."

"Maybe so," I said, taking the carafe out of its holder and refilling my own cup. "After yesterday's event I seem to need even more caffeine."

"Can I see your bruises, Jenna?"

I rolled up my sleeves—I had put on a long-sleeved shirt when I got up—and showed him my arms, which had spots of black-and-blue from my wrists to well above my elbows. "There they are, Oscar."

"Ouch."

"Yeah, ouch. And there are some on my shoulders, my back and my upper chest, too."

"Are you taking anything for it?"

"Mostly just Tylenol. I called a doctor I know, though, and got a prescription for something stronger, but I haven't filled it. I don't think I'll need it."

"Good."

"Enough about my bumps and bruises. I'm anxious to hear what the forensics expert had to say. Is his report in the briefcase?" I pointed to it.

"No, it's in my head. We criminal defense lawyers sometimes ask experts not to write reports now because if they do, and there's a prosecution, under California law we sometimes have to hand the reports over to the DA."

"You just talked to the expert then. I've already forgotten his name."

"Mr. Smith."

"Right."

"Tell me what he said, please."

"Well, aside from validating Primo's handwriting, which we talked about before, he said there's no way to tell if the dates on the diary pages are accurate. There's no test that can distinguish between ink that was laid down a few days ago versus a few weeks ago."

"All right, what else?"

"Let me show you." He opened his briefcase and took out a spiral-bound notebook with a green cover. "This is similar to the one Primo used. I bought it at Ackerman Union yesterday."

"And?"

"Tear a page out of it." He handed it to me.

I took it from him. "Any page?"

"Try one from the middle."

"Okay." I opened the notebook—it was narrow ruled—and ripped out a page.

"Now look inside the spiral spring that held the page you just tore out."

I looked.

"What do you see?"

"Tiny little flecks of paper from where the page used to be before I tore it out, stuck within the spiral metal spring."

"Right."

"I see where you might be going, but as I told you before, there weren't any little flecks in Primo's notebook spring. I looked."

"None that you could see. But there apparently were some. Smith used a special kind of very bright light that allows him to see tiny, almost microscopic paper fragments. It seems someone tore out at least one sheet."

"But we have no way of knowing for sure which sheet was torn out, who did it or when," I said.

"Right. And because you were dumb enough to take possession of the notebook, the police will no doubt suspect you did it."

"So we're stuck with that bad fact."

"Not quite. It turns out that Primo wrote in his diary with a ballpoint pen on paper that's fairly soft. When he pressed on the paper to write, it made a slight depression on the next piece of paper."

"Can you read it?"

"In the old days, they did it by putting a piece of tracing paper on top of the second page and rubbing it with charcoal. Like people do to trace old tombstones. But now there's a laser instrument that lets you read the next-page impression even better, or at least most of it."

"Which page was torn out?"

"It's the missing page from the very end, dated the day before he died."

"What does it say?"

"It says Julie is threatening to kill him because he threw her out at the start of the semester."

"I'm off the hook."

"Maybe not. The laser instrument is new, it doesn't have much of a scientific track record and it might not be admissible in a trial."

"You think this is going to trial?"

"It could."

"That's crazy."

"It would be crazy but for the fact that there was that receipt for the poison in your pocket. And the fact that Charlie Benitez may not like you because you beat him in Robert's trial."

"Last time, Oscar, you said you didn't think he held a grudge."

"No, I said I didn't know if he did or not."

"Well, in any case, I beat him fair and square. And it wasn't his fault. It was the fault of the cops and their lousy investigation."

"Prosecutors have a hard time admitting that people they prosecuted were actually innocent. They tend instead to blame the things that went wrong. And in that case what went wrong was a great defense. Which was you."

After that rather sobering exchange, we spent the next hour going over what I was going to tell Detective Drady. I promised I would try to answer only the questions asked of me, that I'd let Oscar do the persuading if there was any persuading to be done. I also promised that if Oscar held up his hand, I would immediately shut my mouth.

CHAPTER 60

Detective Drady arrived at my office precisely at 8:00 A.M., as we had arranged. After polite greetings and handshakes all around—you might have thought we were there for something a great deal more benign—Drady sat down in one of the two guest chairs, took out a leather-bound notepad and flipped it open. He also took out a black digital recorder about the size of a pack of cigarettes, placed it on my desk and pushed a button. A small red light went on. Oscar whipped out his own identical recorder and put it next to Drady's. Now I was looking at two tiny red lights.

"We're here," Detective Drady said, "to record the interview of Professor Jenna James concerning the death of Primo Giordano on—" He looked at his notepad and mentioned the date of Primo's death and the date of the interview.

"Before we begin," Oscar said, "I'd like to summarize the ground rules that you and I have agreed on, Detective."

"Sure."

"First, we've agreed that if I object to any question, Professor James need not answer it."

"Right. But we've also agreed that, should there be a trial in this matter and should this interview be entered in evidence, I may comment on any question she declines to answer."

"And I can ask the court not to permit that."

"Right."

"Would either of you gentlemen," I asked, "like a cup of coffee before we begin? I just made a full pot." I hadn't cleared that question with Oscar in advance, but I saw a small smile flicker across his face.

"I'd love one," Oscar said.

"I think I'll pass," Drady responded, not making eye contact with me but instead looking down at his notebook.

I poured Oscar a cup and handed it to him. I knew he took it black.

"I want," Oscar said, "to put a couple of other things on the record here. Detective Drady, you've told me that Professor James is not at this time a target of your investigation, nor is she a suspect. Is that correct?"

"That is correct. She is simply a person of interest."

"And you've agreed that, if at any time in the interview, her answers lead you to move her into the category of a target or a suspect, you'll let me know."

"Yes."

I knew what those terms meant because Oscar had explained them to me. If you were a target, it meant the cops believed you committed the crime and were just looking for proof. If you were a suspect, it meant the cops thought there was a good possibility it was you but weren't sure. A person of interest was somehow a click down from that, without a tight definition. As Oscar had explained it, if a wife is found dead in a bathtub with her throat slashed, the husband is always a person of interest. If he's seen driving rapidly away from the house, he's a suspect. If when he's stopped he's got his wife's blood on him and is carrying a large carving knife, he becomes an instant target.

"All right," Drady said, "let's get started."

Oscar took a very loud slurp of his coffee.

"Professor, when did you first meet Primo Giordano?"

"He was a student in my admiralty law course in the spring semester last year. I first met him when he took his seat on the first day of that class."

"Had you ever had any contact with him at all before that?"

"Not that I recall."

"He was taking another class from you this year?"

"Yes, he was a student in my seminar this semester on the law of sunken treasure."

"Did you have any contact with him outside of class?"

"The first time was last week, when I met with him on the day he died."

"How did that come about?"

"He signed up for an appointment to see me during my office hours a week ago Monday."

"How does that work?"

I took a large and noisy sip from my coffee cup before answering. "Every semester I pick two days during the week when I'll have office hours. This semester it's Mondays and Thursdays. I keep a sign-up sheet on the wall outside my office where students can sign up to see me during the available time blocks on those days. Students can sign up for blocks of fifteen minutes."

"Do you put up a schedule a week at a time?"

"No. I'm an optimist, so I put it up for a month at a time."

"What do you mean by saying that you're an optimist?"

"I mean that I imagine that I can predict my schedule a month in advance."

"Can you?"

"Usually."

"Did Primo sign up for one of those slots?"

"Yes, he signed up for the 7:30 A.M. slot that was available a week ago Monday."

"Did you know in advance what he wanted to talk about?"

"No. He had signed up for it during the previous week. I saw him in class the day after he signed up and asked if he could give me a heads-up on the topic, so I could be prepared. He said he'd rather just come in and talk because he had something interesting to talk to me about. I said okay and didn't ask for further details."

"Is it unusual for students to decline to tell you in advance what they want to talk about when they see you?"

"No. Sometimes it's because they haven't yet figured it out. For example, there are some students who just like to check in, so to speak, a couple of times per semester. It's one way for them to help you remember them years later, when they might want a reference for a job or something."

"Had Primo ever signed up for office hours before, in either course?"

"Not that I recall."

"Do you keep the sign-up sheets?"

"No. I throw them out when the month's over."

"Do you have the one from this month?"

"I took it down from the wall and gave it to Mr. Quesana. I later put up a substitute sheet for the balance of the month."

Drady looked over at Oscar, who opened his brown briefcase, extracted a manila envelope and handed it to Drady. "Here you go," Oscar said. Drady clicked open his own briefcase, pulled out a large plastic bag of the size used for freezer storage and dropped the envelope into the plastic bag.

"Had you ever talked to Primo outside of class before he came to see you on the day he died?"

"By outside of class, do you mean outside of the physical classroom in which I teach? Because students often come up to the front of the room to talk to me before or after class, and I have no recollection of whether he ever did that. Certainly he wasn't one of the regulars at that."

"Yes, I mean outside of the physical classroom."

"I think that during the admiralty law class he ran into me in a hallway one day."

I looked over at Oscar to see if it was okay to continue down that path. It wasn't something we had discussed during our preparation. He didn't raise his hand or make any other gesture, so we continued.

"What did he want to talk about?"

"He wanted to know if I could read Spanish texts from the seventeenth century."

"Do you know why he thought you might be able to read them?"

"Because I had mentioned in class that I had had a research grant to spend a summer in the Spanish state archive in Seville to study seventeenth-century documents there related to Spanish treasure ships."

"What did you tell him?"

"I told him I was terrible at it."

"Did he tell you why he wanted to know?"

Oscar held up his hand. "Officer Drady, I think this is going fairly far afield. We're talking about something that happened many months ago. I thought you were investigating a death that took place recently."

"I think this is relevant, and it may actually tend to exonerate your client. But if you don't want me to continue, I won't."

"Okay," Oscar said. "You can go on for a while."

"What was the question again?" I asked.

"Did Primo Giordano tell you why he wanted to know if you could read Spanish from the seventeenth century?"

"No."

"How long did you talk to him about it?"

"Maybe a minute. I'd forgotten about it until just now."

Oscar spoke up. "Why does that tend to exonerate my client?"

"I can't explain that to you until we complete our investigation. Telling you now might compromise it. In any case, I want to move on to another topic. Professor, did you buy a bottle of sodium azide at Angin Chemical Corporation downtown?"

"No."

"You never went down there and purchased it for cash?"

"I don't even know where it is because I've never heard of it."

"We'd like you to participate in a lineup so that the salesclerk can identify you as the purchaser. Or not."

"Whoa." Oscar was on his feet. "I think this interview is at an end. This is some kind of ambush."

"No, Mr. Quesana, we're just trying to get at the facts. If your client will voluntarily participate in a lineup, I think we can resolve all of this one way or another, since the woman who sold the poison to—well, to somebody—has lawyered up and won't talk to us. But both her attorney and her company's attorneys are willing to have her try to identify the person who bought the chemical in a lineup. If she fails to identify your client as the one who bought the chemical, this case is over, at least as far as Professor James goes."

"Even though," Oscar said, "you supposedly found a receipt for it in the pocket of one of her jackets."

"Right, and if she didn't buy it, the receipt had to be planted."

"Do you have a copy of the receipt with you?"

"Sure." There was more unsnapping of briefcase locks, and Drady handed a piece of paper to Oscar. "Here it is."

"This is a copy?" Oscar asked.

"Yes. I'll arrange for you and your expert to examine the original."

"Fine. And now I have something for you." Oscar opened his briefcase again and handed over a plastic bag that contained what I knew to be the original of Primo's diary.

"What is it?" Drady asked.

"It's Primo's diary. You can match the handwriting in it with the handwriting on the sign-up sheet I just gave you. You'll find the diary is genuine."

"What's the bottom line of the diary?"

"Jenna didn't kill him."

"Who did, then?"

"His brother Quinto."

"I'll make a note of it," Drady said.

"My client and I," Oscar said, "need to confer. Would you mind, Detective, stepping out for a few minutes? I'm sure you know the campus well and can find someplace where you can get an untainted cup of coffee. We'll need about ten."

"No problem, Counselor. I'll be back."

CHAPTER 61

After Drady shut the door, I asked Oscar, "Do you want me to do the lineup?"

"Are you nuts? Lineups are for suckers, and they can only force you to do one if you're in custody. Not only that, lineups are often fixed. Either the police indicate by their body language who they want identified, or the person doing the identifying is shown pictures where, one way or another, the message gets through. And speaking of pictures, it will be worse in this case because your picture could soon be in the papers, and if that happens the clerk will see them."

"I've been wondering why there's been almost no news coverage of this."

"It's because Primo wasn't a pretty young white undergraduate woman. He was a late-twenties male foreigner. That's not a story, particularly when he died in the hospital and not here, thank God. To most of the media, without access to the coroner's report, it still reads like a drug overdose. Ho-hum. So far as I know, there was only one small item in the *Bruin* about it."

"Maybe it will stay that way."

"Might, might not. Pretty soon the coroner's office is going to release their report, assuming the police let them. Once our friends in the media read the word *poison*, the headline DID PROF POISON STUDENT? is going to be all over the place. And you didn't help matters yesterday when you talked in the library about someone trying to kill you. That rumor is probably all over Westwood by now."

"I'm sorry."

"Don't be. It's all coming out soon anyway."

"Can we go back to the lineup thing for a moment?"

"Sure."

"Since I didn't buy the poison, don't you think there's a good chance the clerk will fail to identify me, and then it will all be over?"

"Too big a risk. Like I said, lineups are unreliable. Subjecting yourself to one is stupid."

"Maybe they should put Julie in the lineup."

"Maybe, but I'm going to let them figure that one out for themselves, at least for the moment. They have the same technology as my forensics guy, and they'll soon figure out that a page is missing and what it said."

"It's interesting," I said, "that Drady thinks the receipt might have been planted in my jacket."

"It's interesting that he's willing to consider that."

"Tommy was the one with the easiest access to my jacket."

"What's his motive again?"

"You don't buy he's after an inheritance. So I don't know."

Not long after that, Detective Drady returned and resumed his questions, which were benign. He went over in more detail the timeline of my meeting with Primo, and I pretty much repeated what I'd told him the first time he'd interviewed me. He seemed to accept that I'd locked my door when I left the night before my meeting with Primo. Interestingly, he didn't seem that concerned about the map or where it had gone. His final set of questions, though, surprised me.

"Professor," he asked, "do you know if your roommate, Tom James, knows how to pick locks?"

Oscar raised his hand. "Can you give me a little bit of guidance as to where this line of questioning is going, Detective?"

"Isn't it obvious?" Drady asked.

"Whether it's obvious or not, I think I should answer it," I said. Oscar made no attempt to stop me.

"Tommy is the son of my Uncle Freddie. Uncle Freddie is a private detective in Hawaii, and picking locks is kind of a hobby of his. I believe he has taught his children how to do that. But I've never asked Tommy if he was one of his students."

Drady wrote something in his notebook, then asked, "Did your uncle teach you how to do it?"

"She's not going to answer that one," Oscar said. "I can't see that it has anything to do with this investigation, unless you think she picked the lock on her own office door. Do you have anything else?"

"No, that's it. Thank you for your cooperation, Professor, and you as well, Counsel."

He picked up his recorder and put it in his briefcase, along with his tablet. As he was opening the door to leave, I said, "Are you sure you don't want a cup of coffee for the road? I have some Styrofoam cups."

He declined.

After he left I said to Oscar, "So what do you make of that?"

"That they're not very focused on you. For some reason they're focused on Tommy. Maybe they know what his motive was. When they find the missing page in Primo's diary and learn what it said, they're going to start looking hard at Julie, too."

"I feel kind of bad, to use the terminology I see in gangster films, that I 'gave up' Tommy by telling them he probably knows how to pick locks. It doesn't make sense that I feel that way, but I do. I guess it's because he's family."

"You didn't give him up. The police already had him in their sights."

"What happens next?"

"I'm guessing the criminal part of this just goes away as far as you're concerned. It never made any sense in the first place."

"Goes away? What about the crime that hasn't happened yet?"

"What crime?"

"My upcoming murder." I pulled up the sleeve on my right arm and displayed the bruises. "Have you forgotten that the poison was in the coffeepot, too, and that library shelves just happened to fall on me yesterday?"

"I haven't forgotten, Jenna, but I think that's going to turn out to have been some kind of freak accident. Whoever put the poison in the coffeepot was trying to kill Primo, not you. That's what I think."

"I'm glad you think so, but I don't agree," I said.

I couldn't understand why no one else seemed to take seriously that someone was out to kill me. It seemed obvious, and yet no one cared. I wasn't going to get anywhere in making people concerned for my safety, so I changed the subject. "Even if you're right about the criminal case, Oscar, there's still the civil case, remember?"

"Robert and I talked about that. We both have a gut feeling that the whole thing is a scam to get money out of you, the university or various insurance companies."

"Speaking of insurance companies, has Robert heard from mine? I know he submitted a claim."

Oscar laughed. "He told me that he received a typical response—preliminary, of course—via a phone call. Seems your policy, like most homeowners' policies, covers only bodily injury and property damage."

I knew, as a lawyer, what he was going to say next.

"So," Oscar went on, "the insurance company's opening position is that the theft of a map isn't bodily injury, and it's not property damage either, because theft of someone else's property isn't damage to your property. Your policy doesn't have a theft or loss of entrusted property rider."

"That's not a surprising position on their part, Oscar," I said.

"Insurance companies are such thieves, Jenna."

I refrained from telling him that, in my days at Marbury Marfan, I had represented a major insurance company against a claim by policyholders that the insurance company had fraudulently denied their claims. At the time I thought policyholders were the thieves.

"Well," I said, "if there's no insurance coverage, there's not going to be a settlement, and we'll need to defeat the civil suit on the merits. Maybe I can learn more about the scam you suspect from Aldous, since he reviewed the investment proposal. At some point he has to stop hiding behind that confidentiality agreement. Especially if he wants me to go to Buffalo with him."

"I thought you weren't going there ever."

"I seem to go back and forth about it in my own head. One moment he's a suspect, the next I'm at least toying with the idea of joining him in Buffalo. Anyway, let's not talk about that today. Let's focus on what we can do to defeat the civil suit. What about getting info from that guy in Spain Quinto identified?"

"Cabano, you mean? Robert tried to get in touch with him in Seville, but he didn't return his calls."

"The General Archive of the Indies has digitized a lot of their documents from that period. Like I showed you guys, you can just dial them up on your computer. Many of them have been translated to modern Spanish."

"I know. Robert stayed up late Wednesday night looking at them and using a translation program to render them into English. He couldn't find any survivor account from the sinking of the *Ayuda* in 1641, or from any other year, for that matter."

"Maybe I should look at the records."

"You probably should. But in the meantime, Robert is already on his way to Seville to look for the document himself. If it exists."

"Seriously?"

"Yes, seriously. He thought he could do more good there than here. He left at the crack of dawn Thursday morning, with a plane change in Miami. He may even be in Seville by now."

"But Oscar, he doesn't speak the language well, and he won't be able read the archaic Spanish script."

"He's going to do what all lawyers do, my dear."

"Which is?"

"Hire an expert when he gets there."

"Is Tess going with him?"

"No. She told him she thought she could be more useful to you here. Whatever that means."

CHAPTER 62

I wasn't quite ready, psychologically, to teach my 9:00 A.M. seminar on the law of sunken treasure. I was still unnerved by the interview with Drady. Oscar thought it was all going to go away. I wasn't so sure. But classes must go on.

Most days I'm a few minutes early for class. That day I was five minutes late. The first thing I saw on walking in was Julie, sitting in the front row. I noticed she was avoiding making eye contact with me. The thought that went through my head was, precisely: *You little bitch. You killed him yourself and tried to set me up by giving me the diary. But you were too stupid to realize that the writing on the torn-out page can still be read. This is only just beginning for you.*

Instead of saying any of that out loud, though, I stood at the podium and said to the class as a whole, "Apologies for being late. Something came up." Then I put a DVD in the player and projected my image for the day, which was a split picture. On the right-hand side was a picture of the Manila galleon *Nuestra Señora de la Concepción*, which sank along the coast of Saipan in 1638 on its voyage out from the Philippines to Acapulco. On the left-hand side of the screen was a handwritten document from the General Archive of the Indies, written in the cramped script of an early seventeenth-century notary.

The document was a page from the report of an investigation the Spanish Crown undertook after the ship sank. The investigation uncovered a tale of incompetence—the governor of the Philippines had appointed his inexperienced twenty-two-year-old nephew, Don Juan Francisco, as the commander of the ship. It was also a tale of corruption. The governor had secretly shipped more than a thousand pieces of twenty-two-karat gold jewelry to be sold by the nephew in Acapulco, which violated just about every rule in the Spanish rulebook. The jewelry represented bribes paid to the governor for appointing people to office.

Several weeks before, I had passed out to the students the page of handwriting I was now projecting and asked those in the class who said they spoke Spanish to try to read it and translate it into English. This was going to be fun.

I called on a student in the second row. "Henry, I think you said you spoke good Spanish. How did you do in deciphering the document?"

"Miserably. It took me several hours to puzzle out four or five lines."

"Is the problem that you don't understand the words, that they're archaic words?"

"No, it's the handwriting. They didn't put spaces between words, they didn't use punctuation and they used capitals in random ways. Plus some of the letters are quite different."

"What did the lines you managed to read say, in your opinion?"

"Best I can make out, they say that Don Juan Francisco, the nephew who was the master of the ship, was a total idiot."

There was laughter all around.

"I don't assume, Henry, that those are the actual words used?"

"No. I think they use a phrase like 'lacking competence.' In Spanish, of course."

"Yes. And as we discussed when I handed out this assignment several weeks ago—the whole point of which was to show how difficult this is—that Don Juan was basically there to protect the governor's illegal shipment, and to get it sold in Acapulco."

"What I wonder," Henry said, "is how they managed to conduct an investigation of corruption that took place in the Philippines, when the authorities were in Spain."

"Can anyone answer that?"

Candace, a woman in the third row, raised her hand. "The people in the Philippines—in Manila—investigated it themselves and then sent the report to the authorities in Spain and New Spain, that is, Mexico."

"Exactly," I said. "Empires, even in the days before Facebook, managed to keep in touch."

I clicked again and projected a new image from the DVD. This one was of the gold-encrusted jewels—the governor's stash—recovered when the *Concepción* was salvaged in 1987. "Now what I'd like to discuss is one of the issues at the heart of this course: who owns what. The treasures of the *Concepción* were salvaged in 1987. The ship was in territorial waters just off the coast of Saipan. Why is that an issue here, Candace?"

"Because," she said, "Saipan is a territory of the Commonwealth of the Northern Mariana Islands, which is itself a self-governing territory of the United States. The cargo was originally owned by Spain, but it was shipped from what is now the sovereign nation of the Philippines and was headed for New Spain, which is now Mexico. So all of them could have made claims."

"But did they? For the balance of today's class, I'd like to have us pick through the various salvage permits you'd need to obtain from the government of the Marianas, and whether any of the international treaties might apply, even though the wreck was in the territorial waters of the United States."

During the rest of the class we did just that. When the class was over, I saw Julie making a beeline for the door. I practically jumped down from the podium, caught her before she got there and said, "Julie, I'd really like to talk to you."

"Does it have to be right now, Professor? I have a class with Professor Broontz right after this one, and I don't want to be late."

What I wanted to say was, *Why on earth would you want to take a class with that woman?* But I couldn't, of course, denigrate another faculty member to a student, so I just said, "Oh, what course are you taking with her?"

"I'm doing an independent study."

"How's that going?"

"It's going great. She's a brilliant teacher."

"I'm glad to hear that, Julie, but I really do need to talk to you now. And it's private enough that I'd like to chat in my office, even if it makes you a few minutes late for Professor Broontz's class."

"All right."

We walked to my office, saying little to each other.

When we got there, I settled into the chair behind my desk while Julie took one of the guest chairs. I decided not to offer her any coffee, even though there was some left in the pot.

"Julie, why don't you close the door?"

She got up, closed it and returned to her seat. "You don't seem in a very friendly mood today, Professor."

"I'm not. Some of it has to do with you, some of it has to do with other things."

"What's the part about me?"

I knew Oscar wouldn't approve of what I was about to do. He wanted me, I knew, to be a good client and stay out of trying to manage my case. He wanted me to do what all lawyers want from their clients: go home, sleep well, I'll call you when I need you for something. I had tried to do that, but it was starting to drive me crazy. I needed to take charge of my own destiny.

"Let me begin with a very direct question, Julie: Did you tear a page out of the diary you gave me?"

"No."

"I can tell you're lying. We detected the little paper pieces left in the coil when you tore the page out. Not only that but I counted the pages in the notebook. There were ninety-nine. If you go and buy that very same brand of notebook at the student store today, it has an even one hundred pages."

"Oh."

"So let me ask you again, did you tear a page out of that diary?"

"No. Somebody else must have done it. Maybe Primo."

"We gave the diary to the UCLA police, and they'll come to the same conclusion we did."

She sat silent.

"And," I lied, "the police will find your fingerprints on it. You didn't manage to wipe all of them off. So, once again, did you tear out a page?"

"Okay. Yes, I did."

"Do you still have the page?"

"No, I shredded it."

"You realize that if Primo was murdered, or even if he wasn't, your destroying that page is probably obstruction of justice."

"Maybe I should get a lawyer before we talk further."

"If you want to do that, go ahead."

We sat there for a moment, just staring at each other.

"Maybe," she said, "we can talk a little longer without my doing that."

"Okay. What did the page say?"

"I don't remember exactly."

"Didn't Primo write in it that you had threatened to kill him? We could tell that from the imprint on the next page."

"He did. The reason I tore it out is that that's not true."

"What's not true about it?"

"I didn't threaten to kill him. I said that someday he'd be really sorry he kicked me out. He just interpreted it as a threat."

"Were you really angry when you said it?"

"Sort of."

"Sort of?"

"Okay. A lot. But I didn't kill him, and I don't know who did."

"Why should I believe that?"

"We reconciled the night before he died. Patched it up after our six-week separation. Our relationship was always like that. Stormy."

"You patched it up how?"

"Well, we spent the night together. In fact, when Quinto drove Primo over here for your early-morning meeting, I grabbed a ride with them, and I walked with Primo up to your office."

"Was the door open?"

"Yes, it was. We figured you'd just gone down the hall and would be right back."

"What did you do then?"

"I went over to Lu Valle Commons for some coffee and a sweet roll. I told him I'd meet him back at your office around

8:00 A.M. because he didn't think it would take very long. That's why I was hanging around out in the hall when the EMTs came."

"I see."

"Professor?"

"Yes?"

"Is this going to affect my grade?"

I had to resist smacking myself in the forehead. Students had one-track minds. Grades were the be-all and end-all of life.

"No, Julie, it won't." I was able to say that in all honesty because exams at UCLA are graded blind, with just ID numbers on the exams instead of student names. So if Julie didn't kill Primo, her grade would be unaffected, no matter how much of a lying scum I thought she was. If she did kill him, she'd likely be in jail during finals, and I wouldn't have to worry about her grade.

CHAPTER 63

As soon as Julie left my office, I called Robert, expecting to reach his voice mail. To my surprise, he picked up on the second ring.   "Hey, Jenna, what's up?"

"I assumed you were still on a plane somewhere, Robert."

"No, I'm already in Madrid. It's Friday evening here."

"I thought you were going to Seville."

"I am. Tomorrow morning on the train. And I don't mean to be curt, but please tell me what you want to tell me, because I'm badly jet-lagged, and I want to go to bed soon."

"OK. I called to tell you that you screwed up in the deposition."

"Huh?"

"Do you remember when you were teaching me to take depositions that one of the rules you taught me was, 'always ask if anyone else was present'?"

"Sure."

"Well, when you took Quinto's deposition, do you remember he said he drove Primo to the law school?"

"Uh-huh."

"He drove Julie there at the same time."

"I see. So I didn't ask if anyone else was in the car. We screwed up."

"We?"

"You could have passed me a note to remind me."

"Touché."

"Robert, did you really need to go to Spain? Almost all of that stuff is digitized now."

"Not all of it, and I want to find Cabano. He won't return my calls, but I bet I can find him when I get to Seville."

"Why are we bothering with this? Oscar thinks the criminal thing is going to go away, at least in regard to me, and we can just litigate the civil case out 'til it collapses under its own weight."

"Three reasons. One, I think it's important to slay the civil case, too, so that it doesn't come back to haunt you later in some way, including your tenure. Two, the criminal stuff won't truly go away until they figure out for sure who did it."

"And the third reason?"

"I think it will be cool to be in Seville and do the research there. I've been rotting of late, intellectually."

"Okay, but I'm not paying for it."

"Don't worry about that. Anyway, I've really got to go to bed now."

After Robert hung up, I called Oscar, but not before pouring myself a cup of coffee, which was now lukewarm. I needed it because Oscar wasn't going to be happy with me.

He picked up on the first ring. "Hi, Jenna, how's it going?"

"Fine. I just met with Julie. She admits she tore the sheet out of the diary, and it seems she came up to my office with Primo the day he died."

"You shouldn't be investigating the facts yourself."

"I know, but I didn't know if the opportunity to question her and get straight answers would arise again."

"What else did she say?"

"Not much else. But I'm nervous that something more, something we don't know about, is going on. Julie didn't seem sufficiently rattled when I confronted her about tearing a page out of the diary. It's like she knows something we don't."

"I don't think anything else is going on. I'll call the DA and see what I can learn, but I think this is almost over as far as you're concerned. They have no evidence against you."

After that I decided to take care of one piece of business and then take the rest of the day off and go for a bike ride.

The piece of business was retrieving my car. The police had released it, albeit at an impound lot in another part of the city. I drove the Ferrari back to the rental office, returned it and then took a cab to the lot, where I retrieved the car. Except for some leftover fingerprint powder on the steering wheel, it seemed untouched. Then I drove back to the law school, tied my bike to the roof rack and went down to Santa Monica Beach.

It was a glorious day at the beach, the temperature in the 60s. I parked, took my bike down and rode the bike path from Santa Monica to the wetlands of Playa del Rey, riding first by the medical marijuana shops, weight lifters, drum circles and vendors along the oceanfront walk in Venice, and then past the million-dollar beachfront condos on the Marina Peninsula. Then I rode back. All in all, it was about a fifteen-mile round-trip. By the time I finished I was sweaty, exhausted and feeling wonderful. I put the bike back on top of the car, drove home and treated myself to a steak dinner and a bottle of wine.

Just as I was finishing my third glass of wine and telling myself that I wasn't going to have another, Oscar called.

"Hi, Jenna. I have good news."

"Yeah?"

"I talked directly to the DA, and he said they are no longer looking at you. Their focus is on Quinto."

"That's odd, since the diary entry that was torn out said it was Julie who had threatened Primo."

"Right, but don't forget he doesn't know that yet. It's going to take them a couple of days to figure out that there's a page missing and what was on it. The DA mentioned only that the diary makes reference to a threat by Quinto and also said they have other evidence pointing to him."

"Will it change things when they figure out that there's a page missing and what's on it?"

"Only to give them two prime suspects instead of one. But frankly, my friend, if they've ruled you out, this is no longer our problem. The police are going to arrest whomever they're going to arrest, and the DA will indict whomever he's going to indict."

"They've ruled out Tommy, too?"

"Apparently. But, again, this ain't your problem no more."

"You think I'm out of it entirely?"

"No. If they can't arrange a plea bargain, you'll probably be a witness. You'll have to testify about Primo's collapse, and maybe that Julie gave you the diary, so the chain of custody can be established."

"That's great. Thank you, Oscar."

"Don't mention it. I hope we're going to be able to work together on something one of these days when neither you nor Robert is a possible defendant in a criminal matter."

"Me, too. And I want to take you to dinner sometime next week to celebrate."

"We'll do it. Let's talk on Monday and pick a date for that."

"Great. And again, thanks."

After the call ended, I sat and thought about how this would impact the civil suit. If Quinto was indicted, the lawsuit would no doubt quickly go away. If he wasn't, the suit would just wend its way slowly through the courts like most civil suits. And since I didn't have the map, it was hard to see how it could end with anything other than a victory for me. I decided not to worry about it and to have another glass of wine. I thought vaguely about calling Robert back and telling him not to bother to go on to Seville, to just come home. But since he was already in Madrid, that seemed silly. And he'd have a good time, so whatever.

I spent Saturday and Sunday catching up on all the things I'd put on hold the last couple of weeks, including at least starting to think about the exams for my classes, which were due at the registrar's by the end of next week. I slept well Sunday night—without putting the dresser in front of my bedroom door—not only because I was no longer a person of interest in Primo's death but because when I got home I found that Tommy had taken all of his stuff and moved out. He had left his keys on the front desk, along with a note that said, "Thanks for nothing."

CHAPTER 64

Robert Tarza

Week 2—Saturday
Seville, Spain

It had taken me almost twenty hours to get to Madrid. I had left Los Angeles just before 6:00 A.M. on Thursday, changed planes in Miami late Thursday afternoon—there had been no seats left on non-stop flights—and then flown on to Madrid, where I had arrived early in the morning, Madrid time, on Friday.

I hadn't wanted to go immediately to bed—I like to get on local time as soon as possible—so I arranged an early check-in at a hotel near the railroad station, dumped my bags, and, despite my fatigue, spent Friday walking around Madrid. I had spent a semester abroad in Madrid during college, but I hadn't been back since. Spain had changed. When I was there in the late 1960s, it was still a dark, dreary, largely charmless place under the boot of Franco. In what seemed like no time, it had been transformed into a modern country with, at least in Madrid, the hustle and bustle of New York City. Well, okay, it hadn't been no time. It had been forty-four years.

I went to bed mid-evening on Friday, right after a phone call from Jenna in which she chided me about missing something in Quinto's deposition. Then I got up on Saturday morning and took the early high-speed train to Seville. It took only two-and-a-half hours, and I was at my hotel—the Hotel Alfonso XIII, which Tess said was the *only* place to stay in Seville—by 10:00 A.M. The Alfonso was a five-star luxury hotel in the historic center of the city. My room wasn't ready for check in so I left my bags with the valet, obtained a map and a tourist brochure from the concierge and headed out to find the one thing in Seville that I'd always wanted to see—the sarcophagus that held the body, or what was left of it, of Christopher Columbus.

I knew that his tomb was in the Seville Cathedral, which was only about a fifteen-minute walk from my hotel. I found the cathedral easily and then the tomb, which was just inside the front entrance. It consisted of an elaborate sarcophagus, held aloft by four allegorical figures representing the four kingdoms of Spain during Columbus's lifetime. I stopped and looked at it— stared, really—for a couple of minutes. After that I strolled into the cathedral's interior courtyard, the Patio de los Naranjos— the Orange Court—a beautiful space filled with orange trees and with elaborate Moorish tile work all around.

My next stop was the General Archive of the Indies, which was across the street from the cathedral. It was much larger than I had expected and covered the entirety of a huge city block. I've never been much into architecture, but with its red and white stonework, its rectangular windows marching in rows all around the building and its pointed stone towers at each corner, the archive looked vaguely Italianate to me. However, the small booklet the concierge had given me said, when I consulted it, that the building's style was in fact referred to as Spanish Renaissance, and that while the red stuff was stonework, the white stuff was stucco. My mistake was particularly embarrassing since I had long lived in a city that's filled with houses made of stucco. I hoped no one would give me an exam asking me to distinguish between the two architectural styles.

After I had circumnavigated the entire building, I spotted the Café de los Archivos, at which I had agreed to meet my professional archive expert, Gabrielle Muñoz, whom I had contacted via e-mail, introduced by a professor of Spanish literature at UCLA. The café was a small place, with a few tables inside and two wooden ones with matched wooden chairs placed on the sidewalk out front, sheltered by a white awning. The outside walls were covered with colorful tiles.

When I walked up, a woman matching Gabrielle's self-description—tall, blonde and middle-aged—was sitting at one of the sidewalk tables. She was wearing a stylish blood-red dress. I approached the table, and she stood up and said, "You must be Robert Tarza."

"I am," I said, "and you must be Gabrielle Muñoz."

We shook hands, sat down and she said, "Welcome to Seville, Señor Tarza."

"Thank you. But please call me Robert."

"Okay, please call me Gabrielle."

"Are you fluent in English, Gabrielle? If not, I could try out my rusty Spanish."

She laughed. "I'm quite fluent. I was born and grew up in St. Paul, Minnesota."

"Oh. So we can proceed in English."

"Yes, certainly. But before we talk, let's order some coffee."

The waiter appeared, and we ordered coffee and some pastries. When the waiter had departed, she said, "May I ask you a direct question?"

"Sure."

"Are you a treasure hunter?"

"Not exactly. Why?"

"Well, in your e-mail you asked me to arrange for you to look in the archive at some records of a specific seventeenth-century ship—the *Nuestra Señora de Ayuda*. But you didn't say you were looking for information about how to find it, only for crew memoirs."

"Correct."

"That usually would sound like a genealogical project—someone looking to flesh out a long-ago ancestor. Or maybe a history thesis. But in preparing for your visit, I noticed that the particular ship you mentioned sank, and supposedly close to shore. That usually spells treasure hunters, who come here a lot."

"It could be a doctoral history project," I said.

She smiled. "If you'll excuse me, you're a bit old to be pursuing a PhD."

"Sometimes I feel old. But now that I'm here, I'll tell you in more detail what I'm after."

"I'm listening."

"A client of mine is being sued for allegedly stealing a copy of an old Spanish map that shows the exact location of that ship, the *Nuestra Señora de Ayuda*."

"How could such an old map show an exact location?"

"It doesn't. The story is that within the last couple of years someone added data to the copy of the map that lists, by latitude and longitude, the exact location of the ship on the ocean bottom." I figured there was no point in telling her about the two different maps, with supposedly different information on them.

"I see. How did they figure that out?"

"The location was supposedly deduced from a survivor account suggesting that the ship sank somewhere other than the place where it was assumed to have gone down. An assumption that has been around for almost four hundred years."

"Where did people originally think it sank?" she asked.

"Close to shore."

"Well, whether it was close to shore or not, why do you need to see the survivor account—if there is one?"

"Because I think the whole thing is a giant fraud. I don't think there is such a survivor account."

"So you're looking *not* to find something?"

"Something like that."

"As a professional archivist, I can tell you that failing to find it here doesn't mean it doesn't exist."

"How so?"

"Because the system in the sixteen hundreds was that officials in New Spain, as Mexico was called at the time, were supposed to make two copies of everything and send one to the House of Trade—the *Casa de Contratación*—in Seville. The House of Trade controlled all Spanish trade with the Americas and demanded detailed records of everything that was brought to Mexico from the Philippines by the Manila galleons, and records of everything brought back on the return voyage."

"I sense a *but* coming."

"But not absolutely every piece of paper got sent here—there was a lot of fraud and corruption. Some things that actually were sent got lost, a few might be misfiled—there are tens of millions of pages of documents here—and some may have ended up in other archives."

"Which ones?"

"You could always try Mexico."

"Yet it would most likely be here?"

"Yes, and there is one other possibility."

"Which is?"

"Spanish sailors of the seventeenth century had a fairly high rate of literacy, particularly if they were ships' masters. So a survivor account might have been a personal diary or something of that nature and wouldn't have ended up in an official archive at all."

"Where would it have gone instead?"

She shrugged. "Who knows? Into a sea trunk? Stored by the children and the grandchildren and the great-grandchildren and then forgotten? Sold? Centuries-old documents still turn up in antique stores here on occasion."

Our coffee came and we sipped it for a while, and nibbled at sweet rolls while chatting about her career and how she had become a permanent expatriate and a freelance archivist.

Finally, she said, "I've done what I think your e-mails requested. I've talked to the archivists at the General Archive and told them you wanted to see documents related to the Manila galleon *Nuestra Señora de Ayuda*, particularly for the years 1638 and onward. They will have pulled those out for you, and I have asked for an archivist, Cristina Ruiz, who speaks excellent English, to assist you."

"Great."

"You've also reserved more of my time for tomorrow. What do you have in mind for me to do?"

"I was hoping you would help me research this whole issue. Today I'm going to try to plow through some of the documents myself. I know it sounds odd, but if I try myself, even if I fail, I'll have a better understanding of what you do as an expert. That will make it easier for me to explain this to others back in the United States in a litigation setting."

"I see. Interesting. But again, you're expecting not to find a survivor account."

"Correct."

"What will you do if there is one?"

CHAPTER 65

I didn't really know what would happen if I found a survivor account from the sinking of the *Ayuda*. I didn't expect to find one, so I hadn't worried about it, and I was still determined not to worry about it.

After we finished our coffee, Gabrielle took me over to the archive. We walked up the few steps that led to the entrance, a rather plain rectangular doorway with the name—*Archivo General de Indias*—appearing above it in understated script. When I entered I was overwhelmed. The outside of the building is certainly monumental, but not really anything to write home about. The entry hall, by contrast, is a startlingly beautiful room floored in polished polychrome marble. The ceiling is a high, vaulted arch decorated with elaborate, stark white carvings. Down the connecting hallways there is still more marble, laid down in a red-and-black checkerboard. The hallways are lined with tall, walnut-framed bookcases containing what look like hundreds, if not thousands, of bound volumes, presumably archival materials.

"Impressed?" Gabrielle asked.

"Blown away. This place practically shouts, 'I was built by a world empire at its height. Cost was no object.'"

"Not far off," she said. "It was started in 1583 as a place for merchants to meet—the cathedral authorities had become unhappy about their gathering every day in the Orange Court to do business—and completed in 1646."

"I wonder if it had a cost overrun," I said.

She laughed. "No doubt, but the king who authorized it was no longer alive when it was finished, so possibly no one noticed. But let me take you now to the reading room. I've made special arrangements for the archivist to meet us there."

"Is it on the second floor?" I asked, pointing to the marble staircase leading upward.

"No, the reading room and research facilities are in a building next door called *la Cilla*. We can reach it through a tunnel."

We went down a flight, walked through the tunnel, went up a flight and emerged into a room that looked much like a utilitarian reading room in any other archive or library. It had large wooden desks designed to hold six to eight readers at a time, comfortable-looking cloth swivel chairs in blue and, of course, a zillion computers sitting on the desks. Far from the opulence of the archive itself, the room was lit by overhead fluorescents.

Waiting for us was a dark-haired woman I judged to be in her forties, who was introduced to me as Cristina Ruiz.

"I am pleased to meet you, Señor Tarza," Cristina said.

"And I'm pleased to meet you," I responded, "and appreciate your help."

"I am curious, is Tarza a Spanish name?"

"No," I said. "It's Basque. It was originally Istarza but was changed at some point."

There was a small, awkward silence. I had, of course, touched my finger to a live wire of current politics in Spain, since at least some Basques were seeking their independence from Spain. I broke the silence by adding, "But only one of my eight great-grandparents was Basque and, as they say in my country, 'I have no dog in this fight.'"

"That's a nice expression," Cristina said. "In Spanish, I think we would say, '*Nadie me da vela en este entierro.*'"

"Which means?"

"I have no candle in this funeral."

I laughed out loud.

"Well," she said, "in any case, I've talked to *Señora* Muñoz and gathered some documents for you to look at that I think you want. But first I need to explain some of our rules and procedures to you."

"Of course."

"First, you may bring only pencils, pens and paper in here. No markers or highlighters or scissors or sharp objects."

"I understand."

"If you want a document copied, please let me know, and I will have it copied for you. There is a small charge." She handed me a price list.

"We have eighty million documents here, divided into forty-three thousand files. They are well cataloged. Here is a guide in English to the various categories and systems." She handed me another piece of paper and spent several minutes describing the catalog system they used.

"Many of the documents we hold," she said, "have been scanned and digitized. More important, many have been translated into contemporary Spanish, and some have been translated into English."

"Yes," I said, "I know that and I appreciate it. I looked at many before I came here."

"Good," she replied. "Finally, I have gathered for you a set of documents relating to the *Nuestra Señora de Ayuda*, from the year 1638 onward. I assume you know it sank in 1641."

"Yes, I do."

"Okay, then. Just to be sure I have covered what you may want, I started the catalog search in 1630 and ended it in 1660, in case there were investigations of the sinking that took a long time."

"I really appreciate it."

"I've assigned you a spot at one of the desks." She pointed to a wooden desk to the side of the room. "The documents are there for you to look through. Will you be attempting to translate them from the seventeenth-century Spanish?"

"Yes, as best as my rusty modern Spanish will permit."

"I brought you something to help." She handed me a book. "This is a guide to the paleography of seventeenth-century Spanish handwriting and abbreviations. Clerks at the House of Trade and in New Spain used abbreviations all the time, and they are one of the many aspects of Spanish handwriting from that century that give our readers great trouble. The vocabulary has not changed drastically over the years, but the handwriting, and especially the abbreviations, can sometimes make the text almost indecipherable to a modern reader."

"Thank you," I said. "I'll give it a try."

"There are other reference works along the walls," she said. "Most are in Spanish, but a few are in English. Good luck with your research. We have offices around the corner. Please let me know if you need anything. And," she added, "I forgot to mention, if you want to make any of your documents larger when you look at them, you can use the number on the document to see if we have digitized it, using," she pointed, "the computers on the desktops."

Gabrielle had been standing quietly during the whole conversation. When Cristina had departed, she turned to me and said, "I'll leave you for a couple of hours and then return. If you need to reach me before that, here is my cell phone number." She handed me a piece of paper. "Good luck." She said it with a tilt of the head and slightly raised eyebrows that I read as saying *and you'll need it.*

And I did. I spent the next two hours poring over the approximately eighty pieces of paper the archivists had left for me to review. In two hours, even with the help of the book on abbreviations, all I managed to decrypt was the fact that one page was a crew log that listed the shipboard jobs of what looked like fifty or sixty people. What most of the jobs were was utterly unclear to me. The other document I managed to interpret was a cargo manifest that seemed to list how many barrels of water the ship carried when it left port—it was unclear to me which port—in 1636.

Gabrielle returned a couple of hours later and worked with the documents herself for a while. I sat and watched her. By the end of the afternoon she had made good progress and handed me rough translations of about a dozen documents. "If I work all day tomorrow," she said, "I can probably get through most of the rest without much trouble. It's closing time, though, so we really need to go. We can leave the docs here and they'll still be here tomorrow."

"Would you join me for dinner this evening?" I asked.

"Sure," she said. "Where are you staying?"

"At the Alfonso XIII."

"I know a small restaurant near there, so you won't get to bed too late. You're probably still jet-lagged. It opens early by Spanish standards to accommodate tourists."

We walked to the restaurant and had a pleasant dinner, talking mostly about her decision to remain in Spain instead of returning to the United States. I gathered that she liked the diversity of the researchers who washed up at her door from all over the world, seeking the shadows of the past hidden among the archive's eighty million documents—genealogists, treasure hunters, movie producers and historians, among many others.

As we lingered over coffee, I said to her, "Well, there certainly weren't any survivor reports in the documents you decoded today."

"No, but there are many more documents to look at tomorrow."

"I don't know if I want a survivor account to be there or not."

"Don't forget, as I told you this morning, if we don't find it here, there are many more places in the world where it might be lurking."

"Speaking of lurking," I said, "do you know an archivist named Pedro Cabano?"

She stiffened slightly. "Yes, I know him. But I wouldn't call him an archivist."

"What would you call him?"

"A forger."

CHAPTER 66

Week 2—Saturday evening/Sunday
Seville

As we waited for our check, Gabrielle went on to detail Cabano's poor reputation among legitimate archivists and researchers—a reputation of shady dealings, including misleading treasure hunters who couldn't read archaic Spanish, taking a stake in treasure hunts where the value of his services didn't justify his cut and, in one infamous case, actually forging a document from the archive. He was also suspected of stealing archive documents, although that had never been proved, and he had been acquitted on the forgery charge.

She had his address, but she said she'd be surprised if he agreed to talk to me. One of his techniques was to keep people who wanted to see him waiting for days or weeks so they'd think he was important and in demand.

Gabrielle walked me back to my hotel. She promised to return to the archive in the morning—it was open on Sundays to registered researchers—and search herself for a survivor account from the *Ayuda*. We agreed to meet for lunch the next day, at the same place we had had dinner. We said good night, and she started to get into a cab. Right before the valet closed the cab's door, she said, "By the way, he speaks fluent English, but with you he will probably pretend not to."

When I got back to my hotel room, it was almost noon in Los Angeles. I called Marbury Marfan and lucked out: the lawyer I wanted to speak with was in his office. He agreed to put together what I needed and fax it to me at my hotel. I reminded him to put it on A4-size paper, which is the standard size all over Europe.

As I got into bed, I considered whether what I was about to do was legal. I concluded that it wasn't clearly *illegal* and drifted into a sound sleep.

* * *

When I woke up on Sunday morning, the document had arrived. At 10:00 A.M. I called Cabano's number using the hotel's phone system. I didn't expect him to be in on a Sunday but thought I might as well give it a try. When he unexpectedly answered, I hung up. I put the document in my briefcase, grabbed a cab in front of the hotel and was at Cabano's office, which was in the suburbs, in twenty minutes.

I had somehow expected his office to be in a stuccoed, low-rise, classically Spanish building, decorated with bright tile work and surrounded by bougainvillea. Instead, it was in a four-story building that was clad in polished black glass surrounded on all sides by a blacktopped parking lot. Fortunately, there was no building security, so I was able to take the elevator directly to the top floor. I stepped off the elevator into a small lobby that faced four doors, one of which, 402, was Cabano's. There was a button for a bell and I pushed it.

A moment later a dark-complected man with slicked-back dark hair and wearing a bullfighter's shirt and tight black pants opened the door.

"Hi," I said. "I'm Robert Tarza and I need to speak to you."

"*No comprendo.*"

"Excuse me, señor, but I think you *comprende* quite well. You haven't returned my calls and now I'm here, and I'm not leaving until we sit down and talk."

"You're right, señor, I speak English, although not well. I am late for a meeting. You will need to call and make an appointment. I will see you possibly next Friday."

I clicked open my briefcase, extracted the document with a flourish and handed it to him. "This is the draft, in Spanish, of a lawsuit accusing you of conspiracy to defraud investors in connection with the treasure aboard the *Nuestra Señora de Ayuda.*"

He started to page through it.

"You see," I said, "I'm a partner in a large international law firm based in Los Angeles. I have had this lawsuit drafted by our correspondent law firm in Madrid." I named the largest firm in Madrid, which I had looked up on the Net that morning. "I suspect this is something that can be worked out if we can talk. Otherwise I'm going to have that suit filed here in Seville tomorrow morning when the court opens. And then we will talk in a different forum."

He stood reading the lawsuit, which impressed me. Most people would have read only the first page. The truth was, of course, that although Marbury Marfan did have a correspondent firm in Madrid, it was a different one that was much smaller. It was also the case that I had not talked to them. I had, instead, called a Spanish lawyer from our correspondent firm who was doing an exchange internship in Los Angeles for six months, told him the situation and asked him to draft up something that would be appropriate for a Spanish fraud lawsuit, naming Jenna as the plaintiff and Cabano as the defendant.

He looked up from reading the suit. "You have the facts wrong, señor, but we will talk. Come in." He opened the door wider and gestured me inside.

The office was a single large room furnished with a black lacquer desk set on a pedestal, two leather guest chairs and a credenza holding cut-glass bottles filled with dark liquids I presumed were liqueurs. Beneath the credenza were long pullout drawers of the type that usually contain files. The walls of the room were hung all around with color photographs of jewelry encrusted with gold. I assumed they were pictures of treasure that had been recovered from the deep.

I took one of the guest chairs without being asked. Cabano moved up the short step onto the pedestal, sat down in a tall-backed black leather desk chair and stared down at me. "What do you want?" he asked.

"I want the truth about certain things."

"Ask and we will see if I know the truth."

"Fine. I represent a young woman who is being sued by someone named Quinto Giordano. He claims she stole a treasure map from his brother that shows the exact location of a Manila galleon treasure ship called the *Nuestra Señora de Ayuda*. He also claims the location was found by using a survivor account that was found here in Seville, in the archive. We think there is no survivor account and that the map, if it really exists, is a fake."

As soon as I had finished speaking, I realized I had made a mistake.

Cabano folded his hands in front of him and spoke. "The lawsuit says that this woman—Jenna James—is being sued for an investment, not for stealing a map."

"There is an error in the drafting, then. I don't speak Spanish very well, particularly legal Spanish, so I didn't review the paperwork."

He quirked his lips in a sideways smile. "I think this lawsuit is a very clever fake, and you used it to get through my door. I think it will not be filed."

I shrugged.

"You are silent, and I think that means you agree."

"Take it any way you want. I am through your door, and I think you should answer my questions. Is there a survivor account? Is there a map?"

"I suppose there is no harm in answering. You have come a long way to get the answers, and the answers do me no harm. I signed a confidentiality agreement, but they have not paid me, so it is nothing. But I am being impolite. Would you like something to drink?"

"No thank you."

"All right. First, there is a survivor account. You will not find it easily in the archive because it is misfiled."

"I have someone looking for it."

"Who?"

"Gabrielle Muñoz."

"Ah, she is very good. She will maybe find it. We shall see."

"What does the survivor account say?"

"I will show you a copy." He got up, stepped down from the pedestal and walked toward the credenza. He opened one of the long file drawers, bent down and extracted a folder. He stood back up, took a document from the folder and handed it to me.

"This is a copy of the survivor story, or at least the big part of it."

I looked at the document. It was in the same archaic handwriting I had seen the day before in the archive. Which meant I could make out only a word or two of it.

"What does it say?"

"It is written by the navigator of the ship, who survived the disaster." Cabano was standing behind me. He reached over my shoulder and pointed to two words on the page. There is his name, Francisco de Alba."

"What else does the document say?"

Cabano walked back to his desk and sat down again in his chair. "He gives the latitude of the ship when it sank, he estimates the longitude—probably very poorly, because they could not measure it well back then from a ship. And he says how many days he drifted before he came to Catalina Island."

"How many days was that?"

"Ah, there is the thing. The document is at that point smeared. Most people, if they read it, think it is the number 2 there." He pointed at a spot on the page. "They think it says two days. But I asked the original document to be examined with an X-ray scanner, and it says 20 days, not 2."

"Which implies what?"

"If you look at the records from other ships in that area at the time, and weather records from people who lived farther south, you can very roughly estimate the wind speed and water currents and how many kilometers he drifted until he found land."

"What about his own estimate of longitude?"

"You can compare it and you find his own estimate was probably off. That the ship sank at least one hundred kilometers farther west than he estimated."

I looked again at the document. "I see that there's no document number on this. The ones in the archive I looked at yesterday all had document numbers."

"I have taken away the number from the copy so a person cannot find it without the work of finding it."

"So there is no map, there's just a survivor account?"

"Is there a map from 1641? No. Is there a map from now? Anyone can make a map now and put on it the latitude and longitude."

"Do you have a map from now?"

"No."

I realized I wasn't doing a great job of getting the facts, because, really, he was leading the discussion. I needed to regroup.

"Señor Cabano, may I use the restroom?"

"Of course. I will give you the key and point you the way."

CHAPTER 67

Week 2—Sunday
Seville

When I returned from the restroom, I decided to try to take control of the conversation and get to what I most wanted to know: Had the brothers actually done the work needed to find the *Ayuda*, or were they still at the stage of just raising money to find it?

To my surprise, when I got back to the office, Cabano had moved from behind his desk to the other guest chair. He had a map of some kind in his lap. I sat down where I had been sitting before, and he said, "I want to show you something," and then spread out the map so I could see it. It was a map of the California coast.

I realized he was again taking charge but decided to let it roll.

"If you look here," he said, pointing to Santa Catalina Island, "someone who came from a shipwreck to the west and drifted for two days and landed on Catalina came from not too far away." He pointed to a spot not very far off the western shore of

Catalina. "But if he drifted twenty days, then he came from way out here"—he tapped his finger on a spot much farther out into the ocean.

"What about latitude?"

"They knew how to calculate latitude in 1641. They were not so bad at it. And Francisco, he was the navigator. But even if you are mostly right in 1641, without GPS you are not exact. You may be off, north or south, by one hundred kilometers."

"Can you search that much ocean?" I asked. "With so much error in both latitude and longitude?"

"Yes, if you have much money."

"How much?"

He shrugged. "Twenty million euros?"

"Why so expensive? Don't you just run multiple sonar scans across the ocean floor until you find it?"

"Even with the most good side-scan sonar, you must drag your sonar arrays over much ocean bottom because your latitude and longitude, they are not precise. You must search thousands of square kilometers."

"Isn't it just a question of having enough time?"

He sat silent a moment, clearly trying to figure out how to explain the difficulty to me. Finally, he said, "In your briefcase do you have a flashlight?"

"Actually, I do. I always carry one."

"Please may I have it?"

I opened the briefcase, extracted the flashlight and handed it to him.

He walked back to his desk, opened one of the side drawers and took out a ball of white string. He cut off three or four feet of string and tied one end to the pop-up ring at the top of the flashlight.

"If someone tells you a diamond ring is lost on a football field"—I knew he was seeing in his own mind a soccer field instead of a real, American football field, but it didn't matter—"and tells you to find the ring on a black night with the flashlight only, how long will it take?"

"Many hours."

"Now think instead you must hold the flashlight on a string ten thousand feet long and you must search the football field this way." He started walking very slowly around the room, holding the top of the string level with his head and letting the flashlight dangle on the other end, a few inches above the floor.

"Now how long?"

"Longer."

"Now think that you may not look with your eyes, but with only a small lens, three centimeters wide, next to the flashlight. How long?"

"Even longer."

"Now think that on the field there is not only a diamond ring but many bottle tops and other shiny things. Now how long?"

"I see your point. It could take next to forever."

"*Precisamente.* You need, in the end, many people, much expensive equipment, very good GPS and luck."

"Why luck?"

"Because on the ocean bottom there are many things. Rocks. Old ships. Dead whales. Sand bars. They are like the bottle tops. All can look like the ship you look for. A very old ship that is covered much with sand."

"Did the boys ever raise the money to look?"

"No, but they pretend they did, and they pretend that they have found the *Ayuda*. But they have not. It is a fraud to make money."

"How does that work?"

"Señor, if you take money from people and tell them you are taking your boat and looking to recover gold from the bottom of the sea, how will those people know if you truly knew where it was or if you truly went to sea to look?"

"I guess they won't. What would you do instead?"

"You will rent the boat. You will hire the crew. You will sail off. You will go to another port. You will drink with your crew for many, many days. You will pay them something. You will return weeks later. You will—"

I interrupted him. "Tell your investors you tried hard but found nothing."

"*Sí*. And take the money that remains to you from the investors and leave."

"Too bad, so sad," I said.

"What does this mean?"

"It's a way of saying tough shit."

"Ah, I see. I will need to remember this phrase."

"Did you talk to a man named Aldous Hartleb?"

"Yes."

"What did you tell him?"

"I told him more or less the truth."

"Which part of the truth was *more*?"

"That there is no real map. And that they did not find the exact location of the ship."

"What part of the truth did you not tell him?"

"The part that I cannot tell you." He grinned.

"Can you give me a hint?"

"Perhaps there are in the archive other documents that are helpful to find this ship."

I decided he was simply fishing to be paid to do more research and moved on.

"Why did you tell him any of the truth?"

"He was with big investors. I did not wish to end with a lawsuit like the one you brought this morning. Except not fake."

"There is no map at all?"

"The boys have found is my guess some old map of the time. But it is worthless, because you must place on this map the information about where is the ship." He shrugged his shoulders and tossed his hands in the air, as if what he was saying was so obvious as to hardly be worth mentioning.

"Information about longitude and latitude?"

"Yes, yes. This is what they did. Numbers they made up."

"And the map?"

He shrugged again. "Found in the archive? Bought here in the antique store? Bought on the Internet?"

I had learned what I came to learn and decided to end the interview.

"You have been most helpful, señor, and now I must go. May I have my fake lawsuit back?"

"With pleasure," he said. "But before you go, I must also ask, how are the boys?"

"One of them is dead."

"How did he die?"

"He was poisoned."

"This is sad. Which one?"

"Primo."

"Did Quinto kill him?" he asked.

"I don't know. Why do you think Quinto is the one who killed him?"

"Primo was the nice boy. Quinto was not so nice."

"What is not nice about Quinto, Señor Cabano?"

"He is mean."

"Did Quinto threaten Primo?"

"The two, they always threatened each other. It meant nothing."

"Well, again, I don't know yet who killed Primo. But I suppose it's at least possible that Quinto did it."

"I now must go," he said. "To a meeting. Do you want a copy of the document? I have many copies."

"Yes."

He went back to the drawer in the credenza, opened it, took out a different folder and extracted a piece of paper from it. He sat down again in the other guest chair and handed the document to me.

"You have a lot of them," I said.

"When the boys tried to sell this investment, they sent many people to visit me for this document."

"Can I see the original?"

"It is still in the archive, of course."

"How do I know, señor, that this document is not a forgery? That there is nothing at all in the archive?"

He shot out of his chair and threw his arms in the air. "*Dios mio!* I cannot believe this *calumnia*—I do not know the word in English—is still said."

"Slander, I think you mean."

"Yes, slander. Because they are not true, these things people say. These other researchers, they are jealous because I find things they cannot."

"Slander is hard to deal with."

"Did Gabrielle say this to you?"

There was no point in getting Gabrielle in trouble. "No."

He walked to the door of his office and stood there. "I must go, Señor Tarza, and so must you."

I put the document he had given me in my briefcase, stood up and walked to the door. I extended my hand. He looked at it as if it was a dead fish, and it seemed for a second that he was going to decline to shake. Then he apparently thought better of it, put out his own hand and shook mine.

"*Adiós*, Señor Tarza," he said.

"*Adiós*, Señor Cabano."

I took the elevator down to the lobby and realized on exiting the building that I hadn't called a cab. I spotted a bus stop nearby and decided to try the bus. Eventually one came along, and I asked the driver, in my still rusty Spanish, if it went to the *centro de la ciudad*—downtown. It did. I got on and slowly made my way back to my hotel.

In my hotel room I studied the document Cabano had given me. I could no more know if it was a forgery than I could be sure my own birth certificate was real, even with its fancy seal. Perhaps Gabrielle would be able to tell.

CHAPTER 68

At lunch Gabrielle reported that she had been able to find only a few documents about the *Ayuda* in the period from 1638 to 1648, the time frame she and I had agreed upon for her initial search. They were mostly crew manifests, records of port calls and a cargo manifest for the ship's outbound trip from Mexico to Manila in 1640. But she had found no cargo manifest for the return trip to Acapulco. She said there was also a brief report to the House of Trade that the ship had sunk in 1641 on its return voyage, but that it contained no details.

She handed me a thin folder of documents. "These are copies of what I've found so far, although I still have more work to do."

"Did you," I asked, "find anything resembling a survivor account?"

"No, nothing."

"Perhaps not surprising," I said.

"Did you see Cabano?" she asked.

"Yes," I said, "he agreed to see me."

"I'm surprised."

"I tricked him, Gabrielle."

"Congratulations. He deserves to be tricked himself from time to time."

"I don't feel good about it, actually, but it worked. In any case, he gave me this document, which is supposedly a survivor account by the navigator of the *Ayuda*." I handed it to her.

She studied the document for several minutes, and I could tell she was attempting to read it, slowly interpreting the archaic handwriting. After a while she handed it back to me. "I would have to spend much more time with it, but it seems to be an account by the navigator of drifting for two days after the *Ayuda* sank. It's dated in 1641. It says he was dying of thirst and hunger by the time his small raft made land. He thanks God and Our Lady, by which I assume he means Our Lady of Guadalupe, for his survival."

"Is there a smudge next to the number *2*?"

"Let me see it again."

I handed it back to her.

"There's a small black spot next to the number. I wouldn't call it a smudge. Why?"

"He says that if you X-ray it, you can see that it actually says that he drifted for twenty days, not two."

She snorted through her nose. "Excuse my French, but bull-shit. The man who wrote this document—even assuming it's real—says he was floating on some kind of raft he roped together from timbers of the ship, or at least I think that's what it says. The word he uses is archaic, but I think it's a word that means raft. I'll have to look it up. So if that's correct, he wouldn't have had any food or water, or not very much, anyway."

"And after twenty days," I said, "with no food or water, exposed in the open ocean, he would have been dead."

"Yes, or as people like to say around here, *precisamente*."

Just then, in an odd coincidence, the waiter brought the food we had ordered, along with a large bottle of water, and we ate for a while and talked of other things. Then I brought the conversation back to the document.

"So you don't trust the document I got from Cabano?"

"No, and even if it does say twenty days if you use an X-ray, the document doesn't have an archive catalog number on it."

"He said he removed the catalog number from the copies he made so no one else could find it because it was misfiled. And still is, I guess."

"Did he say in what section or folder it was misfiled?"

"No, but I didn't ask him."

"Well, there are a couple of logical possibilities where such a misfiling might take place, and I'll look in those folders, but I think it's likely a lie. After all, there are eighty million pieces of paper over there. So saying it was misfiled, without anything more, is like saying a boat is on the ocean."

"I know. But let me ask you, does the archive keep a record of who checks out which documents when?"

"Yes, but those records are strictly private."

"Are they so private you can't ask a friend to let you have a look?"

"Europeans take privacy restrictions much more seriously than Americans. If I were even to ask, I might lose my privileges at the archive."

"Well, if you think of any way to find that out without putting your livelihood on the line, please let me know."

"I will."

"You know, Gabrielle, there's one thing that bothers me about the idea that that document is a forgery."

"Which is?"

"Well, if you were going to forge a document that suggested someone had drifted on the ocean for twenty days so you could later use the forgery to point to the supposed location of a fake shipwreck site, why would you write in the wrong number of drift days—two—and then have to argue that your fake document really says twenty days?"

"I have no idea," she said, "but it's an interesting point."

"And what's more," I said, "if you were going to say he drifted for twenty days and lived, why would you put the guy on a roped-together raft with no food or water?"

"Again, I don't know."

When we had finished lunch, Gabrielle asked, "What are you going to do now?"

"I'm thinking of going off the grid for a couple of days."

"I'm not sure what you mean."

"When I was a young associate in my law firm, I was burned-out after a big trial and took an actual vacation of two whole weeks. I went to Greece with no hotel reservations. I just hopped from island to island as the mood moved me. There were no cell phones and no Internet, and because I had no fixed itinerary, there was no way for anyone to reach me. I loved it."

"And now?"

"I can be reached every minute of every day in three or four different ways. It's like living in a digital blizzard."

"I don't think there's a lot you can do about that."

"Well, I think I've found out what I came to Seville to find out, so I'm going to call a colleague in Los Angeles, tell him what I've learned and fax him the supposed survivor document."

"And then?"

"Then I'm going to take the train to Madrid, check into a small hotel, turn off my cell phone and my computer and not turn either one back on until I get to Los Angeles."

"Which will be when?"

"I reserved a seat on an early afternoon plane on Wednesday that will get me into LA late afternoon LA time that same day. I'll have two full days to myself in Madrid. Maybe I'll go to the Prado. Or maybe I won't. Who knows?"

CHAPTER 69

Jenna James

Week 3—Monday
Los Angeles

I was in my office, sitting at my desk, continuing to catch up on some work. I had had a wonderful, largely stress-free weekend. Aldous had called and left a few messages, but I hadn't called him back. He was apparently returning on Wednesday. I'd share my good news with him then.

My phone rang. I saw that it was the dean. I sighed and picked it up. He was probably calling again about postponing my tenure application. He'd probably not yet gotten the word that I was no longer the focus of the police investigation.

"Good morning, Jenna."

"Good morning, Dean Blender. What can I do for you?"

"I wanted to talk to you regarding delaying your tenure decision."

"I'm glad you called about that because I've decided not to delay it. I can set out the reasons now if you'd like, but if you'd prefer I'll send a formal letter."

"Actually, I think the decision may now be out of your hands."

"Why?"

"Because Professor Broontz has filed a formal grievance against you under the Faculty Code of Conduct pursuant to both Senate Bylaws 335 and 336. She apparently couldn't make up her mind which one really fit, so she doubled down."

"That's ridiculous. I haven't done a thing to her. I hardly ever even see her."

"She's contending that by murdering Primo Giordano and stealing his map you've, to quote her charge, 'engaged in intentional disruption of functions or activities sponsored by or authorized by the University, to wit teaching.'"

"I'm sorry, what? I haven't interrupted her teaching. I haven't even been to her class. And when she came to mine, she was the one who was disruptive. And I haven't murdered anyone or stolen anything."

"She claims the fact that you allegedly killed a student and so forth has—and I'm quoting again from her grievance—'created a frightening atmosphere in the school that has brought all faculty under suspicion and thereby disrupted teaching.'"

"That's ridiculous, too. Is she seeking some sanction?"

"Yes, that you be dismissed."

"Can she do that?"

"Probably not as an individual faculty member. But I could."

"Under what theory?"

"As the dean, I could bring a disciplinary action under Bylaw 336 based on the same facts. And then the hearing on both her grievance and my charge could be combined. I'd be moving to terminate your contract early on the theory that you killed a student and/or stole his property."

I put the phone on speaker so I could type with both hands and try to look up the rules as we were talking. They were voluminous. I started to scroll through them to try to get some context for the discussion.

"Jenna, are you taking down what I'm saying? I hear keys clicking."

"No. I'm trying to look up the rules myself."

"Okay, because if you're taking notes, I'm going to have to be more cautious about what I'm saying."

"As if you haven't been enormously cautious anyway."

"I'm trying to be candid without disclosing confidences."

"Dean, have you ever read *Alice in Wonderland*?"

"Of course."

"Do you remember what the Cheshire Cat said to Alice?"

"Not precisely."

"He said, 'Everyone's mad here.'"

"Jenna, I can understand how you might think this is all insane, but you have to admit that having a faculty member who's suspected of murdering a student, who hasn't been exonerated and about whom the investigation is 'still open,' is pretty disruptive for a law school. It might even impact our application and acceptance rates and thus our standing in *U.S. News & World Report*'s rankings of the best law schools."

"The police investigation may still be open, but not about me. I've been exonerated."

"That's not how I understand it."

"All right, let me just try to imagine for a moment that we haven't gone down the rabbit hole. What happens now, Dean Blender?"

"I think if you take a leave of absence until this is all cleared up, I could dissuade Professor Broontz from pursuing her grievance, and I certainly wouldn't do anything myself. Two years would probably be best."

"No."

"It's a good solution, Jenna. It seems likely that within an academic year the answer to who murdered Giordano—assuming he didn't kill himself—and what happened to the map will be resolved, and you can come back. Plus all the students who are here now will be gone."

"No."

"I'm also sure I can arrange a research grant of some kind so you can return to Florence and do more research on old documents."

"It was Seville, which is in an entirely different country, but in any case the answer is still no."

"I think you're making a mistake."

"Let me ask you a question, Dean. Do you think there's actually a scary atmosphere in the school?"

"The charge says 'frightening atmosphere,' but I guess the way I'd put it is that there has been some disquiet."

"I haven't noticed it."

"You wouldn't because no one is going to confront you about it. I mean, have you noticed any faculty dropping by your office lately? Or calling you up to arrange a lunch?"

"No, but . . ."

"Please consider my offer."

"I've considered it and rejected it."

"Then we'll have to go to the next step."

"Which is what, a hearing before the Committee on Privilege and Tenure?"

"No, here at UCLA we have something called the Charges Committee, where grievances have to go first. They're much more informal than P&T. They act something like a grand jury. If they think there's probable cause that the grievance is valid, they pass it on to P&T, which holds its own, more formal hearing."

"Does the Charges Committee also consider whether the *type* of charge is even a valid one for them to consider? I mean, are they going to explore whether I killed him and stole the map or just whether there's been disruption on the campus, even if the charge is bogus?"

"I think they consider whatever they want to consider. Like I said, it's very informal."

"This is all insane, and you could put an end to it if you wanted to, *Matt*."

"I don't think so. I've looked at the rules and consulted counsel, and I don't think there's any way to just dump Professor Broontz's grievance in my wastebasket if she wants to push forward with it. The committee may dismiss it out of hand, but that's up to them."

"You could try to persuade Professor Broontz to withdraw her grievance."

"She's already met with the required prehearing counselor, who couldn't dissuade her. And then she met with me, and I failed, too."

"There must be another way."

"Not that I can find."

"I think there would be if you really wanted to find one."

"That is so untrue."

I hung up without saying good-bye. One of the things that's unsatisfying about cell phones is that you can't slam the receiver down in anger. I looked around for a sheet of paper, found one and began folding it. When I finished—I got it folded over five times, with reasonably crisp edges—I went online, ordered a copy of *Alice's Adventures in Wonderland* and had it sent to the dean via overnight delivery, with a fancy gift card that said "NO."

CHAPTER 70

I called Oscar and confirmed that he was in his office. "I'm coming over there," I said. I listened. "No, right now. I'll tell you when I get there. There have been some developments. I'm too angry right now to discuss it. I'll cool down on the ride over."

I went to Lot 3, got in my car and headed to Venice, trying hard to obey the speed limit. Before I left I had printed out the University Academic Personnel Manual, the bylaws of the Academic Senate and the special procedures for hearings before the UCLA Charges Committee. Running collectively to hundreds of pages, they sat in a loose stack beside me, sloshing around on the seat as I accelerated and decelerated.

Oscar answered the door only a few seconds after I knocked. He was a bit more formally dressed than I had been used to seeing him of late. He was wearing a very nice white dress shirt and a red tie of an obviously expensive make.

"Are you okay, Jenna? You didn't sound like yourself on the phone."

"I'm not myself. I'm living inside some kind of insane asylum."

"Do you want a drink?"

"Yes, but I'm not going to have one."

"All right, take a seat at the table and tell me what's happened."

I sat down, tossed the stack of paper on the table and explained it to him.

When I was done, he said, "Show me the key portions of these various regulations."

"Do you have some Post-its?"

"I used to avoid them as too modern, but yes." He rummaged in a drawer under the table and handed me a pad of purple Post-its.

"Purple, Oscar?"

"Nice color, eh?"

"Sort of."

I sat for a few minutes, while Oscar watched, marking off the various sections of the rules I thought applied. I handed the pages to him and he, in turn, began to read what I had marked.

"Do you have a coffeepot?" I asked.

"Sure. It's on the counter in the kitchen. The coffee is up above, in the first cabinet to the right of the sink. It's probably not up to your standards."

"Anything will do."

While Oscar reviewed the documents, I made coffee and watched it drip into the pot for a while, then decided that standing there was too much like being an addict. I went back to the big room with the table.

Oscar slapped down the last of the documents, indicating he'd read what he wanted to read. "Obviously," he said, "this Broontz person is a stalking horse for the dean."

"What makes you say that?"

"These rules aren't designed for the type of dispute that's going on here. Indeed, one part of them seems to say that they're not to be used to determine criminal behavior."

"Right, so why does that make Professor Broontz a stalking horse?"

"I mean only that if the dean wanted to put a stop to this, he could no doubt tell Professor Broontz to cool it, he'd deal with it some other way. Or he'd call the chair of this so-called Charges Committee and tell him to get around to this issue sometime after the Olympics come to Los Angeles again."

"That's not how the university works."

"Not how it works on paper. I'm betting that's how it works in reality."

"I really don't know. Up until now I haven't had to deal with any of this stuff."

Oscar got up and began to pace back and forth in front of the windows, which looked out across several blocks of rooftops to the ocean. "Jenna, do you think there has actually been disruption at the law school as a result of this?"

"I don't really think so. I mean, I'm sure people gossip about it. Who wouldn't? But there's really not very much information out there. There hasn't been much in the papers, the coroner's report hasn't been issued and there's been no memorial service for Primo."

"What about the police investigation? Has that been disruptive?"

"I don't know who they've interviewed, so maybe they've talked to a lot of people and that's generated gossip."

"Do you think parents have been calling the dean?"

"Not likely. We're not a college, and most of these kids are at least in their early to midtwenties."

Oscar stopped pacing, leaned back against the windowsill and folded his arms. "What do *you* think we should do, Jenna?"

"I think we should go to court and try to enjoin this procedure."

"On what grounds?"

"I haven't figured that out yet."

"Well, even if you do figure it out, I think it's gonna fail. Courts don't like to intervene in the internal affairs of universities, especially when you haven't exhausted every step you can take within the university."

"Like what, Oscar?"

"Like going through with this hearing process. A court is likely to say, 'Well, this Charges Committee is like a grand jury. You don't even know if they're going to indict you and pass it on to Privilege and Tenure. So you don't know if this is really going to end your job. Come back if and when that happens.'"

"You're probably right."

"So, my friend, I think we should instead treat this as an opportunity."

I cocked my head. "To do what?"

"If I read these rules correctly, Jenna, we get to call witnesses in your defense, right?"

"Apparently."

"And we can call anyone we want?"

"I guess. Or at least anyone who'll come. There's no subpoena power."

"So, unlike in your usual criminal case," he said, "we can use this to do discovery, not only on the crime—of which you're no longer suspected—but on the missing map suit, which is the only thing still pending against you. We can address the issue of who besides you could have stolen that map."

"Since you think the police aren't pursuing me anymore, Oscar, shouldn't we just let the whole thing lie?"

"That's a reasonable question and a good one," he said.

"Well," I responded, "while you ponder the answer to it, I'm going to see if the coffee is finished. Do you want some?"

"No."

"Be right back." I went into the kitchen and looked for the largest mug Oscar owned. I found an oversize one in the cupboard to the left of the stove, filled it to the brim and took it back with me to the big room.

"Welcome back," Oscar said. "I see you've acquired a supply of your drug of choice."

"I have. Now what about my question?"

"Right. You asked should we just let it lie. I don't think so."

"Why not?"

"The police have said they're leaving the investigation open, which means you're always going to be at least slightly at risk. Broontz is therefore right on one level. This will disrupt the life of Professor Jenna James—that's you—for a long time unless and until they find the real killer. Who's going to give you tenure while there's any suspicion at all hanging over you?"

Oscar was right. Indeed, just as he said it, my cell phone beeped that an e-mail marked urgent had arrived. I clicked it open. It was from the dean and said that with the approval of the chancellor he was "suspending my tenure application indefinitely pending further notice." It cited as authority numerous provisions of the Academic Personnel Manual and told me how to appeal his decision if I didn't like it.

"What was that?" Oscar asked.

"A love note from the dean. Saying my tenure application is suspended. Let's go with your strategy. Where do we start?"

"Let's look up which faculty members are on this Charges Committee."

I put my notebook computer on the table and looked up the current members of the UCLA Charges Committee as Oscar stood behind me. There were twelve of them listed.

"I don't assume," Oscar said, "that all twelve of them sit and hear each matter."

"No, the rule says only that there have to be at least three faculty on each case. It also says they can't be from the same department as the person who's filing the charge or the person who's charged. So the two law profs on this list won't be among the three. Maybe the chair of the committee gets to pick the others."

"And the chair," Oscar said, "is a medical school professor named Rex Wing." He reached out to the touch pad and clicked on Wing's CV. "Wow, he's eighty years old."

"Maybe he's a retired faculty member," I said.

Oscar peered at the screen. "No, apparently not. He's still actively practicing medicine. And he's a proctologist."

"How appropriate," I said.

CHAPTER 71

Oscar pointed to one of the papers lying on the table, which was stickered with one of the purple Post-its. "If you look at Rule 62"—he stabbed at it with his finger—"it says that the Charges Committee procedure is informal."

"Right."

"Let's call Dr. Wing. See what he has to say."

"Seriously?"

"Seriously. I regard systems of rules as things to be used and manipulated to the benefit of my client. If the rules call for informality, fine. I can work with that." As he said it, he unbuttoned his collar, pulled his tie askew and rolled up his sleeves. "Wing's direct-line number," he continued, "is right here on his CV."

Oscar punched the speakerphone button on the handset and dialed Dr. Wing's number. It was picked up on the second ring.

"Rex Wing here," the voice said. It was a rich baritone, betraying not a hint of age.

"Dr. Wing, this is Oscar Quesana. I'm the attorney for Professor Jenna James. I have my speakerphone on. Professor James is sitting here beside me."

"Charmed to meet you both, Mr. Quesana. What can I do for you?"

"Professor James has just received from the law school dean a copy of the grievance—or charge, I'm not sure exactly which it is—that was filed by Professor Broontz."

"I just got that grievance yesterday myself. Peculiar one. Not the dean. The charge."

"Well, since the procedure is informal, I wondered if I could come over and talk with you about the whole thing."

"No reason why not. Bring Professor James with you, if you like."

"I may well do that."

"Out of curiosity, Mr. Quesana, is your goal to get the Charges Committee to dismiss the whole thing?"

"That would work."

"We might just be willing. The entire matter sounds like something to be handled by the police. Of course, it's also up to the other two professors who are going to be on the panel."

"Do you know yet who they'll be?"

"Oh, sure. There aren't many available right now. Several of our roster are off campus on sabbatical, and we have to ex-out the two law profs. That leaves us with five people to choose from, in addition to me. I've already put in a call to two of them—who were chosen by lot—and they've both accepted."

"Who are they?"

"One is Paul Trolder. He's an economist. Very good insights, that guy. And easygoing. I like my panels to be laid-back."

"And the other?"

"Samantha Healey. She's a philosopher. Kind of an odd duck, that one. Never says much. Mutual friends tell me she thinks deep thoughts. Maybe she does, but at the very least she doesn't get in the way of smooth sailing."

"Thanks," Oscar said, as I madly looked up Trolder and Healey to see what I could learn about them.

"Well, Mr. Quesana, when would you and Professor James like to come over and visit with me? I think a prompt sit-down with both sides would be useful in getting into the bone and sinew of this whole thing."

"How about tomorrow, Doctor?"

"Hmm. I have procedures scheduled tomorrow and the next day. How about in about an hour? I'm just doing billing today, and a whole bunch of other boring administrative garbage that takes me away from both teaching and the practice of medicine. This sounds a heap more interesting."

I looked at Oscar and started vigorously shaking my head back and forth in a big no.

"I think that sounds perfect, Dr. Wing. We'll try to be there in about an hour. Can you tell us which building you're in and your office number?"

He told us and then hung up.

"Hey," I said, "I was trying to signal you to say no about meeting today. It's way too early."

"Sometimes, Jenna, clients don't get to make all the decisions. Doing it now gets *informal* rolling. We may never get another chance, and I'm going to take advantage of it. I'm planning to use informality in a proctological fashion on your friend Professor Broontz, and on your dean as well."

An unladylike image popped into my head but quickly dissipated.

Oscar went back to his chair at the end of the table while I worked the keyboard. After a few minutes, I said, "Oscar, I've looked up the details on all three of those people. Trolder, the economist, has a CV that's mostly just his economics articles over the years. Nothing relevant to law or dispute resolution. No picture. I'd guess from his CV that he's in his fifties. U of Chicago undergrad, grad work at Yale."

"High-floor universities."

I ignored the comment and said, "He doesn't, so far as I can find, have a Facebook page."

"What about Healey, the philosopher?"

"Lots of philosophy articles on her CV, including one called—get this—*Deep Philosophy among Indigenous Tribes in the Basin of the Orinoco*. There's a fuzzy picture on her Facebook page of her standing next to a guy who's decked out in feathers. I'm guessing she's about my age, but it's hard to say what she actually looks like because she's wearing baggy tropical fatigues and high jungle boots and most of her head is covered with some kind of mosquito thing. Can't say how old the guy beside her is, although he's not wearing much beyond a loincloth and the feathers."

Oscar got up again and came around to stand behind me so he could see my computer screen. "Huh," he said, "that's really something. The feathered guy must be the philosopher. I gotta read that article."

"Seriously?"

"Hell yes. When I'm in front of a new judge, Jenna, I try to read everything they've written. Especially if it's weird. Most judges actually wanted to be something else, and if you can find out what that something was by reading their writings, you can get ahead with them. What did you find out about our chairman, Dr. Wing?"

"He's been connected to UCLA like forever. He did his undergrad work and med school there, then his internship, residency and fellowship. He started as an assistant prof right out of the fellowship and is still here as a full professor of medicine."

"So Dr. Wing's been at UCLA since he was eighteen."

"Seems like," I said, "and it also mentions that he went to University High School, which is in West LA, about a mile-and-a-half away as the crow flies."

"Does it say anything about his tenure on the Charges Committee?"

"It says he's done various tours on both that one and on the Committee on Privilege and Tenure and has served a total of twenty-seven years on one or the other. What do you make of that, Oscar?"

"He's a judge."

"Meaning what?"

"Meaning he's a guy who gets off on being an elder in the tribe, and UCLA is his tribe."

"Is that good or bad?"

"Jenna, if we can persuade him that the whole charge against you is crazy and bad for UCLA, he'll want to get it dismissed and taken somewhere far away, where no one will ever hear of it again. Perhaps he'll ask Professor Healey to take it with her the next time she goes south and suggest she bury it somewhere along the shores of the Orinoco."

"You're awfully upbeat for you, Oscar."

"Well, I should also have mentioned the other possibility."

"Which is?"

"Dr. Wing will conclude the solution is to have you buried along the banks of the Orinoco."

CHAPTER 72

Before we left to see Dr. Wing, I suggested to Oscar that we get in touch with Robert and bring him up-to-date. "Perhaps," I said, "he's found something in Seville that will be useful."

"Well," Oscar responded, "he called me yesterday from Seville—it must have been very late evening his time—and said he'd learned some useful things, and he wanted to tell me what he'd found. But I was kind of busy, so I suggested that since you were no longer the focus of the criminal investigation, he just wait until he got back."

"He agreed to that? That's not like him."

"He did. But he did fax me an archaic Spanish document from 1641 that he got in Seville. I speak Spanish, but I can't make out the handwriting. I'll give you a copy, and we can talk to him about it when he gets back."

"When will he be back?"

"Late Wednesday I think is what he said."

"Maybe we could call him, now that this idiocy with Greta Broontz has arisen, and see if what he found out will be useful now."

"I don't think we can, Jenna. He said he was going to Madrid for two days of R&R and was going off the grid."

"Off the grid?"

"He's turned off his cell phone and his computer and didn't tell me where he's staying."

"That's ridiculous," I said. "He's a lawyer with an active case. He must be entering a second childhood or something."

"Could be. But it is what it is."

"Maybe Tess knows how to reach him."

"No. When you called me so upset, I figured something bad had happened and that we ought to plug Robert into the conversation. So I called Tess right before you got here to see if she knew how to reach him. He told her the same thing—he's off the grid until his plane lands here late on Wednesday."

"Shit."

"She also said she had an important lead, but it was 'not yet at an end.'"

"On what?"

"On your case. I think that was her way of saying she hadn't quite nailed it down yet."

"I can't imagine what she could find, but I guess we'll find out later what it is."

"Jenna, let's go see Dr. Wing."

Which is what we did.

We found Dr. Wing's office without too much difficulty, considering that it was inside one of the dozens of medical buildings, many connected by tunnels or pedestrian bridges, that festoon the southern portion of the UCLA campus. Some of the buildings are such rabbit warrens that new interns have been known to disappear for hours trying to find their way. We knocked on the door—there was no secretary or receptionist outside his office—heard someone say "come in" and went in.

When we entered it was clear we weren't in a clinical office where Dr. Wing saw patients but in his professorial office. The walls, like those of most professors, were filled with books. Several shelves, however, held unrecognizable medical instruments that looked ominous. There was also a large whiteboard on one wall, with a tray running along the bottom filled with dry-erase markers in various colors.

"Good afternoon," Dr. Wing said. He was lying half-prone in a large, red leather recliner with the footrest up. As a result, it was a little hard to tell how tall he was, but I would've guessed well over six feet. He had a large nimbus of fine gray hair. He was wearing a long-sleeved, checked sport shirt in blue, dark khakis and black loafers.

"You'll excuse me," he continued, "if I don't heave these old bones out of this chair to greet you, but it's been a wearisome day. As you must have guessed, given the name on the door, I'm Dr. Wing, but no title's necessary. Just Rex will do," he said, looking at me, "for a fellow member of the faculty. And you get to ride along on that informality, Mr. Quesana."

"Just plain Oscar will be fine, too."

"And I'm Jenna," I said.

"Good, good. Plop yourselves down on that couch there." He pointed to a black leather couch, much cracked from long wear, which looked to me as if it had been around since Dr. Wing started at UCLA as an undergraduate.

We sat ourselves down, as instructed. The couch was so huge I felt swallowed up in it. My feet actually failed to touch the ground unless I sat far forward toward the front edge. I suspected the couch was installed before women were much in evidence in the medical school.

"Well," Dr. Wing said, "would either of you like something to drink?"

Oscar politely declined, and although I would have loved a cup of coffee, I decided to decline, too. I was anxious to get to the heart of the matter.

"I assume," Dr. Wing continued, "that you two have come to try to persuade me that we shouldn't pass this case on to the Committee on Privilege and Tenure, or P&T, as we call it."

Oscar responded. "At bottom, that's right."

"Good, good. Well, I just got off the phone with the complainant, Professor Broontz. I tried to suggest to her—gently, of course—that the whole thing seemed a tad premature, that the better part of valor might be to put this matter on ice and let the police investigation proceed awhile. She was quite adamant that she didn't want to do so. If she persists in her adamancy, we'll be forced to confront the issues here."

"Well," Oscar said, "that's actually okay with us. Professor James—Jenna—doesn't want this hanging over her head."

Dr. Wing looked at me. "Jenna, do you want to speak for yourself here? It's fine, of course, to bring your lawyer—great American right and all that—but I like to think that these proceedings are more like a conversation among friends than some sort of adversarial proceeding, all tangled up with law and lawyers."

While he was finishing his pitch for me to, in effect, ditch Oscar for now, I thought about how we should respond. On one level, the old let's-just-talk-among-friends thing was attractive. On the other hand, it was a trap. No one at UCLA was currently my friend.

"No, Dr. Wing," I replied, "I'm really quite comfortable having Oscar speak for me. He's not just my lawyer but an old and trusted friend."

"All right, then," Dr. Wing said, "let's get to the heart of it. And do call me Rex, please. I meant that."

"What do you see as the heart of it, Rex?" Oscar asked. "At the heart of it is the question of whether Jenna killed someone."

His statement kind of hung there in midair, reminding me what this was all about. "I didn't kill anyone," I said. Why exactly I had the need to reiterate that every time it came up was unclear to me. Surely everyone understood that I denied it. And yet I needed to say it.

"We agree with that, Rex," Oscar responded. "One hundred percent."

Dr. Wing unlimbered himself from his chair and lumbered to the whiteboard. The guy was huge. Six foot six perhaps, and at least two hundred and fifty pounds. As I watched him, I wondered if his CV had left off some kind of football career as an undergrad.

"So," Dr. Wing said, picking up a marker from the tray, "on the one hand, we have an unsettling death, likely a homicide." He wrote MURDER in large red letters in the middle of the board, dropped the red marker back into the tray and picked up a blue one. "And over here, we have a supposed disruption of campus tranquility." He wrote DISRUPTION in very small blue letters to the right of MURDER.

He tossed the marker high into the air, watched it turn several times and caught it perfectly on its return. "And you can understand, certainly, how murder might cause campus disruption." He drew a quick, slashing arrow from MURDER to DISRUPTION.

He dropped the blue marker back into the tray and turned to face us full on. "And so, class, are we going to try to focus on whether there's a disruption? No, not very much, because in a university who cares if a professor causes disruption? The very nature of the university is to be disruptive. No, the question is what has *caused* the disruption."

I had the sense we were watching a master teacher who probably held his students in thrall.

"We couldn't agree more," Oscar said.

"And would you agree, Oscar," Dr. Wing asked, "that if Jenna caused the disruption by murdering her student, that's a problem for this great university?"

"Of course."

"So the focus of our inquiry must be, must it not, whether Jenna killed her student?"

"Exactly," Oscar said.

"And yet," Dr. Wing said, "how in the world does our small committee, or P&T, for that matter, if we send it on to them with a finding of probable cause, have the resources, the expertise or the acumen to investigate a murder?"

There was a small silence in the room. The obvious answer was that the committee had no business at all investigating a murder.

Finally, Oscar asked, "What's the bottom line?"

"The bottom line, Oscar, is that if Jenna doesn't want to go forward with this, I'm sure my two colleagues on this committee, Professor Trolder and Professor Healey, will be easily persuaded to rule that this is not an appropriate case for us to consider. Is that what you want?"

"No," Oscar said. "If we ask you to do it that way, the matter will be over for you, but not for Jenna. Her tenure decision will still be delayed, and the cloud over her head will remain. And that's true even though the police no longer suspect Jenna of the murder."

"But apparently," Dr. Wing responded, "that information has not reached other people on the campus, particularly not Professor Broontz."

"Apparently not," Oscar said.

"Just to be clear, then," Dr. Wing said, "you want us to consider the crime, not just whether there's disruption from the allegation."

"Yes. Jenna didn't do it. And there's no evidence that she did."

"All right," Dr. Wing said, "we just need to discuss where and when we're going to do this crazy thing." He chuckled. "You know, this reminds me of the start of a joke."

"What joke is that?" Oscar asked.

"Well, I don't know the punch line, but it's one of those jokes that begins, 'A doctor, an economist and a philosopher walk into a bar.'"

I sat there and thought to myself that the punch line in this case would likely be that later they wished they had skipped the bar and gone to a pancake house instead.

We then all tried but failed to come up with a good punch line for the joke, and I decided not to volunteer the pancake-house version. After our failed effort, which certainly did seem collegial and informal—even fun—we returned to the serious business at hand. Dr. Wing gave us a choice. He said we could either start the hearing the next day—Tuesday—or wait until the following February, which is when he'd be back from some mini-sabbatical he was taking to Finland.

Oscar and I went out in the hall to discuss it. My initial reaction was that it was a setup and a trap, because if Greta Broontz and the rest of the Charges Committee were ready to start any time, as Wing claimed, that meant she and the dean—and maybe Wing, too—had been plotting this for a long time. Oscar said we were going to win, that they had no evidence, and we should get

it over with, that if we waited months, it would get more complicated and more difficult. He also said that Wing had practically
promised us they'd listen to the evidence, decide it was nonsense and not send it on to P&T. I acquiesced, although I wished
Robert were around to weigh in on the decision. But he was off
the grid somewhere, the asshole.

We went back in and told Dr. Wing we were good to go for
Tuesday. He looked, frankly, kind of shocked that we had chosen to do it so soon. Maybe Oscar was right.

CHAPTER 73

Week 3—Tuesday

Dr. Wing called Monday evening and told us that the Charges Committee usually met in a conference room in Murphy Hall, the administration building across from the law school. He also told us that in order to keep our hearing informal he was going to move it to a place much farther away from the law school and a lot harder for reporters or anyone else to find. He'd chosen a small conference room on the top floor of the multi-story red-brick pile that was once the UCLA Hospital before it moved down the road to the palace called the Ronald Reagan UCLA Medical Center.

Oscar and I arrived at the conference room at 8:00 A.M. The room had been hard to find, which I guess was the point. *Plain* is too fancy a word to describe it. It had no art on the walls—walls whose color I would describe as blah cream. There was a small conference table in the middle of the room, topped with blah-white plastic of some kind, badly scratched. In addition, there was a large gouge running down the middle. There were seven uncomfortable-looking wooden chairs placed around the table.

The three panel members were already present, seated in chairs that were clustered together at the head of the table. Dr. Wing sat in the middle chair of the three. He was decked out, in contrast to his oh-so-casual attire in his office, in a very nice herringbone suit, white shirt and deep red tie. His suit jacket breast pocket sported a handkerchief with his initials, RW, sewn in red thread.

It was the first time I had gotten a look at the other two panel members in person.

Samantha Healey, the philosopher, didn't look to me at all as I thought a philosopher should, which is to say slightly unkempt and a bit plump, with a distracted air about her. Instead, she was about my height, slim and dressed in a blue knit dress that emphasized her figure. Her hair was blonde, clearly bleached and shellacked into a tight helmet. She was wearing black, three-inch heels. I've never been good at identifying brands, but they looked expensive. Her eyes were green and, far from presenting an air of distraction, seemed almost to bore into you when she caught you in her gaze. It was hard to picture her along the banks of the Orinoco with her arm around a feathered guy. Maybe the person in that Facebook picture was someone else.

Paul Trolder, by contrast, looked more like I expected an economist to look. He was of average height, with average brown hair and scuffed brown loafers. He was wearing an open-necked white shirt and—I'm not making this up—a plastic pocket protector that held several pens. He also looked a bit distracted, if failing to make eye contact with anyone in the room was a sign of distraction.

Professor Broontz arrived shortly after we did and seated herself on the table's right side, just a few feet from the panel members. There was an empty chair next to her that I assumed would be used for witnesses.

When Dr. Wing had first provided us with the address of the conference room, I had asked if there was a coffeepot in it. Dr. Wing said no, but he'd see that one was installed. I glanced over at the small side table against the wall and spied a small coffeepot sitting there. It looked brand-new and still had a Target tag attached to it. I suspected Dr. Wing had probably bought it himself at the store nearby. Next to the pot was a bag of beans with a company logo I didn't recognize. There were also two large carafes of water. Since there was no one else around to make coffee, I assumed I would become the first defendant/coffee girl in history.

Dr. Wing rapped his knuckles on the tabletop. "Ladies and gentlemen," he said, "we have a few important things to take care of before we begin. And those things involve how we're going to go about this hearing. Let's go down the list."

He removed an actual list from his briefcase and placed it on the table in front of him.

"First, we're required to make a tape recording of this and all sessions. So . . ." He took a small digital recorder from the briefcase next to him, placed it on the table and pushed the start button. A red light glowed. "I suggest that if anyone wants their own copy, the most efficient way to obtain one is to make your own recording. This one, though"—he pointed to the recorder he had placed on the table—"is making the *official* copy."

Oscar took out a recorder, placed it on the table and turned it on, as did Professor Broontz, who to that point hadn't spoken a word to anyone. Now there were three red lights glowing.

"Anyone else?" Dr. Wing asked.

No one responded.

"Good, good," he said. "Let's move on to the next thing, then, which is procedure. Usually in this committee we listen to the faculty grievant explain his or her case to us. Then we listen to whoever is on the other side of that grievance—usually an administrator or, in rare cases, another faculty member—tell us their side of the story. If there are witnesses the parties think will be helpful, they invite them to join us, and we question those witnesses. We do that in private without the parties present."

"I don't think," said Oscar, "that—"

"Hold your horses, Oscar," Dr. Wing said. "There's a *but* coming." He paused for what he clearly regarded as the drama of it. "But this time my colleagues and I have decided to let the parties remain when the witnesses testify, unless the witness objects. Any problem with that?"

Professor Broontz spoke up for the first time. "I object. I think you get more honest testimony if people can speak in private."

"What makes you think that, Greta?" Dr. Wing asked.

"Because they aren't subject to retaliation."

Professor Healey leaned forward—I noticed her helmet of hair seemed slightly delayed in moving forward along with her head—and said, "Surely, Greta, you don't think people in a great university would retaliate against colleagues, do you?"

"I assume," Greta replied, "that you're being sarcastic, Samantha. As you and I both know, there are a lot of long knives on this campus, and quite a few people skilled in their use."

Professor Healey sat back in her seat. Again her hair seemed delayed in following her head. "I see your point, sort of."

Oscar raised his hand. "May I interject something here?"

"Of course, Oscar," Dr. Wing said.

"My profession has had a thousand years of experience with this issue. While Professor Broontz's argument has a certain amount of initial appeal, experience demonstrates that things done in secret tend, in the long run, not to hold up in the bright light of history. As my grandmother used to say, 'If you can't say it out loud, don't say it.'"

Count me as dubious that Oscar's grandmother had ever said any such thing. My cynical thoughts along those lines were interrupted by a sharp knock on the door. Everyone's head swung toward the sound.

CHAPTER 74

Professor Trolder, who was apparently the appointed doorman, got up to answer the knock. He opened the door, peered at someone standing to the side—I, at least, couldn't see who it was—said something inaudible to the person and closed the door. He walked back to the table, leaned over and whispered in Dr. Wing's ear. Dr. Wing nodded his head in acknowledgment and then picked right up where he had left off.

"We were discussing whether the parties should stay to hear the witnesses. My co-panelists and I discussed this earlier and came to the conclusion that it's better if the parties stay for the witnesses, particularly in something this fraught." He looked to his left at Professor Trolder, then to the right at Professor Healey. "Has either of you changed your mind after hearing the discussion we've just had?" Both shook their heads in the negative.

"All right, then," Dr. Wing said. "It's settled. The parties will stay for the witnesses, long knives and all. Now, let's see, what's next?"

"I think what's next," I said, standing up, "is coffee. I'm happy to make it. Anyone else want any?"

There was a small silence.

"To put you all at ease," I said, "someone else bought the beans."

"Actually," Professor Healey said, "I brought them. They're grown by an Amazonian nonprofit that got its start with a microloan."

"Oh, joy," Professor Trolder said. "Those microloans don't actually help to grow an economy."

I stood there waiting for resolution of the budding economic dispute.

"Well," Dr. Wing said, "I'm going to exercise the power of the chair to rule that coffee will be had without discussion of its economic roots. How many want coffee?" All hands went up except Professor Broontz's.

"All right," I said, "that's five coffees. I'll make a full pot and pour it"—I pointed to the stack of Styrofoam cups—"and then you can all come over and add cream or sugar if you want." The truth is, I just wanted the excuse to stand up and move around, and I wanted to break up the formality of the room even more.

While I walked over to the table that held the coffeepot, Dr. Wing continued. "The next item on my list," he said, "is the issue of who will question the witnesses. We conferred on that, too, and agreed that, to keep this informal, we'll just ask the witnesses to tell us what they know. If there are questions to be asked, we'll ask them. In the unlikely event there's anything still to ask when we're done, we'll permit the parties to pose a *few* questions. We want to keep this friendly and professional."

Oscar spoke up. "So cross-examination will be left to the end?"

"I don't, Oscar, see it as cross-examination, just the parties asking a few questions. Call it a very gentle cross-examination."

"That," Oscar said, "is something of an oxymoron. Because, again, the learning of my profession is that if you press someone hard on their answers, you get better answers."

"I kind of agree with him," Professor Broontz said. "I want to be able to press people hard because I think a lot of hard lies are being told here."

"You want to be able to use your long knives, Greta?" Professor Healey asked.

"That's not the way I would put it, Samantha," Professor Broontz replied.

"I think," Dr. Wing said, "we'll stick with the way we've agreed to do it. I can always cut off questions that I think don't comply with our standards of professionalism and civility. And with that, I have only one item left on my list. Normally, we don't apply the rules of evidence here. And in any case that would be difficult to do because I don't know them." He turned to Professor Trolder. "Paul, do you know them?" Trolder shook his head in the negative. He then turned to Professor Healey, on his other side. "Samantha, do you know the rules?"

"I do, actually," she said, "but I have some fundamental complaints about them. They're really an epistemological set that explores how we know what we know, and I think they're misguided attempts to apply a medieval philosophical construct in the twenty-first century."

Dr. Wing had remained looking at her while she spoke. He raised his eyebrows—I thought I also saw his lips twitch slightly—and said, "All well and good, Samantha. But the real question is, do you want to apply those rules here?"

"Certainly not."

"Good, good. So we have that out of the way."

Oscar raised his hand.

"Oscar, what pearl of wisdom do you have for us on this?"

"It's okay with us if you don't apply the formal rules of evidence here. But I'd like to remind the panel—and if this is a pearl, please accept it with my compliments—that the principles underlying those rules—such as being suspicious of speculation and suspicious of hearsay, to name only two of the many things the rules of evidence concern themselves with—are important principles to keep in mind."

Professor Healey started to speak up. "Well, I don't know that I agree that those principles—"

"Samantha," Dr. Wing said, interrupting, "I think we'll just consider ourselves reminded, okay?"

"All right, I suppose so."

I listened to all of this with some trepidation. Professor Healey seemed to me someone who was going to be difficult for us. I wished that Oscar hadn't spoken up and, clearly, irritated her. It was an unusual mistake for him, since he was usually so good at reading people.

"The coffee's ready," I said. "Please come help yourselves."

As often happens when caffeine is available, everything stopped and everyone came over to the table to get some. I noticed that everyone took their coffee black except Professor Trolder, who put in enough milk to make his coffee almost white and then added two heaping teaspoons of sugar.

When everyone was again seated, Dr. Wing said, "All right, let's get going. Greta, you're the one who brought this insanity our way. Who's your first witness?"

"My first witness," she said, "is waiting in the hall."

CHAPTER 75

Professor Broontz got up, went to the door and opened it. In walked George Skillings, the UCLA security guy, who I hadn't seen since the day Primo died. He looked around and stood waiting.

"Welcome, Mr. Skillings," Dr. Wing said. "Please take a seat in that vacant chair there." He pointed to the empty chair next to Professor Broontz.

After Skillings had taken his seat, Dr. Wing said, "Mr. Skillings, as I think you know, we're here investigating—in a sort of indirect way—the death of Primo Giordano."

"I understand."

I noticed that Skillings had not made eye contact with me. Which worried me.

"Before we get started," Dr. Wing continued, "I want to remind you that although we have no power to put anyone under oath, we do expect you to testify fully and truthfully."

"That's fine."

"I understand you were with Professor James the morning that a student, Primo Giordano, took sick."

"That's right."

"Can you tell us what you remember about that?"

I could feel my body wanting to jump up and object. In a courtroom I would have objected to the question as vague and calling for a narrative. Here no one seemed to care, and Skillings was busy answering.

"Pretty early, I think it was around 8:00 A.M., maybe a little before, I got a call from my supervisor saying that a law professor had locked herself out of her office. He gave me the office number and asked if I could take my master key and let her in. I wasn't far away, so I said sure and went over to the law school. When I got there, Professor James was standing in front of her office. She said she had left the office to take a phone call and locked herself out."

I looked over at Greta Broontz. She was looking down, taking copious notes. I knew she knew I was looking at her, but she didn't look up.

Skillings was continuing. "When I let the professor in, there was a student sitting in the chair who was half-unconscious, breathing irregularly and drooling. We put him on the floor and I called the EMTs, who came pretty much right away and took him to the hospital. Professor James went with them. Oh, and one more thing: while we were waiting for them, I asked her how long the phone call had kept her out of her office. She claimed it was only six or seven minutes."

I immediately noticed his use of the word *claimed*. It's the kind of word witnesses use when they don't believe someone. Had it been longer? I hadn't thought to check my phone records to find out. Until that moment it had never occurred to me that it was important.

"What happened," Dr. Wing asked, "after that?"

"I went back to my station and then a while later got a call from the police department asking me what had happened—the dispatches for the EMTs go to the police station—and I told them. They said they would send someone over and asked me, in the meantime, if I'd go back and secure the office. So I went back, opened it up and waited there awhile. At about the same time, Professor James came back. I told her I was suspicious the coffee might have caused the student's medical problem. In fact, I told her that's why I had come back. I didn't mention the police request. She gave me a couple of plastic bags, and I bagged the student's coffee cup, including the little splash of coffee that was left in it. I also took a sample from the sugar bowl."

"Anything else, Mr. Skillings?"

"Not much. The professor left again, and I waited for a policeman to arrive and take over, then I left."

"Did you do anything else, Mr. Skillings?" Dr. Wing asked.

"The only thing I can think of is that I bagged some of the coffee beans, too. Professor James had a bag of them there, still."

Dr. Wing looked at first one, then the other of his two colleagues. "Do either of you have any questions?" They shook their heads in the negative.

"I have a question," Professor Broontz said. "Do you know, Mr. Skillings, if Professor James drank any of that coffee herself?"

"Come to think of it, she said she didn't."

I can smell a planted question, and that one had a distinct aroma about it. Skillings was, for whatever reason, clearly cooperating with Greta Broontz.

"Well," Professor Broontz asked, "didn't that seem suspicious to you?"

"I object!" It was Oscar, back from the dead. "That's an outrageous question. I mean, this man isn't an expert on how people behave in particular situations. He has no idea why Professor James did or didn't drink the coffee, assuming for the moment his recollection about that is even correct."

Dr. Wing smiled down at him from his full height. "Well, Oscar, this is informal, remember? So I'm going to let him answer. Go ahead, Mr. Skillings."

"Yeah," he said, "it did seem kind of suspicious, especially because I've heard since that Professor James is kind of a coffee addict."

As he said that, I realized, of course, that my having volunteered to make the coffee a few minutes earlier had cooked my own goose on that one.

"Any other questions, Greta?" Dr. Wing asked.

"No, I'm done."

"Good," Dr. Wing said. "Then we can move on to . . ."

"I have a question," Oscar said. "Since we're going to let people speculate, let's try this one on. Mr. Skillings, if Professor James poisoned the student's coffee, as I think Professor Broontz's question was meant to imply, why do you think she was dumb enough to call you and ask you to open up her office, where the student was dying, before she had a chance to clean up the evidence?"

"Huh," Skillings said, "that's a good one. I really don't know."

I looked over at Greta Broontz, who was still taking notes. Then I looked at Dr. Wing, who had cocked his head, pursed his lips and was clearly cogitating about Oscar's question. After a few seconds, he straightened up and asked, "Who's your next witness, Greta?"

"It's Detective Drady," she said.

CHAPTER 76

Without so much as a knock, the door opened and Detective Drady walked into the room, looked around and stood there, waiting.

"Welcome, Detective," Dr. Wing said. "Please take a seat in that vacant chair there." He pointed to the empty chair next to Professor Broontz.

After Drady had taken his seat, Dr. Wing said, "Detective, as I think you know, we're here investigating—indirectly—the death of Primo Giordano."

"I understand."

"Before we get started, I want to remind you that although we have no power to put anyone under oath, we do expect you to testify fully and truthfully."

"I will certainly try to do that, Dr. Wing. Of course, there's a still-open police investigation into this matter going on, so there may be some things I won't be able to share."

Oh, great, I thought to myself, *he's pledging to tell the truth but not the whole truth, so help him God.* I looked over at Oscar, who was stoically taking notes and seemed disinclined to jump up and scream at the ridiculousness of what Drady had just said.

"We understand you won't be able to share everything," Dr. Wing replied. "Also, please note that your testimony is being recorded." He pointed to the three digital recorders on the table.

"Understood. I assume the recording's digital. Can someone e-mail me a copy?"

"Of your own testimony?"

"No, of the whole hearing."

"Well," Dr. Wing said, "this is a confidential hearing, so I don't think so."

"All right, I'm sure we can get it later with a search warrant, or the DA can get it with a subpoena if we need it."

"I don't think so, Detective. These things are truly confidential, and I think a subpoena would be squashed."

I decided not to correct the chairman and tell him that the word is quashed, not squashed—a common error made by non-lawyers. In any case, I suspected the university's confidentiality claim would, in the face of a criminal subpoena, provide about as much resistance as a fly presents to a flyswatter. It would be squashed.

"Could you start, Detective," Dr. Wing continued, "by just stating your name and your relationship to all of this?"

"Sure. I'm Detective Von Drady of the UCLA Police Department. I'm one of the officers investigating the death of Mr. Giordano."

"Thank you. You know Professor James, right?"

"Yes."

"Okay. Could you tell us what you know about that student's death and about Professor James's role in it?"

"If any," Oscar muttered, almost under his breath.

Dr. Wing seemed to take no offense at Oscar's barely heard amendment of his question, and said, "Of course, if any."

"All right," Drady said. "Earlier this month I got a call that a student had been removed unconscious from a professor's office at the law school. I was asked by my supervisor to go to investigate. I went to Professor James's office and found a UCLA security officer, George Skillings, already there. He brought me up to date on the situation, and I began to survey the crime scene. Shortly after I arrived, I learned that the student had died."

"May I," Oscar said, "—not to ask a question, but just to clarify something, so someone listening to this later won't be confused—be permitted to state my understanding that there was no crime scene at that point because there was no suspicion of a crime?"

"Is that right, Detective?" Dr. Wing asked.

"Well, yes, that's right. At that time it was just an unexplained student death caused by an unexplained illness. I used the term *crime scene* just to mean a place where we were looking for evidence related to the death."

"Well," Dr. Wing said, "I'm a doctor, and I'm aware there are lots of students taken ill on campus every year, isn't that so, Detective?"

"Yes, of course."

·"And you don't usually consider their dorm rooms crime scenes, do you?"

"No."

I was happy. Dr. Wing seemed to have picked up on what an attempted setup this whole thing was.

"Okay, thanks. Please return to your narrative, Detective."

"Well, eventually, I treated it as a potential crime scene, especially after Mr. Skillings told me he suspected the coffee the student drank was somehow tainted."

"Then what happened?" Dr. Wing asked.

"I took the coffee sample Mr. Skillings had collected into my possession, along with the sugar and the beans. Shortly after that Professor James showed up and told me what had happened. One of the things she mentioned was that Mr. Giordano had brought a treasure map with him, but that it was now missing. That later became of very great interest to us."

At the mention of treasure, Professor Healey's eyes lit up, and she asked her first question. "Did you ever find the map, Detective?"

"No, ma'am, we didn't. But I did learn later that Professor James had hidden the information about the map from the EMTs and hadn't told Mr. Skillings about it either. And now I understand Mr. Giordano's brother has sued her for the return of the map."

I sat there and cursed myself for my decision, taken what seemed like ages ago now, to keep the map story to myself initially—a decision I had made not to protect myself but to protect the confidentiality that Primo had seemed so concerned about. It was a lesson I kept having to relearn: stop worrying about other people and worry more about yourself.

Dr. Wing then returned to asking questions. The examination, if you could call it that, wandered on for a while, with nothing much being said that I didn't already know and eliciting nothing that seemed very damaging. Then Professor Broontz had another question.

"Detective, isn't it the case that you learned later that Professor James had taken what coffee was left in the pot and tossed it out, along with the coffeepot?"

"Yes, I did learn that."

"Did that seem suspicious to you?"

"Not necessarily."

Wow, I thought to myself, that was a straightforward, honest answer.

"Why not?"

"We just didn't know—and don't know—all the circumstances of how she came to discard the coffee and the pot. Plus Mr. Skillings had already collected some of that evidence."

It didn't seem that anyone else had any further questions of Drady and, as usual, Dr. Wing seemed about to move on without asking Oscar if he had any questions. I looked over at Oscar, because we had discussed a few days ago what had really happened with the discarded coffeepot.

"Detective," Oscar asked, "do you recall that when you were in Professor James's office and were about to leave, Professor James asked you what she should do with the remaining coffee?"

"No, I don't recall that."

"Maybe I can try to refresh your recollection a bit."

Dr. Wing interrupted. "You know, Oscar, it seems to me you're about to try to cross-examine the witness, which is not our approach in this informal setting. I think the detective has tried to answer your question as best he can, and we should just leave it at that for now."

"Okay, thank you," Oscar said. "I have nothing further."

I knew, of course, that had we been in a real courtroom, Oscar would have pressed Drady to the wall about his answer. "I don't recall that" is one of the most weaselly answers a witness can give. It can mean "I don't recall one way or the other." It can mean "I don't recall that exactly, but I recall something else." Or it can mean "I don't recall right now because I don't want to recall"—as well as a whole host of other things. All of which leave the witness free to recall a more precise answer later on. I truly hated this way of doing things. I thought we were done when Professor Broontz asked one final question.

"Detective," she asked, "did Professor James tell you she'd been out of the office on a phone call and had left the student alone in her office for a while?"

"Yes."

"Did she say how long that phone call had taken?"

"She said about six or seven minutes. And George Skillings later told me she'd given him the same estimate."

"Have you had the opportunity to check her estimate against her phone records?"

"Yes, we obtained her cell phone records from her phone company."

"What did you find?"

"We found a record of an incoming call to Professor James's number that started at 7:36 A.M. on the day of Mr. Giordano's death and ended at 7:53 A.M."

Professor Trolder spoke up for the first time. "So the call was seventeen minutes long, not seven?"

"Yes."

I guess math was Trolder's thing.

I looked at Oscar and he looked at me. I was dumbstruck; he appeared merely surprised. This must be the real reason Broontz had brought Drady in to testify. But why had she left the question to the very end? And what inference was going to be drawn from the answer? That I lied? But why would I? While I was pondering all of that, Oscar gave it the old college try.

"Detective," he asked, "do you know what happens to the call time record if someone receives a cell phone call but doesn't click off at the end of the call?"

"No, I don't."

I didn't know either, but I suspected that the call had indeed lasted that long. I just hadn't thought about it since I gave my initial rough time estimate to Skillings. Nor had I thought it was important. Until now.

Broontz was no doubt going to argue later that I blatantly lied about the length of the phone call, even if she didn't know—yet—exactly why I felt the need to lie about it, or even if it was obvious I'd be caught. But, she'd argue, lie I surely had. And then she'd add, "Once a liar, always a liar."

As a civil procedure teacher, she was no doubt aware of the California jury instruction that tells jurors: if you think a witness lied about one thing, you're entitled to disbelieve them about everything else. This wasn't a jury, of course, but she'd make the same argument to the panel, and she might just get them to buy it. And then who knew what else they'd conclude I lied about? How the receipt for the poison got in my pocket? Whether I had the map?

Shortly after that Dr. Wing declared a lunch break. Before we left he asked Professor Broontz who the next witness would be. She said she couldn't tell him exactly because of scheduling issues, and she didn't want to give him a bunch of names and then not be able to bring any of them in. Dr. Wing said okay, that we'd just wait to see who showed up after lunch.

CHAPTER 77

The medical school complex is on the southern end of the UCLA campus, not far from Westwood Village. Oscar and I walked the two blocks into the Village to have lunch. We chose the Corner Bakery, which has good, quick food and large tables, some of which, if you pick the right one, have a reasonable amount of privacy. We grabbed one by the windows.

The Corner Bakery is a place where you stand in line and order, and then they bring your food to you. I ordered a chicken panino and a large coffee. Oscar ordered an apple.

Back at our table, I said, "All you're having for lunch is an apple?"

"That's what I usually eat, Jenna. Well, sometimes I'll have a peach, if they have them."

"Okay. I need more sustenance than that."

"An apple a day keeps the doctor away."

"Do you know where that saying comes from, Oscar?"

"No, where?"

"It was an old proverb popularized in the early 1900s by an ad agency for the apple industry to try to persuade people that apples were healthy."

"Didn't people already think they were healthy?"

"Not really. At that time apples were primarily used to make alcoholic apple cider. Carry Nation and her friends in the temperance movement were chopping down not only saloons but apple trees. So the industry decided to promote apples as healthy."

Oscar took a bite out of his apple. "Huh, who knew? You know, you're becoming as filled with esoteric information as your friend Robert."

"It's a hazard of being a law professor."

"Well, what does the law professor think so far about our bizarre hearing?"

"It's driving me crazy. I mean, the information is so squishy it's junk. I also think it was a mistake to agree to participate and that we should depart."

"That won't stop the hearing. If we stay we learn what the police and others are thinking. It will be helpful in any defense."

"I thought you said they were no longer looking at me, that this was over. If that's so why do I need to think about a defense, Mr. Criminal Defense Attorney?"

"After listening to this morning's testimony, I'm wondering if the DA was shining me on. That they're still looking at you."

"Great."

"Jenna, what did you make of the testimony about the length of your phone call?"

"I was shocked. I do remember that guy from the law review just wouldn't get off the phone, and that the call took a long time. But I would have sworn it was well under ten minutes, not seventeen. I assume Greta's just going to argue that if I lied about one thing, I'm lying about everything else."

"Maybe," Oscar said, "if the information about the timing is correct—and I have no reason right now to think Drady's lying about it—it should make us rethink what happened here."

"Please explain."

"We've been working with a time line that says you locked the door the night before and that someone with a key opened it or someone picked the lock. On purpose. Let's assume instead that you simply forgot to lock it the night before or maybe the cleaning people accidentally left it open or whatever."

"Where would that get us?"

"If we assume that someone had to pick the lock or use an illegal key, it strongly suggests they were after you, and that they came in the night before and spiked the ingredients for the not-yet-made coffee with sodium azide, hoping you'd drink it."

"Which is what I've been assuming."

"Right. But if we assume instead that you accidentally left the door open the night before, it erodes that assumption and means that whatever was done to the coffee was likely done either right after Primo got there or right after you left to take the phone call."

I thought about it. "That could make sense. Particularly if Dr. Nightingale is correct that sodium azide is too dangerously unstable to grind in the coffee grinder and too heat sensitive to be exposed to the high heat of the coffeemaker."

"Right. It means the poison was most likely dumped directly into Primo's coffee cup. And if you were out of that office for seventeen minutes instead of only six or seven, it leaves a lot of time for someone to show up and do that."

Just then our food arrived and was set down in front of us by the server. I began to eat my panino, and Oscar started in on his apple. Before biting into it, he used his knife to peel all the skin away.

"You're taking off the skin?"

"Sure."

"But that's the part that keeps the doctor away. It's got most of the vitamins and fiber."

"I do what I do, Jenna. I'm too old to adopt newfangled approaches like eating the skin of an apple."

"You just throw it away?"

"No. At home I might use some of it to make an apple martini for guests."

"Oh."

"Weren't we discussing," Oscar said, "who poisoned Primo?"

"Yes. I suppose I'm just trying to take my mind off the whole thing. Three days ago I thought this was over, and now it's returned."

"Let's get back to the analysis, Jenna. First of all, you think you left your office door open when you went across the hall to take the phone call, right?"

"I'm sure I did."

"If you were gone for seventeen minutes, that means Primo was sitting there by himself for seventeen minutes with the door open, and almost anyone could have come by and seen him."

"True."

"Jenna, isn't this just like when the cops find people murdered in their own house and there's no sign of forced entry? What do they always say in those cases?"

"I don't know, Oscar, what do they say?"

"That the killers were probably someone the victims knew, and that the victims let them in."

"You're saying if my office door was open for all that time, the person who poisoned the coffee was someone Primo knew who came by and saw him sitting there and invited himself in to chat. Or herself. And Primo made no objection."

"Exactly, and, while chatting, whoever that was surreptitiously dumped the poison in Primo's coffee, waited for him to get in too much distress to call for help and then left and locked the door behind them."

"The only problem with that," I said, "is that there was clearly poison in the coffeepot itself, too, because it burned the leaves of the plant I dumped it in."

"All right," Oscar said, "let's modify my theory. After Primo was disabled, the killer dumped the poison in the pot, too, in order to frame you, or maybe kill you. That way, it got into the pot without having to be brewed and exposed to too much heat."

"If you're right, Oscar," I said, "that leaves us with two very likely suspects: Julie and Quinto. Both were in the vicinity and both had reason to kill Primo. Julie out of anger and Quinto to get Primo's copy of the map, with the longitude of the sunken *Ayuda* written on it."

"Exactly. The problem is that while we now have a plausible scenario, we have no direct evidence against either of them."

"Except," I said, "that Julie tore out the diary page on which Primo wrote that Julie had threatened to kill him. And in the diary Primo also wrote that Quinto threatened to kill him if he showed the map to me."

"Actually," Oscar said, "that's not quite what Primo wrote, or not all of it, anyway. You can check the copy of the diary, but, if I recall correctly, what Primo actually said was that Quinto had threatened to kill him if Primo showed you the map in order to 'involve you' in 'our project.'"

"What's the difference?"

"Your interpretation focuses on Quinto being worried that you'd see the map. I think what Quinto was worried about—assuming the diary reports all of this correctly—was not that you'd see the map but that once you got involved, you would investigate the true facts of their project. Whatever they are. And that perhaps Aldous, who already knew a lot, would help you."

Just then my cell rang. I answered and listened.

"A drink tomorrow? Sure, I could do that. Five o'clock sounds fine. If I'm going to run late for some reason, I'll call you on the number you just called me on."

"Who was that?" Oscar asked.

"It was Tess. She says she's discovered something I'll find very interesting."

CHAPTER 78

Oscar and I returned to the small conference room at about 1:30 P.M. Only Dr. Wing was present.

"I think the others," he said, "will be back shortly."

"I'm going to make some fresh coffee," I said. "We need more water, though, so I'll take one of the carafes and get it refilled. I noticed there was a water fountain down the hall."

"Okay," Dr. Wing said. "That would be appreciated. I wanted to ask you, though, how do you think we're doing?"

My initial inclination was to tell him what I assumed he wanted to hear—that everything was going great, he was doing a good job on presiding over a wonderful, just-among-friends hearing and that all was well. And then I thought to myself, *well, what's the point in that?*

"What is it they say in the military?" I asked. "Or at least in military movies? Permission to speak freely?"

Dr. Wing laughed. "Granted."

"I think this whole thing is a joke. The witnesses are walking all over you and the panel, and you're not learning half of what you need to know."

"Jenna," Oscar said, "I think—"

"No, Oscar, I'm not stopping. For example, Rex, let's talk about that detective, Drady. He came in here and basically said from the get-go that he'd tell you some things but not others, and he didn't even tell you what category of things he was holding back on. In any self-respecting courtroom the judge would either have kicked his butt out of the courtroom or put him in jail until he wised up. And then you wouldn't let Oscar go after his wimpy I-don't-recall-that answer."

Dr. Wing grinned at me. "Ah," he said, "now I see the hard-bitten, brilliant law professor I've been hearing about on the grapevine. What do you suggest we do to correct these deficiencies, Professor?"

"Let Oscar cross-examine the witnesses when they're finished telling their mushy stories."

"Maybe we'll give that a try," he said. "I've been a little dissatisfied myself with the quality of information that's been coming out."

I looked over at Oscar, who had taken his seat. His face was frozen. I couldn't read it one way or the other.

"Well," I said, "I'm now going to go down the hall and get some water for fresh coffee." Which is what I did.

When I got back, everyone was back and seated, but there was as yet no witness in the vacant chair. I walked around the table, poured the water into the coffeepot receptacle, dumped the ground coffee into the filter, pushed the on button and took my seat.

Dr. Wing looked at Professor Broontz. "Well, Greta, do you have a witness for us?"

"Yes. I want to recall Detective Drady."

"Is it," Dr. Wing asked, "absolutely necessary? We already heard quite a bit of testimony from him."

"He has something new to tell us," she said.

"All right, then, let's have him back."

A sudden chill ran up my back. Whatever was coming could not be good.

The door opened and Detective Drady sauntered back in, took a seat, smiled broadly and nodded at Professor Broontz, as if to say, "I'm ready to roll."

And roll he did, with Broontz's first question.

"Detective," she asked, "have you learned anything new about the case against Professor James?"

"Yes, I have. Over the lunch break I learned the results of a forensic analysis of an item taken from Professor James's apartment during a search."

"And what was the item?"

"A jar of dark liquid that was in her refrigerator."

"What did the report show?"

"It showed that it was coffee, and that it contained a high level of sodium azide. It also showed that, in terms of its other chemical constituents, it was an exact match to the coffee found in the victim's coffee cup."

I wanted to put my head in my hands, but I resisted the urge and just sat there gritting my teeth and wishing we had never agreed to the hearing.

"Can we," Oscar asked, "get a copy of the report?"

"I don't have one yet," Drady said. "It was read to me over the phone by a colleague."

"Then I move," Oscar said, looking at Dr. Wing, "that Detective Drady's testimony be struck from this record. This is hearsay on hearsay on hearsay. The report itself is hearsay, and Detective Drady admits he hasn't even read it himself. He is reporting what someone else says is in it. This testimony is outrageously unreliable totem-pole hearsay, as we call it in my profession. Stacked hearsay."

"Well," Dr. Wing said, "because this is an informal proceeding, I think we'll admit it and weigh its value later. Greta, do you have more questions?"

"No, I don't."

"How about you, Oscar?"

"Oh, I have several," Oscar said. "And let me start with this one: Detective, do you have any evidence that Professor James is the one who put the jar of coffee in her refrigerator?"

"No, I don't, not directly. But it was in her refrigerator, eh? So who else would have put it there?"

"Are you aware that Professor James has a roommate?"

"Yes."

"Who majors in molecular chemistry?"

"Yes, we're aware of all of that. But so far as we are aware, the roommate didn't even know the victim. So why would he poison him, eh?"

Drady's affectation of the *eh* at the end of his sentences, as if he were a newly minted Canadian, irritated me. Almost as much as the fact that Oscar knew very well who had put the coffee in the refrigerator because I had told him several days before that I had put it there, and that the police had taken it during their search.

"Oscar," Dr. Wing asked, "do you have anything further?"

"Just two more questions. Detective, even assuming Professor James put the jar of coffee in the refrigerator, do you have any evidence as to when she put it there?"

"No, I don't. But I don't know what difference it would make because it was her refrigerator in her apartment, eh? And most people don't have poisoned coffee in their refrigerators."

"Detective," Oscar asked, ignoring the sarcasm, "when did you first learn of the analysis of the coffee taken from the refrigerator?"

"Today."

"Did anyone else know earlier?"

"Not to my knowledge."

"Why did it take so long? The police department has had that jar of coffee for over ten days now."

"The LAPD lab does the analysis for us, and they're backed up. They did the analysis of the coffee in the victim's cup first, and then the sugar and the coffee beans. They only just now finished various items taken from the defendant's—sorry, I mean Professor James's—apartment."

"Anything else, Oscar?" Dr. Wing asked.

"Not at the moment, but I may call Detective Drady as our witness later on."

"Oh, that's fine," Dr. Wing said. "Are you willing to come back, Detective?"

"Of course."

"Good. Then you're excused for now."

If the whole thing hadn't turned so serious, I would have laughed at watching Dr. Wing fall into the lingo of formal courts, now *excusing* the witness instead of just telling him he could go.

"Greta," Dr. Wing asked, "are you ready with your next witness?"

"She's a couple of minutes late, apparently. Let me make a call."

"In that case," Oscar said, "I'd like to take a brief break."

"Sounds good," Dr. Wing said. "Let's meet back here in ten." And with that, he pushed back his chair, got up and left the room, as did the other members of the panel. That left only me, Oscar and Greta in the room.

"Who," I asked, "is your next witness, Greta?"

"That will just have to be a surprise, dear."

I wanted to protest, but with Dr. Wing and the rest of the panel gone, there was no one to protest to. In the meantime I could feel my stomach knotting up.

Oscar got up and started to leave the room, and I followed. We walked down the hall and once again went into the nearly empty conference room.

"Oscar, why did you bother trying to mess up Drady's testimony about where the jar of coffee came from? We both know where it came from. As I told you earlier in the week, I put it there."

"It always helps to sow doubt," he said and smiled.

"Maybe," I said. "But I think we should just pull out of this hearing. We went into it thinking we'd learn some things that would help in the civil case. Now it's turning into a serious preliminary hearing on my possible guilt in a murder, for God's sake. We're now worse off than we were before they told you I was no longer on their list."

"Jenna, you've forgotten everything I taught you about criminal law. Whether this turns back into a criminal case or remains just a civil case against you, it's free discovery for us. You don't have to testify, and we get to listen to the potential witnesses against you and ask them questions. Nothing could be better."

"What would be better, Oscar, would be for you to have figured out—before we agreed to this hearing—that the police hadn't yet tested the coffee jar from my refrigerator."

"Ouch. That was a fair comment, Jenna. I admit I didn't think to ask, when the DA said you were no longer a person of interest, whether they'd already processed all of the evidence they seized. I just assumed they had. My mistake, and I apologize."

"So do you think I'm again a serious person of interest?"

"No. Candidly, you're now at least a suspect, and maybe even a target."

CHAPTER 79

We went back to the hearing room and took our seats. The others, including the panel members, filtered in over the next few minutes. After everyone was seated, Dr. Wing asked, "Greta, is your next witness ready?"

"She's just arriving, I think," Greta said.

Just then there was a knock at the door. Professor Trolder got up to answer it and admitted a petite Asian woman.

"This is Thu Nguyen," Broontz said.

"Welcome, Ms. Nguyen," Dr. Wing said. "Please have a seat in the chair next to Professor Broontz."

She went and sat down in the chair. I looked at her but couldn't immediately place her.

Dr. Wing then went through his usual drill about what we were doing, how she had to tell the truth, the fact that we were recording the session, how informal it all was and to please feel at home and all the other baloney.

"Now, Ms. Nguyen," he said, "could you tell us your occupation?"

"Yes. I own a nail salon on Westwood Boulevard south of Wilshire. It's called Only Nails. I'm both the owner and the manager."

"What can you tell us, if anything, about Professor James's relationship to the unfortunate death of her student, Primo Giordano?"

"Nothing. I don't know the student and I don't know about his death."

"May I ask some questions?" Professor Broontz asked.

"Of course, Greta," Dr. Wing said.

"Okay. First, Ms. Nguyen, have you seen Professor James before? She's sitting right there." Broontz pointed at me.

"Objection," Oscar said. "You can't ask someone if they've ever seen a person with a certain name before and then point to the person."

"That does seem an awkward way to go about it," Trolder said. "It's like doing an economics survey where you tell the respondents the answer you're looking for."

I had been looking at Thu Nguyen and had finally recognized her. She was the woman who had arranged for me to get my hands waxed when they had been so red the day that Primo died. I had no clue what relevance her testimony could have, but I saw no reason to avoid the fact that we had met. And I said so.

"Excuse me," I said, "I think we can short-circuit all of this. I know Ms. Nguyen. We met on the day that Primo died."

"Is that correct, Ms. Nguyen?" Dr. Wing asked.

"Yes, it is."

"Can you tell us about that, please?"

"Yes. Professor James—I didn't know her full name until now—came into my salon and complained that her hands were red. She asked if we had some treatment. We used a hot wax treatment on her hands. She seemed pleased."

Professor Broontz resumed her questions. "Did she pay with a credit card or with cash?"

"I told you the other day when you interviewed me. She paid with cash."

"Did she mention," Professor Broontz asked, "whether she had gotten something on her hands that had irritated them?"

"I also told you the other day. No, she didn't say that."

I suddenly saw where this was going. Greta was going to argue that I had gone to the salon to get any traces of sodium azide washed off my hands, because I must have spilled some of it on them.

"But," Greta persisted, "if Professor James had something on her hands, the wax would remove that, right?"

"I guess so, but I don't really know."

"Okay," Greta said. "I don't have anything further. Let's move on to the next witness."

"One moment," Dr. Wing said. "Do you have any questions, Oscar?"

"Yes," Oscar said. "A few. Ms. Nguyen," he asked, "do women often come to your salon because their hands are red?"

"Yes."

"Because their skin is irritated?"

"Yes."

"How many times this week has your spa given a hot wax treatment to women who complained about red or irritated hands?"

She stopped and thought for a moment. "Maybe five?"

"So you might do two hundred and fifty hot wax treatments in a year?"

"Maybe more."

"Finally, is it unusual for someone to pay in cash in your salon?"

"No. And we prefer it, because then we do not pay a percentage to the credit-card company."

"Thank you. That's all I have."

"I have a question," I said. "How did Professor Broontz contact you?"

"She came into the shop one day and brought a picture of you. She asked if we had ever seen you. We said yes."

"Did she ask you anything else?"

"She asked if you had gotten a hot wax treatment from us."

"Did Professor Broontz say how she knew I might have had a hot wax treatment?"

"No."

She didn't know. But I knew. Tommy must have told her. He was the only person on the planet, besides the employees of the salon, who knew that I'd had a hot wax treatment that day. And after Tommy told her, Greta must have gone around to all the nail shops in the area with my picture. And hadn't Tommy also been the person in the best position to plant the sodium azide receipt in my pocket, despite his denial? He was now at the very tip-top of my list of suspects. No, he wasn't a suspect. He was *the target.*

I wanted to leap out of my chair and scream, "Case solved!" But instead, I calmed myself and went on questioning the salon owner. "Did she ask you anything else, Ms. Nguyen?"

"Yes. She asked if your hands were really red."

"What did you tell her?"

"I said they were red, but I had seen hands more red."

"Thank you. That's all I have."

Dr. Wing looked at her. "Thank you, Ms. Nguyen. We appreciate your coming."

"No problem." And then Ms. Nguyen looked at Professor Broontz and said, "I will see you for your nails next week, right?"

Broontz looked taken aback. "Oh, of course."

"I think," Dr. Wing said, "that we're at a good breaking point for the day. Greta, who will you have for us tomorrow as the first witness?"

"Quinto Giordano."

"That won't work well for us," Oscar said. "One of Professor James's other lawyers, Robert Tarza, is particularly familiar with Mr. Giordano's issues, but he's out of town. So we'd like to postpone him until Mr. Tarza is back, which won't be until Wednesday night."

"Isn't he," Trolder asked, "the guy who was charged with murder a number of years back? And then escaped the charge somehow?"

I couldn't stand it. "Yes" I said, "he was that guy. And he escaped the charge because he wasn't guilty. Kind of like me, ya know?"

Dr. Wing intervened. "I think there's no need to go into this. Mr. Tarza is welcome here without regard to all of that." He gave Trolder a look that said *Please shut up, Paul.*

"Well," Oscar said, "what shall we do about scheduling?"

Wing looked thoughtful. "You know, we've accomplished quite a lot today, I think. Why don't we adjourn now and meet again on Thursday, maybe 10:00 A.M.?"

There were nods of agreement all around, and we adjourned until Thursday morning. I hoped Robert would be back by then because Quinto had it in for me, and, I had to grudgingly admit, he was capable of being persuasive.

CHAPTER 80

Week 3—Wednesday

It was almost 9:00 A.M., and I was still in bed when the ringing of my landline woke me from a ragged sleep. Oscar had kept me up late the night before planning strategy for Thursday and talking about who *our* witnesses were going to be—if any—when Broontz finished with hers.

To my disappointment, Oscar wasn't impressed with my Tommy-did-it theory. He pointed out that Greta, who, he noted, was also on my suspect list, could simply have followed me and seen me go into the salon. I argued that she had no reason to follow me and no reason to ask if I'd had a hot wax treatment. I finally dropped it after Oscar said he would let the police know my theory.

We also talked about the fact that if they dared to call Julie as a witness, we were going to have to find a way to immolate her. I hadn't slept well at all. And I had pushed the dresser back in front of the door, because if the police were focusing on me again as their prime suspect in Primo's death, it meant the real killer was still out there, unconcerned and free to act.

The phone was still in its cradle and continuing to ring. I punched the speakerphone button so I wouldn't have to hold the thing up to my ear. It was Aldous.

"Hey," he said, "I'm back from Buffalo. Sorry I was gone so much longer than I expected."

"Welcome back."

"That didn't sound all that friendly."

"No, no. It's just that you kind of woke me up. I've had a sleepless night. Greta Broontz has brought charges against me, contending that my alleged murder of Primo has disrupted the teaching environment on campus, and we're in the middle of a hearing about it."

"You're kidding."

"No, I'm not. Three days ago I thought this was all over, and that I was no longer a focus of the police investigation. Now I'm again apparently at least a serious suspect, and I'm also the focus of an investigation by the Charges Committee."

"That's ridiculous. Why didn't you call me and tell me what was going on?"

"Well, why didn't you call *me*, Aldous, and ask how things were going back here?"

"I'm sorry. I've been in meetings and meals from dawn to dusk. Well past dusk, actually. Anyway, these charges against you are ridiculous."

"Yes, they are. I've also gone back to thinking that maybe someone was trying to poison me, and that the library thing wasn't just an accident."

"What library thing?"

"While you were gone, a shelf of books fell on me. I'll tell you about it when I see you."

"What about the civil suit for stealing the map, Jenna?"

"Allegedly stealing the map."

"That's what I meant."

"Who knows? I'll have to deal with that later. How was Buffalo?"

"It was great. It's going to be just what I've always wanted. A school that combines a great legal education and a great business education for each and every student."

Aldous began to describe his whole trip to me in glorious detail. While I listened, or tried to, I climbed out of bed, snatched the portable phone from its cradle so that the speakerphone clicked off and transferred the sound to the handset. I pulled the dresser away from the door and went into the bathroom. My mouth tasted foul. I continued listening—now Aldous was talking about the great facilities they were renting, and how they were going to build their own building within three years—while trying to brush my teeth, but quietly, so he couldn't hear. I should have put the mute on, but I forgot.

"Jenna, are you brushing your teeth?"

"Uh, yeah. My mouth tasted horrible. I was afraid you'd be able to detect my bad breath even over the phone."

"Very funny. But listen, I won't keep you."

"Hey, Aldous, I'm sorry, don't be that way. It's like being stuck in a long tunnel when I thought I'd already come out of it."

"All right. I understand. How about lunch today, Jenna?"

"Sure."

"It's a really beautiful day, and I think you need to do something to cheer yourself up. I propose a picnic in the sculpture garden."

"Sounds great. What time?"

"I'll meet you there at noon."

"Okay. Shall I bring something?"

"No, I'll put it all together."

"Good. See you there."

I spent the rest of the morning drafting end-of-semester exams. Normally by this time in the semester I would already have written near-final drafts of both exams.

At about eleven the doorbell rang, which was an almost unheard of event. Usually, if I was expecting visitors, the front desk called and asked me if it was okay for them to come up. And, in any case, I wasn't expecting anyone. I walked to the front door and peered out through the little glass peephole. It was Tommy.

I didn't open the door. Instead, I just raised my voice and yelled through it, "How did you get up here, Tommy?"

"The usual way. I took the elevator. They know me at the front desk, and I guess you didn't tell them I've moved out."

He was right, of course. "Well, what do you want?"

"I left a set of walking sticks in the closet of my room. I need them for a hike I'm taking tomorrow."

"I might get them for you, Tommy, but before I do, did you tell Greta Broontz that I had my hands waxed the day my student died?"

"Who is Greta Broontz?"

"One of my colleagues at the law school."

"I've never heard of her."

"You didn't tell her about the hot wax?"

"No. Why would I? And how could I if I don't know her?"

"Are you sure?"

"Of course I'm sure. Can I have my poles now?"

"Wait there, please."

I walked back to his bedroom and, sure enough, there was a pair of walking sticks leaning against the back corner of his closet. I hadn't noticed them when I checked his room after he moved out. I picked them up, went to the kitchen and grabbed a knife, then returned to the front door with the poles in one hand and the knife in the other.

"Tommy," I yelled, "move down the hallway to the very end, where I can see you, and I'll toss them out."

He actually rolled his eyes, or at least I think that's what he did, since his face looked weird in the distorted visual field of the peephole. As requested, he moved far down the hallway, so that he was just a speck in the eyepiece. I opened the door a crack, heaved the poles out and slammed the door.

I watched Tommy return and pick up the poles. When he turned around, he gave me the finger, then walked off down the hallway. I watched until he turned the corner.

Oscar was right: I was losing it.

CHAPTER 81

After Tommy left I went back to working on my exams, although I had trouble focusing on them. About 11:30 I put them aside, grabbed my bike from the study and headed for the front door. Right before I reached it, I thought about calling Aldous and canceling. I rejected that and instead went back to the kitchen, grabbed a six-inch knife and put it in my saddlebag. If someone came after me with a gun, it would be useless, of course. But so far it had been poison and library books, so maybe it would be helpful in a nongun situation.

I left the building and rode my bike up to the sculpture garden, which is at the north end of the campus. It's named for the UCLA chancellor, Franklin D. Murphy, who founded it. Its five acres of grass, planted with flowers and trees, spreads over gentle hillocks crisscrossed by winding walkways. Amid all of it are dozens of exquisite sculptures from the world's most famous sculptors, from Rodin to Calder. It's the most calming place on campus. On any day you can see young couples watching their small children run, students studying and people picnicking. It's a place where the grass seems to say *Please walk on me.*

I spotted Aldous right away. He was sitting toward the bottom of one of the small hillocks and had already spread out a green blanket and a checkered tablecloth. On top of the tablecloth was one of those classic, rounded wicker picnic baskets with a split wooden top and polished double wooden handles.

He got up as I approached and we hugged. He was still hugging when I broke it off and sat down.

"Hi, Aldous, it's good to have you back." I knew as soon as I said it that it wasn't the kind of thing someone would say on her lover's return, and that it meant our relationship was, if not over, very close to over. I felt a wave of sadness wash over me. The relationship had seemed to have such promise when it started.

I think Aldous sensed the end coming, too, because all he said in response was, "Good to be back."

Neither one of us said anything more as he pulled back the basket's wooden handles and flipped open the wooden tops. He took out bright red plastic plates, two red plastic cups and what looked like coleslaw packed in a plastic container he'd picked up at one of the campus eateries. I could also see sandwiches inside the basket, which he'd clearly made himself and carefully wrapped in Saran Wrap. And, finally, there was a white thermos that I knew must hold coffee, plus a couple of soft drinks.

"What are the sandwiches?" I asked.

"Ham and cheese, salami and your favorite, peanut butter and jelly."

"On white, I hope."

"Yep, on WASP white. Guaranteed stale in one day."

He knew I loved peanut butter and jelly. I'd eaten it all through my childhood and had seen no reason to stop just because I passed the age of eighteen and eventually became a law professor. On the salvage boat that past summer, the sailors aboard, who preferred heartier fare, had derisively dubbed me the PB&J girl. By the end of the summer, though, I'd converted two of them and even drawn them into the ultimate PB&J discussion topic—which peanut butter was best and whether you should eat smooth or chunky.

I took out one of the PB&Js, unwrapped it, poured myself some coffee and began to eat. Aldous picked up a ham and cheese and pulled a can of Coke out of the basket. After we'd both munched for a while, I said, "I gather from the call this morning that you're definitely going to Buffalo."

"Yes. It looks like a perfect opportunity."

"It probably fits. You've always been as much a businessman as a lawyer."

"True. I'm hoping to persuade you to come, too, Jenna. The founder told me that, to get you, he'd be willing to build you a world-class center for admiralty law. There'd be three faculty positions to fill, and the funding for some scholarships and an academic journal."

"You think they'd want a suspected murderer?"

"That's going to go away, I'm sure."

"Aldous, I appreciate your saying that, but may I speak bluntly?"

He laughed. "Have you ever done otherwise?"

"That's not fair. I can be subtle."

He just looked at me.

"Okay, not very often, but I can." I paused. "Anyway, I would die in Buffalo. I'm sure it's a very nice place, but it would remind me too much of Cleveland. I need a much bigger city."

"I figured you would say something like that."

"Also, and here's the blunt part, if I thought our relationship was going somewhere, I might consider it, despite Buffalo. But even with our many attempts to work things out—and I kept thinking we would work it out—our relationship still seems mostly to be about the great sex. I know we have fun together, too, and we travel well together, and we have a lot of things in common. Maybe it's mostly my fault, but it's just not enough, at least for me. So—there's no easy way to say it—we need this to be over."

He took a bite out of his sandwich, as if to give himself some time to think, a gesture that sort of summed up what was wrong in our relationship. After a while he said, "I don't feel that way, Jenna, but it takes two, and if I've learned anything about you, it's that once you make a final decision about something, you rarely change your mind. And your decision sounds final."

"It is."

"I can't say I'm not hurt, because I am. But I know you don't mean it to hurt."

"I don't."

"Will we still be friends, Jenna?"

"Of course we will." I scooted my butt over on the blanket and gave him a big hug, much warmer than the one with which I'd greeted him.

"Good," he said after we broke the hug. "Because I wouldn't like to lose our friendship. Maybe I can even persuade you to visit me in Buffalo at some point."

"Visiting is certainly doable. In late spring."

He laughed. "By the way, I have a present for you."

"Oh?"

"Yep. It's in an envelope in the picnic basket. Check it out."

I leaned over and looked into the basket. There was a white business-size envelope on the bottom of the basket. I picked it up. "Is it the offer for the admiralty professorship?"

"Nope. Open it."

I tore it open and pulled out several folded pieces of paper stapled together. I unfolded them and saw that it was a long multipage list of Internet addresses. "What is it?"

"Do you remember that you were pissed off at me when I refused to break the confidentiality agreement I had when I investigated Primo and Quinto's treasure salvage deal?"

"Yes. Are you about to break it now?"

"No. But I wanted to make that up to you, so I hacked Julie's notebook computer and looked at her Internet search history."

"What?"

"Don't act so shocked. You know I have those skills."

"Yes, but you have strange ethics. You won't break the confidentiality agreement, but you'll break various federal and state laws to hack someone's computer."

"Sometime I'll explain to you why I think they're different."

"I don't expect to be persuaded. But since you've already done it, I guess I need to ask what you found."

"I found out that about two weeks before Primo died, Julie went online and Googled the topic *poisons soluble in coffee*. It's the sixth item on the list I just handed you."

"Are you able to tell what she did with that?"

"Yes. She linked from the results for that search to several newspaper articles about an incident that took place at Harvard a number of years ago. Somehow sodium azide got into a coffeepot in a research lab there, and six people were poisoned, although none of them died."

"Who did it?"

"The articles say Harvard did an investigation but never figured out how the poison got into the coffeepot."

"Oh my God. That means Julie did this."

"I wouldn't jump to that conclusion quite so quickly."

"Why not?"

"Because Julie was living with Primo and Quinto, and if you look at all the searches, it's pretty clear from the topics searched that some of them were done by Primo or Quinto. They're searches of multiple Italian websites. So we can't know for sure if Julie did the poison search or if one of them did it using her computer."

"Why would Primo have done it?"

"To kill himself?"

CHAPTER 82

Week 3—Wednesday Afternoon

I thanked Aldous for the picnic, gave him a peck on the cheek—it's amazing how a relationship can cool as quickly as thin-crust pizza—and went back to my condo. I had come up with a plan, but if I was going to implement it, I needed to do it quickly.

Oscar had given me a copy of the receipt for the sodium azide that had supposedly been found in the pocket of my jacket. The name of the company from which it was bought was at the top of the page—Angin Chemical. It was located near downtown LA. The salesperson's name wasn't on the receipt, but the salesperson's number was.

I called the company and when someone answered, I said, "Hi, this is January Bigelow." (January Bigelow was the name of my long-ago freshman college roommate.)

"I bought some chemicals the other day from one of your salespeople. I came in personally to pick up the order. I can't recall the name, but the number is 2385. Can you tell me who that is so I can talk directly to them again? I have a couple of questions."

I listened. "No, no, it's not a complaint, just a question."

After a moment the person came back on the line and said, "That would be Sylvia Menendez. Let me connect you."

I hung up.

Next I went back to the website and tried to find the most benign thing the company sold over the counter. Then I ordered up my car from the valet, got in and drove to my bank, where I took out four hundred dollars from the ATM. Then I drove downtown to Angin Chemical. When I got there, I parked in one of the three spaces labeled CUSTOMERS ONLY, got out of my car and walked in through the double glass doors at the front. As I expected, there was a service counter in the back, and I made a beeline for it.

Luck was with me. The woman standing behind the counter had a nametag that said Sylvia Menendez. She looked to be in her early twenties. She was shorter than me, maybe five foot three, with dark hair cut short and green eyes. She was wearing the kind of button-up blue smock you often see on employees of places where there can be a lot of dust around.

"Hi," I said. "I'm Annej Semaj." (I had been amusing myself since childhood pronouncing my name backward. I thought it sounded vaguely East Indian. I always pronounce the *j* in both words like the *g* in Geronimo.) "I saw on your website that you sell Decon AquaPur ST Sterile Purified USP-Grade Water. Is it in stock?"

"I'm pretty sure it is," she said, looking down at her computer screen as she typed in a query. She glanced again at the screen display and said, "Yes, we do have it in. What size would you like?"

"What are the available sizes?"

"It comes in one-gallon containers, four containers to a case."

"I'll take one case."

"Okay, let me get it from the stockroom." She turned and disappeared into the back.

I had ordered the four-container case because I knew that a gallon of water weighs almost eight-and-a-half pounds, and I wanted the entire thing to be heavy enough that it would be reasonable for me to ask for help carrying it out to my car.

Sylvia emerged from the back, pushing the case of USP-grade water on a dolly.

"Will you be paying by cash, credit card or check?" she asked. "Oh, I should add that we only accept checks if your company has an account with us. Do you?"

"No. I'll pay with cash. How much is it?"

"It's $180 plus sales tax. You can pay here or at the front."

"Here is fine."

With tax the bill came to $196.20. She took the two hundred dollars I proffered her and gave me change. "For your receipt," she asked, "what name should I use? Yours or a company name?"

"Oh, just my name, Annej Semaj." I spelled it for her and then pronounced it again, slowly.

She handed me a receipt that looked just like the one found in my pocket.

"Will you need some help," she asked, "getting this to your truck?"

"Oh, I don't have a truck. Just an old Land Cruiser, but yes, I could use some help. I'm parked right out front."

"I'll push it out for you," she said.

I headed for the front door and she followed. When we got to my Land Cruiser, I popped open the back, lifted the hatch and together we lifted up the heavy box and slid it in.

I was trying to think of some small talk to engage in that would make my visit memorable when she saved me the trouble. "It's unusual," she said, "for individuals to buy this much highly purified water. If you don't mind my asking, what do you do with it?"

"Oh, I work in a medical research lab at UCLA. We use purified water to dilute sterile disinfectants. We ran out of it this afternoon, and my boss was bitching about how long it would take to reorder it through normal channels."

"So you just said you'd go and get some?"

"Exactly."

"Medical research. Wow, maybe I should try to get a job like that. One day I'd like to go to med school."

"What do you do now?"

"I'll be graduating from LACC next spring and I'm hoping to transfer to UCLA."

"Well, give me your card, if you have one, and I'll send you a link to the UCLA job postings board."

"That would be great. Let me run back in and get you one."

She was gone a couple of minutes and then came back with a card. She handed it to me and said, "This is actually the company's card, but I've written my name and e-mail address on the back."

"Great."

"Do you have a card?"

"Not with me. But now that I've got your e-mail address, I can send you my contact info."

"Thanks."

As I drove away, I thought to myself that I had taken a risk. Sylvia might have recognized me if the police had already shown her my photo. Oscar had told me that the police used to show photos but now tried to avoid it because it could screw up the credibility of later identification. But it had still been a risk. Or the clerk could have seen a picture of me in the paper or online, although I thought that the only picture connecting me with Primo's death had been in a brief article in the *Bruin* on an inside page. Anyway, it had worked. She thought my name was Annej Semaj, and she had shown no hint of knowing who I really was.

CHAPTER 83

Tess had asked me to meet her at the Bel-Air at five. I hadn't been there since Marbury Marfan had taken me to a recruiting dinner at the hotel almost fifteen years earlier. I arrived a few minutes before five, gave my car to the valet and walked across the bridge toward the main building. The place was still beautiful. The hotel had been remodeled a few years before, but its essential character had been preserved. Even the ducks and swans remained.

Tess was waiting for me in the wood-paneled bar. She was sitting at a table for two in a corner, sipping a drink and picking at a plate of olives.

"Please sit," she said.

I did, and said to her, "I feel as if I really ought to reintroduce myself, since we met so briefly at Craft."

"Yes, it was rapid," she said. "So let us do it properly. I am Tess Devrais." She put out her hand to shake mine.

"And I'm Jenna James." I took her hand and shook it. "Pleased to meet you, Tess."

We both laughed out loud. So loud that the bartender turned and looked at us.

"When I saw you that night," Tess said, "I had a small jealousy. Because you have a necklace with the same design as the bracelet which I have. A gift to you, I think by the same man, yes? Is that not stupid?"

"Yes, it was the same man, and it is stupid. In fact, I would be happy to give you the necklace if you'd like. Maybe the necklace and the bracelet need to live together again, as they must once have done."

"Ah, this is a nice thing you think to do, but it is not necessary. Not at all."

Just then the waiter appeared and asked me for my order. I ordered a vodka martini with a twist.

"How long have you known Robert?" I asked

"I think it is sixteen years. Maybe more years. I will have to count. And you?"

I thought about it. "Well, I met him when I was in my second year of law school, so let's see, that's maybe thirteen years ago? I, too, would need to count to make it exact."

"Jenna, were you in a romance with Robert?"

I tried to look as horrified as possible. "Oh no, never. Nothing like that. We were professional colleagues. He was my mentor. He taught me a lot, but there was not an ounce of romance."

"I believe you," she said.

I wondered briefly to myself what possible difference it would have made if I had had a romance with Robert. After all, she was in France. But I put it out of my mind.

"Tess," I said, "before I called Robert that night in Paris, had he ever mentioned me to you?"

"Never. I wonder why he did not?"

"It's because he was angry at me for leaving the firm to go to UCLA to teach. I thought at the time that it was stupid for him to be angry about that. But I can see now that Robert thought of the firm as his family, and he thought of me as one of his favorite children. So it's like I was breaking up his family. He wanted to grow old with his family."

"Men, they are bizarre," she said.

The waiter put my martini in front of me at that very moment. I lifted it up and said, "Let's drink to that."

We clinked our glasses.

"We can talk about Robert more later perhaps," Tess said.

I smiled. "Or we can talk about something more important."

"Yes. I will drink to that, too."

We clinked glasses again.

"Now," Tess said, "I will tell you something I think you will like to know."

"I'm listening," I said.

"Before he left for Spain, Robert told me of your troubles. And he explained some of the things—strange things—that have happened."

"Uh-huh."

"And I told him that I wanted to help you. And I thought to myself there was one thing I could solve."

"Which is?"

"The answer to who is wishing secretly to buy your apartment."

"Oh. I have been curious about that. Did you figure it out?"

"Yes."

"How?"

"I am rich, you know. I got from Robert the name of the real-estate agent who came to see you so often. I rented a

Rolls-Royce and went to see him. I told him I liked your building. I let him take me to lunch. I let him think I was *très intéressé* in him."

"Were you?"

"*Mais non*! Or how do you say?"

"No way."

"*Exactement*. But I let him think this. I asked him again and again about your building. Who owned each apartment. Who would buy. Who would sell. Finally, he told me that the person who wants your apartment is someone named Greta Broontz."

"Oh my God."

"Is she a bad person?"

"Maybe. But she's one of my law-school faculty colleagues."

"*Mon dieu*."

"Why does she want my apartment, Tess? I mean, she already lives in the building, and I think her view is almost as good as mine. It's only one floor below me."

"She wishes to have an apartment of two floors. She will, I am not sure of the right verb . . ."

"Break through from her apartment to mine?"

"Yes."

I thought to myself that I had now identified a motive for Greta Broontz to poison me. But would she really be willing to kill me for my apartment? I decided not to utter the thought aloud because it was too absurd.

"Do you think," Tess asked, "that this woman wishes to kill you for your apartment?"

"No one is that crazy, Tess."

CHAPTER 84

Week 3—Wednesday Evening

Around 6:00 P.M. I got a text message from Robert. It said, "Hi, I'm back and back on the grid."

I texted back:

"u r ahol 4 leaving. we needed u."

He texted back:

"Let's meet at Oscar's at 8."

I texted:

"Okay."

Then I called Oscar and arranged it.

When I got to Oscar's promptly at eight, Robert was already there. He and Robert were both sitting at the big table. Robert's briefcase was on the table in front of him, unopened.

"Hi," Robert said. "I gather you're mad at me."

"Yes," I said, marshaling the iciest voice I was capable of.

"Well, Jenna, I come bearing gifts, so perhaps you'll end up forgiving me."

"What gifts?"

"Information about what's really going on with Quinto and Primo. You'll be pleased, I'm sure."

"Primo's dead is what's going on with him."

Oscar interceded. "Hey, my friends, you both need to cool it. Jenna, Robert has some good information, so muffle your ire. And Robert, it wasn't cool to disappear for three days in the middle of a case. It would help if you admitted that."

"I admit it," Robert said. "But I thought the criminal case was over, and I had no idea there'd be a UCLA hearing."

"You're right," I said. "Please tell me what you found out."

"I found out that there really is a survivor account—by the navigator of the *Ayuda*. Apparently it's been misfiled for centuries." He unsnapped the briefcase on the table, pulled out a document and handed it to me.

I looked at it and saw that it was written in archaic seventeenth-century Spanish. With effort I'd be able to decrypt it, but not while sitting at Oscar's large table.

I handed the document back to Robert. "What does it say?"

"My researcher says it is indeed an account written by the navigator. It gives a very approximate latitude of the *Ayuda* when it sank, and it says the number of days he drifted before reaching land."

"How many?"

"Twenty, if you believe the X-ray of the document."

Oscar broke in. "Which means, Jenna, that the *Ayuda* really did sink somewhere far out in the Pacific, not near Catalina. Hard to figure out exactly where, though."

"How," I asked, "does that fit in with Primo bringing me a map with the location?"

Robert's face lit up in a big grin. "Here's my theory: there's no real map, or at least no map with a true location of the *Ayuda* on it. That's what Cabano said. And I'm guessing they just picked a place far out in the Pacific along the same line of latitude, took a nautical chart and drew an X on that spot."

"So you suspect the whole thing was a fraud?"

"Yes. I think they were trying to persuade investors that they had located the ship on the bottom—with precision—and needed a couple of million dollars to go down and get what was in it. Then they were going to pretend to launch a salvage operation, tell people they failed, take most of the money and go to Mexico."

"Why would they try to defraud me? I have no money to invest."

"I don't think they wanted your money. They were getting rebuffed by investors, and it makes sense that they would want to associate a prominent admiralty lawyer with their venture in order to beef up their credibility, the better to try again with new investors."

"So you think I was a mark."

"Exactly."

"I'm not sure," I said, "even if it's true, where that will get us in this stupid Charges Committee hearing."

"Well," Oscar said, "if it's true, it seems to me it eliminates one possible suspect. Quinto would have had no reason to kill you. In fact, if Robert's right, he and Primo would have very much wanted you alive to help them with their scam."

"Maybe," I said, "Quinto himself had some other reason to kill Primo. Primo's diary says Quinto threatened him."

"Yes," Oscar said. "But as you and I discussed, Jenna, I think Quinto just didn't want you involved at all because of your connection to Aldous, who knew at least some of the truth. So if Quinto wanted to prevent your involvement, he would have needed to kill Primo *before* he met with you."

"I have something to add to that," Robert said. "The guy I spoke with in Spain says they threatened each other all the time, but that it meant nothing."

"Well, how much time," Oscar asked, "did you spend with that guy?"

"Maybe an hour," Robert said, "but I think he was very credible. Even if he was himself something of a crook."

I sat there for a moment and thought about it. Did I want to eliminate Quinto as a suspect in Primo's murder on just the say-so of someone I'd never met, with whom Robert had spent an hour, who he thought was a crook but credible on this one point? Quinto was testifying tomorrow, and I wanted him to be friendly, and help me nail the other suspect—Julie.

"I guess that leaves Julie," I said. "After all, we know she had the opportunity because she rode up to the campus with Primo and Quinto, so she was around, waiting, or so she says, for Primo to finish talking to me. And I've learned—never mind how—that she looked up something to do with the poison on her computer."

Oscar just looked at me. "That's a key piece of evidence, and you're not going to tell us how you got it?"

"Well, Oscar," I said, "this hearing is just an informal chat among friends, remember? Surely where evidence came from can't be important, can it?"

Oscar got up and went into the kitchen. "I think," he said, "that this whole thing has descended to such a level of absurdity that we might as well just drink martinis while we plot tomorrow. And I think Plan B is the way we should go."

"What's Plan B?" Robert asked.

"It is," Oscar said, "a criminal-defense ploy. When your client looks guilty, blame it on someone else. Anyone, really, who is even remotely plausible. It tends to distract the jury and sometimes gets the guilty client off the hook."

"Are you saying, Oscar," I asked, "that I look guilty?"

"No, not at all, Jenna. But you're the person in the dock, so to speak. So we need to distract the panel to someone else in order to be sure that they don't find you did it."

"So who is it going to be?" I asked.

Robert spoke up. "From everything I know, we should target Julie."

"Can't we target Quinto, too?" I asked.

"No," Oscar said. "Plan B doesn't work with more than one target."

So while we drank martinis, we all agreed the name of the game would be pin the crime on Julie.

I, of course, had my own little plan on that. I kept it to myself.

CHAPTER 85

Week 3—Thursday

Our hearing, originally scheduled for 10:00 A.M., didn't get started until 11:00 A.M. Professor Trolder had an unexpected departmental meeting of some kind that delayed us. I had made a certain call at 9:00 on the expectation we'd start at 10:00. I made a second call that fixed the problem. Or so I hoped.

When everyone was in place, Robert had been introduced and I had duly made coffee for all, Dr. Wing asked Professor Broontz if she was ready with her next witness. She said she was and called Quinto Giordano. Professor Trolder, now a truly expert doorman, went out into the hallway, found Quinto and brought him in. Watching Trolder operate, I wondered what kind of economics paper he'd generate out of this. No academic likes a new experience to go to waste.

Dr. Wing went through the usual drone about what a friendly group we all were, blah blah, and Greta posed her first question to Quinto.

"Mr. Giordano," she asked, "can you tell us what you believe happened to your brother Primo?"

Oscar said, "I object. That question has no foundation, calls for speculation and is just generally bad."

Dr. Wing looked over at him. "Generally bad? Is that really a standard objection?"

"No," Oscar said, "it's not. It was designed to indicate how useless the answer is likely to be. Mr. Giordano's evidence, if he has any, has to start with some basis—something he saw or heard or knew. The question, as posed, invites utter flights of fancy."

"All right," Dr. Wing said, "I see your point, but I'm going to allow him to answer. It's more efficient that way, I think. You can ask him questions when he's done, as you did with the last witness on Tuesday."

I thought I actually saw Oscar roll his eyes, although perhaps I was just imagining it.

"Well," Quinto said, "on the morning he died, I helped my brother roll up a map, which we put in a big red mailing tube. It was a map that showed some of the information necessary to find the resting place of the Spanish galleon *Ayuda*, which sank in 1641."

"Please go on," Greta said.

"Okay, well, I dropped Primo off at the law school, and he said he was headed for Professor James's office. He had an appointment at 7:30 A.M."

"Then what happened?" Greta asked.

"I went into Westwood to get some breakfast. A couple of hours later, I got a call from the Reagan Medical Center saying Primo was dead. I went over and identified his body."

"Was anything missing?"

"Yes. They gave me Primo's wallet and other personal things, but the map wasn't among them. I assumed Professor James had taken it. But she later claimed, according to Dean Blender, that she never got the map from Primo and that it had gone missing."

"Do you know what happened to it?"

"I assume Professor James stole it and still has it. It's very valuable."

"Do you know how your brother died?"

"The coroner's preliminary report said Primo died from acute poisoning by sodium azide, and that it was in coffee he drank. It was Professor James's coffee that did it. She poisoned him."

I noticed that he had not once looked at me during his testimony. Mainly he stared at the table in front of him.

Greta put her hand gently on his shoulder and said, "I'm sorry, Quinto, that you have to go through this in your period of grief."

I wanted to throw up.

"But," she said, continuing, "please allow me to ask you one final question. How do you know it was Professor James's coffee that poisoned your brother?"

"Easy," he said. "The preliminary coroner's report said it was poisoned coffee, and I know my brother had no coffee before I dropped him off. Professor James has admitted she gave him a cup of coffee to drink, and traces of that poison were found in the cup Primo drank from. So it's obvious."

The panel, to my disgust, had been riveted by Quinto's testimony. Professor Healey and her helmet of hair had leaned so far out over the edge of the table that I thought she might fall over.

"I have nothing further," Greta said.

"I have a question," Dr. Wing said. "Young man, what makes you think it was Professor James who put the poison in the coffee cup?"

"Obviously," Quinto replied, "so she could get the map. Once she has that and puts it together with the navigator's survival account, she'll be able to figure out the location of the ship, just like we did, and go salvage it herself."

"Does she have any salvage experience?" Professor Healey asked.

"Yes, she does. She worked on a treasure salvage ship last summer."

I couldn't help it. "As a deckhand!" I yelled out.

"Please, Professor," Dr. Wing said, "you'll get your chance."

"Can you show us a copy of the map?" Professor Trolder asked.

"No, because only Professor James knows where it is. And even if I did have it, there's confidential information on it, and I wouldn't want to show it to you."

"I don't understand," Trolder said, "what's so confidential about the map."

"My brother's copy, wherever Professor James has hidden it, has the exact longitude of the shipwreck written on it."

"What about your copy of the map?" Trolder asked.

"My copy has the exact latitude written on it. The 1641 survivor account only roughly estimated the latitude of the wreck—that's all they could really do back then. The precise latitude, which we figured out with a modern sonar search we commissioned, is written on my copy of the map. So if someone were to steal both copies, they'd know where the shipwreck is, and they could go salvage it before we do. We spent much too much money to locate the ship to permit someone else to go grab the spoils."

"But you don't contend," Trolder asked, "that Professor James has stolen your copy, too, do you? The one with the latitude?"

"No, but I'm actually afraid of her, and I have my copy under lock and key outside the state."

I suppressed a laugh. The idea that Quinto was afraid of me was really too much. The fantasy that was being spun in the room was beyond belief. I hoped soon to unspin it.

"I see," Trolder said, although he looked far from satisfied. "I have one more question: Why haven't we seen a copy of the preliminary coroner's report?"

"It's still confidential," Quinto said. "I haven't seen it either. It's simply been described to my lawyer because I'm a family member of the victim."

"Well," Trolder said, "as an economist, I've learned not to rely too heavily on anecdote, and this seems very anecdotal."

Professor Healey emerged from her cocoon. "I don't know about that, Paul. Sometimes anecdotal accounts provide powerful clues to the fundamental memes of culture."

Dr. Wing turned and looked at her. "This isn't about memes, Samantha. It's about a murder."

Oscar had put his hands behind his head and had been listening to the academic banter with a bemused look on his face. "If I may interrupt," he said, "I have a couple of questions for the witness."

"Of course, Oscar," Dr. Wing said. "Please proceed."

Oscar kept his hands behind his head. "You said, Mr. Giordano, didn't you, that Professor James, with the map and the survivor account, would be able to find the ship 'just like we did.'"

"Yes."

My question is, did you actually find the ship, or did you just make this all up?"

"Yes, of course we found it."

"Where is it exactly, by longitude and latitude?"

"That's confidential, and anyway, I only have the latitude. I need Primo's map to get the longitude."

"How deep is the water where the ship is?"

"That's confidential, too."

"Well, can you at least tell us how you found the ship, or is that confidential, too?"

"I can tell you that," Quinto said. "We hired a company that does sonar searching on the ocean bottom, gave them the general location where we believed the ship was, based on a survivor account, and asked them to search."

"What's the name of the company?"

"That's confidential."

"How long did it take them, whoever they are, to find it?"

"About three months."

"What did that cost?"

He hesitated. "About four million dollars."

"Where did you get the money?"

"From investors."

"Who are they?"

"That's confidential?"

"Why, Mr. Giordano, should the names of your investors be kept confidential?"

"That's the way they want it."

"So we have a ship on the bottom of the ocean in a confidential location at a confidential depth, found by a search conducted by a confidential company financed by people whose names you won't tell us."

Quinto didn't answer immediately. Finally, he said, "That's not the way I'd put it, but that's correct overall."

"You said correct overall," Oscar said. "Is there some way *underall* in which it's not correct?"

"No."

Oscar turned to the panel. "Lady and gentlemen, I move that this witness's testimony be totally excluded. You can't come into a court—and this certainly is a court—and tell the court, 'Hey, I want you to believe me about something very important, but I won't tell you any of the details that would allow you to test whether I'm telling the truth.' And then, just for a little icing on the mystery cake, the witness adds, 'with regard to the coroner's report, I can tell you a detail, but I haven't actually seen it, and you can't see it either.'"

Dr. Wing looked at Professor Broontz. "Greta, what do you have to say about that?"

"I don't think that's correct at all," Greta said. "Mr. Quesana is wrong. This isn't a court. It's an informal procedure in which you can sort the information into reliable and unreliable testimony and make a decision based on what you find reliable."

I thought to myself, as I listened to the back and forth, that Greta was, after all, a civil procedure teacher, and she knew how to distinguish between what courts do and what more informal panels do. It was the old divide between courts, who are picky about evidence, and arbitration panels, who say, "Well, we'll listen to everything, including the junk, and sort it out later."

Dr. Wing looked at Trolder and then at Healey and said, "I think this is important enough that the panel should take a few minutes to discuss it. We'll take ten, adjourn to another office and return with a decision."

I poked Oscar. "Ask who their next witness will be."

"Excuse me," Oscar said, "may I ask who the next witness will be?"

"It will be Julie Gattner," Greta said.

CHAPTER 86

Oscar," I said, after Greta, Quinto and the panel had left the room, "I need to make another phone call. I'll be right back."

"What have you got up your sleeve, Jenna?" Oscar asked.

"Nothing, Oscar." As I said it, I considered telling him, but then I thought better of it, for fear he and Robert would object, cautious souls that they were, and we'd have a row about it. And somehow my plan would be derailed. But I was sure it was the right thing to do, and I didn't want anything to interfere.

Robert grinned. "It must be something. During my trial you were always off on some private project."

"Right," I said, "which got the charges against you dismissed."

"True."

"Anyway, I need to make this call." I went out the door and looked for a spot where I wouldn't be overheard. When I got back ten minutes later, everyone had reassembled, and it was clear they were just waiting for me.

Dr. Wing looked around, no doubt ready to announce his ruling. In looking at him, it was clear to me he was relishing the role of judge. He'd probably missed his calling.

"Well," he said, "we've caucused and agreed that we'll let Mr. Giordano's testimony stand. Although we're skeptical about it, we can always weigh it, and that seems fairer in this informal setting than applying some obscure rules of evidence and excluding his testimony entirely."

"I would argue," Oscar said, "that those rules are hardly obscure. With all due respect, they're common sense. But I'll accept the panel's ruling and move on to my final questions.

"Mr. Giordano," Oscar asked, "do you know a gentleman by the name of Cabano who lives in Seville, Spain?"

"Like I told you in my deposition, I know of him, but I don't know him personally, and I've never communicated with him."

"If I were to tell you that my colleague here, Mr. Tarza"—Oscar pointed at Robert—"had gone to Spain and met with Mr. Cabano, and that Mr. Cabano had told Mr. Tarza that he had met with both you and your brother, would you be surprised?"

I smiled to myself, because that was the kind of question you couldn't get away with asking in a courtroom without objection. No one on the panel even blinked, and to my surprise, Professor Broontz said nothing.

Quinto hesitated not even a second. "I would be surprised."

I noticed that he hadn't said it wasn't true.

Oscar followed up. "Is what Mr. Cabano said to Mr. Tarza true? Did you meet with Cabano?"

"No."

I thought back to the question Robert had asked Quinto in the deposition concerning the penalty for perjury. Because if Cabano had told Robert the truth, Quinto had lied in the depo and he was lying now. At least he was lying consistently.

Professor Trolder spoke up. "Where is this going, if I might ask? We on the panel don't even know who Mr. Cabano is, or why this is important."

I smiled inwardly. These guys were becoming more like real judges every minute.

"I'll move on," Oscar said, "and come back and link that up later." He looked directly at Quinto. "Mr. Giordano, it's correct, isn't it, that you inherited this confidential map from your grandfather?"

"Yes."

"His name was Sven Johannsen, I think you said in your deposition?"

"Yes."

"And he died, I think you said, several years ago?"

"Yes."

Oscar was doing what good lawyers do all the time. He was asking the witness a series of seemingly softball questions, but to me it had the feel of setting him up for something. Perhaps Oscar had his own secret plan.

"Would it surprise you to learn, Mr. Giordano, that I spoke to your grandfather yesterday?"

"Yes, because he's dead."

"Well, since this is an informal hearing, I think I'll just testify a bit and say that a private investigator located your grandfather Sven, who is now living in a small village in Norway, where he's been for the last ten years or so."

"You were talking to an impostor."

"If so, he's a very good impostor, because he was able, without prompting, to name you, your brother Primo—even though Primo was only his stepgrandson—all of your other siblings and your mother and father. He also knew your mother's address in Pittsburgh."

"I don't know how he got that information, but my grandfather is dead."

Professor Broontz woke up from the dead. "What does this have to do with anything? We're trying to learn who killed his brother. Whether his grandfather is alive or dead is irrelevant."

"No," Oscar said, "I have a fax from Sven Johannsen in my briefcase, confirming everything I've just said. What it demonstrates is that Mr. Giordano is an outright liar. About everything. There is indeed a survivor account in the archive in Seville, but there was no expedition to find the *Ayuda*. The whole thing is a scam."

"Well," Dr. Wing said, "this is indeed both interesting and, if true, distressing, but, like Professor Broontz, I'm not sure how it ties into how Primo Giordano died."

"An educated guess," Oscar said, "is that Primo was about to blow the scam wide open and Quinto killed him to shut him up."

I was as surprised about everything Oscar had just revealed as everyone else in the room appeared to be. And puzzled as to where it was leading or how it would end up pointing to Julie as the killer. I leaned over to Oscar and whispered, "I thought we were implementing Plan B, which was to target Julie."

"This is Plan C," Oscar said. "I only got the info from Sven this morning."

"Well," I said, "our original Plan B is underway, and I have no intention of stopping it, because I still think it's the right plan."

CHAPTER 87

Quinto had been silent through the entire exchange between Oscar and Dr. Wing. As Oscar finished, he rose from his chair and said, "I haven't lied about anything. My brother is dead, and this whole proceeding is a joke. I'm leaving."

"I think you said your next witness would be Julie Gattner," Oscar said. "I'm ready for her right now."

I had to admire the approach. Oscar had decided simply to ignore Quinto's departure and let everyone think about it as he moved on to the next witness, as if nothing out of the ordinary had transpired.

Trolder went to the door, went out, found Julie in the hallway and brought her in. As soon as Julie came in, I sent a text from my cell phone that I had already keyed in. Then I keyed in a second text but held off sending it.

Dr. Wing went through the usual, after which Greta started in on her first question.

"Ms. Gattner," she asked, "can you tell us your relationship to Primo Giordano?"

Before Julie could answer, Oscar interrupted and addressed Dr. Wing. "Dr. Wing, I know it's out of the ordinary, but since this is so informal, I wondered if I might ask Julie a question of my own before she answers Professor Broontz's question. I think it will clear up her relationship with Primo and save us all a lot of time."

"Any objection, Greta?" Dr. Wing asked.

"I guess not," she said.

"Good," Oscar said. "My question is this: Ms. Gattner, isn't it the case that you poisoned Primo and did it because he had dumped you a few days earlier?"

Julie looked stunned. For a moment she seemed unable to answer. "I didn't kill anyone," she said.

"Well," Oscar said, "let me point out a few things to the panel. Informally, of course."

There was a knock on the door.

"Professor Trolder," I said, "that's a defense witness who's a bit early. May I go and let her in and tell her to come back a bit later?"

"Sure," he said.

I got up, walked around to the other side of the table and opened the door. In the background Oscar was trying to get Julie to answer another question, and she was responding with outrage. When I opened the door, Sylvia Menendez was standing there. "Come in," I said, "and I'll explain."

"I thought," she said, looking around at all the people, "that this was a job interview."

"It will be in a moment. There's a delay while we finish a meeting." I said it really loudly, and everyone in the room stopped talking and looked at us.

"Grab a seat in that chair over there, Sylvia." I pointed to the other side of the table. As Sylvia began to walk toward the chair

I had pointed to, I swiveled my hand and pointed to Julie. "Ms. Menendez, is that the woman who bought the sodium azide from you?"

Sylvia stopped, turned her head and looked at Julie. "No, she's not. What is this about?" She looked around the room, seeking to make some sense of it. "You tricked me, and I think I should go." She turned around and started to head back toward the door. Then she stopped in her tracks and pointed at Greta Broontz. "That's the woman who bought the chemical from me."

I pushed send on the text I had preprepared.

"Excuse me," Dr. Wing said, "how can you be so sure?"

"The woman who bought the chemical from me had one brown eye and one blue one, just like she does. And a, uh, craggy face."

"That is absolutely not true," Greta said. "This is an outrage."

"You see," Julie said, "it wasn't me!"

Sylvia looked again at Julie. "You were in the store, too, but you were hanging back. I saw the two of you come in and leave together."

The door to the room opened, and Detective Drady walked in, accompanied by four other UCLA police officers, all in uniform. Two were men, two were women.

"Detective," I said, "this woman is an employee of the chemical company from which the sodium azide was bought. She has just identified the woman who bought it as Professor Broontz, and the woman who was her accomplice as Julie Gattner."

Drady looked at Sylvia. "Is that true, ma'am?"

"I don't know their names, but yes. That one, there, bought it." She pointed at Greta. "And that one, there, was with her." She pointed at Julie.

"I'm placing you both under arrest for the murder of Primo Giordano," Drady said. He nodded at the two female police officers, who proceeded to pat down Greta and Julie and, aided by the two male officers, handcuff them. They were reading them their rights as they were led out of the room.

Julie said nothing, but Greta was screaming at the top of her lungs that the whole thing was an outrage, and she was going to sue everyone, especially me.

Dr. Wing looked at me and said, "I guess this proceeding is over, with a finding of nonresponsibility on your part, Professor James. And I suppose it's none of our business, really, but what was Professor Broontz's motive?"

I thought to myself that I could respond by telling him I didn't know, or I could tell him what I had pieced together since Tess had told me that Greta was the person secretly trying to buy my apartment. I opted to tell him what appeared to be the truth, so far as I could understand it.

"Dr. Wing, it's hard for me to wrap my head around it all, but it seems Greta wanted my condo, in order to create a two-story condo with a fabulous view. And whether I was framed for killing Primo or just failed to get tenure and had to leave town, either way, she figured I'd sell."

"Is that all there was to it?" Dr. Wing asked.

"No. On top of that she hated me, and somehow the mixture of hatred and real-estate envy—my condo is the penthouse—made her snap. I don't know, maybe this kind of thing can only happen in Los Angeles."

"It could easily happen in New York, too," Professor Healey said.

"What about Ms. Gattner?" Dr. Wing asked.

"She just wanted Primo dead. For dumping her."

Professor Healey asked the last question. "Just as a matter of understanding relationships on this campus, how did the two of them figure out they had a compatible mutual interest?"

"Oh," I said, "Julie was taking an independent study from Greta. I assume they managed to achieve what graduate faculties are always trying to bring about: true bonding between faculty and students.

"Dr. Wing," I said, "there's one more thing. This young woman, Sylvia Menendez, who's been so helpful to us, is actually here for a job interview. She wants to apply for the opening in your lab for a trainee med tech."

"Job opening?"

"Yes, you know the one I'm referring to."

A broad smile broke out on his face. "Oh, of course. Ms. Menendez, please come with me to my office, and we'll get you set up for the interview. I think you'll like working here."

Oscar leaned over to me. "Which plan of yours was that, Jenna?"

"Plan D."

"Did you know it was both of them?"

"No."

"Which one did you think it was when you thought it was only one of them?"

"I'm not saying."

I wasn't saying because, in truth, I was so elated that the whole thing was finally over that I couldn't in the instant really remember who I'd most suspected. I looked down at my hands and saw they were shaking again. But this time, at least, they were shaking from the adrenaline generated by relief instead of fear.

"Let's," Robert said, "go to the Bel-Air and celebrate. Tess will be waiting for us. Jenna, will Aldous be joining us?"

"No, but I think there's someone else I'd like to invite."

EPILOGUE

The ensuing months have been busy ones for me. Early in the New Year, I testified in Greta Broontz's sanity hearing. According to the psychologist's report, which I read with great interest, Julie and Greta did in fact hatch the whole thing in the independent study Julie took from Greta in the fall semester. Exactly how and why they decided to act together isn't yet fully known.

To my disappointment, Greta was ruled unfit to stand trial for murder and is now committed to a state mental facility. It seems she had been off her meds for months (although no one at the law school other than the dean had seemed aware she was even on them). Her motives, so far as anyone could make them out, were exactly as I had described them to Dr. Wing. She simply hated my guts and became fixated on getting my condo so she could have a two-story place with great views. Since I have some fixations of my own, I can kind of understand.

Julie, according to the indictment, wanted to kill Primo simply because he had dumped her, apparently in a not-so-nice way. She's awaiting trial for first-degree murder. The Twitterverse commentary about her, which is extensive, suggests she's planning to present a defense based on allegations that she was abused as a child and by Primo, too. I hope to avoid testifying in that trial because it will waste a lot of my time. On the other hand, if that's what I need to do to keep her off the street, I will. Oh, and believe it or not, she somehow got her hands on a copy of the final exam for my Law of Sunken Treasure seminar and mailed in her answers from jail. I didn't bother to read them.

One of the things I've wondered about is how the attack on Primo came about when he was sitting in my office drinking my coffee. As near as I can figure out from the extensive testimony at the sanity hearing, the attempt on me and Primo simultaneously was pure serendipity. Greta and Julie had been planning to get both of us separately some time later that week, but when Julie found Primo alone in my office while I was on the phone across the hall, she managed to dump the poison in his coffee without his seeing her do it. Then, when Primo fell quickly into a semiconscious state, she dumped some of it in the coffeepot, too, hoping I'd drink it later.

Had I done so, Greta would have expected to buy my condo from my estate. Because I didn't drink it and didn't die, she later figured she could force me out by framing me for Primo's murder and buying the condo when I went to jail. Barring that, she figured I'd at least have to look for a new job in another city—if I could find a job at all.

Oh, and I think I figured out how the receipt for the chemical got in my jacket pocket. Julie must have dropped it in right after she poisoned Primo. The jacket—one of four I have that are identical—was hanging on the back of my office door. Later on I took it home and hung it in my closet, where the police found it when they did their search.

I've tried to patch things up with Tommy, but he hasn't returned any of my phone calls or responded to my e-mails or texts. And he's never cashed the check I left for him at the Chemistry Department to reimburse him for the dead-bolt lock. But he hasn't blocked my e-mails or texts, so perhaps there's still hope there. So far as I know, he had nothing to do with the crimes. He did, however, tell the police about my having gotten my hands waxed, and the police apparently told Greta. I've forgiven Tommy for that, though. He was just being a good citizen. Maybe he'll forgive me one day.

The dean, in his own way, has tried to make amends. A few days after the arrests, he took me to lunch at the Faculty Center instead of Oroco's and assured me that my tenure application was back on track. When, not long after, I got tenure, he threw a big party for me at his house. Even better, he tells me he has located an alum, the wife of a wealthy shipping magnate, who wants to endow a chair in admiralty law and fund an admiralty studies center. Frankly, I think the school is being so nice because they're worried I'm going to sue them.

One thing that continues to bother me is the library episode. The official engineering report says there was a minor earthquake at the time the shelves fell on me, and they fell because the bolts were missing and the earthquake tipped them over. Supposedly the bolts on all the shelves had been replaced the week before in a seismic upgrade, but they'd missed replacing them on that one shelving section. A mistake, nothing more. The two things came together in, as the report put it, "a most unfortunate way." Do I believe it? Not really, but with Greta out of the way, I'm no longer worried about it.

Robert has gone back to France with Tess, although he claims he's not planning to stay there forever. He's also promised to pay up on the bet he lost and take me and Oscar to dinner at

At.mosphere at the top of the Burj Khalifa in Dubai. I told Tess she was welcome to join us, but that Robert had to pay for the trip himself.

Oscar has gone back to New York to be with Pandy. I do hope to meet that woman someday.

Aldous gave the law school notice in early December that he was departing in January for "a great opportunity" in Buffalo. We've exchanged a few e-mails, but I assume they will peter out, and he'll soon become someone I used to know.

You probably wonder about the map. It's never been found. Neither has the red mailing tube. My own theory is that Julie took it and ditched it somewhere after she poisoned Primo. I heard the police did extensive searches of Julie's apartment, locker and storage unit, so maybe they have it and will use it as evidence in her trial. If so, they're not telling.

You probably also wonder what happened to Quinto. He transferred to USC and is pursuing new investors there. I suggested to the DA that Quinto be investigated for fraud, plus perjury in his deposition. But, so far as I know, no investigation is underway.

As for me on a personal level, I've put my condo on the market. As soon as it sells, I'm planning to get a cool place at the beach. There have already been three offers, and it's only been on the market for a week. And I'm dating Dr. N. It seems to be going well. So well that we're planning to go to France together for a month in the summer. Maybe we'll even drop in on Robert and Tess while we're there. Mainly I'm looking forward to spending lots of time with Bill, eating good bread and great cheese, drinking fine wine and doing not much at all. I deserve it.

THE END

ACKNOWLEDGMENTS

I am indebted to my agent, Erica Silverman, for encouraging me to write a sequel to *Death on a High Floor*, to my editor at Thomas & Mercer, Alan Turkus, for taking the chance that I could actually write one, and to the rest of the crew at Thomas & Mercer, especially Jacque Ben-Zekry and Anh Schluep, for making the publishing experience such a pleasure. I must also express my deep appreciation to my developmental editor, Charlotte Herscher, who wields an edit pen that is somehow both gentle and, at the same time, razor sharp and wonderfully effective, and to my copyeditor, Randy Ladenheim-Gil, who did such a splendid job, not only of sharpening and smoothing the writing, but of managing to identify even the smallest error, from a minor biblical misquotation to the misspelling of an obscure type of purified water, to the incorrect name of a UCLA academic document. They both improved the manuscript immensely. And, last but very much not least, to my excellent proofreader, Rebecca Jaynes, who found not only the many little things, but one big thing, too.

Special thanks are due Deanna Wilcox—one of the best lawyers I know—for the suggestion that in her new job as a professor Jenna become an expert on the law of marine salvage and sunken treasure.

I also want to acknowledge the many friends who provided encouragement, who read the manuscript in its various stages and drafts and then gave me such helpful, candid notes, as well as those friends, old and new, who were kind enough to share their expertise. The entire list is long, but it includes especially Roger and Susan Chittum, Linda and John Brown, Melanie and Doug Chancellor, Roger Rosen, Amy Huggins, Marty Beech, Brinton Rowdybush, Joyce Mendlin, Julie Rutiz, Michael Haines, Krista Perry, Dan Wershow, Becky Novelli, Alison Anderson, Paul Bergman, Joanna Schwartz, Cameron Furey, Maxine Nunes, Julie Serquinia, Maureen Gustafson, Doreen Weisenhaus, Rodney King, Prucia Buscell, Diana Wright, Susan Nero, Lauren Gwin, Nona Dhawan, Dick Birnbaum, Christine Ong, Brad Hansen, Yoko Miyamoto, Joyce Mendlin, Deborah Coonts, Tom and Juanita Ringer, Harriet Young, Dale Franklin, Patty Nolan, Maria Elena Frances-Benitez and Ruben Benitez, Harold Kwalwasser, Melissa Lee, Holly D'Lane Miller, Lu Ann Homza, and Carlos Galvez-Pena.

And with thanks to my son, Joe, for his perceptive comments on voice, pacing and story arc in the early drafts, and, as always, to my wife, Sally Anne, for her patient and perceptive comments as the chapters emerged, one by one, into the initial drafts, as well as her encouragement when words sometimes failed me.

ABOUT THE AUTHOR

Charles Rosenberg is the author of the bestselling legal thriller *Death on a High Floor* and the 1994 viewer's guide to watching a criminal trial, *The Trial of O. J.: How to Watch the Trial and Understand What's Really Going On.* He was one of two on-air legal analysts for E! Television's live coverage of the O. J. Simpson criminal and civil trials. Rosenberg has also been credited as the legal script consultant for television shows *Boston Legal, L.A. Law, The Practice* and *The Paper Chase.* After graduating from Antioch College and Harvard Law School, where he was an editor of the law review, Rosenberg has had a long career as a partner in large law firms and as an adjunct law professor at several prominent law schools, including Loyola, UCLA and Pepperdine. He is currently a partner in a three-lawyer firm in the Los Angeles area, where he lives with his wife. This is his second novel.